ILLER

The
Principle
of Evil

T.M.E. W

ALSO AVAILABLE FROM T.M.E. WALSH

For All Our Sins

Trial by Execution

The
Principle
of Evil

T.M.E. WALSH

ONE PLACE. MANY STORIES

ONE PLACE. MANY STORIES

This novel is entirely a work of fiction. The names, characters
and incidents portrayed in it are the work of the author's
imagination. Any resemblance to actual persons, living or
dead, events or localities is entirely coincidental.

HQ
An imprint of HarperCollins*Publishers* Ltd.
1 London Bridge Street
London SE1 9GF

This paperback edition 2017
1
First published in Great Britain by
HQ, an imprint of HarperCollins*Publishers* Ltd. 2016

ISBN: 978-0-263-92774-0

Set by CPI - Group(UK) Limited,
Printed and bound CPI Group (UK) Ltd, Croydon, CR0 4YY

Tania (T. M. E.) Walsh began writing full-time after becoming a casualty to the recession in late 2008. She successfully self-published the first two novels in the DCI Claire Winters series before being picked up by HQ - a division of HarperCollins - in 2015.

Tania is currently working on a new thriller, and a fourth book in the DCI Claire Winters series, with a further two books in the series, coming soon.

Tania lives in Hertfordshire with her husband and young daughter. For the latest information on T. M. E. Walsh, you can follow her on Twitter @tmewalsh, or visit her website www.tmewalsh.com and Facebook page www.facebook.com/tmewalsh

For my parents, Sandra and Stewart.

Also in loving memory of Angela Walsh – truly the luck

of the Irish – who would've got such a kick out of this.

'He got inside my head. He twisted it, danced around in it, leaving nothing behind but bad memories and bloody footprints.'

31st October

She tasted the earth, the dead leaves and the damp as she crawled on her belly.

The bitter wind rose. It raged through the trees like something possessed, scattering the last remaining dead leaves that had once clung to the skeletal branches. Shivering uncontrollably, she pressed her body harder to the ground, willing it to open and swallow her whole.

Don't let him see me from here.

Was she hoping or praying? She didn't know any more.

God hadn't been with her when she needed Him the most, not for a long time. Not since the accident. Nothing had come to ease her grief then and nothing would come now. Why wait for some divine intervention to carry her from this wretched place? She could only rely on herself, and look where that had got her. There wasn't any hope of escape. Not now. The gash on her ankle had seen to that. Nothing left now except the time before he killed her.

He'd desecrate her body, but not her soul. A soul that had already been ripped to shreds and lain broken, slowly dying a piece at a time since the day of the accident. The day her life broke down into nothing meaningful, just something wretched, languishing in self-pity.

The man who was tracking her would be following the trail of blood, seeping from the wound on her ankle. For all she knew, he could be standing right behind her now, watching in silence, waiting to strike the final blow. The great calm before the storm.

Her bruised ribs prevented her from rolling on her back. She sucked in a deep breath against the dank earth, soil creeping inside her mouth, between parched lips. She dug her fingers in deep, nails raking through the mud.

She pulled.

Just a little further towards the bushes. I can make it. I have to. Ignore the pain.

Then she heard it. She froze with the fright and the possibility that death was coming even sooner than imagined. She wondered if it was delirium or if the noise close behind her was as real as the hot tears falling down her face.

No, the sound of crushing twigs was much closer now. It was as real as the heat of his breath now upon her neck.

He appeared almost from nowhere, creeping through the oily blackness.

He was determined.

He would kill her.

The hairs on the back of her neck rose, gooseflesh puckering her skin. There was a moment there in the darkness when she thought he might speak to her. She heard his sharp intake of breath... but nothing more. She hadn't the courage to look into his cold dark eyes again. The weight of his boot pressed down on her neck, burying her face deeper into the soil.

Sweet Jesus, just let this be over quickly.

He stooped down close, replaced his boot with an icy hand. She braced herself. Her eyes squeezed shut when she felt the sharp tip of the blade, the cold edge of steel.

She felt no pain at first, just a forceful punch to the neck.

Then came the pain.

She felt her warm blood pouring down her neck, onto the ground, drenching the earth. Then the rain came. Icy fat droplets, pattering over her bare skin.

As her mind took her beyond the pain, spiriting her away high above the violence below, the last thoughts that ran through her head were of her husband and their two children.

She could see them clearly, as alive now as they had been a year ago. They were playing in the cornfield behind the house where she had grown up. A year without them had felt like an eternity, but she knew they had always been with her and would be until the very end.

Isabelle and Jasmine, my beautiful girls. And Anthony. I've missed you all so much. I'm coming back to you.

The vision of her husband blurred with reality but she was sure he was walking towards her, hands reaching out, lips greeting her with a smile. Her fingers splayed and ached for the touch of his skin, just as the darkness carried her away.

PART ONE
Present Day
5th November

'Don't run... don't run from me.'

There, deep in the wood, she hears the voice again. The same voice that had haunted her, followed her desperately. Relentlessly for months.

'Don't run, wait for me. I can offer you so much more if you'd only let me.'

But she cannot stop. She cannot learn to walk through this world again, not while the fear has a hold of her body, heart and soul.

She runs down the track through the trees. She cannot place the voice, nor tell if it's male or female. It rings like a cacophony of sounds in her head.

She risks a glance down at her feet. They are bare once again, deep in the snow. The forest floor beneath the ice scratches at her skin, and she leaves drops of blood in her wake.

She panics.

Someone will follow her home, chasing the scarlet trail left behind. But where is home? She cannot find it. Ahead, there is nothing but forest.

The mist circles the trees around her, the same as every time she sees them.

This world is stripped. Void of colour. Void of time.

Her heart pounds in her chest, but she can never understand who or what she runs from. Inside, the only thing that is always certain, is the fear. It relentlessly courses through her veins.

She sees the clearing ahead. She wants to turn the other way. She has been here time and time before, but never understands why. A force is driving her forward, which she cannot control. She runs as if the hounds of hell were at her heels.

She reaches the clearing... stops.

The voice is there, behind her.

She turns; ready to confront whatever it is that hunts her…
It's Him.

As she feared it would be; a ghost from the past.

She's almost afraid to look into his eyes, but when she does, she sees there is nothing there but darkness. Hollow pits where brilliant eyes once shone.

He reaches out, and before she can stop him, his hand grabs her hair, ripping clumps out by the roots.

Then fingers are at her chest. They tear through icy flesh, nails scratching against bone, against ribs, hungry for her heart.

As she cries out, his mouth opens in a silent scream, blood pouring out from within.

CHAPTER 1

Detective Chief Inspector Claire Winters bolted upright, eyes snapping open.

She was shrouded in darkness and it took her several seconds to realise where she was as her eyes adjusted to her surroundings.

Her head was spinning but soon the shadows stopped moving and became solid shapes, pieces of furniture she soon began to recognise in her living room.

Her hands grabbed at her chest, which was slick with sweat despite the chill of the room. A sigh of relief shuddered through her body when she realised her skin, flesh and bone were still intact.

She pushed back the stray strands of blonde hair from her face, and then held her head in her hands. Night terrors had become part of her, almost feeling as physical as something she wore, but it was no badge of honour.

That one had been one of the worst she'd had in the last year. Usually, they followed the same familiar pattern, but with subtle differences.

She sucked in a deep breath, held it until her chest ached.

Despite knowing who it was she ran from by the end of each frantic nightmare, this was the first time she'd actually seen Him – or at least some twisted version of Him.

Her hands slid down her face, wiping back tears that had begun to fall. Ice-blue coloured eyes glassed over as she eventually let the tears fall freely, staining the pale flesh of her cheeks.

A loud bang outside made her jump, bolting off the sofa, stumbling over the blanket that had fallen at her feet. A series of smaller hissing sounds then followed, erupting in a series of loud bangs, and bright lights flashed behind the curtains that she had drawn earlier.

She hugged her arms tightly around her torso and shivered. She wore a rough knit jumper, its coarseness scratching at her skin, with skinny jeans that were slack at the waist and had begun to bag at the knees. She'd lost a stone in weight in the last year, but she refused to buy new clothes.

She was startled by the cracking sound as sparks seemed to dance across the roof of her house, raining down in a night so cold it stole your breath away.

She pulled back the curtain of the nearest window and saw the bright coloured fragments scatter in the sky.

Fireworks had been let off from the house somewhere across the road, at the bottom of the drive.

She released the breath she hadn't realised she had been holding. She caught her reflection in the cold glass. Dark circles rimmed her eyes, and what little lines she did have across her forehead had deepened.

She imagined she saw Him beside her, staring at their reflections. His eyes, seen moments before in the nightmare, still black pits.

Hollow.

That summed up how she felt.

She looked at Him, then squeezed her eyes shut. 'Go away,' she said. When she opened them again, she felt the fog in her mind begin to clear a little. 'It's just a nightmare,' she said in the darkness.

After several moments passed she went back to the sofa and felt for her phone, her head feeling thick, disorientated. She unlocked the screen and checked the time:

18:36.

She had less than an hour before she was due to be at the annual firework display in Haverbridge. She contemplated not going, and pulled up the last text message she had sent, about to send her excuses.

She flicked on the light, and looked around the room, phone clutched in a sweaty palm. The house looked as it had done a few hours ago when she'd decided to just rest her eyes.

The night terrors took their toll on her. Rarely a week went past without being woken by them. Grabbing a short sleep here and there when she could had been her way of coping with it for many months now.

She knew it couldn't go on like this, but no way would she ask for help.

This was something she had to overcome on her own... and she would, in her own time.

*

She headed up the stairs and put on clean clothes, dumping the sweat drenched ones in the laundry basket, before heading to the bathroom.

She stared at her reflection in the mirror of the medicine cabinet.

Her skin had taken on a grey tinge of late and her frame appeared gaunt. Others had noticed, made comments. She lowered her eyes, casting a critical eye over her stomach when she lifted her jumper.

For someone who had once taken so much pride in her appearance, even she knew her standards had slipped a little.

She could hear her colleagues' comments in her head, whispering their concerns when they thought she couldn't hear them.

The self-pity crept in briefly, before it was pushed aside by the resilience she was known for. Soft, kind eyes became hard once again, a steely glare cast at her reflection in the mirror.

Fuck them, she thought.

She splashed cold water on her cheeks, determined she would leave the house and at least appear to be social.

This is not me, she told herself inwardly. I am in control.

Minutes later she was sitting in her car, engine running, heaters clearing the fog from the windows, tapping out a text.

You twisted my arm. On my way.

She pressed send before she could change her mind, put the phone in her pocket, and headed down the drive, mindful of the ice on the ground that twinkled in the brightness of the headlights.

She headed out of Hexton, and on towards Haverbridge, taking the scenic route, passing another sleepy village before the road cut through open fields.

She sucked in deep breaths when her mind started to clog with the familiar uneasiness of before. When she breathed, she could see the faintness of her breath expelled like puffs of smoke from between parched lips.

She turned the heating up a little more and tried to relax her body. Tight muscles soon began to relax into the seat. She felt the ache in her jaw and realised she'd been clenching her teeth together. She swallowed hard, focusing on the stillness of the country road, where frosty skeletal trees and bushes hugged it from both sides.

This year autumn appeared to have bypassed the UK entirely, and winter seemed to have taken the Hertfordshire town of Haverbridge, where she worked, into its relentless clutches much earlier than anticipated.

The large town had a population just short of 100,000 people and was situated some thirty miles from London. Haverbridge had grown over the years, becoming a commuters' paradise for those who worked in the capital but didn't want the bright lights of the colourful city in their backyard at home time. They wanted to say goodnight and really mean it.

Haverbridge was beautiful, yet ugly in so many ways – not dissimilar to other towns and cities up and down the UK – but Haverbridge had a different side to it. It was exceptionally beautiful in the darker months. What made it so striking, you couldn't easily describe; it just was.

The summer sun had long disappeared and the threat of early snowfall was a very real one.

For Claire, it was bad news. It made her fall easily into an abyss of self-loathing and bitterness, something she was prone to. The cold haunted her like a restless spirit and the chill was not good for her bones.

She glanced at the clock on the dash. She'd be a little late, but she knew Stefan would understand. She took the road leading to the motorway, and as she travelled at a steady 60mph, she looked at the road ahead, bright lights and traffic rushing past, through eyes that didn't quite feel like her own.

ONE DAY EARLIER

The man glanced around the car park and stifled a yawn as he looked down at his watch. He snuggled down further in the driver's seat; his thick padded coat was warm and inviting. He was sleepy and wished he could close his eyes.

The body in the boot – it's now or never.

His car was the only one there, almost hidden in the darkness. The cold air hit his face when he emerged from the car. It caught him unawares and he gasped instinctively, clasping his hands tightly together, rubbing them for warmth.

When he stood in front of the boot, his hand hovered over it as if he had second thoughts about what he was about to do, as if the final act were any worse than what came before it.

The light inside the boot cast a dull light on what was inside. He looked down at the black bin liners, wrapped crudely around the majority of the body. Only the bottom half of the legs were left uncovered.

The once soft skin now looked waxy. He thought back to when those legs had kicked out at him, before he'd secured them together.

Shame, really.

This one had had such spirit.

His hands reached in and grabbed cold limbs. He began to haul the body carefully out onto the frozen ground.

CHAPTER 2

5th November

There was a huge whizz followed by a violent crack in the night sky as the firework exploded high above their heads.

Claire jumped, instinctively closing the gap between herself and Detective Inspector Stefan Fletcher. He glanced down at her, his tall thin frame buried in an oversized padded coat against the cold. He saw her tense, and ease herself a step or two away from his personal space.

He smiled inwardly.

Aloof and sometimes proud, with walls built so high that they could rarely be penetrated. These were Claire's bad points, but she wore the traits with pride, giving off the impression that nothing could faze her.

Stefan knew different though.

After a high-profile case the previous year, Claire had put Haverbridge back on the map. Not always for the right reasons, but in Claire's case, any publicity had turned out to be fairly good publicity. She'd become one of Haverbridge CID's best, and had ridden out the storm, forging some close allies amongst her team, and Stefan was one of those people.

Despite Claire's misgivings about herself, she was extremely good at her job, and respected. No one would've been justified in calling her incompetent, or an easy target.

But Stefan had seen the signs, seen the cracks appear since that investigation. It had exhausted her, changed her forever in some ways.

The murdered priest case – how could anyone come back from that completely unscathed?

More fireworks whizzed skywards, drawing appreciation from the assembled mass around them. Stefan watched Claire from the corner of his eye. Whilst she looked to the heavens with everyone else, he saw the glassy look of her eyes. She was there in body but the mind was elsewhere.

'The kids would've loved this,' he said, his blue eyes scrutinising every twitch in her face when she heard him speak.

She glanced at him, gave a weak smile.

Stefan would normally take his kids to Haverbridge Lake's annual firework display, but his ex had changed her plans and he was expected to fall in line. He felt sad at not seeing his children but, surprisingly, he was very glad to have Claire's company.

In the past, Claire had had a few detective sergeants as her subordinates. Most hadn't lived up to her expectations but Stefan had been different. Having watched him come into his own, and making DI in recent years, she'd relished the chance to work alongside him permanently, where possible, as an equal, despite the difference in rank.

'They wouldn't have liked the cold, Fletch,' she said, at length. 'The kids I mean.'

Stefan shook his head. 'Kids are tougher than they look.'

He saw her bite her lip. Claire didn't have children, or was ever likely to. Sometimes he felt like he was walking on eggshells in the last year. He didn't know what might upset her, so topics of conversation sometimes felt stilted.

Claire had her vulnerabilities as much as the next person. She had closed the gap between them earlier, something she'd never admit to if he called her out on it.

He'd noticed her weight loss, although he'd never say so. Her face had become more chiseled, cheek bones sharp.

Those ice-blue eyes looked permanently sad.

Stefan pushed his hands deeper into his pockets, trying to draw the life back into them. The night air was bone-chilling and the breath of the eager crowd hung in the air like thick white smoke.

He breathed in deeply; the air was heavy with the smell of bonfire smoke and fast food. He followed the line of people surrounding the huge lake and caught sight of the fast-food stands. His stomach growled.

'Do you want anything to eat?'

Claire was rubbing her gloved hands together for warmth and her breath cast out in clouds around her face. She shook her head.

'Mind if I?'

Claire either didn't hear him or was too cold to answer. He shrugged and pushed his way through the crowd.

When he returned, hotdog in hand, Claire saw he looked troubled.

'What's wrong?'

Stefan gave half a shrug as he bit into his hotdog. 'I wanted to talk about DS Crest.'

Claire waved her hand, dismissing the very mention of his name. 'Not while I'm enjoying myself.'

'He speaks highly of you too.'

'Look, I really don't need this right now.' Her voice turned hard. 'I couldn't care less what that Armani-wearing-metrosexual-walking-cliché thinks of me.' She turned to face him.

Detective Sergeant Elias Crest was a new addition to her team.

The last man Detective Superintendent Clifton Donahue had placed under Claire's watchful eye had lasted barely six months. Claire had hoped DS Crest would be different, but they hadn't exactly hit it off.

Elias had transferred from Merseyside after spending five years in Liverpool South's CID team. There were official reasons given for the transfer, but the real reason wasn't quite so clear cut.

Claire knew that more than anyone.

A steeliness had returned to her voice. 'I take it by you mentioning him, he's been kicking off?'

'He's found a few things out about you from your reputation alone. He thinks you hate him.'

'He's close… Hate is such a terrible word. He knows where the door is and it's open any time, day or night, if he wants to walk…'

Stefan nodded to himself, taking in her words. Then his eyes met hers. He saw the seriousness in her face.

'I'm sure it's nothing,' he said. 'Just wanted you to know he's not happy.'

'Boo-fucking-hoo.' Stefan rolled his eyes and she leaned in closer to him. 'I'm not going to apologise for who I am, Fletch. I have to be hard and when arrogant screw-ups like him are sent my way, they need to learn to toe the line.'

Stefan narrowed his eyes. 'Screw-ups?'

She fell silent.

'Is it something to do with why he was transferred? 'Cos you do realise not everybody is buying into the close-to-family excuse?'

She kept her face neutral.

Stefan shrugged. 'People talk, that's all I'm saying.'

'It's nothing, Fletch, forget I said anything.' She felt the weight of his stare but avoided his eyes. 'So,' she said, trying to deflect attention away from Crest, 'what happened to that girl you were dating? Doesn't she like fireworks?'

Stefan grimaced. 'Leigh couldn't make it. I think she's about to chuck me anyway.'

'Really?'

Stefan gave a mock laugh. 'Don't pretend to care.'

'You're questioning my sincerity?'

'Personally, I always thought that divorce of yours left you dead inside.'

She gave half a smile. 'Touché, Stefan.'

'Oh, first name for once. I'm flattered. Did I touch a nerve?'

'Simon didn't cut it enough as a husband to even come close to touching a nerve, Fletcher.'

Stefan glanced at her. 'I heard DCI Forester is dating again.'

Claire raised an eyebrow and sniffed with indifference. 'You shouldn't listen to gossip.' She knew he was talking in jest and on the surface she grinned, but inside she felt a little sad.

Claire had been married to DCI Simon Forester for three years. He served at Welwyn Garden City police station, some eight miles from Haverbridge. They'd met at a charity ball, and after a brief engagement, they'd married too quickly without really knowing anything about each other.

The relationship had turned sour after the first year and the pressure of their jobs helped drive a wedge between them, and they became more friends than lovers.

When Claire had risked an affair with another man, they became even less than that and it was Claire who filed for divorce, and immediately reverted back to her maiden name.

Surprisingly, despite feeling little for Simon, she felt the twinge of jealousy. It wasn't as if her love life was flourishing. Her dedication to her job didn't allow much time for a personal life, but she hated the thought there could be anyone else in her ex's life. Certainly not someone who could compare to her anyway.

As more fireworks erupted overhead, Claire pushed Stefan towards the edge of the lake, until they stood just feet from the edge of the frozen water.

He shoved the rest of his hotdog into his mouth and grinned. 'You're aware you're supposed to be playing the part of the submissive Leigh, aren't you?'

'Submissive? You're well shot of her, Fletch, by the sounds of it.'

'When I spend my working days with you, I need dominant like a hole in the head.'

'It's less crowded here, stop moaning,' Claire said. Then she saw Stefan's eye was trained on something else off to their left.

'You see that?' he said.

CHAPTER 3

The group of teenage boys continued to shove each other, shouting and laughing, goading each other towards the lake's frozen edge. One of them, Sean, who was much fatter than the rest, shoved his shoulder into his friend, Harry, with such brute force that the boy spilt his drink.

'You fat fucker,' Harry said, wiping the beer from his jeans.

'Such a hard man,' Sean jeered, the rest of the pack laughing and jumping around in a drunken mess. 'Too scared to go on the ice.'

'Don't see you on it, you fat twat,' Harry said, shoving his fist hard into an ample shoulder. Standing a good head taller than Harry, who was thin and wiry, Sean squared his large frame up to his opponent.

'Twenty quid says you're a fucking wimp.' His voice was low and the alcohol seemed to roll off his tongue in an invisible boozy haze. Harry looked over Sean's shoulder at their peers.

One boy was trying to chat to a group of young girls, who clearly weren't interested. The rest were lighting up, drinking or pushing each other closer to the lake's edge, laughing like a pack of hyenas.

Looking back into Sean's eyes, Harry raised his chin. 'Make it thirty. You'd better have the money.'

*

'You see that?' he said.

Claire followed Stefan's gaze and sighed.

A boy, aged around thirteen, was walking on the ice, about twenty feet from the embankment. Even from this distance, they could see that the ice grew thin towards the middle of the lake.

Claire shook her head. 'Why are kids so bloody stupid?'

Stefan sighed and dusted his hands free of crumbs. 'Come on,' he said, 'we'd better break this up.'

*

Harry, the boy on the ice, barely registered any fear, even when the ice underneath his feet started to crack. He looked back to his friends on the bank and laughed.

Trying to play the hard man, he took another step towards the middle of the lake and slipped, crashing down on the ice with brute force.

He felt the cold seep through his clothes almost immediately. He looked towards the embankment and heard his friends shouting.

A sea of faces now watched him in horror, just as he heard a cracking sound underneath him.

Before he could think, the ice gave way and he sank into the freezing cold water.

His head disappeared under the ice.

He gasped involuntarily with shock, his mouth filling with water. He kicked his legs until his head broke the surface, spitting the water from his mouth, before he went under again.

On the embankment, Stefan had slowly begun to edge himself out onto the ice, trying to distribute his weight evenly, while Claire called for an ambulance.

Harry was growing tired, his body shutting down, but he still managed to grab hold of the edge of the ice, trying to haul his body from the water.

Stefan heard the ice creaking under his own weight. He paused, dropped slowly to his knees and straightened his body out along the ice and shuffled closer on his belly.

Harry's head went under water again, and Stefan moved faster, putting the sound of the creaking ice to the back of his mind.

Underneath the water, Harry was losing the fight.

His body ached to shut down, as the cold tore through his flesh. He was holding his breath, lungs aching for air.

Then he felt something against his foot catch and drag him. He kicked out, his foot colliding against something solid.

He risked opening his eyes and peered down. The light from the fireworks overhead sent down little chinks of light that fractured in the water.

He saw a face, pale and ghost-like.

Instinct caught him.

He opened his mouth to scream, water flooding into his airways, as he stared down into dark dead eyes.

Scared, and knowing this would be his last effort, he mustered his last ounce of strength and kicked his legs hard.

On the surface, Stefan was shivering, his breath coming in short sharp bursts as he edged as close as he dared to the hole in the ice.

Harry's head then broke the surface, his body propelling forward, landing with his arms outstretched, flailing for something to grasp on the slippery surface. He began to slip back down again, but Stefan grasped his wrist.

'Kick with your legs!' he shouted, reaching out his other hand to grip the boy's right arm. Harry kicked again and again, and even when his body was out on the ice, clear of the water, he didn't stop.

Stefan pulled him to the embankment.

'I need blankets,' Claire shouted out to the gathered crowd. 'Coats, anything.'

A few men took theirs off and started to wrap them around Harry. He'd been in the water less than ninety seconds, but to Harry it had felt like hours of having needles pushed underneath his skin.

He coughed up some water when Claire sat him forward, and before she could speak, she heard his rasping voice from behind his chattering teeth.

'B… b… body.'

Stefan looked confused and lowered his face to the boy's eye level. 'What did you say?'

Harry grabbed Claire's hand and looked deep into her eyes.

'Body… in the water… Dead. Body.'

Claire saw the fear in his eyes, just before they closed and he fell unconscious in her arms.

FOUR DAYS EARLIER

1st NOVEMBER – 11:02 P.M.

'It's your time.'

He stood watching her from the street corner, icy rain soaking him to the bone. He could have gone back to his car, chosen another night, but no matter how hard reason pleaded with him, he couldn't tear his eyes away.

Everything about her disgusted him. The way she walked, the way she dressed, the way she talked.

Everything.

To him, her whole life was just a game determined by how much someone was willing to pay for her. The fact she was now with child complicated things, but also gave further justification to carry out what he'd planned for her.

Nola Grant stood at the side of the road. Her lanky, painfully thin frame cut a sombre stance under the street lamp. The fluorescent light cast shadows across her face but strangers could still see her wide-eyed vacant stare. She was tall and her bones jutted out at sharp angles, which were further exaggerated by her tight-fitting clothes.

She wore a low-rise, sleeveless top, no coat despite the cold, flaunting her many tattoos. The ink covered nearly all the flesh up both arms, and also found its way over her left shoulder and down onto her breast. Her light brown skin made the faded designs appear more muted in colour, but still made her stand out more than the other girls. Many men seemed intrigued to know just where else she had been scarred by the tattooist's needle.

As a car pulled to a stop in front of her, she bent her head to see inside the open window. The harsh night made her even more eager to get away, to seek shelter from the rain that grew heavier by the second.

A price was quickly agreed, and the man across the road saw her disappear inside the car. He wondered how far gone she was with child, spawned by an unknown faceless punter. He hazarded a guess at no more than eleven weeks, since her belly showed no signs of swelling.

As the car pulled away into the unforgiving night, something inside spurred him on. He charged across the road, giving chase. The driver put his foot down before he could get close enough.

The man stood staring after the lights as they grew smaller by the second. What had he been thinking? He would have to make his move later, and promised himself that she would not leave him until he knew she was ready and she'd earned the right of safe passage.

*

Inside the car, Nola lit up a rolled cigarette, relishing the small amount of warmth and comfort it gave her. The sickly scent of cannabis swirled into the punter's face and his mouth pulled into a hard line of disgust. He took one hand off the wheel, violently plucked the cigarette from her mouth, and discarded it out the window.

Nola risked a sideways glance at his face but stayed silent. He had paid for submissive and she had agreed to play the part in his twisted fantasy, no questions asked. As she sat in the passenger seat, rainwater dripping from her tightly curled hair, she was indifferent when the car turned down a dark lonely side street.

Deep down she had never felt any shame in the fact that sometimes she enjoyed this job. The fact that she now carried another life inside her never even crossed her selfish mind and had no bearing on her decisions. Little did she know, or could have ever imagined, just how quickly this was about to change.

11:57 p.m.

It was nearly midnight when she was pushed from the car as it parked up outside the back entrance to a nightclub down another dark side-road. She hit the concrete, landing hard on her knees, cutting holes in her leggings.

The car door slammed shut behind her and tyres screeched on the wet tarmac. She pulled herself up, but fell forward onto her hands, feeling the raw sting as the surface cut her flesh. As if to add insult to injury, the heavens opened once again, and large drops of rain engulfed her.

'*You fucking prick!*' she screamed, as the car's headlights disappeared into the darkness. She looked up to the night sky, but saw no moon. It had been raining heavily since early October with no signs of letting up. The bleak weather was in keeping with her mood.

She pulled herself to her feet, teetering on her thin high heels. She winced as a sharp surge of pain ran up through her groin. Nola was hurt, inside as well as out. If she hadn't needed the money so bad, she'd never have got into that man's car.

She inspected the grazes on her knees through the holes in her leggings, and then held her hands out in front of her. The falling rain stung the cuts on her palms, and she tucked both hands under her armpits. She was trying to get her bearings when she suddenly felt she was not alone.

'Are you OK?'

The calm voice came from the darkness. Nola whipped her head around and saw a man approach her through the torrent of rain.

'I saw what happened.'

Wary, she took a few steps back and the man slowed his pace, holding out his hands to calm her. 'It's OK. I just wanted to check you were all right.'

She searched his face, but it was hard to make anything out in the shadows.

She felt a flicker of recognition as she looked into his eyes and listened to his well-spoken, controlled voice, but it quickly passed. He wasn't from Haverbridge, not this part anyway. She could see it in his clothes, the way he held his head high, the way he carried himself.

Cars whipped past down the main street several yards away, tyres cutting through puddles. Shrieks from those caught in the downpour rang out in the distance and the smell of fast food filled the air, carried on the wind, down towards them.

Nola longed to be anywhere but here with this man.

'You're bleeding,' he said, venturing forward.

She took a step back. 'Stay away.'

'I just want to help.'

'And I said stay the fuck away.'

'But you're hurt.'

She stepped back again and looked for an exit. There was none. He was blocking any hope of getting to the busy street ahead. 'Let me help you, please.' His voice sounded gentle enough.

'I don't need your help!' she spat. 'I'm fine. It's just a few scratches.'

He looked away, deep in thought. Her eyes never left his face. 'I… I can pay you.'

'What?' Her face twisted. 'Thought you were offering me help?'

'I am, but since you seem reluctant to accept my help at face value, I thought I'd offer you something you weren't used to turning down.'

Nola's face screwed up with disgust. 'Just fuck off,' she said, her arm waving him away. She edged around him but he blocked her path.

'You misunderstand me. I meant I'll pay you if you let me help you.' He reached out and lightly touched her arm.

'Don't touch me.'

'Please, I just want to help.'

'Fucking weirdo,' she said, pushing him aside.

'Don't be like that, Nola.'

She froze. The weight of his stare was crushing. 'How'd you know my name?'

He smiled, stepping closer. 'I know many things… Let me help you.'

2nd NOVEMBER – 00:48 A.M.

It was a welcome relief, as she slipped down lower into the hot bathwater. The man, who said his name was Aaron, had taken her back to his home and tended her wounds, fed her well, and explained how he'd watched her for some time now and felt he had to help her. Nola had thought it was creepy at first but the pull of a hot meal and a bath had been too great for her to dwell on it much.

She smiled as he handed her a bottle of shampoo. He returned the smile, for appearance's sake, and went to leave her in peace.

'Wait,' she said, sitting up in the bath. 'Would you mind?' She held the shampoo bottle towards him. He looked down at her, his face blank. Only a few soapy bubbles covered her modesty, and he felt embarrassed. Eventually, he nodded. He lathered up the liquid in his hands as he perched on the edge of the bath.

When he massaged the shampoo into her hair, he felt her shoulders relax beneath his touch. He realised that no matter how much mental and physical torture this whore could endure, deep down, when it came to it, at every opportunity she would use her body to her advantage. It made him sick. Still, it was this flaw that had made it easier for him to lure her into his house.

Stupid bitch.

Nola had no knowledge of his actions behind her, and he was free to cover her nose and mouth with the chloroform-soaked

cloth he'd concealed inside his trouser pocket. She whipped
her hands back, scratching at his arms as he held the rag
tighter against her face. Bathwater sloshed over the sides as
she thrashed her legs, until she became limp, sliding deeper
into the unknown.

He dragged her body from the tub and let her fall, her
limbs hitting the cold tiles, hard.

Nola Grant was not destined to drown in her own filth.
All he knew was that she would be tested and she alone
would decide the outcome. He would make her responsible
for either her life or her death.

His face remained resolute as he dried her body and
pulled her clothes on roughly, disgusted by her thin nylon
underwear.

*

He barely struggled down the stairs to his basement; she
was so light to carry. Once he had shackled her wrists, he
looked down on her sleeping face and pushed stray strands of
wet hair away from her eyes. In another life, she might
have been pretty. Maybe she would have made her parents
proud. Yes, maybe in another life. For now at least, Nola was
going nowhere.

As he reached the top of the stairs, he looked back.
His eyes did one final sweep of the room, then her body, before
switching out the light and locking the door behind him.

02:03 a.m.

She was freezing.

That was Nola's first thought when she opened her eyes
for the first time since being attacked in the bath. She didn't
know how long she'd been out cold. There was no concept of

time down there with so little light, just a sense of dread and heaviness in the air.

She noticed the small lamp on a table in the corner. She tried to think but her head felt heavy, especially when she tried to pull herself up from the floor. She felt a sharp tug at her skin when she moved her hands.

She stared at the medieval-style shackles that circled around a pipe fixed to the wall and, instinctively, pulled the chain hard. The pipe vibrated, and metal bit tighter into her skin. She stifled a groan of desperation and pulled at the shackles again and again until she broke the skin and her wrists ached. She felt tears wash her cheeks as she began to sob.

*

Upstairs, the man smiled as he turned the volume down low on his television set. He wanted to imagine her pain, her desperation. It felt empowering. Although the basement was carefully soundproofed, he still heard the rumble in the pipe. Nola was finally awake, and probably cold and hungry. She would also be very scared… perfect.

*

She heard the floorboards creak above her, and sucked in a deep breath before screaming. It wasn't until her throat felt red-raw that she stopped. She swallowed hard, the sensation akin to swallowing ground glass.

She heard the door at the top of the stairs groan, as locks were turned and a bolt drawn back. Her heart thundered against her chest, and she realised she was holding her breath. The door swung open and she saw his feet on the top of the wooden stairs. She pulled herself to her feet, the chain ringing against the pipe.

She backed against the wall.

The man slowly came down the stairs, taking his time, prolonging the agony inside her. Each creak of the wood under his weight made her nerves alive with fear.

'Aaron?'

He stopped.

Inside, she cursed herself. She may not be the brightest but she felt really stupid for not realising that 'Aaron' was not his real name. Everything about this man was a lie, and she'd fallen for it, hook, line and sinker.

He continued down the stairs. She pushed herself further back against the wall, as if she could melt and hide inside the walls themselves.

He approached her with caution, and she noted the tray he was carrying, balancing a jug of water and a plate with a lid. It was like one of the stainless steel plates containing food she'd had in hospital once.

Underneath one arm, he clutched neatly folded clothes. He stopped a few feet in front of her, watching her recoil. He frowned as he went to the table. She watched him like a hawk as he sat the tray down. Unfolding the clothes from under his arm, he turned to her, eyes hidden in the shadows cast across his face.

'Are you thirsty?'

Silence.

Neither could hear anything but the sound of their own breathing. His eyes met hers. Nola Grant was scared all right. Scared to death almost.

'You must stay hydrated to keep your strength up.'

She almost buckled at his words. 'You're not going to kill me?' she said, a new wave of hope flooding her senses. His eyes narrowed, before looking back at the table.

'I didn't say that.'

Pause. 'I just want to go home.'

He breathed in sharply and went to speak, but firmly shut his mouth and she immediately felt her heart sink. A fearful sweat took hold of her. Whatever nasty thought he had in his head quickly disappeared as he held up a pair of jeans and a thin jumper.

'I've brought you a different set of clothes,' he said, as he looked at her from head to toe. 'Yours are… unsuitable.'

He edged closer, until he stood within a few inches of touching her. 'I think I got your size right. I got the smallest in the shop, size six.' Her eyes were silently questioning him. 'Here, let me help you.'

As he reached out to touch her, she sank to the floor, drew up her legs towards her torso, raising her arms to protect herself.

'Don't touch me!'

'Don't be silly,' he said, kneeling beside her on the rough cold concrete. He slipped his fingers down the waistband of her leggings, but she kicked him hard in the jaw, sending his head reeling to one side with a crack.

Then there was silence.

She pulled herself upright. His face was turned away from her, and he was bent forward to one side.

'Now you know why I took those heels off you.'

She froze at the tone of his voice.

He swung his head back around to stare at her. His eyes were darker than before. They were frightening, almost no iris, just pupils dark and wide, bottomless holes.

He spat blood from his mouth onto the floor, narrowly missing her leg. She watched him arch a finger inside his mouth, pull it out and inspect the blood on his fingertip. He'd bitten his cheek with the force of her blow. It took every ounce of strength to suppress his inner rage.

For a brief moment he recalled his mother's words from when he was about twelve years old – 'Jekyll and Hyde'. That was the only way she could ever describe him to anyone.

'Don't try that again, or I'll have to shackle your ankles as well.' He spoke quietly, but Nola recognised the very real threat behind his words. She recoiled as he reached out for her again. This was part of the humiliation he wanted her to feel, right down to her core.

'I don't want to change my clothes.' She rushed her words, and even to her own ears, she could hear as the sentence tumbled from her mouth that the words sounded jumbled. Almost incoherent. She was losing her control.

'Your clothes offend me, Nola. You will change or you won't eat. That's how it is. How it has to be.' He sat forward and pulled her leggings over her small hips.

She squirmed. 'No, please, let me change myself.' She tried to push his hands away. The chain around the pipe vibrated under the strain. He looked at her, then the shackles. 'Give me this one bit of dignity, please, I beg you.'

He weighed up her request. It wasn't unreasonable and he didn't want to touch her any more than was necessary. He nodded and he could visibly see her relief.

He moved so close, she could feel the heat of his breath. 'I'm going to unlock your shackles. I'll be waiting right outside the door whilst you change. When you're decent, sit back on the floor and call for me.'

Nola nodded obediently, forcing a grateful smile.

He suddenly reached out and gripped her chin in his hand, twisting her face towards his. She felt flecks of spit on her lips as he spoke.

'Listen to me carefully, Nola, this is very important… there is no other way out of this basement other than the door up those stairs.'

He saw her eyes glaze over again and a tear roll down her cheek. He watched it slide over her skin and felt an urge simmering inside him. He stretched out his tongue, catching the teardrops on the tip, and licked up the length of her cheek.

He closed his eyes, heard a desperate whimper escape her mouth. His eyes fluttered open. Hers were wide. Fearful.

'I will always be right behind that door.' He squeezed her chin hard. 'Make sure you don't forget that... Do you understand what I'm telling you?'

She blinked hard. She understood.

He produced a key from his pocket, held it in front of her eyes, then unlocked her shackles. He watched her rub each wrist before he passed her the clothes. When he reached the top of the stairs, he turned and glared at her.

'Remember what I said.'

*

Nola changed quickly, never taking her eyes from the door. Her legs were trembling as she pulled the jeans up and over her hips. They were a perfect fit; the man had chosen well. When she pulled the jumper on, it also fit seamlessly. The man had guessed her size, which unnerved her even more.

Just how long has he been watching me?

Her eyes took in the room. She was desperate for a way out but was mindful of what he'd said to her, and she believed every word. She called out to him, and after a long pause he opened the door and came down the stairs towards her. He stared at her from head to toe, and nodded, pleased with himself.

'You look much better. More respectable.' Nola didn't know why, but she found herself smiling at him, as if she needed his approval. She watched him pick up the shackles and raise them towards her. 'Back in these, please.'

He saw her face fall.

'It's a necessity.'

Once he pulled the shackles around the pipe and cuffed her again, he retrieved the tray from the table and set it on the floor by her feet. He removed the lid, and steam from a hot casserole swirled up towards her, and her stomach tightened with pangs of hunger.

He looked at her face thoughtfully before pointing at the food. 'Please eat.'

She sat on the floor cross-legged but hesitated. He smiled. 'It's fine. I've not poisoned it.' He produced a plastic spoon, threw it into her lap. 'Eat now, because there won't be anything else for a while, and you'll only get fed if you're good.'

'How long have I been out?'

His face was serious. 'Not long enough for anyone to notice you've gone.'

She shivered at the words but found the strength to press him further. 'Why am I here? What've I done?' He twitched at her tone of voice, as if it were painful to his ears. He paused.

'You'll find out soon enough, just eat.' He retrieved the water from the table and poured some into a plastic cup, then sat it down beside her. 'Make sure you drink,' he said, before climbing back up the stairs. When he reached the top he looked down at her and scanned the room, checking for anything that might be out of place. 'You've got twenty minutes, then I'll be taking your plate.'

She looked away, holding back her tears. 'Don't try anything stupid, and remember what I've told you.' Then he slammed the door after him. As she heard the turn of a key and a bolt lock her away again, she flung her head back, letting out a guttural cry.

02:06 a.m.

'They say we should get snow.'

Rachel Larson was hugging her coat tighter around her body, bracing herself against the strong wind. She'd given up trying to light her cigarette after several attempts against the gale. The yellow flame from her lighter appeared fleetingly in small sparks before dying.

'I should give up,' she said, pulling the cigarette from her dry lips and throwing it to the floor.

'Hey, I would've had that,' said her friend, Olivia Jones, who stooped to pick it up. Her cold fingers barely felt the cigarette between them as she put it in her coat pocket.

'Livi, that's been on the floor.'

'Your point?' She turned her back to the wind, wild blonde hair thrashing around her face.

'The pavement's dirty.'

'I'm sure I've had worse in my mouth, Rach,' she laughed, turning to face her again. 'In fact, I know I have.'

'You skank.'

'Isn't that what punters pay for?'

Rachel forced herself to bury her smile. Olivia grinned then checked her watch. 'Where are all the desperate lonely men?' Rachel shrugged and checked her own watch. 'Have you managed to get hold of Nola yet?' Olivia asked, seeing the worried expression on her friend's face.

'No.'

'I'm sure she's fine.'

Rachel shook her head. 'It's just not like her. We have, like, this unwritten rule to always check in with each other when we see a new client.'

Olivia shrugged, then caught the eye of a man lingering around the local Nisa supermarket opposite where they stood. He gestured towards her, a simple nod of his head.

'Customer at last,' she said, turning to face Rachel. 'I'll see you in a bit, yeah?' Rachel forced herself to smile but could not hide the worry in her eyes. Olivia reached out and rubbed her shoulder. 'She'll be all right, Rach, you'll see. She may be back at the flat by now. You know Nola. She's like a bad fucking penny… she always comes back.'

'Maybe.'

The feeling that all was not well pinched Rachel's body. She shivered but was unable to shake the feeling. As Olivia turned to leave, she reached out for her arm. 'You'll be careful, won't you?'

Olivia smiled and nodded. 'I'll see you later, Rach.'

She watched Olivia disappear from view towards the back of the Nisa with the man. She looked at her watch for the hundredth time then checked the streets around her.

It was definitely quiet tonight and the thought of going back to her flat, which she'd shared with Nola this past year, was a comforting one. As the wind picked up again, the blast of icy cold made the decision for her.

She turned off down the high street and followed the road around, walking the next three blocks to her home very quickly, passing the rundown blocks of flats and maisonettes with some dread. She'd had a few near misses around here. The dark corners and dead ends were a breeding ground for dark deeds.

It was a relief when she finally climbed the iron stairs that ran up the side of the local shops to her flat. She closed the front door, blocking out the cold behind her. She could smell the pungent scent of fat as she took her boots off in the cramped hallway.

She hated living here, but being directly above a chip shop did have the advantage of keeping the flat reasonably warm during the cold weather, which helped keep her heating bills down. The less her bills cost, the fewer times she had to lie on her back to pay them.

Tonight, though, felt extra chilly so she plugged in the electric heaters in each room, turning them up high. She went to Nola's bedroom, and smiled a little at the QUEEN OF FUCKING EVERYTHING sign on the door, before she knocked.

Silence.

'Nola? You in there?'

She tapped her knuckles on the door again and pulled the door handle. The room was how Nola had left it the day before. Clothes were strewn across the unmade bed, make-up left out on the floor in front of a full length mirror, along with her hair dryer and a wrap of something white and powdery. Rachel's heart sank and she took out her mobile from the pocket in her jeans.

'Nola, it's Rach,' she said as her call was immediately diverted to voicemail. 'I'm worried.' She didn't know what else to say and left a long pause before finding her voice again. 'Please, call me as soon as you get this.' She checked her watch again:

02:43 a.m.

'If you've not been in touch by midday—' She broke off mid-sentence. 'Just call me.' She hung up, pushed the mobile back in her pocket and went to the kitchen.

After she'd eaten and got ready for bed, she checked her mobile again. There was one text message from Olivia, saying she was OK, but nothing else. Unable to ignore the feeling of dread inside her belly, she curled up in her bed, the duvet wrapped tightly around her, but was unable to sleep.

02:43 a.m.

Her feet were like blocks of ice. Nola flexed her toes to ease the numbness. She'd wolfed down her food, without a moment's thought to savour the taste. When she heard the door unlocking again, she closed her eyes with dread. The man was soon beside her and she noticed he was carrying a large leather pouch. He laid it on the table carefully, his fingers lingering on the drawstring cord. He was trembling. He forced himself to move away.

She shut her eyes tight, as if it would make him disappear when she opened them again. She prayed silently that this was all a dream. A twisted nightmare she would safely wake from.

She'd be frightened but unharmed.

He cleared a space for himself on the floor in front of her and waited for her to look at him. When she finally did, it was through bloodshot eyes.

'Can I have some socks and shoes, please? My feet are so cold... so cold.' Her heart sank when he shook his head. She sat up straight and leaned closer. He seemed so normal towards her most of the time. It was only if she pressed him, or became agitated, that he changed, like a switch being flicked on and off. She guessed if she played along with him, acted normal – or as normal as she could be – she might find a way out of this.

'I won't try to escape,' she said. His eyes narrowed, suspicious. 'If you promise you won't hurt me, I won't try to escape.' She spoke with such conviction that he almost believed her.

He shook his head.

'Do not make promises you have no intention of keeping.' He paused, allowing his words to sink in. 'Now's the time when you should be thinking about the life that grows inside of you, rather than yourself.'

His words visibly shook her.

Her eyes widened. 'How'd you...? How could you know...?

'How do I know that you're pregnant?' He smiled. 'You should dispose of your rubbish more carefully. You can tell a lot about someone by what they throw out each week.'

He saw the shock on her face. She spent the next few moments thinking back to the longest three minutes of her life, when she'd taken that pregnancy test. She knew what the answer would be before the double lines appeared in the results window.

She'd been throwing up regularly and her body ached all the time, like she was expecting her period, but it hadn't come. The aches continued and she was so tired, much more than usual. When the test had shown positive, she'd discarded it and buried her head in her hands, feeling nothing but despair.

She knew if Daryl found out there would be big trouble and she could kiss goodbye to her earnings. Then there was her life. It wouldn't be worth living. This business had a strong hold on her and she doubted she had the strength to fight it.

'How far gone are you?' he asked. When she didn't reply, he looked at her, eyes fierce. 'You've been to see a doctor, haven't you?' Her head lowered and she shook it solemnly.

He got to his feet and glared down on her. 'Why not? Don't you care?'

'No, I don't care. Why should I? I obviously don't know who the father is. It could be anybody.'

He looked exasperated, turning away with a mock laugh, running his hands roughly through his dark hair. He paced up and down, before turning on his heels and peering down at her.

'So, you were going to carry to full term then drop it down some side alley like it's rubbish and carry on business as usual?'

Nola snapped. 'Who the fucking hell do you think you are?'

When she saw the surprised look in his eyes, she felt a wave of confidence grow inside her. She pulled herself to her feet. 'It's not as if I was planning on going full term. Not that this has anything to do with you,' she said, jabbing her finger hard in his chest. 'Who are you to judge me?'

He rushed at her then. He gripped her face with both his hands, forced her eyes to look at his.

Inside, he was reeling at the insolence. It took all his strength not to lose control completely and snap her delicate neck. He tried to focus on why he was doing this, why she was there.

'I'm trying to help you. Give that life inside you a chance, yet you mock me,' he spat, his mouth just inches away from hers.

A look of defiance washed over her face. 'I'll scream the place down before you even lay another finger on me!'

A cruel grin spread across his face. He pulled her head violently to the side and whispered in her ear. 'Soundproof room, Nola. Do your worst.' He released her head and took a step back, before swinging his fist square into her jaw.

*

03:36 a.m.

Second chances. Second chances. They could be tricky things. Obstacles almost. He wondered if it was a sign of weakness to break his own rules, bend to anyone and suffer the consequences. He'd given people second chances before. His mother had been one of them.

No, he thought. His mother had more than a second chance. She'd had many, and failed each time. They'd been wasted on her. He didn't want to be tested. He was the teacher, not the pupil. She would bend to him and if she didn't, that was it. Literally, game over, even if it did hurt him a little.

Sometimes a conscience, be it small and almost invisible, had its drawbacks. Its hidden problems. A conscience was overrated.

He'd tried. It wasn't working.

Despite wanting to offer her a second chance, he found she was leaving him with little choice. He'd expected some resistance, but unlike the woman before Nola, he'd expected her to fight for her life to save the baby that grew inside her.

Nola Grant wanted to live, but for herself, not for her child. He could see it in her eyes, feel it in her body when he touched her skin. The need to survive radiated from every pore but she was only making it harder and harder for him to justify letting her live.

He felt sad, desperate, and that he'd failed. Failed her, the child, himself… and because of this, he could feel the familiar knot of shame pull at his insides.

A conscience is overrated. He was trying to believe his own thoughts, but his heart tugged away at him inside.

Nola Grant must die. She must die, so that others might stand a chance to be touched by his hand and steered back to the right path.

She must die… she has to.

*

04:06 a.m.

Nola had spent the last half hour swearing at him, spitting her filth like a person possessed. Her legs lashed out at him violently whenever he tried to come near and calm her.

Inside his head, he could hear his mother's voice screaming obscenities at him back when he was a small boy. Nowadays, he couldn't abide the language. It tapped into a pain deep within him and he knew he couldn't stand much more. He was nearly at breaking point.

'I won't tell you again,' he said, turning to face her, his finger pointing. 'This is your last warning.'

Her head shot backwards as she laughed. It didn't sound human.

He used his hands to cover his ears, drowning her out.

She couldn't believe what she was seeing. He was acting like a little child. She half expected him to start stomping his feet in a paddy and she felt more confident the more he seemed to crumble in front of her.

His spine stretched upright, as if he'd just been shocked. He looked at the pouch he'd put on the table earlier, then at her mouth.

Sound seemed to be sucked from the room, and all he could see was her mouth moving, spouting more poison.

Open. Shut. Open. Shut.

He reached for the pouch, pulled away the cord, and took out a pair of scissors. He hadn't intended on using any of the items in the bag: the knuckleduster, the pliers, the lighter. He was only going to frighten her with them, so that she'd fear what he might do if she didn't obey him. If she didn't see reason.

Nola Grant was beyond seeing reason by now.

He thought she'd have been ideal for his plans. That she would embrace the new life offered to her. A second chance to teach her. A chance to leave her current way of life behind and raise her child with none of the trappings that life entailed. But she was pure filth, inside and out, and she would never change. She didn't want to… There were others. Others more worthy, deserving, more in need. He'd had enough of her abuse.

He clasped the scissors in his palm.

He edged closer.

She kicked out, screaming insults at him. He blocked out her words, let them wash over him. She meant nothing to him any more.

A conscience is overrated.

As her leg kicked out again, she caught him in the thigh. He stifled a groan, but remained focused. He grabbed her leg, pulling hard, knocking her off balance.

Her body crashed to the floor, collapsing in a heap at his feet. Before she could react, he was down on her, grasping her in a headlock with one arm. With his other hand he gripped the scissors in his sweaty palm, and weighted her body down with his own.

He released her head, pried open her mouth and pulled at her tongue.

She gagged, spluttered, but he maintained his grip, forcing the scissor blades either side of the thrashing muscle.

She froze.

She felt the metal edges scrape her soft flesh. She whimpered, helpless.

'Hold your tongue or lose it!'

He roared so close to her ear, she thought the drum might burst. 'Do you understand me?' He felt her head nod. He could feel the fear radiate from her body in waves so strong, he could almost taste it.

She had to die. He knew this now, but it had changed his plans somewhat. Nola had been a mistake, but he'd learn from it.

She whimpered when he removed the scissors and released her body from under him.

She curled herself up into a ball, her back towards the wall, head tucked down with her chin resting on her chest. He saw her body shake violently as sobs overcame her. He allowed her a few moments of respite before the inevitable came.

08:32 a.m.

Rachel woke to the sound of someone banging on her front door. She bolted from the bed and ran. She flung open the front door, ignoring the cold that flooded in from outside.

'Nola?'

'Erm, no,' replied Olivia, standing with a large McDonald's paper bag under one arm. She stared at Rachel from head to toe. 'You may wanna put more clothes on, Rach,' she said, pushing her way over the threshold. 'It's like minus ten or something.'

Rachel looked down at her thin pyjama bottoms and bra, but she didn't care. The cold was nothing compared to the inner torment she'd had to put up with all night.

'I got us breakfast,' Olivia said, heading towards the kitchen. She started pulling out the cardboard cartons from the paper bag. 'I hope you're hungry.' She took a large bite of her burger. 'Oh, that's good,' she said with her mouth full.

Rachel looked at her, despondent. 'I thought you were Nola.'

Olivia stopped chewing, keeping her eyes trained to the floor.

'I've still not heard from her.'

Finishing her mouthful, Olivia turned to face her. 'You told Daryl yet?'

'Have I hell,' Rachel said, reaching for her burger. 'He's been calling though.'

'What you been telling him?'

'I've been avoiding answering.'

Olivia gave a mock laugh. 'FYI, that's not wise.' Rachel threw her burger down on the counter and rested her face in her hands.

'I know, I know,' she said. 'I've left him a voicemail saying she's been with a punter for a few days, that she'd been paid up front, but I can't keep it up much longer.' She picked up her burger again and took a large bite. 'He's started leaving me nasty messages already,' she said between mouthfuls.

'Course he has, that's Daryl.' Olivia chewed the last mouthful of her Big Mac and dusted her hands together, sending crumbs to the floor. 'Look, way I see it, Nola's gone AWOL 'cos she don't want to be found. You can't force her, Rach. She knows the price she'll pay if she runs out on Daryl – we all do.' She placed a hand on Rachel's shoulder.

Sadly, Rachel knew from personal experience just what he was capable of. Daryl Thomas was their pimp. He ran their lives for them, as he did with all of his girls. He took a big percentage of what they earned on the street, dictated to them what to wear, how to act, and told them who they could talk to, and what he would do if any of them tried to walk out on him.

Rachel had tried it once – a long time ago now it seemed – and she had nearly got away from him. If it hadn't been for another girl giving her away (Rachel never did find out who), she would've been free of him. On that occasion it had taken seventeen stitches to put her head wound back together and another five in her split lip, followed by several trips back and forth to the hospital until her arm was fixed again after a difficult break. All things considered, she'd got off lightly, compared to what Daryl had done to others.

She watched Olivia pull out her hairbrush from her bag and run it through her long hair, and wished she could be more like her; living each day as it came, and never really worrying about anything.

Despite her slight frame, Olivia was tough and streetwise. Rachel was the opposite; her long auburn hair, with large curls, made her look younger than her twenty years. Her build was average, and she was taller than Olivia, but she wasn't anywhere near as robust.

She was about to ask Olivia what she thought she should do about Daryl, when they both heard Nancy Boy by Placebo echoing from Rachel's room.

They stared at each other, motionless as statues.

Rachel shrieked: 'My phone!'

Both girls nearly fell over themselves, as they skidded across the hall and into the bedroom. Rachel's mobile was flashing on her bedside cabinet, but the call diverted to voicemail as she picked it up. She pressed the answer button anyway.

'Hello? Nola?'

'You missed the call,' Olivia sighed as she launched herself onto Rachel's bed. 'You should've kept it on you.'

'The caller ID says unknown; it might not have been her.'

'Probably Daryl then.'

Rachel was silent and stared at her phone, willing it to ring again. After a few minutes, the phone lit up and let out a beep.

1 New Voicemail Msg

Both girls looked at each other, then the phone.

Rachel hesitated.

'You gonna listen to that, or what?'

Rachel looked at Olivia then the phone again. She swallowed hard as she pressed the button to retrieve the message. Warily, she held the mobile to her ear.

Her eyes widened as the message played out. It sounded so surreal, she didn't even know whether to believe it or not. She remained silent and when the message finished, she felt tears pricking at the surface of her eyes, like thousands of tiny red-hot needles.

*

08:45 a.m.

Nola wailed as the man hung up her mobile and tossed it to the floor. The lid of the battery compartment came away on impact and cracked, but the phone itself seemed to be intact and working. He'd deliberately withheld the number when placing the call moments ago.

As she hung upside down, tethered to a steel framework attached to the ceiling, her arms hung down, hands grasping at nothing but air. She knew she was too far from the mobile to reach it but still she tried.

She saw his big black boots come into view. He placed his foot on her mobile, then raised it high before bringing it crashing down. The cracking sound from her only source of help resounded in her ears. Her eyes clamped shut, her mouth pinched, as she fought back fresh tears.

Her senses were tingling. She was so cold. A draught was coming from a gap under the wooden door to the building. She'd been stripped naked and was now hanging precariously from the rafters, open to whatever torment was to come.

Her blood rushed to her head and she prayed she would black out.

The man watched her, eyes looking like dark holes. The pits of hell set deep in his pale face. She pleaded with him as he drew nearer but it was pointless. He held the knife at his side for her to see. The best she could now hope for was that it would be over quickly. She closed her eyes tight, bracing herself.

Then she felt the blade.

*

08:46 a.m.

'We've got to go to the police.'

'And tell them what?'

Olivia was now losing patience, and paced the room. Rachel was already getting dressed, stumbling as she pulled her trainers on her feet.

'I'll tell them Nola's missing and about the call,' she rushed, grabbing her coat as she made her way to the front door. 'They'll help.' Olivia, following behind, reached out and grabbed her hand as she touched the door handle.

'We've got to work, Rach,' she said, her eyes looking deadly serious. 'Daryl wants to see us.'

Rachel was frozen by her words. Daryl wanting to see them suddenly meant one thing – trouble. 'What've you told him, Livi?'

'Nothing,' she said, averting her glance from Rachel.

'You're lying to me.'

Olivia was silent, but her face gave her away. Rachel's body tensed and she raced back into her bedroom and went to the bed. 'I can't believe you've told him what's been going on, that I've lied to him.' She reached under her pillow and pulled out a knife.

Olivia's eyes widened. 'What the fuck, Rach? You're not taking that out with you. I'm not letting you.' She grabbed her wrist, squeezing hard, but Rachel refused to drop the blade.

'Don't you remember how long it took me to heal the last time Daryl messed me up?'

'He won't touch you this time, I promise.'

'I'm going to help Nola. I'm going to help myself.' Tears were now falling down her cheeks. 'I need to get away from Daryl, from all of this.'

'You don't know if the voicemail's real or fake, Rach. Wake up!'

'I heard her screams in the background.' Her words ensured a long desperate silence between them both, until Rachel managed to find her voice again.

This time she spoke softly. 'I heard her. She was crying for help. She said he was going to kill her, whoever he is,' she said, dropping her knife to the floor. 'I can't ignore that. She wouldn't joke about something like this.'

Olivia's face softened. 'I'll go with you to the police, but let me call Daryl first.'

'*No!*'

'All right, no phone call,' she conceded, putting her mobile back in her pocket, 'but you got to talk to him sometime.'

Rachel nodded. 'I know… let's just find Nola first.'

CHAPTER 4

Present Day

6th November

Ice crunched under her feet as she walked over the grass verge, towards the lake where the body had been pulled from the water. Smoke from the fireworks still hung heavy in the air.

The winter sun was just beginning to break through the darkness, lying low on the horizon, and as she walked towards the white incident tent ahead, she stifled a yawn.

It had been a long night for forensic pathologist Dr Danika Schreiber, having been on call, and she could barely keep her eyes open. She was met by Claire, who was shivering in the cold, puffing on a cigarette.

'Thought you were giving up?' Danika said as she placed her case on the ground next to her. Her faint German accent was still audible, despite the fact she had lived in England for several years.

'It's been a long night.' Claire stomped her feet against the ground, trying to revive her frozen toes.

'For us both. That's why I'm late. The last job took longer than expected.' She peered over Claire's shoulder and stared out towards the broken ice floating on the water. 'Is that where you found the body?'

Claire flicked her cigarette from her fingers and it rolled across the ground. She nodded as she exhaled a plume of smoke. 'Yep, and it wasn't easy dragging her up either. You're bloody lucky it's only one body as well.'

'Yes, I heard you had to rescue a boy who'd fallen through,' she said, pulling the hood of her Tyvek suit over her long black hair. 'Where is DI Fletcher? He's OK, I hope?'

'He's gone with the boy to the hospital until we can locate the boy's parents. From what information we got out of those drunken friends of his, the mother's a lush and the father's not much better. We're having trouble finding them.'

They walked under the police tape and towards the incident tent. Danika pulled on a pair of overshoes, then thin blue plastic gloves, and followed Claire inside the tent. She was careful not to disturb any potential evidence, keeping to the plastic walkway which led towards the body. She squinted under the glare of the large spotlights, one in each of the four corners of the tent.

Both women looked down at the body. The face of a young girl stared back at them. Her body was naked, with a thick chain around her ankles. Danika stared at the heavy coiled links.

'Someone weighted her down,' she said, kneeling next to the body. Her eyes glanced over the girl's face and down to her toes. Then she returned to the deep cut to the side of the neck. The remains of dried blood were partially spattered down the dead woman's neck and chest, still visible despite having been in the lake. The water had given the blood a dull hue against the skin.

'How long do you think she's been under the ice?' Claire said.

'It's hard to say at this stage. When someone has been in cold storage, it slows the process of decomposition. It will be hard to pinpoint a time of death.'

'She's not been in a fridge, Danika.'

'Yes, but being under the ice has had the same effect to some degree. If she had been found elsewhere, there would be larvae, maggots... I could pinpoint the time period. There are no obvious signs of scavengers having tampered with the body, although I'll know more when I've examined her properly, but it suggests maybe she's not been in the water very long.

'There's a little orange tinge to the skin, which is to be expected as she's been submerged, but it's minimal. Again this would indicate she's not been here long.' She paused, frowning hard. 'That chain's a bit excessive. Even with it weighting her down, she'd have risen to the surface eventually, but you were lucky to find her now before the skin started to peel.'

Danika looked up. 'It's looking likely loss of blood is the cause of death.' Claire cocked her head, looking at the body at a new angle as Danika continued: 'She has a deep laceration to the side of the neck, most likely severing a jugular vein, carotid artery and the trachea. Death would have occurred within seconds, but she was probably killed somewhere else and dumped in the lake.'

'Ensuring most of the evidence is washed away.' Claire's voice was stern. Danika nodded in agreement.

'That's why there isn't as much blood here as there should be.' She pulled herself up and snapped a glove off over her hand. 'Wherever your crime scene is, it would've been a bloodbath.'

'The blood would've been cleared up.'

'Yes, but with the best will in the world it would be practically impossible to clear every last drop of it. There'll be a scrap or fine trace of it left somewhere. It's your job to find it.'

CHAPTER 5

Detective Sergeant Elias Crest rolled the biro he'd been chewing over his teeth, staring blankly at the newspaper on the table in front of him.

He'd been in Haverbridge CID less than a week and still he felt on edge. Moving back down south after living in Liverpool for the best part of eight years – five spent in CID – it was taking him time to adjust to his new surroundings.

It would take him even longer to adjust to working under yet another female DCI. His old Guv, DCI Meredith Glass, had been tough but she at least gave him the benefit of the doubt.

DCI Winters, however… He chewed his bottom lip as he cast his mind back to his first morning. She'd shaken his hand, but gripped it tight. He'd wondered if that had been her way of asserting her authority without the need for words to be spoken.

He knew she would have seen his file. Seen the reason he was transferring. Not that he gave a shit about what she thought in that respect but still, it bothered him. He didn't want her to have something she could hold over him, something she could use as leverage if she wanted.

Meredith Glass had tried that once.

He had smiled at Claire, in a vain attempt to hide his reservations. He'd asked her to call him by his first name, when she'd addressed him merely as 'Crest', but it had the opposite of the desired effect.

Her grip had tightened around his hand further, her face dropping any hint of a smile she may have expressed.

'I try to make it a habit never to go by first names, Crest,' she had said. He remembered how she'd given him the once over, head to toe, without any subtlety.

'To you, I'm 'Ma'am', 'Guv', 'Boss'… yes?' she'd said.

Elias had remained silent. 'And 'Bitch'?' he'd thought, suppressing a wry smile.

He remembered feeling a boiling heat rise up inside him as she had explained what was expected of him.

'You'll be mainly under the supervision of DI Fletcher, a very competent and respected member of my team,' she had said, watching his face carefully.

Elias had kept his eyes focused ahead. He knew when to pick his fights and when to merely observe.

And what was that last part she'd said? Something that had made him question what he was doing here. He grimaced as he remembered, her words echoing inside his head.

'I have no time for men who find it hard to work under the authority of a woman.'

She had deliberately let that sentence hang there in silence a moment longer than she'd needed to.

Elias figured he'd deserved that. Still, his eyes narrowed, the memory fresh in his mind, eating away at him.

I wish I knew exactly what was in my file.

Then there had been that parting shot – 'I won't tolerate mavericks.'

It was these words that jolted him out of his reverie, back to the lunch room.

He eyed the few people that were gathered around the vending machine, and plucked the biro from his mouth, flicking it across the table with irritation.

He'd decided to sit on his own. He wasn't in the mood for making friends. He'd had friends before he transferred, or so he thought. Where had they been when he needed someone to cover his arse? Watching their own backs, that's where. Doing everything by the book. Sometimes rules had to be broken for the greater good.

He tried to push the thought from his mind, staring down at his lunch, but although the hot meal smelled delicious, he didn't feel very hungry. Instead he added five heaped teaspoons of sugar to his coffee cup and slowly began to stir. He barely noticed DI David Matthews as he sat in the chair opposite him.

'You'll come crashing down about five o'clock if you're not careful,' he said, as he poured milk into his own cup. Elias stopped stirring, raising his eyes wearily, face blank.

'Sugar rush,' Matthews said. 'You'll be crashing in so many hours, mate.' He gestured to the coffee. When Elias failed to acknowledge him, Matthews pushed his own cup to one side and folded his arms on the table. 'She really isn't that bad.'

Elias scoffed and shook his head in disagreement. 'Why do you assume I have a problem with Claire?'

Matthews cocked an eyebrow. 'Written on your face.'

'Don't take the piss.'

Matthews held up his hands. 'I'm serious, mate, she's just testing you. She likes to see how tough you are, and no offence, but you're kinda falling at the first hurdle.'

Elias was having none of it. 'I grew up in Brixton, mate. I don't have to prove I'm tough enough. I've nothing to prove to her and my credentials speak for themselves. I'm not an idiot.'

Matthews sat back in his chair. 'Look, I know she's hard to get along with at first, but everyone agrees once they get to know her... Claire wouldn't be Claire if she was any different.'

'I have no intentions of getting to know her on a personal level.'

Matthews chewed his bottom lip, carefully taking in the new DS.

Elias was in his mid-thirties, dressed smartly, with fashionably messy hair that was streaked with blonde highlights.

A pair of large hazel-coloured eyes looked back at Matthews, with a steely edge to them.

'You got a problem or something, working under a woman?'

Elias practically scowled. 'No.'

Matthews raised his eyebrows. 'You sure about that, mate?' Silence hung heavy in the air. ''Cos if it's a gender thing—'

'It's not.'

'It's pretty old-school, thinking like that.'

'I respect women officers… good ones.'

'DCI Winters not good enough?'

Elias paused, being careful. 'I never said that.'

'But?'

'But… she does have a reputation.'

Matthews saw a little of himself in the new recruit, back when he first started his career as a PC. He also recalled his first impression of Claire when he started in CID. It would be hypocritical of him to be completely hard on Elias for his initial thoughts on their Guv. He ran his hand back through his brown hair and said, 'You definitely won't last five minutes with that attitude. She'll eat you for breakfast, lunch and dinner.'

'Who's eating who for what now?' asked Stefan, as he approached the table.

'Claire,' said Matthews, not taking his eyes from Elias.

'Ah. He's having reservations about his transfer.'

'Yep.'

'To be expected, I guess.'

'We've all been through it.'

'Yeah, I remember it well.'

'You know I am sitting right here,' Elias interjected. 'You needn't talk as if I wasn't.'

Exchanging glances with Matthews, Stefan looked apologetic.

'You're right. Sorry, it was meant as a joke,' he said, taking a seat beside Matthews. 'Guv's called a team brief in twenty minutes; see where we are with the body in the lake.' He glanced at Elias. 'You ever see anything like it before?'

Elias shook his head, but avoided Stefan's eyes. 'Saw my fair share of depravity, but this has a different feel to it.'

Stefan eyed Elias closely, noted his pale drawn face, and then glanced at the untouched food in front of him.

'Did Claire actually have the power to make you lose your appetite as well?' Stefan asked. Elias glanced up, and then looked at Matthews, who hid a smile in his coffee cup. He returned his gaze to Stefan and glowered.

'Hey, I'm being serious,' Stefan said, jabbing Matthews hard in the ribs. 'Ignore him. He's just glad Claire's taken the heat off him in favour of you.'

'That's not fair, Fletch.'

'Come off it, you love the banter, you practically ask for it,' he said, winking at Elias. Matthews ignored him and picked up the newspaper on the table.

Stefan looked at Elias and thought he caught a hint of a smile.

'You gonna eat that?' Stefan pointed his fork at the full plate. Elias shrugged, then shook his head, pushed the plate aside and sipped his coffee.

Stefan sat back in his chair. 'Did she give you the 'no first name' spiel?' Elias remained silent. 'She does give that speech to everyone.'

Elias sat back in his chair, jutted out his chin in defiance. 'You think I'm taking myself too seriously.' It was a statement rather than a question.

'Well, you said it,' Matthews quipped.

'Ignore him,' said Stefan. 'Best thing you can do is not take Claire's attempts to destroy you seriously. She's as harmless as a kitten really.'

'As far as harmless sharp-clawed kittens go,' Matthews added, nose still buried in the newspaper. Stefan rolled his eyes at him.

'Cut her some slack. She's really been through it in the last year. What with all that uncertainty with her father and… '

He trailed off when he saw he'd piqued Elias's interest.

'She's tough,' he said at length, 'but she's good. I'd trust her with my life, Crest. You just got to earn her trust and respect.'

Elias sat forward and looked stern again, his hands now clasped in front of him on the table. 'You know respect works both ways, right?'

Stefan's eyes narrowed, silently questioning.

'I mean, I can see you're her biggest fan n' all that but I don't need to know the inner workings inside her head. I'll deal with her in my own way.'

There was a long pause as the two men stared at each other. Stefan raked his fingers through his floppy light brown hair, trying to work Elias out. Realising he might have spoken too harshly, Elias added, 'Thanks, though… for the advice.'

He stood, drained the last dregs of his coffee and set the cup back down onto the table with a bang. 'Team briefing now, yes?' he said as he left.

Stefan felt Matthews looking at him.

'Are we taking bets on how long it takes him to walk?'

Stefan watched Elias leave the canteen. 'I think he's gonna need training wheels that's for sure.'

CHAPTER 6

From his desk, back in CID, Elias watched her through the floor-to-ceiling glass wall of her office, talking into the phone glued to her ear.

Claire must have felt eyes on her, because she looked up, straight in his direction.

He looked away first.

'And what're you doing for Christmas? Have you been a good girl this year?'

Elias glanced up, saw Matthews was beside Claire as soon as she came out of her office. Her face turned from a frown to what he thought was the faintest hint of a smile.

'I'll probably be in my straitjacket,' she said.

He cocked an eyebrow. 'Do I even want to know?'

'My mother's staying… probably right up until Christmas.'

He laughed. 'Don't tell me Iris managed to prise herself away from the Costa Brava?'

'Her once-a-year jaunt.'

'When it's this cold as well.'

'She's full of surprises,' she said, as she took her place at the front of the room. After several seconds the room quietened down.

'By a stroke of luck, we've already got some news on the body,' Claire said, as she circulated some photographs of a young woman who, despite smiling, had eyes that remained dark pits, captured in time, the light never reaching them.

'Nola Grant, twenty-three years old, prostitute.'

'So, our Jane Doe has a name,' Stefan said, crossing his legs when he sat down in his chair.

Claire nodded. 'Switchboard took a call from a girl claiming to be her flatmate, who reported her missing on the second. Her name's Rachel Larson. She heard about the body in the lake and she said it had to be Nola, based on the significant tattoos described on the body.

'We ran the name. Grant was known to police for soliciting and has been cautioned for drug offences. Looking at the photograph we have on file and this one provided by Larson, it sure looks like the girl we pulled from the lake this morning. The post mortem should confirm her identity with the records we have on the system. Nola went missing in the early hours of Friday morning, and guess who her pimp is?'

Everyone in the room looked expectant.

'Daryl Thomas.'

Nobody spoke at first. Claire looked at Stefan.

He paused. 'Christ…'

'Yeah, I thought the same,' she said. 'The 'filth beater' as he's affectionately known since that assault on PC Southgate the other year.' She paused. 'That's not the best bit either.'

She explained the missing persons report and the voicemail left on Rachel Larson's mobile.

'You've listened to the voicemail?' Matthews said.

Claire shook her head. 'No, I haven't yet, and Nola was still being treated as a missing person. It couldn't be established whether the call was legit and not a prank. We need to get Larson's and Nola's phone records. Larson should tell us who Nola's network provider was. We also need her mobile, which leads me to my next question.'

She glanced at Elias.

'Larson refused to say whether she'd formally ID the body and now her phone is switched off. I want you, Fletch, to head down to her flat – and take DS Crest with you.'

After allocating various other tasks to the rest of the team, Stefan was soon close beside her, pulling his coat on. Claire followed his line of vision.

It was firmly set on Elias.

'Is this his test run?'

She paused. 'You could say that.' She stared at Elias. 'Keep an eye on him, Fletch.'

He raised an eyebrow. 'Are you expecting trouble?'

'Truth be told,' she said, looking away when Elias glanced in her direction, 'I'm not sure yet.'

CHAPTER 7

Elias looked out of the window and sighed as Stefan drove his car towards Rachel Larson's flat. The tired-looking buildings that ran through the heart of the industrial area did little to enhance an already rundown part of Haverbridge. As they headed towards Haverbridge North, Stefan squinted at the bright shafts of light penetrating through random gaps in the gunmetal grey clouds above.

He hadn't offered Elias any conversation and he felt uncomfortable. Racking his brains for something to chat about, he couldn't think of anything that didn't sound contrived or insincere.

'Ice Maiden gave you permission to take me out with you, did she?'

Stefan's face shot around to look at him, feeling Elias had somehow read his mind. He returned Stefan's gaze. 'I mean Claire, of course.'

'Don't know what you're talking about.' Stefan was never really any good at lying, not even telling little white ones.

'Sure you don't. Why would you? It's all in my head, I get it,' Elias said. Stefan remained quiet, concentrating on the traffic. 'Is she like this with everyone she first meets?'

Stefan felt his face flush a little as he drew near a roundabout. 'It's the third exit here, isn't it?'

Elias laughed. 'Don't change the subject.'

Stefan sighed as he followed the road away from the roundabout and slowed the car as he approached some local shops, pulling into one of three parking spaces outside a chip shop.

'Larson's flat is one of them over the shops,' he said, looking Elias hard in the face. 'And with Claire, just cut her some slack. You're new to a tight-knit team, she's naturally wary.'

Elias looked incredulous. 'Everyone's so far up her arse and I just don't get it.'

Stefan had heard enough and as Elias got out of the car, Stefan followed after him. 'Word of advice: just drop it.'

'Drop what?'

'Your petty vendetta against Claire. She's got the respect of those in high places, not to mention from those who work directly with her, me included. My advice to you is to make the most of the time you've got left at Haverbridge.'

Stefan started towards the stairs which led to the flats above the shops, when he felt Elias pull at his shoulder.

'You're threatening me?'

'I don't need to. Your attitude alone is gonna get you the push.' Elias was silent but his eyes bore into Stefan's. 'Why are you starting something with Claire? That's what I don't get.'

'I'm not. I just can't seem to find any common ground with her. I don't know what I've got to do or who I have to become to get her to say, 'You know what, Crest? You've done a good job today.'

Stefan's eyes widened with amusement. 'You're expecting a pat on the back every time you do something good?'

'What, you think I don't deserve her thanks?'

'Wow, your arrogance knows no bounds, does it?'

Elias dismissed him with a gesture of his hands and started up the stairs. 'You may like being pussy-whipped by a woman but I don't.' Stefan stared at him, face blank. 'Let's just see the Larson girl, shall we?'

CHAPTER 8

Daryl Thomas watched from the window of his old beat-up BMW, parked across the road, eyes narrowing as the two men, dressed in suits, moved towards her.

Rachel was sitting in the bus shelter on her usual daytime patch, looking at her mobile phone when the two men approached her. She seemed nervous and he saw her eyes flash across the street in his direction.

It meant one thing.

Trouble.

The black eye he'd given her for lying to him about Nola had started to fade but he could still see it from the car. He'd cursed himself inwardly for damaging her where people could see. This wasn't out of some new-found sense of sympathy for her, but purely from a business point of view. It might put the punters off.

One of the men stood in front of her, blocking his view.

Daryl lit a cigarette, took a deep drag and exhaled, revealing his stale-yellow teeth, and got out of the car. He walked a short way up the road and leaned up against the wall of a house on the edge of the turning towards the main street. He could now see Rachel's face clearly and she appeared on edge. Her eyes kept darting back and forth towards him and, after a short while, he crushed the cigarette under his foot and crossed the road.

*

'We could go back to your flat, if that'd make you more comfortable,' Stefan said, more than aware of the fear in her eyes. 'We could talk more openly then.' Rachel shook her head and, when she saw Daryl closing in on them, she sprang from her seat.

'You need to leave. Now.'

Stefan and Elias exchanged glances. They saw the panic in her eyes. They knew what they needed from her and the sooner she ID'd the body, the better.

'Look,' Elias said, 'I don't think you understand. We need to talk to you about your friend. It'd be better if we went back to your flat.'

'No, you don't understand,' she said, edging closer. 'Please, leave now. I'll call the station later, I promise.' She gently pushed Elias out of her way, but it was too late.

'You two paying or not?' Elias turned to look behind him. 'If you're not, just fuck off, yeah? You understand me, boys?'

Elias sneered at the sight of the shabby, dirty-looking man and reached inside his pocket. He showed the man his warrant card.

'DS Crest, meet Daryl Thomas,' said Stefan. Daryl's face turned sour and his eyes narrowed at Elias's credentials.

'She's done nothing wrong, sitting 'ere minding her own business. You got nothing.' He folded his arms in defiance.

'Miss Larson isn't in trouble, Daryl. An associate told us she was here after we got no answer at her flat. We're here about Nola Grant,' Stefan said.

Daryl swaggered around Elias to stand beside Rachel. 'You tell that silly slag to get her skinny arse back round 'ere 'n see me.'

'That's not possible,' Elias said. He saw Stefan shake his head and his jaw set firm as Rachel began to cry.

Daryl saw their faces and edged closer. 'What you two hiding?' he said, raising his finger, pointing at both of them. 'Where is she?'

Stefan ignored him and focused on Rachel. 'We'd like to talk to you back at your flat. We'll give you a lift.'

'Stay out of the fucking car,' Daryl said, grabbing her roughly by the arm. 'Whatever you say to her, you can say in front of me.'

'Careful, Thomas. You don't want another assault charge under your belt.'

'Fuck off! I'm just looking out for the lady, aren't I, Rach?'

'Shall I add using offensive language to an officer as well?' Elias asked Stefan. Daryl puffed out his chest and pushed strands of his thinning brown hair out of his eyes.

'What's your name again?' Daryl let go of Rachel's arm and she rubbed it instinctively through her thick coat. Daryl squared his tall wiry frame up to Elias. Stefan took the opportunity to move Rachel, and helped her into his car.

'Hey!' Daryl called out and Stefan used his key fob to lock the automatic doors as Daryl reached for the passenger-door handle.

'She'll be fine, Daryl, settle down.'

Elias reached out and gently pushed Daryl back when he tried to round on Stefan.

'Get your fucking dirty hands off me.'

'You want to get a new profession, Thomas. Real men don't beat women.'

'You wanna fucking have a go, pig?' He shoved his hand hard into Elias's chest. 'What does it matter to you? Plenty of your lot are serviced by my girls.'

Elias's face dropped. He reached out and grabbed Daryl by the front of his jacket, pulling him forward, until his face was just inches from his own.

'She's dead.'

He watched Daryl's eyes now searching his own. He went to speak, but Elias stopped him, tightening his grip. 'Nola. Is. Dead.'

Daryl's face grew serious. 'You're lying.'

'She's laid out on the slab in the morgue. She's been murdered, Daryl, and I'll be coming back to speak with you about it personally. I'll make sure of it.'

PART TWO

02:58 A.M.

A deep pounding echo. A rush of blood through the ears. Breathing is hard and rapid.

She can see her own feet when looking down with eyes that don't quite feel like her own. The ground is drenched in melting ice and snow. There are trees, so many trees, skeletal branches and trunks like twisted figures in the grey. Her surroundings are void of colour, entwined in a thickening mist.

Running.

She runs across the woodland floor. She has no shoes, and her feet are turning numb. Her legs are heavy. They can't keep up with the will of her heart, the pull of her soul.

Her eyes scan the surroundings and everything whips past in a blur. A panoramic view of no way out, no place to hide. Her heart slams harder against her ribcage, fear driving her on.

All she can hear now is the sound of her own breathing, a fearful rush through the depths of her body.

A body too tired to run for much longer.

She sees the path ahead.

A path dense with trees, their roots stretching far and wide. She doesn't see the twisting, dark root, snaking its way above the earth, and crossing her path. It's too late now to stop herself.

Her foot is hooked. Her legs pull from under her. She is no more than a rag doll, cast aside. She panics as the ground rushes up to meet her. She can hear a voice as she falls.

She knows she can't fight any more.

Still the ground rushes towards her. She feels like she is endlessly falling in slow motion, the wind pulling through a mass of blonde tangled hair.

CHAPTER 9

7th November

The first November snow started to fall at exactly 5:31 a.m. Claire knew the time, having been up since 3:00 a.m., unable to sleep after yet another night terror. It was her third that week.

This time, she was sure the man with no eyes that haunted her, who she ran from, was some twisted version of her father – Peter.

How long had it been now since they'd spoken?

She couldn't remember and part of her felt guilty for not caring. Everything that had happened last year he'd brought upon himself, Claire knew that.

I did all I could, she reasoned with herself. Then why do I see the two of them – Father and the Other, whose name I can't bring myself to speak – in every nightmare?

Sweat cooled against her skin, and she felt the shiver travel up her spine.

It was the morning of Nola Grant's PM. She'd concentrate on that. It was all that mattered right now, not her broken inner self.

After she wiped the sweat from her face and chest, she headed downstairs. She then sat curled up in the window seat of the bay window in the living room, swathed in a blanket, nose buried in a book.

There was a small lamp dimly lit beside her and the curtains were open, despite it still being dark outside. A cup of coffee that rested beside her had long gone cold and she'd pushed it aside. When the first snowflake had settled on the window, she set aside her book in favour of watching the snow cover her garden in a blanket of white.

She could hear her mother, Iris, get up and start down the stairs, then her feet shuffling in her slippers against the hardwood floor as she entered the kitchen. When she heard the coffee machine whir into life, she sighed to herself, her solitude soon to be broken. She snapped her book shut and stood just as Iris entered the room.

Iris had invited herself to stay with Claire, forcing herself away from her home in Spain. Claire had never been to her mother's house on the Costa Brava, and didn't intend to if she could help it.

Since Iris had been divorced, she rarely made the effort to see her only child, and even when Claire had gone through her own messy divorce, Iris practically left her to go it alone.

Knowing how her mother felt about England nowadays meant Claire could relax, safe in the knowledge her mother only made an effort to visit once a year, at a time of her own choosing.

She insisted Claire never take days off to spend time with her while she was here, and was quite content to amuse herself. As long as she stayed in Claire's house, she'd be happy left to her own devices.

Claire's father, Peter, had moved to Aberdeen in Scotland, into a warden-controlled complex. It saddened Claire immensely but her decision to sever all ties had been for the best.

The last time they'd spoken had ended with cross words after he'd said some rather nasty things about Iris. Despite knowing her mother had been difficult to live with, Claire was having none of it, and had defended her.

'It's snowing,' Iris said, with some irritation, wrapping her dressing gown tightly around her small frame.

'It's been forecast for over a week now.'

'You seem to get snow earlier each year. Bloody global warming.' She raised her finger at her daughter. 'You should move out to Spain, love, much warmer climate. Not like England's changeable weather. It's bloody tedious.' Claire rolled her eyes and turned on the television.

Iris paused, watching her closely. 'You're up early. Couldn't you sleep?'

'No. I had a nightmare... Silly really.'

'Weren't you supposed to be seeing some doctor about all this?'

Claire shuddered, suddenly feeling very cold. 'I'm fine.'

Iris's face softened a little. 'What happened wasn't your fault, you know. Everything that went on with that man and that thing, that woman, what she did—'

'I said I was fine, Mum, really. You talking about it doesn't help me, it takes me back there, and it's not somewhere I want to go.'

'I just think—'

'Anyway,' Claire cut in, 'I've got to attend the post mortem of Nola Grant and it's an early one. I didn't see much point in staying in bed when I couldn't sleep.'

She flicked through the channels until she found Sky News. 'Are you going to be able to amuse yourself today, Mum? I'll be away until late this evening.'

Iris looked up, frowned but backed down. She sat in a nearby chair and nodded. 'I'll be all right. I may pop into town, do some early Christmas shopping.' She paused to listen to the headlines, then said, 'Who's Nola Grant?'

Claire's eyes narrowed. 'Since when do you take an interest in my work? Thought it depressed you?'

'Oh, it does,' she said, now more animated. 'But that doesn't mean I can't ask, does it?' Claire looked at the television screen ahead.

She knew her mother was just making idle small talk, pissed off Claire wouldn't talk to her about last year. Iris needn't have felt offended. Claire made it a habit never to discuss it with anyone. It was officially off limits.

The only part of Claire's life Iris usually showed interest in was either her love life (or lack of) or the house. When her eyes crossed back to her mother's, she noticed Iris genuinely looked intrigued.

'Grant was a prostitute. Her body was found dumped in Haverbridge on Bonfire Night.'

Iris held up her hands, and shook her head. 'OK, sorry I asked. It's far too early for gore. Nasty business.' There was a long pause. 'I take it she was murdered?'

Claire stopped and stared at her from the living room door. 'Some things never change with you, do they, Mum?'

CHAPTER 10

Stefan Fletcher hated standing in on autopsies. It wasn't because watching the whole process unfold was unpleasant – nobody liked doing it, not even the ones with an iron stomach – but because it made him think about his own life and regrets. Life was fragile. Death could take anyone of any age at any time.

Death didn't discriminate.

He thought about Nola's life, cut short having never achieved much. She had no second chances, no time to say her goodbyes. It wasn't as if death had claimed her after a battle with illness, when she had time to prepare for the inevitable. Death had struck quickly and indiscriminately. There was no coming back. She had no time to lay to rest any past grievances, or right any wrongs.

Life was cruel and the motto 'Live each day as if it were your last' felt evermore poignant. Today would be no different, and as soon as he saw the naked body of Nola Grant laid out on the slab in Haverbridge Hospital's morgue he suppressed the urge to walk out.

He stood alongside Claire, dressed in protective clothing, masks over their mouths. Danika had come to escort them from reception and down to the mortuary. She was one of the good guys: respected, intelligent and one of the best Claire had ever worked with by a long shot.

She didn't hold grudges and Claire sometimes wished she could be more like her in that respect. Claire could take a grudge and bury it deep inside her, but it never went away. If you wronged her, she'd take the hurt it caused her to the grave.

Danika appeared as normal: hair tied back, face and body clear of make-up and jewellery. The mortuary technician, Paul Farringdon, had already helped her photograph and swab the body in the external examination and now stood patiently beside the body, hands clasped loosely in front of him.

'While we waited for you,' Danika said, turning to address Claire and Stefan head on, 'the body was photographed, samples taken from under the fingernails, and surface traces of debris collected from her body and hair. Despite being in the water, we still managed to collect some samples.

'We also used the ultraviolet light. Mainly to check for any signs of sexual activity, which came up negative for any traces of semen externally, but since she was in the water, this could have easily washed away or been contaminated. I will check internally for any signs of trauma, but so far, I'm not convinced she was raped. I know some people have already been speculating,' she said, casting a sly look at Paul before continuing. 'She does have some minimal bruising around the groin, but given her choice of job, it's to be expected.'

'Some men like it rough,' Paul said.

Stefan smirked.

Claire's face was stony.

Danika visibly shuddered. 'Yes, thank you for that.'

'OK,' Claire cut in, 'let's assume the bruising is old until you check internally.'

'It's not old,' Danika said. 'It's recent, but could have been caused before she was taken off the street by the killer.'

Claire wrinkled her nose. She hated cases involving rape even more than murder, no matter how vicious it was. She moved Danika's attention on.

'Anything else?'

Danika nodded and pointed to Nola's body. 'External examination shows she put up some resistance, but she was restrained by the wrists. Handcuffs, maybe,' she said, pointing to the bruising around each wrist.

'This obviously restricted her ability to effectively fend off whoever did this. You already know she was found weighted down by that heavy chain, and there are marks around her ankles which are consistent with her being bound, but not by the chain.' She pointed to the dark-coloured bruises around Nola's ankles. 'I believe the chain was added afterwards.'

Claire lowered her head for a closer look. 'How'd you know that?'

'The width of the chain. The links themselves are much thicker than the marks around her ankles, which means it was added afterwards.'

'To make sure she stayed at the bottom of the water,' Stefan said.

Danika nodded again. 'Yes, and for a while, she would have done. But whatever was used to bind her before death was much thinner.'

Claire's eyes wandered back to Nola's skin and her eyes narrowed. 'These ligature marks,' she said, pointing so Stefan could have a look, but directing her question to Danika. 'The surface is uneven.'

'Yes, well spotted. I think her ankles supported her weight at some point, when she was tied up. It looks as though she was suspended.'

Stefan looked at her and cocked an eyebrow. 'Why?'

'Ready for the kill?' Claire offered.

Danika nodded. 'Yes, it's a reasonable assumption.'

'But she could've been dragged by her feet, couldn't she? That would also leave the same uneven marks.'

'You're right, but then I would expect to see scratch marks up her body: back, legs, hips, arms...' she said, trailing off. 'Although her skin had begun to deteriorate in the water, I can still see there's nothing consistent with her being dragged. The only other cuts and bruises that she does have are on the face, along with the defence wounds.

'I also inspected her mouth and found some abrasions to the tongue, not to dissimilar to razor blade cuts, small little nicks in the flesh.'

'Did she do it herself inadvertently with her teeth? Maybe when she struggled?' Stefan asked.

'These cuts are too perfect. I'm guessing someone else inflicted those wounds. The cuts are neat and identical. The cut on the right side of the tongue is an exact mirror-image to the cut on the left. They are the same length and depth.'

'The cuts were inflicted at the same time,' Claire said.

'Yes, with something sharp, placed either side of the tongue.' Danika paused for breath. 'Cause of death was through exsanguination, I'm ninety-nine per cent sure of it. Once I've performed the internal and had a toxicology report, I'll be—' She cut her sentence short and paused, staring at the wound at the side of Nola's neck. She shook her head.

Claire exchanged a look with Stefan. 'Something wrong?'

Danika looked up. 'I don't know really. I mean, the killer could have got lucky, I suppose.'

'Lucky?'

Danika pointed to the wound. 'The killer only made one incision, cutting in just behind the point of the jaw. This severed a jugular, carotid artery, and trachea, in one fluid, forward motion.'

She looked up at them to emphasise her point. 'There are no other attempts made, no hesitation marks. This person got it right first time and with a very sharp instrument.'

'Is that really so unusual?' Stefan said.

'Inspector, this method of dispatch takes practice. Cutting like this is generally seen in something like animal slaughter. When it's performed correctly, blood flows freely, draining the body. Death occurs in a very short space of time. We're talking seconds here – not hours – for her to bleed to death.'

'It's almost like a mercy killing, then. Is that what you're saying?' Claire asked, her eyes narrowing as she looked at Nola's throat.

Danika shook her head and looked pained as she said, 'I'd hardly call it a 'mercy' killing. The killer stuck her like a pig.' Claire held up her hand for her to calm down.

'You know what I meant. You could view it as a more humane way of killing her, rather than prolonging her agony. This was quick. You say this would take some skill to perform, so maybe the person we're looking for is well educated or trained?'

She looked at Danika, expectantly.

'It's cruel, that's what it is.'

There was a long silence between them. Paul, who had remained quiet throughout, could only look down at the floor. When he risked a glance at Danika again, he saw her body visibly harden once more.

This was her job: to examine and find the causes, find the facts. She knew it was fruitless to become emotionally involved. Normally she was good at keeping her personal emotions buried inside her. Why Nola Grant was any different, she didn't know and couldn't understand. She seemed to shake off her personal feelings as quickly as they'd arrived.

'If this was someone's definition of mercy, they've got a sick sense of humour.'

CHAPTER 11

Paul carefully placed the body block under Nola's back, allowing her chest to arch up, her arms and neck falling back against the cold autopsy table. Stefan looked away as the wound at her neck briefly opened wider, reminding him of a mouth opening, puckering and shutting again.

Danika committed a few details to tape before making her first incisions with her scalpel. She cut the large Y shape into Nola's torso and with the help of Paul, cut through and removed the sternum and ribs as one whole breastplate. After removing and taking further samples from the other main organs, Danika was ready to remove and open the stomach.

She carefully sliced into the tissue and inspected the contents. Stefan looked away, and swallowed hard. He saw Claire eye him with curiosity, and he looked sheepish.

'I should've skipped breakfast.'

Claire gave a wry smile.

'She'd eaten recently before she died, her stomach is fairly full,' Danika said, raising her eyes to them. 'I can tell more once I've looked at the intestinal contents, but I'd hazard a guess she'd eaten not much more than an hour before she was killed.'

'Are we any closer to a time of death?' Claire said.

Danika frowned.

'Roughly?'

'She's been in extremely cold water. The bacterial process that causes the body to bloat is slowed. The cold would also have encouraged the formation of adipocere, which slows decomposition.'

'Which means?'

'A substance formed from fat in the body helps to protect it. I need more time.' She studied Stefan's face. 'Inspector, if you need a time out, I'm sure DCI Winters won't mind. You don't need to be present. My full report will be ready within the next day or so.'

Exchanging glances with Claire, he nodded, reaching for the door.

'Wait, I'll come back with you,' Claire said. 'Save you the extra journey in the snow. I think I've seen all I need to here.' She gestured to Danika and Paul. 'I'll leave you to it and wait for the report.'

*

As soon as Stefan reached the pool car, his foot slid on the ice, the bottom of his trouser legs dipping into the snow. He cursed as he brushed the fabric clean, but his ankles instantly felt cold.

'I hate this weather,' he said, climbing into the passenger seat beside Claire.

She grinned as she pulled off over the forecourt, towards the exit. 'Did you get anything else from the boys at the firework display?'

His eyes remained focused on the road ahead. 'Harry's parents didn't seem too bothered about what happened.'

'Figured as much.'

'Well, you should've heard his mother. She made sure she pointed out that if her beloved son hadn't been messing around on the ice in the first place, we wouldn't have found the body for weeks. Essentially trying to justify that it's a good thing her son's a little shit.'

He turned to face her. 'I know Melissa and I have had our differences but we've kept it friendly for the kids' sake. God forbid my babies turn out like that Harry.'

Claire glanced over his face.

This had been the second time in months he had mentioned his ex-girlfriend in relation to their children. Although in his mid-thirties, Stefan looked too baby-faced to have one kid, let alone two. He had been with Melissa since meeting her at university and shortly after he'd joined the police she'd quickly fallen pregnant with their son, Phoenix, now aged ten.

It'd been a happy five years for him and Melissa, watching Phoenix grow before they decided to try for another baby. Soon they were blessed with Melody, now aged five, to make their little family complete. It had been over a year since Stefan and Melissa had separated but Stefan was right – they had kept it amicable, despite a difficult break-up.

Claire knew better than to question him about it. He kept his private life out of sight as much as possible. She decided to ask how the kids were, and kept Melissa's name out of the conversation as much as possible on the short drive back to the station.

*

Paul leaned over Danika's shoulder to get a better view, as if he didn't believe what she'd found. She was hunched over, which made it hard for him to see anything other than a little blood on her gloved hands.

'You can't be serious?' he said, moving round the table to get a better view.

'Look for yourself. Tell me I've made a mistake.'

There was no chance of that.

He looked into her dark eyes and frowned, before nervously risking a glance at her findings. When he saw what lay in front of her, he sighed and looked away, his eyes sad. 'I wish I could tell you I'm wrong,' she said. 'The poor girl.'

'Maybe the killer didn't know. She wasn't showing at all.'

'You think it would've made a difference if he did know?'

Paul shrugged, leaning back against the counter, arms folded.

'I don't know, I'm not a murderer. Who knows what goes on in some psycho's head?' He studied her face and guessed what she was thinking. 'I know I'm just the assistant, and please, don't think I'm trying to tell you how to do your job, but I don't think this is something that should wait until the report. You should inform DCI Winters. Now.'

Danika looked back at her hands and shut her eyes tight. After a long pause, she nodded.

CHAPTER 12

The incident room was large, busy and noisy. Phones were ringing and people were rushing around. There was a flat-screen monitor on a podium, and an image of Nola Grant flickered across the LCD screen.

There were several workstations in the four corners of the room, divided up into areas for detective constables, sergeants and inspectors. In the centre was another workstation, lined with computers and with staff trawling through CCTV footage.

There were more pictures of Nola Grant on the boards along the main wall, together with 'before' shots that Rachel Larson had given Stefan the day before and shots from when Nola's body was found. There was a list of known associates written beside the board and a pile of statements ready to be typed up, read and cross-referenced.

Claire wasted no time pulling everyone together for a briefing to give them the information they had so far from the post mortem and the details of the voicemail message left on Rachel Larson's phone. After she'd finished, she opened the briefing up for contribution.

'I want to start putting together a rough character profile on the killer,' she said, her eyes sweeping the room. 'I know profiles can hinder a case if we don't think outside the box, but I think we need to start with some basics.

'The killer is almost certainly a man. If the motive was sexual in nature, perhaps the killer has had a bad relationship with women all his life. Nola was a prostitute, so maybe a client asked for something she wasn't willing to give.'

Detective Constable Gabriel Harper stepped in. 'Do we think it could've been an accident and the killer panicked?'

Claire shook her head. 'It wasn't an accident. The effort was made to dump her body and weight her down. There's an amount of foresight and planning.'

'Textbook stuff then?' said Matthews.

'If it were a crime committed in the heat of the moment then the killer would most likely have left her where she fell, whether it be sexually orientated or otherwise,' Claire said. 'But this appears to be cold, calculated.' She paused. 'It's significant that she was naked. She was a target.'

'And that makes you restless?' Stefan said.

Claire stared at him. 'Everything about it makes me restless. Aren't you?'

Stefan shook his head and placed his coffee on a table in front of him. 'No. I think it may be a one-off. We've had prostitutes turn up dead before.'

'But not like this… Dead in an alley, yes. Dead in some crack den, or dead at the hands of a pimp, yes, but not dumped in a lake. Not the way she was found.'

The room fell silent. Outside it was snowing again, white flakes hitting the window in the strong wind.

'The warden at the parkland said the lake started to freeze on the first and was completely frozen over by the morning of the fifth. He's going to provide us with the CCTV footage from his Portakabin,' Claire said.

Matthews then jumped in, standing up to address the team. He scratched the back of his head as he read from a sheet of paper in his other hand.

'Uniform has conducted a house-to-house in the area where Nola was believed to have been seen last and from the houses around the lake. DC Harper will be leading another round of interviews, with DC Roberts.' He looked up at Claire, who was leaning up against a table opposite him, arms folded. She nodded for him to continue.

'I've got more CCTV footage to start trawling through from the town centre and from the shops below Grant's flat. The chippy and newsagent both have cameras inside and outside their premises, but I also found this an hour ago,' he said.

He held up a grainy black-and-white 10x8 shot of part of the town centre. A date and time were stamped across the bottom and judging by the angle and neon sign, it was taken from a CCTV camera opposite a McDonald's.

The last time Nola Grant was seen alive.

The street was virtually empty with only four people, grainy shadows almost, in the frame. There were more people in the McDonald's itself, but all Claire could see at that angle was the bottom of their legs through the glass window.

There was a car parked outside but the number plate was obscured and the picture was of such bad quality, she couldn't correctly identify the make and colour, or anything else.

'What am I meant to be looking at, Matthews?'

He grinned. She'd studied the photo briefly and missed what had caught his eye instantly.

'This guy here,' he said. She followed his finger across the photograph and squinted. Matthews then circled a few copies amongst the team. They stared at the photograph.

Leaning up against the wall of the McDonald's, which led down a side alley, was a black smudge, which, after closer inspection, they all recognised as a man.

'Can you tell me who he is?' Claire said.

Matthews shook his head.

'No name, but he was noticed by two witnesses, employees at that McDonald's. They say they saw him hanging around

Nola in the week leading up to her disappearance. Nola was a regular in there, the two guys knew her. They said the last time they saw her was when she got into a car the night she went missing, and this guy,' he said, pointing at the figure again, 'ran after the vehicle, before giving up and getting in his car… which happens to be this one here.'

He pointed to the parked car in the photo, the one with the obscured plate.

'Here are their statements,' he added, handing them across to Claire. 'I know what you're going to ask and the answer is no.' He leaned back against his desk. 'They can't remember the make, model, colour or even a partial plate number of the man's car… or a decent description of the man, except that he wore a black-and-red checked hooded jacket with a baseball cap. Usually with the jacket hood pulled up over the cap, obscuring his face.'

Claire eyed him carefully then looked back at the man in the photo.

'Let me get this straight… two people both notice a man tailing Nola. Notice enough to know a man chased after a car she got into on the last night she's seen alive, but neither of them have any real description of this man's face, height, colour? Nothing on his vehicle?'

Matthews shrugged. 'They serve a lot of customers, and they said they didn't think it relevant. Apparently, it's not the first time Nola's had admirers. Maccy D's is very busy, Claire, sea of faces and all that. Fast food, fast paced. Their story sounds credible.'

'What about the other car, the one she got into?'

'We picked it up on CCTV on the first of November, same spot.' Matthews turned towards Detective Constable Jane Cleaver. 'Jane?'

Everybody turned to face Jane as she spoke.

'The last car Nola got into was a silver E-Class Mercedes, registered to forty-five-year-old Kenneth Philips, of 92 Magenta Drive, Stevenage.'

Jane accessed the CCTV footage and resumed playback. The LCD screen at the front of the room changed to show grainy footage, taken across the street from the McDonald's.

Everyone watched the mystery man from the photograph Matthews had shown them. He was looking at Nola from the side of the McDonald's, before running across the road after a car as it pulled off. The footage offered no further help in terms of a description of the man.

They watched him go to his parked car, sitting almost out of the shot, and hoped that as he drove off, they could pull a plate from the grainy footage.

Claire spoke first. 'Could anyone make that out?'

Everyone muttered a negative.

Stefan shook his head. 'Footage is too grainy, lighting's bad. I think I could make out an R and maybe a five and even that I wouldn't swear to. I'll get image enhancement to have a look at it.'

Claire jabbed a finger towards the screen. 'I want the other cameras in the area checked. Find this man's car. Get me a number plate, if he's not using fake ones. Which direction does he head in? Find him.'

She looked back at Jane. 'Does this Kenneth Philips have any previous convictions?'

'One speeding conviction last year and a history of unpaid parking tickets.'

'Kenny came in voluntarily this morning,' said Harper, 'although he seemed more concerned that his wife would find out about his night-time activities than the fact he was the last person to see Grant before she was murdered.'

There were a few raised smiles and knowing glances.

'Aren't they always,' Claire said. 'Carry on, Harper.'

'Kenny picked Nola up and took her down the side street next to the Wickes warehouse in Haverbridge industrial area. After about an hour in his back seat, he dropped her off.'

'You showed him the shots of the man chasing his car? Did he say if Nola recognised him?'

Harper shook his head. 'Apparently, Grant barely looked at the guy. She told Kenny she had no idea who he was. It was then that Kenny started worrying about the fact this could make the papers, then his wife would know what he'd done. He said he should've forgotten the whole thing and dropped her off when he'd had the chance.'

'Did he provide a description of the man?' Stefan asked.

Harper shook his head. 'Not really,' he said, passing the statement to Claire.

She read over it as Harper continued. 'He says he was looking through his wing mirror so he didn't see a great deal. It was dark and raining. He gave the same description as what we've seen in the footage.'

'He thinks he could be about five-eight, average build, but he was wearing a thick coat, so he could've been thinner,' Claire said, skimming over the statement. 'Mr-fucking-average. He's like any other man on the street.'

She turned to Matthews.

'Matthews, check the CCTV footage in Haverbridge industrial area, concentrating on the Wickes warehouse and Turner Street. That's where Kenny says he dropped her off.'

'Yes, Guv, but I don't think there's any cameras down Turner Street.'

'You'll be able to pick him up around that area.' She looked back at the photograph of the shadowy figure. 'If he is our man, he's taking risks, being sloppy, out in the open like this. Have this circulated to the local press. See if we can't draw in any more eye witnesses. Right now he's a person of interest.'

'First mention of Nola's death has already gone to the local news,' said Matthews.

Claire handed him back the photograph. 'They'll print that photo. It may, if we're lucky, flush out our man sooner rather than later. If he has anything else planned, he'll change his plans accordingly if he thinks his time is running out.'

She paused a moment. 'That car and the van on the other side of the street that are parked up, see if we can get clear shots of the number plates. Who owns them? Someone must remember something.

'I want someone to speak to the two employees at McDonald's again, push them harder this time.' She paused as she looked around the room. 'I also think we need to look at cold case.'

A few murmurs sounded around the room, nobody really relishing the thought of being assigned the task.

'It's just a thought,' Claire said, trying to quiet their discord, 'especially if we think the killer planned Nola's murder. Matthews, can you organise it, see if we have any unsolved murders like this one. Look for similar MO and social class of victim. Nola Grant was a prostitute. It may be the reason she was chosen.'

She looked around the room and pointed at DC Richard Lloyd. 'Lloyd, I want you to assist DI Matthews.'

While Claire was talking, Stefan was watching Elias from the far side of the room. He didn't miss the look Elias gave Claire as she spoke. When she paused for breath, Elias raised his hand. Claire gave him a sideways glance.

'Crest?'

'I'd assume that cold case is a waste of time.'

Claire paused, giving him the once over. 'I need to be sure we don't overlook something that could be waiting to be found in the old files.'

'You can't be sure Grant isn't just the first and last victim.'

'And you can't be sure she is, Crest.'

She pushed herself off the table and walked over to him. 'The killer may have done this before, and his MO might have changed. If he made any errors, our man may strike again and correct what went wrong the first time. She may not be the only victim. She may be part of something bigger.'

'It's a novice, not a pro,' Crest said, and looked away from her with contempt. 'If the man from the CCTV footage is the killer, he might as well have had a neon sign over his head.' He shook his head. 'You're just not seeing it.'

This stirred a few murmurs from the rest of the team. Those who had worked with Claire previously had seen colleagues like Elias challenge her before, and knew he was skating on thin ice.

They knew it wasn't so much the content of what he was saying. It was a reasonable assumption that Grant's murder was a one-off and she'd died by the hands of a first-timer, but it was more the way in which he was behaving and speaking to Claire that niggled.

She leaned back against the table opposite Elias's desk and her eyes bore into his. 'Perhaps you can tell me who I should be looking for, Sergeant, since you seem to have a wealth of experience that rivals my own?'

Elias leaned back in his chair, wanting to distance himself from her as much as possible. 'Daryl Thomas might be a good place to start.'

'Yes, I've heard you had the pleasure of making his acquaintance.'

'He's got priors for assault. We know he's smashed up his girls before… What's to stop him making that final leap?'

'Daryl's a nasty piece of work, Crest, I'll give you that, but he's not a murderer.'

Elias took in her face for a moment before he spoke again. This time he lowered his voice and tapped his pen on the desk in front of him, as if driving the point home.

'He's stupid. He's stupid and careless enough to rouse suspicion, and it'd be presumptuous of us not to question him, even if it is to merely cross him off our list.'

'The killer's not stupid. He managed to kill Nola Grant with one expert cut of his knife,' Stefan said, coming to Claire's aid.

The last sentence hung heavy in the air. A few nodded their heads in agreement with Stefan. Claire saw the eyes around the room watching her carefully and when her gaze fell back to Elias, she saw the twitch in his mouth. It was a silent 'fuck you' and it made her blood boil.

'Can I speak with you privately?' Elias said.

She met his stare and gave a sharp nod. 'When we're done here and I've seen DI Fletcher. Now,' she said, looking to Matthews, 'I want a Family Liaison Officer assigned to Rachel Larson. See if they can find out any more information that might shed light on the last few days before Nola disappeared.

'I want the CCTV footage processed ASAP. Statements on HOLMES, any inconsistencies I want flagged and followed up.'

The Home Office Large Major Enquiry System (HOLMES), developed in the 1980s, held all the information gathered for the investigation, consisting of evidence, such as statements, to intelligence. It made it far less likely that the investigation could succumb to human error and made sure any coincidences or inconsistencies were flagged up.

Claire had a real fixation about it and made sure it was always referred to and scrutinised for a possible hole, link or lead in any case.

She looked at Elias, who sat staring at his desk, avoiding her gaze. 'Crest, I want you to gather intelligence on Grant's and Larson's mobile phone records for the last few weeks, and get a location where Grant's phone was when the voicemail was left on Larson's phone.'

'Whatever you say,' he said in a flat voice, without looking up at her.

She glared at him, but took a deep breath, pushing her anger down inside her, right to the pit of her stomach.

CHAPTER 13

Stefan followed Claire into her office, but no sooner had he shut the door after him than it was open again. Stefan frowned as Elias came in, looking frustrated.

'I thought I told you I'd see you later,' Claire snapped. She sat back in her chair, arms folded. 'And, next time, I'd prefer you knock on my door before you barge in.'

'I need to speak with you, it's important,' he said, ignoring her words and body language.

'It can wait.'

'No, it can't.'

The tone of his voice surprised her. She eyed him curiously. 'Fletcher, would you mind waiting outside a minute?'

Stefan said nothing, but cast Elias a warning glare as he left.

In the incident room, Stefan went straight over to Matthews, who stood over DC Morgan Roberts as she fast-forwarded through some CCTV footage. She was about to hit Play when Matthews stopped her as Stefan approached.

'You got a minute?'

Matthews didn't look surprised. He nodded. 'Sure.'

They wandered towards the water cooler on the far side of the room, out of anyone's earshot.

'You're gonna have to rein in Crest, and fast. If there's any more shit with Claire, something's going to blow up... most likely Crest.'

Matthews grinned. 'Don't worry, I'll get him on the mobile records, keep him busy. Then if he fucks up, it's my arse the Guv's gonna be grilling.'

'It's not your arse Claire's after.'

'Look, I understand. Don't worry.'

Stefan nodded and gave a half-smile as Matthews poured himself water from the cooler. He gripped the plastic cup and stared at the glass partition wall, one side of Claire's office that didn't have closed blinds. 'She looks pissed.'

Stephan sighed. 'Pissed is an understatement.'

CHAPTER 14

'Forget it, Crest. Daryl Thomas is no murderer.' Claire picked up her pen and tapped it against her desk, exasperated. 'What's the beef between you and Thomas anyway?'

Elias shifted his weight to the other foot, and his head told him to bite his tongue and swallow his pride. For now at least. He'd just started here. He didn't need the aggro so soon. He tried to control his voice.

'Look, I've met the bastard, and Rachel Larson has told us that Thomas gave her the shiner she's now sporting.' Claire tapped her teeth with the pen, buying time before she spoke. Or exploded. Either was possible.

'Is she pressing charges?'

'No, of course she's not. Too scared of him.'

'Then it's irrelevant, isn't it? We can't help her if she's not willing to help herself. She's coming in to formally ID Nola. I'll go through her options, but I can't force her to do anything she doesn't want to.'

Elias stared hard at Claire for a few seconds, then shook his head. He didn't understand how she could just completely rule Daryl out as a suspect, without even questioning him once.

He thought back to when he'd asked Rachel about Nola's family.

Nola had no one, and the girls on the street were her family, all she needed. Those had been Rachel's words. When they'd asked her if she would formally identify the body, she'd cried a fresh wave of tears and reluctantly said, yes.

Elias broke away from his thoughts when he felt Claire's hard gaze.

'DI Fletcher told me you didn't take to Thomas. Not that I can blame you, but I've heard you let him berate you. You let him get to you and you showed it.'

Elias's eyes narrowed and his face flushed with anger. Stefan, he could go to hell. Reporting back to her over something insignificant. This is why he thought it best not to get close to work colleagues.

'Why are you not bothering to speak to Thomas first, before ruling him out as a suspect? It's good practice.'

Her eyes shot to his. 'Is it good practice to question a superior officer?' she asked, raising an eyebrow. 'I'm the SIO on this case, Crest. Best you not forget it.'

'Oh, it's clear where I stand in all this.'

Her gaze was hard. She looked him up and down.

She let his outburst slide and said, 'The real question you should be asking is, why bite the hand that feeds you?'

'What?'

'Daryl Thomas and Nola Grant. She brought in a lot of money for him, why would he kill her? From what I understand, Thomas has got himself a nice little set-up with those girls. He's not going to murder his source of income, is he?'

Elias thought for a minute, knew it was the most logical argument, but countered her point all the same.

'What if that's what he wanted us to think? You know there are more Nola Grants and Rachel Larsons out there to pimp out to the next man willing to pay.'

'You've met the guy, and you're telling me you think he deserves that amount of credit? That he's able to think it through himself, and actually murder one of his girls?'

Elias was silent.

'You've clearly got a lot to learn, Crest, if that's what you really think. I've dealt with idiots like Thomas before and whilst capable of many nasty things, murder is not one of them. That man in particular is a coward.'

'I was just putting the question to you,' he protested. Claire stood abruptly and Elias felt himself unconsciously take a step back.

'Yes, I'm sure you were doing what you thought best.'

He was silent and looked down at the floor.

'I'll be sending an officer out to speak to Thomas, but it's not a priority at the moment and we don't have the manpower to have officers everywhere, what with the government's budget cuts.'

She let the statement hang for a few moments. 'Are we done?'

Elias nodded but kept his eyes trained on the floor as Stefan came through the door. 'Danika's on line two. Says it's urgent.' Claire nodded a thank you in his direction then stared at Elias.

Your time to leave.

Taking the hint, Elias scowled at Stefan before slamming the door behind him as he left. Stefan looked at Claire, confused, his brow furrowed.

'Don't ask, Fletch, just don't ask,' she said, sitting down again. She picked up the telephone receiver and clasped it to her ear. She pressed the button next to the flashing light on the cradle and waited.

CHAPTER 15

Stefan's eyes grew wide when he saw Claire's reaction to the voice at the other end of the phone. The receiver still stuck to her ear even after the line was dead.

'Is everything OK?' he said, pulling the phone from her hand.

It took her a moment to register his words. She looked up at him, eyes serious. 'Nola was pregnant.'

He hesitated. 'Jesus! How far gone was she? She didn't look remotely pregnant – you saw her stomach.'

'Not far from twelve weeks, Danika thinks.' She rubbed her fingers hard across her brow. 'This just makes her murder even more poignant. We're going to be under even more pressure.'

Stefan sat down in front of her, feeling numb. He thought back to when Melissa had been pregnant with Phoenix and how vulnerable she'd been. 'Press will have a field day.'

Claire nodded. 'Can you imagine the headlines? It's bad enough trying to deal with the death of a young girl. When you add an unborn life into the equation people will be gunning for this person's blood. It makes Nola's death even more tragic. This could turn into a media circus.'

Stefan ran his hands through his hair as he arched his neck back, sighing.

'I've seen that look before,' Claire said. 'If you've got an idea running through that head of yours, you'd better share it with me.'

'You want to know what I'd do?' he clarified.

She remained silent.

He looked down at his hands, as if contemplating how to phrase his words.

'There're two ways of looking at it. We could tell the media, which may help bring in the killer more quickly, what with people's emotions running high—'

'Which will also bring the crazies out the woodwork,' she said, cutting him off. 'Hoax callers, people wanting their five minutes of fame. I can do without that.' She swung her chair around so she could look out the window.

'Yeah, I know it could be counterproductive – so the other option is, we simply don't say anything.'

She gave him a sideways glance and chewed on her bottom lip.

'Either way, I think you should swallow your pride and see Donahue.'

CHAPTER 16

Detective Superintendent Clifton Donahue was well into his fifties, and although a fairly ostentatious figure, he was also as fair as he was firm. Well respected in the force, Donahue was not a man you would want to fall out with, but equally was a valued friend if you worked hard and earned your position, proving to him you always put your heart and soul into each case.

Claire and Donahue had a mutual understanding. Each was stubborn with a will of iron. Each had different ideas and techniques that sometimes worked together but often clashed.

New and old.

A bone of contention for some.

They both knew it was pointless to go against the other unless absolutely necessary but they also had a deep and mutual respect for each other, both as colleagues and on a personal level.

Claire took a seat when he offered her a chair in his office. He sat back and eyed her with interest. Donahue was a tall man, and his legs were now stretched out in front of him under his desk, the tips of his shoes nearly reaching Claire's.

He was average in build, except for his belly, which showed his love for fine wine and dining. His large nose was slightly red and crows' feet were set deep either side of his brown eyes. The lines around his mouth were a product of years of smoking, although he'd given up some ten years ago. He still retained his smoker's cough, which served as a constant reminder to himself never to fall back into bad habits whenever he was tempted by a pack of B&H.

His hair was thinning on top but despite this he still had a good thatch of silver-grey hair, turning white at the temples. His face still had something about it that made Claire feel like she was in good company.

He leaned forward and clasped his big hands together, his fingers on his right hand turning his gold wedding band around his left index finger, unconsciously. Claire noticed he did this whenever he was anxious.

'What can I do for you, Claire? How's DS Crest settling in so far?'

She felt her stomach roll when he mentioned Elias.

'My team's working hard on the Grant murder, but we've hit a snag, and I need to run something by you first, see what you think about it.'

Donahue let out a low chuckle, which turned into a coarse smoker's cough, and he hacked into his clenched fist. 'I'm honoured you want my approval,' he said, smiling. 'What's it going to cost me?'

'Don't be like that, Sir, you've not heard what I have to say yet.'

'If it's something you think you need to see me about first, I expect to be nervous.'

Claire explained the details compiled on the case so far and when she reached Nola's pregnancy, he squirmed. 'I see,' he said, shaking his head. 'There are some sick bastards out there.' His voice sounded gruff and he coughed hard into his hand again.

'OK, this is what I think,' he said, swallowing warm water from the glass on his desk. 'We keep this to ourselves, for the time being. Make sure your team is briefed and know not to talk to anyone outside the investigation about it.'

His eyes then turned more serious.

'You may want to think about this Daryl Thomas, Grant's pimp. Your gut feeling that he isn't involved can't be relied on as gospel, Claire, you know that.'

He lowered his eyes, avoiding her gaze, and she knew something was wrong.

'We've done a door-to-door around the neighbourhood, Cliff. We've got a witness placing Nola not far from the town centre area. There's no description of a man loitering on Nola's patch before she disappeared that matches Thomas. Besides, he has more sense than to murder one of his girls.'

'But where was he? Does he have an alibi?'

Claire looked at him, exasperated.

'I'm merely throwing the question out there, Claire,' he added. 'DS Crest is right. We can't rule him out just yet, although I agree with what you're saying.'

Claire's head shot up, her face glowing crimson.

'*Crest?*' she said, practically spitting his name. Donahue went to speak, but nodded a response instead, his fingers working overtime on his wedding band.

'Crest was in here? He's been to see you?' She leaned forward across his desk. 'Today?'

'Don't get angry, it's nothing against you.'

'I don't bloody believe this. I just spoke with him before I came up here myself.'

'Yes, I know. You just missed each other,' he said with some trepidation.

'The devious little bastard. After what I did for…' She stopped herself, avoiding his eyes.

Donahue frowned at her words.

'After you did what?' he said. 'Finish what you were going to say.'

Claire got to her feet, and her knuckles turned white as she leaned heavily on Donahue's desk. 'All I meant was he's gone over my head. I'm not having it.'

'Don't you dare pull rank with me.'

His tone silenced her and she knew not to push her luck. He raised his hand, his finger now pointing at her square in the face. 'You forget, I don't care about your personal differences with anyone, providing it doesn't impair your judgment or compromise a case. We do this by the book.'

'I'm planning to speak with Thomas but my instinct is telling me it's a waste of time.'

'You've been wrong before, remember?'

As much as it needed to be said, he felt a twinge of guilt when he saw the hurt in her face. She knew instantly what he was referring to.

The murdered priest investigation the previous year.

It'd been a setback for her to say the least, although it hadn't completely been her fault, but Donahue felt it necessary to bring it up every so often if she needed to hear it. If he needed to quell her arrogance.

He lowered his hand, sinking back against his chair, but eyed her sternly. He wasn't the type of person to show too much compassion.

'I know you never went to all those meetings you were told to attend. You've got me to thank that you escaped any internal investigation by the skin of your teeth.'

Claire's eyes rose to meet his. She swallowed hard.

'Look, Claire, back down off your hunches, get out of my office and get someone on Daryl Thomas.'

It took Claire every effort to swallow her anger. Her lips pursed together, then stretched in a tight line across her face. She looked down at the table, took a deep breath, and returned her eyes to his.

'Yes, Sir.'

He stole a few moments to look at her, grimaced at her thinner frame, not the Claire he'd known before. Then he waved his hand, silently dismissing her. As she pulled at the door handle to leave he sat forward in his seat.

'And Winters?'

He saw her body stiffen, but she didn't turn around to face him. Instead her eyes remained fixed on the door, her fingers gripping the door handle. 'You know my office is always open…' He couldn't finish the sentence, but he knew she understood.

At least he hoped she did.

CHAPTER 17

'It's a shit-storm in a teacup, Claire. Don't show him you're easily wound up.' Claire heard Stefan's words, but was barely interested.

'Who the fuck does he think is? I feel like I'm back at school!'

Stefan winced as she roared the last part, making people look up from their workstations, peering through the glass partition wall of her office.

'Calm down.'

'I'll give him something to complain to Cliff about, the cocky twat.'

Stefan watched her pace her office, feet scuffing the carpet, fury building inside her. When he saw Elias walk into the incident room, he tried to distract her.

'So, where are you taking your mother for dinner tonight?' She shot him a hard stare but didn't answer him, and sat back down instead. He raised his arms dismissively in the air. 'OK, I'm going to leave you to it, let you ride out the storm on your own.'

He caught her staring out across the office.

Her eyes landed on Elias.

She slowly stood up.

Stefan swore under his breath when she pushed past him and strode out of her office. He guessed Elias's heart skipped a beat when he saw Claire striding up in front of his desk and glaring down at him.

He stiffened in his seat and rested his interlocked hands over his stomach.

'What can I do for you, Guv?' Elias's voice sounded normal but inside his mind was working overtime, preparing to defend himself if she'd come to dish out a verbal onslaught.

'Daryl Thomas,' she said.

'What about him?'

'Pay him a visit.'

'You're serious? Why the sudden change?' He was pushing her and she knew it. She felt the anger boiling just under her cool exterior. She kept it suppressed, aware that all eyes were on them.

She leaned in closer, voice low. 'Don't get clever. You wanted Thomas, now I'm handing him over to you. I'd hate to be proven incompetent if he has a motive and no alibi on the night Nola was last seen.' She paused. 'Take DC Harper with you tomorrow.'

Elias looked away, lowering his face and smiling inwardly. She watched his face, dissecting him with her eyes.

'Yes, Guv.'

She gave a sharp nod, turned to leave, then came back full circle. He looked up expectantly as she leaned across his desk.

'And, Crest,' she said, almost whispering in his ear. 'The next time you go over my head…'

He looked into her eyes.

She deliberately let the sentence hang in mid-air, unfinished. His face grew dark, but he nodded his head once. She was practically pissing all over him, marking her territory. Strategically placing herself higher than him, leaning over his desk, invading his personal space.

I'm bigger than you. Don't you forget it.

He knew it then.

He knew the battle lines had just been drawn.

CHAPTER 18

Iris eyed the waiter suspiciously as he took her order, repeating it back to her in a thick Italian accent. After he'd brought her the wine Claire had persuaded her to try, she watched him head off towards the kitchen. She leaned in closer to her daughter.

'Don't suppose he's legal?' she whispered. Claire narrowed her eyes and buried her face in the menu.

'Why, because he's Italian? This is an Italian restaurant, Mum.'

'Even more reason to do a spot check or something.'

Claire snapped the menu shut and stared at her. She would never get used to her mother's bigotry or narrow-mindedness. It was something Iris had inherited from her own mother. Claire's grandmother had been a force to be reckoned with, and had determined the main characteristics of the women that were to follow down the family bloodline. Claire was many things, but there was not a hint of racism in her body.

'You know, Mother, you're not exactly the pinnacle of 'Englishness', if there is such a thing.'

'Don't be so ridiculous. Whatever has got into you this evening?'

Claire ran her hand through her hair, twisted strands around her fingers. 'I'm sorry. Bad day.'

Iris scowled at her, and they sat in an awkward silence until their dinner had been served. The waiter topped up

Iris's wine glass, and grinned at her. Claire smiled inwardly. Watching her mother's face was priceless. The waiter left them alone, and Iris leaned in closer. She watched Claire picking at her pasta dish.

'You know, you should have had pizza.'

'Why?'

'Because it's got more fat in it and you've lost far too much weight since I saw you last.' Claire pulled a face. 'You can look at me like that all you want, it's true. You're looking gaunt. Look at you – picking at the food, rather than eating it.'

Claire shoved a huge forkful of pasta in her mouth, cheeks bulging as if to prove a point.

Iris tutted, shaking her head.

When Claire had finished her mouthful she said, 'I've got too much on my mind right now to worry about what I'm eating. So, please, just drop it.'

Iris frowned, creating deep furrows in her brow. 'You going to tell me about it or not?'

'You'll just tell me I'm being stupid.'

'Probably, but I'll listen nonetheless.'

After a brief pause, she reached out and placed her palm on Claire's hand, forcing her to make eye contact. 'I know I would never win mother of the year, but I am here to listen.' It melted Claire's exterior a little and her face softened.

'DSI Donahue gave me a dressing-down today. It's nothing, really.'

Iris's eyes widened and she spooned a mouthful of spaghetti into her mouth. 'He must have had his reasons. That's not like him. What did you do?'

'It's not me, it's the new DS. Elias Crest. He went over my head, stirred up some shit. We don't like each other, that much is clear. He knows I know the reason he transferred to Haverbridge, and now he's made everything personal and it's really not what he thinks… I'm not going to forgive and forget, so don't even bother suggesting it,' she said, pointing her fork at Iris, anticipating her reaction.

Iris went to speak but ate another mouthful of food instead. She took her time chewing and eyed her daughter from the corner of her eye. After a few moments, Claire caught her line of vision. Iris's grey eyes were silently questioning.

'I can see your mind ticking over. Come on, out with it.' She rested her knife and fork down on her plate, and leaned closer. 'You're going to say I asked for it.'

'Well, did you?'

'No,' she said. 'Jumped-up little shite is testing me.'

'And, obviously, you're biting and living up to your reputation.' Her tone left Claire feeling she was being chastised. 'Sometimes you might want to take some of what you dish out. You've got nothing to prove and nothing to gain by hammering the shit out of him, just because he's the new guy.'

'Language, Mother,' Claire said, trying to divert attention away from herself.

'I'm not perfect, Claire, and neither are you... and neither is this new man, Crest, by all accounts. That's my point.' Studying her mother's lined face, Claire sighed. Iris mistook her change in demeanour. 'You can tell me to shut up if you like. I'm just trying to offer some advice.'

Claire smiled. 'Have you ever thought about a career in counselling?'

Iris's face was serious for a brief moment but soon felt her lips pull into a smile.

Then a grin.

Then a laugh, which was genuine.

'You cheeky sod.' She playfully pushed Claire's arm and felt her face flush.

When they'd finished their meal, and had settled at a table in the bar area, Iris sipped her wine, watching Claire over the rim of the glass.

'I can see you staring at me,' Claire said, turning her gaze to her mother. 'Is this some kind of intervention? First my weight, then work…'

Iris winced. 'I was only going to ask after your father.'

Claire shifted in her seat.

Iris explained, 'The care home called the other week. They said I was a last resort! Can't say I felt too good about that.'

'What did they want?'

'They asked if they had the right number for you, only they'd tried calling you on and off over the last few months. They said you rarely responded to emails, and even then it was only if it was about the money to keep up with his care plan.'

Claire looked at her, a little worried.

'Nothing's wrong, they just said your father's been asking after you.'

Claire sipped her Coke. 'He sent a text message to me. A year ago now.' She snorted a laugh then. 'Or rather, he must've got someone else to text it, considering his fingers are gnarled to useless stumps.'

Iris bit her lip.

'Too harsh?' Claire said, eyebrows raised.

'Considering how he left things with you, no, I don't think so. I'm sure I've said worse.' She paused. 'In fact, I know I have.'

Claire drained the last of the Coke from her glass. 'I can't talk about him, Mum. It opens up too many old wounds and they've only just begun to heal.'

*

After the meal, Claire drove them back as promised. As she put the kettle on, Iris noticed her reflection in the kitchen window, turned sideways and frowned. She ran her palm over her stomach. 'Do you think I'm getting fat?' Claire half turned towards her, glanced at her mother's petite frame and rolled her eyes.

'I've seen more fat on a greasy chip.'

'I shouldn't have had the spaghetti. I'm gaining weight and you're losing it!' Iris said, ignoring her. She turned to face her reflection head on. 'And I'm shrinking.'

'What?'

'Look at me,' Iris said, turning to face her. 'I look shorter than the last time I was here, admit it.'

'Oh, Mum.'

'Now don't try to sugar-coat anything – I can take it.'

Claire sighed, turning to face her, hand set firmly on her hip. 'You're five-three… same as last year.'

Iris screwed up her face, checked her reflection again, then headed off into the living room, muttering to herself.

Claire grinned as she made the tea. Although she never liked to admit it, Iris was as image conscious as the average teenager. Her hair was fashionably styled and dyed a soft shade of blonde, which suited her complexion. Her clothes hung well on her petite frame and her make-up was always flawless.

Although approaching her sixties, Iris was still an attractive woman, despite being hard to get along with. Claire just wished her mother could see herself as everyone else did, but then she could hardly talk.

Claire was tall, more slender than she'd been in a very long time now, with strong features, something she inherited from her father, and the polar opposite from her mother, and sometimes people struggled to see any resemblance at all.

After they retired to bed, Iris found it hard to sleep. She lay there in the darkness, listening to the sound of her own breathing.

After a long time had passed, she felt sleep begin to take her. In the back of her mind, however, she could hear the faintest of sounds. At first it sounded like whimpering, as if someone or something was in pain. Trying to block out the noise, convinced she was imagining it, she rolled on to her side, facing away from the door.

The sound grew louder, more desperate. She could hear the panic in a woman's voice.

Claire?

Sliding her legs out from under the warm duvet, she shivered as the cold air touched her bare legs under her nightdress. Despite the radiator, the room was chilled, and fresh snow was once again falling outside her window.

She threw on her dressing gown and slowly turned the door handle. She paused then stepped out on to the landing. She crept towards the sound, balancing on her tiptoes, pulling her dressing gown around her tighter still.

The noise grew louder, more alarming. Someone was in pain.

It was coming from her daughter's bedroom.

*

The mother called out to her as she ran ahead off into the woods.

The little girl slowed down to a skip, her smile wide across a wind-chapped face.

A thick mist clung to the tall thin trees around her, and she was lost to the world within seconds.

The mother stood, eyes squinting against the bitter wind, damp strands of hair sticking across her forehead.

'Where are you?' she called out. She heard voices, whispered. It sounded like her daughter. She was not alone.

The mother panicked.

She saw a flash of blonde hair and started to run.

'Where are you?' Her breath caught in her throat and tears stung her eyes.

The wind brought with it the faint voice in return. 'I'm here, Mummy.' The child was running back, hair flailing behind her, a smile on her face.

The mother dropped to her knees, clutching at her child as she fell into her.

'Don't run off like that,' she said. 'Stay where I can see you.' She kissed her cheeks, pushed back wild tangled hair. 'Baby, who were you talking to?'

'The lady.'

The mother held her daughter at arm's length 'What are you talking about? What lady?'

'The lady on the other side of the trees. I think she's asleep. She didn't open her eyes or get up when I called out her name.'

The mother's face crumpled in confusion. 'What are you talking about? Who is it, what's her name?'

The child gripped her hand and pulled. 'We have the same name, Mummy! Come, I'll show you.'

They ran, child leading mother – through the trees, the mist, the grey miserable world they were trapped in – until they came to the clearing, where barely any light could penetrate.

There was a frozen lake, cutting them off from whatever lay ahead over the horizon.

It was then the mother saw her.

A naked woman was slumped over, bent awkwardly at the waist. Her legs disappeared beneath the frozen water, so only her torso was visible. It was as if the woman had been pulling herself to safety, and in an instant the lake had been frozen by some kind of dark magic.

Twisted pale arms had been reaching for the shore – now frozen, bent at odd angles. Long blonde hair cascaded over stiff shoulders, messy, brought forward in the wind, strands obscuring the face.

'Claire?' the mother said, gripping her daughter by the hand tightly. Claire pulled against her arm, towards the woman.

'Do you want to play?'

'Don't speak to her,' the mother said.

'Maybe she's just tired, Mummy.' Before she could be stopped, the girl pulled free from her mother and ran to the woman.

The mother tried to run, stop her, but her legs were rooted to the spot, and when she opened her mouth to call after her, no sound escaped.

The girl knelt down just in front of the lake woman's outstretched hand with its twisted fingers, bent and misshapen, nails broken and filthy.

The girl reached out to touch her hand.

The woman's fingers twitched, then grabbed her wrist. The girl screamed as the woman stirred; back contorting, the ice cracking releasing her legs.

Her head reared up, revealing her face. Eyes wide, mouth open, matching the girl's screams.

*

Claire screamed, bolting upright, straight into her mother's arms. Sweat poured from her body, and her T-shirt clung to her, painted onto her skin. She could hear Iris's voice, calming and soothing her, brushing back her sweaty hair with her hands.

'I'm here, it's OK. You need to calm down.' She prised her arms from Claire's hands and held her back firmly, forcing her to remain lucid.

It took a few minutes to gain her composure, then Claire found herself staring back into the familiar eyes of her mother. She sighed and pushed herself back, flopping onto the bed.

'God, I'm sorry, Mum,' she said, pushing away strands of hair, glued to her forehead with sweat. 'I hope I didn't scare you.'

'You're the one who was scared. What was that all about?'

'A nightmare, that's all.'

'Seemed pretty intense for just a nightmare. Are you sure you're not on anything,' Iris said, eyeing her with caution.

'I'm not on anything.' She was breathless. 'It was just a stupid dream. I've had it before. It's nothing, really.'

'It didn't look like nothing. It looked like you were having a panic attack in your sleep.'

'I'm fine.'

'I can call out a doctor.'

'I'm fine!'

Iris recoiled and sat further back on the bed, looking at the floor. Claire felt guilty and when she tried to sit up, Iris hooked her arm with hers and hauled her upright.

'How long has this been going on?'

'Really, Mum, I'm fine. You go back to bed, get your sleep.'

Iris shook her head. 'No. You're going to tell me what happened.' Her eyes wandered over her daughter's face. 'I mean, look at the state of you. You were scared.'

Claire's defence mechanism kicked in, and she glared at Iris. 'Go. To. Bed.'

'Don't you dare talk to me like that.' Her finger rose up, pointed in Claire's face. 'I've heard enough to know there's more to it. It's not normal to have bad dreams every night.'

'I don't like where this conversation's going.' Claire pulled her duvet back up over her legs. 'I'm going to sleep.'

'And what happens later, when you wake up screaming, drenched in sweat?'

Her mother's words stopped her then. She couldn't bear to look her in the eye and pretend everything was all right, because it wasn't.

'Why don't you tell me what it is you see? It might help.'

For the first time since Claire could remember, her mother's voice actually sounded concerned, anxious. There was even a hint of compassion in her voice. Maybe the maternal instinct wasn't completely long dead and buried.

'It feels so real… and I don't know why.'

Claire explained what happened every night and what had played out in her mind for months, every time she closed her eyes. All her days were blurring into one. She couldn't remember the last time she'd fallen asleep and not dreamed about being in that damn wood, running from someone. Someone she could usually only hear, never see.

Lately, though, the voice had manifested itself to become a solid figure and she recognised their every shape, every line.

'You know what I'm going to say, don't you?' Iris said.

'Work?' Claire shook her head. 'All the years I've been doing this, and after all the things I've seen… nothing like this has happened before.'

'Maybe you've reached your breaking point.'

'It doesn't affect me during the day. I forget about it until I'm alone at night.'

'And what do you see?'

Claire swallowed hard, throat dry, raw. 'Just the wood, mist and trees, the usual…'

When she trailed off, Iris cast a knowing look. 'Except this time something was different?'

Claire's eyes misted over. 'I was a little girl, running, playing with you, except this person didn't look like you at all.'

Iris held her hand. 'I'm worried about you.'

'There was a woman,' Claire said, not listening. 'She was half submerged in a frozen lake.' Her eyes locked with her mother's. 'Almost like Nola Grant.'

'Jesus!' Iris shook her head. Then she saw a look in her daughter's eyes that made her blood run cold. 'There's more?'

Claire stared ahead, not really focusing on anything any more. 'That woman in the lake. She looked dead. *Was* dead... I went to her, reached for her hand, then I saw who she was.'

She squeezed her mother's hand.

'As I am now... that woman was me.'

*

When Iris crawled back into her bed, she glanced at the clock beside her and the green glow showed it was 1:00 a.m.

She rolled over to face away from the door once again and although extremely tired, found it difficult to sleep after what she'd just witnessed.

CHAPTER 19

8th November

Elias Crest parked the silver pool car on the opposite side of the road to where Daryl Thomas lived, and took a moment to compose himself. He was unfamiliar with this side of town and he certainly didn't know anyone from this area. He'd half expected Daryl's house to be on some rundown estate, where he imagined stray dogs roamed the street and kids scavenged through overflowing bins, searching for scraps because their mothers had spent their Income Support money on fags and booze instead of food.

The Thomas household didn't live up to the stereotype, which annoyed Elias somewhat. There was no beat-up washing machine or sofa discarded in the front garden. No overflowing rubbish, broken beer bottles, fag-ends or dog shit up the path to a dishevelled house.

This place was anything but.

Elias had read Daryl's file on his past dealings with the police, his minor offences and the assault on PC Southgate, but he knew Daryl's mother lived with him, which was the issue he couldn't get his head around. Did she know what her son had become?

He didn't come from a rough background and had gone to one of the best state schools in Haverbridge. He'd taken the council-estate stereotype, chewed it up and spat it out.

The house across the street looked impressive, with a well-kept front garden. The street itself looked respectable, not rough and rundown. He was intrigued to see what the house looked like inside. He was so lost in his thoughts he'd forgotten DC Harper sitting in the passenger seat staring at him.

'Earth to Planet Crest.'

Elias blinked hard. 'Sorry.'

Harper had been to the Thomas house before and already knew what lay ahead. He leaned closer towards Elias and grinned. 'Whatever you've prepared yourself for, you may want to have a rethink,' he said.

'Somehow I doubt that,' Elias said as he stepped out of the car. Harper followed him across the street. 'You've been inside this house before. Did you ever meet the mother?'

'Sure.'

'And?'

'She's a force to be reckoned with, but not in the way you might think.' He grinned at Elias, who eyed him suspiciously as they walked to the front door. The grin didn't fade when Mrs Thomas opened the door to them either.

'Gabriel, hello!'

'Ello, Mrs Thomas.'

'Oh, you make me sound so old,' she said, her face glowing. 'I've told you before, call me Heather.' Elias stood gobsmacked. He half expected the woman to reach for Harper with open arms and give him a bear hug.

Heather Thomas was about fifty with dyed, but well-groomed, blonde hair. She looked expensive; her clothes complemented her well and her make-up was expertly applied. Her body was fairly trim but her face was hard, after years of smoking and sun abuse. Any sign that she'd once been beautiful had long vanished.

Elias exchanged glances with Harper, who shrugged. Heather soon turned her attention to Elias then back to Harper.

Her face dropped.

'What's my Daryl done now?'

The question was directed at Harper, which annoyed Elias, considering he was superior in rank. 'We just need to ask him a few questions, Mrs Thomas,' Elias said. She stared at him again, and gave him the once-over with her pale eyes.

'Don't think I know you,' she sniffed. Elias smiled, producing his warrant card, holding it up for her to see.

She leaned forward and squinted. Her glasses hung around her neck on a cord, and she placed them on her face before studying his ID again. Her eyes slowly rose to look at his face and she grunted. Elias guessed she'd seen enough. 'Is your son in, Mrs Thomas?'

Heather stared at him in silence, her eyes narrowing. She was thinking before she answered. She gave a sharp nod of her head and stood aside.

'You'd better come in.' She smiled at Harper but frowned at Elias, pointing at his shoes. 'Wipe your feet, Sergeant. Daryl's just had cream carpets put in for me.'

CHAPTER 20

Heather showed them into a large, well-decorated living room equipped with modern furniture and appliances. There was no doubt in Elias's mind that this was all paid for by Daryl and his little enterprise of exploitation. It made him feel sick to his stomach.

Harper declined the offer of a drink from Heather, and she made a point of not asking Elias. Instead, she invited them to sit and went to get Daryl.

'I feel like I've stepped into the Twilight Zone. What was that all about?' said Elias after she left the room.

Harper smiled. 'I did warn you. Dispel your belief and leave your preconceptions at the door.' He looked around the room before his eyes came wandering back to Elias's bewildered face. 'I've lost count how many times I've been in this room, and so has she, probably.'

'She's clearly taken a shine to you,' Elias said, 'and on first name terms as well. Lucky you.'

Heather reappeared and this time she offered Elias a drink. He declined. She folded her arms tightly and seemed to look past him, out of the window that looked onto the back garden. Her demeanour had changed – she now seemed more anxious and definitely less buoyant.

'My son will be with you in a minute. He's in the garden.' She studied Elias's face, making him feel self-conscious.

'My Daryl's a good boy, Sergeant,' she added, in a low hushed voice.

Hardly a boy, Elias thought, the man's thirty-five. He kept quiet, avoiding her stare.

'What's this about? Whatever it is, I'm sure there's been some mistake.'

'I'd rather wait until Daryl is here, Mrs Thomas, before I discuss anything.'

'It's nothing to do with that girl they found in the lake, is it?'

Elias and Harper exchanged glances.

Elias edged closer to her. 'What do you mean by that, Mrs Thomas?'

'She didn't mean anything, did ya, Mother?'

All three turned and saw Daryl leaning against the door that led from the hall. He gave half a smile, walked towards his mother and wrapped his arm around her tightly. He gave her a small but firm shake, seeming to comfort her, but Elias understood the real meaning of the gesture.

Let me do the talking.

'Mum knew Nola and I were friends… of sorts,' he said, baring his yellowing teeth in a wide grin. 'Didn't ya, Mum?'

Heather nodded slowly, avoiding his eyes. Daryl paused, watching her closely. 'How about you go and meet up with one of your friends, Mum, just for a few hours?' He took his wallet from his trouser pocket, pulled out a few twenty-pound notes and stuffed them into her hand. 'Treat yourself.'

Elias noted that Heather kept her eyes from her son's. 'Yeah, why not? I'll see if Tina's in and fancies a ride into town.'

'Before you go, Mrs Thomas...' Elias said, stepping in front of her. 'Where were you on the night of the first of November?' She stopped dead in her tracks and her eyes stole a quick look at her son.

'I was at home all day. Daryl and I had a takeaway pizza for dinner and watched a Blu-ray.'

Crest looked sceptical. 'What Blu-ray?'

She hesitated. '*Pirates of the Caribbean*. The new one.'

'And the pizza?' Elias made no attempt to hide the disbelief in his voice.

Daryl bristled and Heather looked at the floor, trying to find her voice.

Harper rose to his feet quickly, notebook in hand. 'I love pizza,' he said, smiling at her. 'Do you have the name and number for the place you ordered from?' She looked at Daryl and he answered for her.

'Leaflet's on the kitchen counter. Help yourself, Constable, you know the way.' Harper went to the kitchen and quickly reappeared holding a leaflet. There was silence as he copied the name and telephone number into his notebook.

'Can I go now?' Heather asked, risking a glance into Elias's eyes. He nodded. After she left the house, Daryl watched her drive away in her car before he turned and scowled at Elias.

'Before you say anything, I didn't do it.'

Elias's eyes widened. He gave a look of mock surprise. 'Didn't do what?'

Daryl laughed and circled both men, heading to the drinks cabinet in the corner. 'Nola,' he said, as he poured himself a large whisky. 'You want to know if I killed her.'

'Did you?'

'Nope.'

'You're sure about that?'

Daryl regarded him for a moment before grinning. 'Cocky cunt, aint ya?'

'What did you say?' Elias said, rounding on him.

Daryl held his hand up into his face. 'Easy. Said it in jest, mate. Get back on ya leash.'

'You're not doing yourself any favours, Daryl,' Harper said, his face showing his apprehension. Daryl shot him a grin, then nodded. He gestured to Elias to continue.

'It's all good, Sergeant.'

Elias's voice was low when he spoke, as he tried to contain the urge to floor the dirty pimp where he stood and to hell with the consequences. 'Know anyone who might wish her any harm?'

Daryl grinned. 'I could give ya a list.'

'Care to elaborate?'

Daryl took a large mouthful of the spirit and plumped out his cheeks, washing the liquid around his mouth, staring at Elias the whole time. At length he swallowed, flopped down in a chair and plucked a cigarette from the pack on the table. He lit it and began to take deep drags.

'Nola pissed off her fair share of punters in the past,' he said, expelling a stream of smoke. 'She didn't always perform well, if ya know what I'm sayin'? Didn't always give out the money's worth.'

'And any money she did make, you took from her,' Elias said, leaning so he looked down on Daryl, 'didn't you?'

Daryl kept quiet, studying Elias carefully, while he smoked his cigarette.

'How else could you afford to keep mummy happy? This house, for instance,' he said, looking around, 'you've certainly done well, Daryl, I'll give you that. Just a pity it's not by honest means.'

Daryl shifted in his seat. His face grew dark, his eyes appearing almost black. 'You couldn't wait to have another pop at me, could ya, Sergeant?'

Harper shifted uneasily on his feet. He didn't like the way this was going. He'd seen what happened to people who wound Daryl up the wrong way on many occasions, and Elias was treading precariously close to the edge.

'When was the last time you saw Nola alive?' he asked Daryl, stepping in, going over Elias's head.

'Found your voice, Gabriel?'

'You'll address me as DC Harper.'

'Oh, I'm sorry, DC Harper, Sir,' he said. 'I last saw Nola early the morning before she disappeared.' He was grinning, not taking anything seriously.

'Where?'

Daryl seemed to think generally at this point. 'It was by the chip shop where she lived. She'd just bought some fags from the newsagent next door.'

'Can anyone confirm that?' Elias asked, stepping in again. Daryl stared at him, his eyes hard, unrelenting.

'Rachel Larson. She was there. I was with her all day, if ya know what I mean?' He puffed on his cigarette and blew a long stream of smoke up into Elias's face, winking suggestively. 'There's cameras at the shops, Sergeant. You might wanna check them.'

Elias was angry. Daryl was a cocky bastard of the worst kind. Elias's lips pulled into a thin line and his eyes narrowed. He gave Daryl a well-rehearsed sneer, a look of contempt.

Try a different tack.

'Your mum seems nice, Daryl.'

'Leave her out of it.'

'Very hospitable lady, by all accounts. Wouldn't you agree, Harper?' he asked, tilting his head towards the constable. Harper was unsure where this was heading, and he stuttered at first, before clearing his throat and speaking again.

'How relevant is this?'

Daryl nodded. 'I'd listen to him, mate. Chats a lot of sense for a copper, like.'

'She doesn't know what you do, does she?' Elias continued.

'She knows what she needs to know,' Daryl said, grinning again. 'Why? Ya threatening to tell me mummy, is that it?'

'I think she'd be devastated if she found out, don't you?' Elias looked around, gestured to the fine surroundings. 'I mean, can you imagine how she'd feel if she found out that all this came from trading girls like Nola from one sicko to the next?'

Daryl frowned hard, his brow deeply creased. He felt anger boiling within his gut. He wanted Elias to stop, but he carried on.

'Your mum looks like she has high standards... I reckon she'd make sure things went quite bad for you, Daryl... son or no son. Blood isn't always thicker than water.'

'I think we're done here, don't you, Crest?' Harper's voice expressed his concern but the other men ignored him. Instead, their eyes bore into one another for what seemed like an eternity. Eventually, Daryl rose to his feet, took a deep drag on his cigarette, and blew more smoke into Elias's face, making his eyelids flutter.

'Are ya gonna charge me for anything, mate?'

'I'm not your mate, Daryl, far from it—'

''Cos if you're not, you and the constable 'ere can piss off. I'm a busy man.'

'We should go,' Harper said, touching his colleague's arm, but Elias shook him off.

Daryl smiled. 'You'd do well to listen to him,' he said, jabbing a finger hard into Elias's chest.

As soon as he'd made contact with the hard mass of muscle, Elias grabbed Daryl's fingers, twisted them around and snapped them back, sending shooting pain through his hand. Daryl howled, balled his free hand into a fist, and struck Elias hard in the ribs.

Elias fell to the floor in a heap. He was winded, lungs aching for air.

'I'd stay down, pig, if I were you.' Daryl squeezed his fingers together, easing life back into them again, suppressing the pain, then leaned forward and spat into Elias's face. 'You wanted to cross that line, and now you're the fool on the ground.'

He looked at Harper, who was stunned to silence, glued to the spot. 'I didn't kill Nola. I wouldn't kill her even if I knew I could get away with it.'

A switch seemed to flick in Harper's head and he quickly reached for Elias. 'That was foolish, Daryl.'

'What you gonna do, filth? You serious? He was pushing me, you saw it. He could've broke my fuckin' fingers.'

Harper reached for his arm, pulling him closer. 'Daryl Thomas, I'm arresting you for assault on a police officer. You do not have to say anything, but it may harm your defence if you do not mention when questioned something which you later rely on in court…'

'You're fuckin' jokin'?'

'…anything you do say may be given in evidence.' Harper pulled Daryl by the arm. 'I trust handcuffs won't be necessary.'

Daryl looked down at Elias, who was slowly catching his breath, his hand clutched to his chest. Underneath the mask of pain, he was grinning.

'You fuckin' bastard. You did that on purpose.'

'Come on, Daryl,' Harper said, pulling him towards the front door, 'let's keep this civil.' He cast a dark look at Elias, before escorting Daryl out into the snow.

CHAPTER 21

In the incident room, Elias looked self-assured when Harper approached. Any hope he had of a breakthrough with Daryl was quickly dashed when he caught the look on Harper's face.

'News isn't good, is it?'

'Perfect Pizza confirmed that a delivery was made to Thomas's address the night Nola went missing, at nine o'clock. A large Margarita deep-pan, with free Coke and garlic bread.'

'Yes, yes,' he said, 'it just means they ordered it, doesn't mean Thomas was there at the time and he could've gone out later. His mum could be covering for him. You saw the hold he has on her.'

Harper shrugged. 'Delivery driver gave a good description of Thomas. The only reason he remembered him was 'cos he tipped so well. Plus, I spoke to his neighbour next door. She said she would've heard if Thomas left the house as they share the same path. Thomas's alibi holds up.'

'So far.'

'I don't think he's our man, Crest.' He paused. 'It's like you want it to be him. What the hell was going on back at Thomas's house anyway? You ripped his fingers back.'

Elias threw his hand up, dismissing Harper's words. 'You're just as bad as the Guv.'

'My ears are burning.'

Both men looked up as Claire walked up to their desks. She stopped in front of Crest, her demeanour frosty. 'You've something to say, Crest?'

'Thomas is in custody.'

There was a brief flicker of surprise across her face, but it quickly vanished. 'Why?'

'Assaulting an officer,' Harper said.

Claire looked at him. 'He's keeping with tradition then.' Her eyes crossed back to Elias. 'Who did he assault?'

'Me.'

'You?'

'Yes. That surprise you? He took a swing at me in the ribs.'

'Why would he do that?'

'Because he's a thug,' he said.

She paused. 'Harper?' Her eyes met his again. 'Why did Thomas assault DS Crest?'

Harper was silent. He looked at the floor, then at Elias, who watched him carefully.

'Well?'

'DS Crest questioned him on his alibi… that's all. Thomas was edgy, he didn't like it.'

'So he swung a punch?'

'I guess.'

'Are you sure?'

'What's that supposed to mean?' Elias interjected. 'You heard what Harper said.' Claire eyed him with suspicion. She looked to Harper and he gave her Daryl Thomas's statement.

'Does his alibi hold up?'

'Yes, Guv.'

'Then he's not our guy.'

'You still can't say for sure. He could've got someone else to do the dirty work for him if he didn't sneak out,' Elias protested.

Claire sighed, flung the statement back at Harper. 'For Christ's sake, let it go, Crest.'

She disappeared into her office, Elias hot on her heels. 'We're done here,' she said, as she sat down at her desk. She brought up the HOLMES software and accessed the statements compiled so far relating to Grant's murder.

'I'm pressing charges on Thomas.' He heard her sharp intake of breath, but no words followed. 'What? You don't approve?'

Claire looked up at him. 'What's it going to achieve? With his previous record, he'll get up to six months or a fine. Meanwhile, you're here with a face like a smacked arse because you let him get to you, and mouthing off about how he should've got a tougher sentence… Are you seeing where I'm going with this?'

'The guy is scum.'

'But you can't lock someone up just for being that.'

Elias was taken aback by her tone. He stared at her, wide-eyed. 'So glad I've got your support.'

'That's something you've got to earn, Crest.' Her voice was different now. It sounded heartfelt. 'I've read up on your history with the force so far and let me tell you,' she said, as she rubbed her forehead with her fingers, 'I think you've got great potential, despite the reason you transferred here.'

His face darkened but he said nothing. He didn't want to think about his reasons and he certainly didn't like the fact that she knew about them either.

'You could go as far as you want to,' she continued. 'You won't hear that from me very often.'

Elias scoffed, but then saw the look in her eyes. Is that sincerity?

She wasn't finished. 'But first there are some things you've got to learn, and managing your aggression is one of them.' His eyes were hard at first, unrelenting as she held his stare, but then they softened a little.

He nodded but couldn't bring himself to say anything. His ribs still ached from Daryl's fist, and he was tired.

Very tired. He didn't want to say anything he might come to regret.

He left her office, and gave Harper a frown as he sat at his desk. He picked up a pen and chewed it at the corner of his mouth.

After a short while, Claire called another team briefing. As she confirmed to the team, Rachel Larson had formally ID'd Nola's body with her friend, Olivia Jones. Elias kept quiet, not even bothering to look at her when he gave her the last-known information he'd collected from Nola's mobile-phone records.

Nola's mobile signal had been scrambled by something, most likely some device bought over the Internet, when the call was placed to Rachel's phone and there was nothing untoward in her text messages or phone calls during the last few weeks leading up to her murder.

'Image-enhancement unit is working on getting a better look at the man seen running after Kenny Philips's car the night Nola was abducted. Matthews, stay on that,' Claire said, folding her arms and leaning against Stefan's desk.

She went quiet and when every face was searching hers, knowing there was more, she straightened herself out, her voice low when she spoke.

'What I'm about to tell you all goes no further. It stays within these four walls.'

The silence of anticipation was almost crushing.

'Grant was pregnant. Approximately, twelve weeks.'

Elias shook his head. 'It's better off out of it. Our man did it a favour.'

Claire's eyes narrowed. 'It?'

He nodded.

'You unimaginable bastard,' said Jane. 'Don't have kids do you, Crest?'

'Tell me you'd feel the same way if you had a son or daughter? Can't, can you?' asked Harper.

Elias sneered. 'What're you lot? Mother Earth?' He sat forward, pointing his finger, driving the point home. 'Grant would've either had an abortion or dragged the poor kid into the same downward spiral she was riding. You lot want to get things into perspective.' He paused, and looked at Claire. 'I'm sorry if it sounds cold, but you know I'm right.'

'What's important now is to keep it from the press for the time being.'

The room was silent, a few people nodding or making notes. Elias looked around at everyone, then back to Claire. He looked exasperated.

'Why?'

Claire's eyes snapped up in his direction. Her eyebrows rose. 'You seriously need to ask?'

'Seems pointless holding it back. It could work to our advantage.'

'Or the opposite. This order has come from above. It's not up for negotiation.' Elias shook his head. 'I'm sorry, Sergeant, was there something else you wanted to add?'

'Nah, it's all right, Guv.'

Claire's face was tightly controlled, taut with tension, and she addressed the whole room when she said, in a low calm voice, 'If I find out that anyone in this room has leaked this information, you'll think a holiday in Somalia's a trip to fucking paradise compared to the hell I'll rain down on your head.'

PART THREE

CHAPTER 22

The man watched from behind the window in Bayley's coffee house, across the road from her office building. He knew Barratt & Causeland, Solicitors occupied the first and second floors of the building, and he knew she'd be leaving any time within the next half-hour, having watched her movements, like he'd watched all his chosen ones.

Dealing with Nola had thrown him. He hadn't expected her to have such a difficult spirit to break, but he was adamant he'd learn from his mistakes and put what had happened with Nola down as another practice run.

It was almost 8:00 p.m. He cast his eyes back towards the office block, just as she emerged. He sighed inwardly. She was so beautiful.

Sara Thornton's light-ginger hair, tied up in a sleek ponytail, swayed as a gust of bitterly cold wind hit her when she stepped outside. Although dressed appropriately in her winter clothes, she felt chilled to the bone.

She stopped under the shelter of a convenience store and pulled her hood up over her head. He watched her as she put on her leather gloves and walked down the street, clutching a large folder under her arm.

He kicked the stool out from underneath him, left Bayley's and followed her at a distance, keeping his baseball cap pulled low over his face, coat hood pulled over the top. The cold hit him like a smack in the face, his skin feeling taut and frozen.

His heart felt like it was dancing, the beat reverberating inside his chest with excitement. He quickened his pace, both to fight the cold as well as to keep her in his sights.

When she headed off the main high street, towards the multi-storey car park, her mobile phone rang.

The man hung back, slowing his pace as she fished around inside her bag. She stopped, grimaced at the caller ID, then answered the phone.

'I know I'm late, I'm sorry,' she said, when she held the mobile to her ear. 'You may as well just go without me, I'll meet you there.' She fell silent, then visibly bristled. 'It's not my fault. I couldn't just up and leave, Gregg. I'll be there as soon as I can.'

Whatever the reply, Sara clearly didn't like it. She hung up and flung the mobile back into her bag in anger.

The man knew Gregg was her husband of five years. They'd planned a night out – 'date night', they called it. Trying to inject some much needed spark back into their short marriage. The thought raised a smile.

As she turned into the street that led to the car park, his hand disappeared inside his pocket.

Keys. Mobile. Wallet. Cloth.

Chloroform...

CHAPTER 23

Elias glanced over his shoulder. Everyone was either too busy to care what he was doing, or running around with phones glued to their ears. His eyes darted towards Claire's office.

She was talking with Stefan.

Her favourite.

He was beginning to despise them both. His face hardened, watching their body language. What the hell did she see in Stefan that she didn't even bother to look for in him?

He had aggression, sure, but he didn't see much of the alpha male in Stefan. He seemed too nice... Maybe that was his cover and deep down there was a darker, devious side? Elias didn't know and right now didn't care.

He accessed Google, typed in a search and brought up the website for Haverbridge's local newspaper. Chewing on the end of his biro, he scanned the various headlines scrolling across the screen. He read the article on Nola, and noted the reporter's name. He clicked on their contact details and wrote down a number and email address on a scrap piece of paper.

He clicked and closed the webpage, and turned the paper over when Matthews approached his desk. He kept his motions slow, drawing no undue attention towards himself.

Matthews perched on the edge of his desk and passed Elias a handful of paperwork.

'There're some discrepancies about who may have had access to the parkland while the firework company and council were rigging everything up for the display. It was supposed to be closed to the public in the early hours of the morning on the fifth, but seems it wasn't.'

Elias pulled a face and checked his watch.

'I'm sorry, did you have to be somewhere?' Matthews snapped.

Elias checked the top page on the bundle of headed A4 paper: MILLENNIUM FIREWORKS. He read further along. 'They're closed.'

'Call them tomorrow. You can do that before you go and see the park warden. See why the security wasn't as tight as it should've been and if he's got the CCTV footage from his Portakabin ready for us yet.'

Elias nodded, and flung the paperwork down on top of the scrap paper he wanted hidden.

Matthews noted the expression on Elias's face and crossed his arms tight across his chest. 'Is there a problem?'

'It's Claire.'

Matthews laughed. 'I'm beginning to think you like torture. I can't decide whether you're brave, very stupid or—'

'DCI Simon Forester,' Elias cut in.

Matthews looked perplexed at first, then the realisation hit him. 'What're you bringing him up for? Don't let Claire hear you chatting about him.'

'I heard she cheated on him. May have even compromised a case while she did it as well. What's that about?'

Matthews shrugged. 'Rumour, mate.'

'There's always an element of truth in a rumour.'

'Look,' Matthews said, lowering his face to stare into Elias's eyes. 'I may be a lot of things but ratting out the Guv, or spreading gossip about her private life, isn't my thing.'

Elias smiled and looked away towards Claire's office, then back to Matthews's face. 'She did compromise a case, didn't she?' Matthews blinked. 'Her relationship with DSI Donahue has taken a battering over it as well, hasn't it?'

Matthews said nothing.

'See, she has her secrets too, you know?'

'What are you doing, Crest?' he said, shaking his head.

Elias stood up and pulled his suit jacket on. He gathered up the paperwork on his desk and shoved it under one arm. 'She knows my secrets. It's only right I know hers too.'

CHAPTER 24

The road that led to the car park was dead. The further Sara headed towards the entrance, the quieter everything became, and all she could hear was the sound of her heels against the pavement.

She was very close to his car now, parked on the left against the curb. A quick look over the man's shoulder confirmed they were alone.

He readied himself.

His face seemed to shrink back even further under his hood, as he pulled the peak of his cap lower, shielding his face from the CCTV camera perched up high on a building several feet away from them.

He reached for her.

He caught her off-balance as she tripped on her heels, slipping on the ice. Her knees went from under her as he dragged her against him. He stifled her screams, pressing the chloroform-soaked cloth harder over her mouth.

She clawed at his arms and the folder she'd been carrying fell to the floor, skittering across the pavement, loose paper spilling into the road.

Soon her movements slowed. Her body went limp in his arms.

Backing up towards the back door of his car, he stooped and pulled the door handle. He pushed her along the length of the back seat.

Sitting in the driver's seat, he looked around again. He didn't see anyone, which relaxed him a little. He was still new to all this... Well, fairly new. He felt conscious of the lone CCTV camera but he'd kept their backs to it, as planned. The fake plates he'd acquired would slow the police. He was aware that the cameras were usually manned 24/7, so quickly turned the key in the ignition.

Then he heard a muffled sound. Sounded like something by Queen.

Sara's mobile was ringing.

He arched around in the seat and retrieved the phone from her bag, fumbling in his haste.

He checked the caller ID:

Gregg... The name flashed across the screen and he grinned. Too late for apologies.

Arrogance and a smug satisfaction swarmed inside him. Even the threat of being caught at this crucial moment didn't deter him. It did the polar opposite. The thrill of getting caught felt delicious.

He hit the Answer button.

Raising the phone to his ear, he waited in silence.

'Sara?' Gregg's voice sounded strained, tight.

The man smiled to himself.

'Sara, I'm sorry for what I said. I know how hard you've been working.' He let out a deep sigh. 'Let's not fight like this. We've been making such good progress with the therapy. I just wanted tonight to be special. I thought...' He broke off. Paused. 'God, I don't know what I thought.'

The man smiled at Gregg's words. 'Too late for apologies,' he said, before he could stop himself. He could almost feel the fear in Gregg's rapid breathing.

'Who is this? Where's Sara?'

Silence. A cruel smile appeared.

'She belongs to me now.'

His words hit Gregg like a gunshot wound to the chest, his insides exploding. The man began to pull away from the curb, Sara's mobile now on the dashboard. Gregg was shouting now, a mixture of obscenities then beseeching.

He sounded desperate, like he might shatter.

As the car turned the street corner, the man rolled down the window. It'd started to snow again, the drops pattering across the windscreen and through the driver's side window, cutting across his face.

'She's mine.'

He hung up, and guided the steering wheel with his raised knees as he wiped his prints from the phone. Then he dropped it out of the window. It smashed against the concrete, sending fragments of plastic and metal across the tarmac. Then the car disappeared into the bitter night.

*

The phone went dead. Gregg's heart was pounding.

'Sara?'

He screamed again and again, until his voice was hoarse. He dropped the phone. It hit the carpet with a dull thud. He stared at his reflection in the mirror in the hallway. He was streaked with sweat. His hair was plastered to his forehead and his face burned but inside he was cold.

Numb.

A void deep within him.

Sara...

He retrieved the phone from the floor. It seemed an eternity, waiting for the emergency services to pick up his call. After he'd hung up, he found himself sliding down the wall, onto the floor in despair.

CHAPTER 25

He parked the car in the usual spot. Behind the town houses there was a row of garages and a small forecourt for residents who paid for the privilege of a car parking space each month. The man couldn't afford for his car to be spotted on the road so it had become a necessity to pay for the garage.

It was dark and secluded, and he rarely saw anyone else there. It was the perfect place to drag a body unseen, through his back garden and into the kitchen via the back door.

Sara was slender but she was heavier than he'd thought she would be. He struggled to hold her weight as he pulled her through the door and onto the kitchen floor. She lay there in the half-light, like a sleeping doll. He locked the back door, heaved her up over his shoulder, his legs giving a little as he took the strain, and took her down the stairs to the basement.

He removed her coat, gloves and boots, then her jewellery. He shackled her wrists, rolled her on her side, then swept away hair from her face that had worked its way loose from her ponytail.

He retrieved her things, switched off the light at the top of the stairs and locked the door behind him.

*

It was nearly midnight when he heard a noise that woke him from a light sleep, and he found himself still in his armchair.

The only light in the room came from the television in front of him, sound turned down low. At first he wasn't sure what had woken him, until he heard the sound again.

The sound of metal against metal.

Sara was awake.

Testing the shackles and the pipe, as Nola had done before her… Then there had been the first one of course.

He smiled, rose from his chair and went into the kitchen. He warmed up the meal he'd cooked earlier, in the microwave. When it was ready, he set it on a tray with a plastic spoon. He unlocked the basement door and the banging against the pipe below stopped instantly.

She's waiting for me.

He picked up the tray, balanced it across one arm, and pushed the door open. He slowly walked down the steps into the semi-darkness.

CRUEL BEGINNINGS

September 1981

'Boys don't cry?' the vile mother said to her son in his bedroom, as the song played out over the radio. The voice of The Cure's Robert Smith crackled out of the old speakers and the mother sneered at the sight of her son's tears. 'Boys don't cry. That's fucking ironic, looking at the state of you.'

'You've been drinking again,' said the boy's grandmother, her tone harsh as usual. She kneeled down to comfort him. 'It's his sixth birthday. His father should be here.' She looked up. Her face was serious. 'One day of sobriety, that's all I asked of you.'

'That's half your trouble, Mother. You're always asking the impossible.'

'He said he'd come,' whimpered the boy. 'He promised me.'

His mother stooped down to his eye level. 'A promise doesn't mean anything when it comes from a man.' As the song came to the chorus again, she nodded her head towards the radio. 'I'm glad your father's not here to see this. His only son, crying like a little girl and listening to that nancy.'

The grandmother's hand rested on the mother's wrist. 'Leave him be.'

'He's an embarrassment.'

'He is your son.'

'Regrettably.'

The grandmother's face grew dark. Her hand flew out, slapping the mother hard across the face. 'That was an evil thing to say.'

'Careful, we don't want him growing up anything like you,' the mother said, rubbing her cheek. The boy buried his face in his grandmother's bony shoulder, his body jerking with uncontrollable sobs. The mother smiled as she left the room, slamming the bedroom door behind her.

The grandmother pulled the boy from her, ignoring the large damp patch left on her blouse, and stared hard into his face.

'You know she can't help it, don't you? She's just not grateful for what she has. You are perfect.' She kissed his forehead. 'Do not let her tell you any different.' She raised his chin from his chest so she could look into his eyes. 'Do not let her make you believe you are worthless. You are special, and someday she will realise just how much.'

She reached forward, taking from the floor the box of space Lego she had bought him. He smiled as his small hands gripped the box.

'I hope I got the right one?'

A small nod. 'You did, Nanna. He leaned up and kissed her cheek. 'Thank you.'

'That's not all,' she said, her face now beaming. She left the room then came back with another present, wrapped in bright birthday paper. She dropped it into his eager hands and sat back down beside him. 'Do not tell your mother about this. It will be our little secret.'

He smiled as his fingers tore through the paper, and froze when he saw a tape recorder underneath. His face shot to hers, a smile spreading from ear to ear.

'Do *not* tell your mother,' she said again.

'Thank you,' he said, flinging his arms around her. 'I didn't think I'd ever have one of these.'

'You've had a rough year and I thought you deserved it for being so strong.'

She put her arm around his shoulders. 'I know you wanted your dad here today, but we do not always get what we want in life. It is about being grateful for the life we do have.'

He sniffed, and wiped his eyes. 'I didn't want Dad to leave. Mum blames me. She said life was perfect until I ruined it.'

'That was a wicked thing to say,' she said, stroking his hair. Her voice was soft, nurturing. 'It wasn't her talking. It's the drink, but we can try to help her. We must always try to help others, but sometimes, some people are beyond help or just don't want it.'

He squeezed his eyes shut, then opened them again. He looked up into her face, his brow furrowed.

'What happens if they don't want help?'

The grandmother sighed, cradled him in her arms, and began rocking him back and forth. Her eyes were staring straight ahead at the wall, her jaw set firm and her eyes unrelenting.

What she would tell him next would change him forever.

CHAPTER 26

9th November

The next morning dawned with a fresh blanket of snow on the ground and most of Claire's team was late into CID to take over from the night team. There had been one significant development overnight and as Claire briefed her colleagues, she felt a mixture of emotions as she explained about Sara Thornton.

'Uniform managed to track Sara's journey from CCTV footage and nothing seemed to be out of the ordinary until they noticed a man following her. That's when uniform put two and two together, with the Grant investigation. The man's wearing the same coat and hat as our suspect who was tracking Nola, and it appears to be the same car as before.'

Stefan's eyes immediately lit up. 'Number plates?'

'It would appear he's using fake ones.'

'Can you see his face?' Elias spoke this time.

'Barely,' Claire said. 'He has his back towards the camera ninety-nine per cent of the time. Plus, he was wearing his hood up, with a baseball cap pulled low underneath it. He knows where the cameras are. He's done his homework.'

Claire moved towards the LCD screen at the front of the room. 'Everyone needs to see the footage.' She turned to face Crest. 'I want you to get Image Enhancement on the stills from the footage. I want to see what this snake looks like.'

'Yes, Guv.'

The team then waited for Claire to hit the Playback button.

They saw the scenes unfold before them with bated breath. They watched Sara and the man right up until the point when he grabbed her, drawing a few gasps from some of the team at the sheer ferocity of the attack.

'What's that he's doing there? Is that a cloth over her face?' asked Harper.

'Judging by the way Sara reacts here,' Claire said, pointing to the screen as Sara slumped to one side, almost lifeless, 'he's using some form of sedative. Possibly chloroform. It's easily available if you know where to look.'

'What about the folder she was carrying?'

'It was missing when uniform went to retrieve it, but was handed in this morning by a member of the public to Barratt & Causeland, Solicitors, where she works. The file had their headed paper inside.'

She froze the footage just after the man had pushed Sara into the back seat. Everyone stared at the still image, then at Claire as she spoke.

'You've all seen the footage. We don't have one clear image of this man, and he's planned it this way. He's being brazen – cocky – taking her in a public place. Despite it being late evening, there was still the risk he could've been disturbed.'

She looked around at the faces before her. 'Why does he take these risks? We need to start building a profile on Sara Thornton and comparing it to Nola Grant. So far they seem to come from completely different walks of life. Their backgrounds differ completely, but there must be something they have in common, no matter how random we may think our man has been.

'Where does Sara hang out? Who with? Sara lives in Willian, Letchworth. I know I don't need to point out that it's an affluent area. In contrast, Nola lived in a rough part of Haverbridge. There may not seem to be any link but Sara is a solicitor. Nola has been in trouble before. Did Sara ever represent her? There may be a reason their paths have crossed.'

Jane cut in, voicing what most people had on their minds. 'Are we treating Sara as a potential murder victim?'

Claire saw all eyes were on her. 'We know this is the same man who had an interest in Nola Grant and most likely killed her or knows who did. We need to be prepared for the possibility that Sara's next.' There were a few more murmurs, and Claire raised her hands, her signal to quieten down.

'OK, here's what I want to happen,' she said. 'Harper and Cleaver, I want you to go to Barratt & Causeland. Speak to anyone who was around when she left last night. Show them the stills taken from the CCTV. Sara stayed in work out of normal office hours, which means the cleaners would have been in. Speak to the cleaning company and talk to whoever was working last night.'

She paused for breath, then continued: 'Bayley's. It's opposite Sara's work. From the CCTV taken outside the office block, we were able to find out the man was waiting in there before she left.'

'They'll have cameras,' Crest said.

Claire nodded. 'Yes, and hopefully we might be able to get a better angle on his face. Also talk to the staff. Someone must remember something about him.'

Claire looked back at the LCD screen and rewound the recording a little, until she got to the place where the man grabbed Sara.

'The news has already started to circulate to the local press and news stations,' she said, turning to face the team. 'This may go national. Sara Thornton is a totally different class of missing person. For obvious reasons, the public and media will be more sympathetic to finding this man.'

'There's a reason to be sympathetic to Nola, too,' Stefan said.

Claire knew what he meant. 'Nola's pregnancy, yes, I know. Tensions will be running high. The pregnancy still goes no further than these four walls at the moment, is that clear?' A few more murmurs of agreement. Claire moved on quickly.

She finished giving out instructions, then began to close the briefing. 'To quickly bring people up to speed, I've had Nola's tox report from the pathologist. There were traces of cannabis found in her body, but nothing else was detected. The results of the PM confirm she died from loss of blood.'

She stared at Elias until he made eye contact. He knew something was up.

'Daryl Thomas is being released.'

The words didn't quite sink in, and Elias gave her a blank look. 'You can't do that.'

'Yes, I can, and we can't hold him for much longer anyway.'

'I want to press charges for assault.'

'But you're not going to do that, Crest. Daryl's account of what happened doesn't look favourably on you either.' Harper shifted uncomfortably. Elias went to protest but she cut him short. 'This is not negotiable.'

Her eyes remained cold as she held his gaze. 'We've too much going on with this investigation, and the fact Sara Thornton was taken by the same man as Nola Grant, somewhat blows a hole in your theory about Thomas. He was in custody when Sara was taken. He's not a part of this. You've ensured he had a cast-iron alibi.'

Elias shook his head. 'I don't like this. What message are we sending out if I let him walk out of here with a slap on the wrist?'

'This is just your ego talking, Crest... let it go.'

His eyes narrowed in anger.

Patronising bitch.

After an awkward silence, Claire looked around the room. 'Any more questions?' No one raised anything. 'OK,' she continued, 'DI Fletcher and I will be visiting Sara's husband. If anyone needs me, I'm on my BlackBerry.'

CHAPTER 27

The pain in her stomach had built steadily over the last few hours, and despite its intensity, she couldn't bring herself to scream any longer.

It was pointless.

Sara had spent hours crying for help, despite the man telling her the room was soundproofed, and she'd now run out of steam. She was huddled in a heap on the cold floor, leaning up against the wall, fighting sleep.

What if I don't wake up again?

She'd asked herself the same question, over and over, whenever she felt her eyelids begin to close under the heavy weight of exhaustion. She'd seen the man only briefly since she'd woken in the basement. He had brought her food, but it had upset her stomach. Either that or it was the pure fear that was eating away at her limbs, chewing away at her flesh.

She had no idea how long she'd been awake. He'd taken her watch and there was no window, so she couldn't even hazard a guess at the time of day. She'd asked the time, but he'd ignored her. She yanked on the chain around the pipe, haphazardly, hoping it might suddenly break and free her.

It didn't.

She found herself sinking lower within herself. Sleep was winning out. After fighting with her body to stay awake for several more minutes, she found herself resisting the urge to wrestle with the idea any more.

She let her eyes close.

*

'Do you remember me?' The voice seemed to penetrate inside her head and rattle around, shaking her back to life. Her eyes began to open. She saw nothing at first, except white lights dancing in a haze, her eyes beginning to focus in the dim light.

She heard a man's voice say her name, and like a flick of a switch, she bolted upright, suddenly remembering everything.

His cold eyes met hers.

He was sitting cross-legged in front of her, watching her every movement. 'I asked if you remembered me?' he said. 'It hasn't been that long since I saw you last, has it?'

Part of her knew the voice was familiar. His face had familiar features, but she couldn't place them. It was the voice… definitely the voice.

'Do you remember me?'

His eyes searched the room, then shot back to hers when she didn't answer him. He threw himself forward, his face inches from hers.

'DO YOU KNOW WHO I AM?'

She screamed back at him: 'NO! … No, I don't know who you are, or what you want.' Her voice gave away the fear she felt inside, but she tried to keep her face neutral. 'Where am I?'

The man shook his head. 'You don't recall me at all?'

She shook her head.

'That… disappoints me, Sara, it really does.'

'Don't.'

He looked at her curiously at first, then a smile spread across his lips. 'Don't what?'

'Don't you say my name, you animal.' Her voice was strained and she knew he could see her trembling.

'You know nothing about me,' he said, his mouth set in a cruel line. 'You can't even remember seeing me before, yet you call me an animal all the same?'

'I've never met you. You must have confused me with someone else. It's not too late to let me go. I promise I won't say anything to anybody.'

The man laughed and looked away. 'They all say that.'

His words silenced her.

She felt a tear begin to roll down her cheek. 'What do you want with me?'

His face seemed to soften a little as he looked back at her pale face. Her hair now looked ragged, stray strands plastered across her forehead. Her make-up had run and black mascara lines had dried on her cheeks. She shook her head.

'I don't understand.'

'You will soon enough,' he said, voice almost tender. He eased himself to his feet, and was amused when she backed herself closer against the wall.

He grabbed a wooden chair that he'd brought down to the basement while she slept, and placed it in the middle of the floor. He turned the back of it to face her, adjusted it a little until he was satisfied, then straddled it. His arms folded over the backrest and he supported his chin on his forearms. He watched her closely but she avoided his stare.

He knew she was intimidated, but she needed to know he was the teacher and she would be his student… whether she liked it or not.

'Do you like your job, Sara?'

The question took her off guard. She hesitated, staring at his face for any hint of what his intentions might be. She saw nothing but curiosity in his eyes.

'What kind of question is that? How do you even know what I do?' Silence. His eyes seemed to silently repeat the question. 'Yes,' she said, 'I like my job.'

'You consider yourself valued?'

'I'm a solicitor. I help people.'

'What about your marriage?' He saw her tense. 'I think you need the help, Sara, but not in the way you might think.' She looked away from him and brought her knees up towards her chin.

Her thoughts turned back to Gregg. How he must be worried for her. She tried to forget the weight of the man's stare, despite feeling as if he was looking deep inside her, raping her soul.

'You have a lot of arrogance,' he said at length, 'but you mustn't worry, I can help you with that.'

'All I want to do is go home.'

'And you will, when I'm done with you.' He got off the chair and paced the room. 'I'm not a monster, Sara.' He paused, the next words painful to say. 'Parts of my childhood were… less than desirable, but I had an angel watching over me.' He laughed then. 'Not the feather-winged variety – I don't believe they're real – but I mean in a metaphorical sense.' His eyes turned serious. 'There was a woman in my life who showed me the way. She helped me. She moulded me into a better person.'

He stopped in front of her. He smiled. 'This is how I plan to help you, dearest Sara.' He paced the room again. His face was pained when the distant memory resurfaced and it was hard to bear.

Sara watched him carefully.

She'd seen a programme on television years ago that said, if you ever found yourself in a situation like this, where you were abducted, stolen away, for whatever purpose, you should always try and leave as much evidence behind for those who try to find you. Show them that you were there.

That you did exist.

Sara had thought of the possibility that she might never make it out of the basement. That these hours might be her last. She knew Gregg would have contacted the police and that people were looking for her.

She knew she should start leaving traces of herself wherever she could. She had no doubt that this man would clean up, try to cover his tracks if he did kill her, but he couldn't guarantee eradicating everything.

She cast a look over her shoulder.

The man was pouring her a glass of water from the jug on the table in the middle of the room. His back was to her.

She raised her fingers to her mouth. She nibbled on the nail of her right index finger until it broke away, leaving a jagged edge. She kept the nail in her mouth a moment, looked around, and discreetly placed it behind the pipe on the floor.

Leave evidence you were here. Leave evidence you existed.

The man came back over, handing her a plastic cup of water. 'You must be thirsty.'

Her mouth felt like a desert and as much as she didn't want to accept anything from him, she grabbed at the cup.

She took a large mouthful.

He sat down on the floor in front of her again, leaned forward and smiled. 'I've waited a long time for this moment. To hear you speak to me properly, tell me about your fears, your hopes, your dreams.'

'We've spoken before?'

'Oh, yes.' He smiled.

She sneered at him. 'I've nothing to tell you.'

His face dropped, eyes growing dark again. He shook his head.

'Now we both know that's not true, Sara, my darling.'

CHAPTER 28

Gregg Thornton was barely thirty years old. He had married Sara after a short engagement, and at first it had been a fairy tale dream come true. They were both successful; Sara a solicitor and he an accountant for the company he co-owned with his friend and business partner, Mason Clarke.

Both were from wealthy families and both had a taste for the finer things in life. They frequented expensive restaurants and stayed in luxurious hotels on holiday to which they flew first class. They owned expensive cars and took pride in their appearance. Both belonged to a top gym, wore designer clothes and were envied by many.

They were the beautiful couple, in the perfect marriage, or so everyone thought. But, as is often the case, there were flaws, and after a few blissful months, the cracks had begun to appear.

Barely having the time for each other due to their busy work schedules, the romance was brief and fleeting. They had spent the last five years becoming more like friends than husband and wife and lately, not even that.

Gregg had suggested they try psychotherapy after hearing about it through a mutual friend, and Sara had agreed. Whilst he thought they had been making progress, she had her doubts, but kept them to herself. Last night had been their 'date night,' and he felt numb sitting on the sofa thinking about the last words he'd said to her. He had been cruel and harsh, and he deeply regretted it.

Claire studied Gregg, sitting in front of her, then turned to his friend.

Mason Clarke was doing all the talking, answering all their questions with ease, and seeming in complete control. Gregg Thornton, however, was a mess.

He kept running his hands through his blond hair, then sniffing away imaginary tears, as if he'd cried every drop of moisture from his body, and all that remained was dry bone and withered tissue. His skin was pallid, his eyes red-raw, lips bloodless and his body was bent almost double in a heap on the sofa.

Claire had asked the basic questions, but she was now concentrating on the voice of the caller. 'You don't recall anything about the man's voice? No accent or distinguishing tone?'

Gregg shook his head, then said, 'Maybe.' Then another shake of the head, followed by, 'No. Nothing.'

'This is getting us nowhere,' Mason said. 'Why is this relevant?' He stood and folded his arms as he paced around the sofa. 'Surely you have eye witnesses? You already have him on CCTV and a car reg.'

'No one has come forward yet. The images on camera are hazy at best, with perfect shots of the back of his head, and he's using fake plates,' Claire said, breaking off as Mason's face began to register the problem she was faced with. 'We really need Mr Thornton to remember anything he can, no matter how insignificant he thinks it might be, if we are to find his wife.'

Gregg suddenly dropped his head in his hands. 'Would you not talk about me as if I wasn't here?' His hands trembled as he looked up at Mason, then at Claire. 'He said Sara was his now.' He looked at Stefan, who was sitting beside Claire. 'God knows what he's doing to her.' His voice faltered, as fresh tears welled in his eyes.

'This is a joke,' Mason said, shaking his head. Claire looked at him. He was a heavy-set man, with dark features and olive skin. His hair was shoulder-length, curly and almost black. He had large brown eyes to match.

He rested his arm on the mantle above the fireplace. He stared at a wedding picture of Gregg and Sara. His eyes looked sad as he stared at her smiling face. She did look beautiful. The look didn't go unnoticed by Claire.

'Was there any kind of trouble in your marriage, Mr Thornton?' Her eyes watched Mason, despite aiming the question at Gregg. She saw Mason's shoulders tense and his eyes glance back towards them, but he remained silent.

'What do you mean?' Gregg asked, defiant. 'I had nothing to do with this.' Claire's face remained unreadable. 'My marriage isn't perfect, Chief Inspector, but I love my wife very much.' He looked at Stefan. 'I'd never hurt her.' His eyes shot back to Claire.

She raised her eyebrows. He felt flustered then embarrassed. He looked at the floor and sighed. 'All right, all right.' Deep breath. 'Sara and I are going through a rough patch.'

Mason swung around to stare at him. 'What?'

Gregg gave a slight nod, looking at his friend. 'We've been seeing a psychotherapist.'

'Where?' Mason looked exasperated. Claire was sat quietly, saying nothing.

'Letchworth,' Gregg said, sorrow in his voice. 'F. B. C. on Broadway.'

Mason shook his head. 'I just don't get it.'

Claire sat forward, gaining Gregg's attention. 'What is F. B. C.?'

'Focus Being (Counselling & Psychotherapy) Centre.'

'How long have you been seeing a psychotherapist?'

'Eighteen months.'

'And who do you see?' Claire asked.

'I'm sorry, but how is this relevant?' Mason spoke now, cutting in and sitting next to Gregg.

'I'm trying to gain an insight into Sara and Gregg's relationship.'

'I don't think that is any of your business.'

'And I don't believe I was asking you.'

She looked back to Gregg, who didn't appear to be listening to either of them, absorbed in his own world, which until last night was fairly uncomplicated. 'Could you answer the question, Mr Thornton? I need to know the facts if we're to help Sara.'

He looked back at her. 'We saw Stephanie Curran. I have her number around here somewhere.' He stood and went to the table in the hallway and began rifling through a messy drawer.

Claire rose to her feet, a signal to Stefan they were done for now. She gave Mason a dark look and left the room.

'It's OK, Mr Thornton,' she said, as she neared the front door. 'We can easily find the office number should I need to speak to Stephanie Curran.'

Gregg continued to search, his face tense, his brow furrowed. 'No, no,' he said glancing up at her, 'it is in here somewhere.' He threw a stack of paper onto the floor. 'I know it's here.'

Claire and Stefan exchanged glances. Stefan put his hand on Gregg's shoulder. 'This isn't necessary right now, don't worry about it.'

'It is necessary. If I had listened to Sara, I would have it right now.' He looked Stefan hard in the face. All of a sudden his eyes welled up with tears again. 'She's always telling me to sort a filing system for important numbers, and I always put it off.' He looked away, shoulders hunched, and tears began to fall.

'Mr Thornton, please,' Claire said, trailing off when she saw him violently shake his head.

'No, it is here somewhere!'

Mason appeared in the doorway as Gregg thrust something into Claire's face.

'Here.' He handed her a white business card. 'I knew it was here.' He wiped tears off his cheek with the back of his hand. Claire glanced at the card and gave a thin smile and handed him her own.

'We'll be in touch, Mr Thornton, and get a Family Liaison Officer to you, but should you think of anything else in the meantime, please contact me. It doesn't matter what time it is.' She broke off as his sad eyes met hers. 'We will find her.'

'Alive, I hope,' Mason said. The look on Stefan's face told Claire to leave the last word with Mason. She nodded to Gregg before letting herself and Stefan out into the cold street.

*

'He refers to her in the present tense, not past. I don't think he's lying.'

Claire sat in Stefan's car and rubbed her hands together and exhaled. 'His friend, however, is another case entirely.'

Stefan began backing his car out the drive and onto the road. He paused before driving off. 'We're not far from the psychotherapy centre.' Claire turned to stare at him. 'Want to check it out? Maybe we can speak to Curran.'

CHAPTER 29

Focus Being (Counselling & Psychotherapy) Centre, or F. B. C. for short, sat nestled away up a short driveway on a turning off Broadway in Letchworth Garden City. The huge picturesque building was built in the 1980s and was now a well-established centre for people from all walks of life, seeking help for a wide variety of life's different problems.

As Stefan pulled his car up the drive and followed the road around towards the visitor car park, he caught the look on Claire's face as they parked up.

'Thoughts?' he said.

Claire wrinkled her nose, peering out of the window up at the top floor of the building.

'It looks as pretentious as it sounds, that's what I think.'

Stefan smiled as they got out of the car and headed towards the main entrance.

*

Alice Hathaway stared hard at Claire and Stefan, then her eyes dropped to their warrant cards. She frowned, removed her glasses from her pinched nose, rested them carefully on her desk, and clasped her bony hands together.

'Mrs Curran is a very busy woman. She doesn't see anyone without an appointment.'

Claire's face remained stony. 'We're not here as clients, Mrs Hathaway.'

'That doesn't make a difference.' Alice had a raspy edge to her voice, indicating she was a heavy smoker. Her nails were yellow and brittle, and her skin was heavily lined and sallow. Her grey eyes were small and beady, reminding Claire of a bird.

Alice was painfully thin, shoulder blades jutting out through her tired-looking blouse. Claire guessed she was in her fifties, and that she was a very hard and difficult woman to please. She was the office manager and as soon as Claire had spoken to the receptionist, they had been quickly ushered into Alice's office.

The silence was broken when Stefan leaned forward, making Alice recoil slightly. 'It won't take long. Perhaps if Mrs Curran was informed that this is just a routine visit, she wouldn't mind sparing ten minutes.'

Alice sighed and shook her head. 'I don't make a habit of breaking the rules, Inspector,' she said, picking up the phone on her desk. 'If she is with a client, I can't expect her to interrupt.' She avoided Claire's eyes, despite feeling the full weight of her stare. She gripped the receiver tight, her knuckles white.

After several seconds ticked by, Alice put the phone down with force. 'She must be with someone, she's not answering.' She stood. 'I suggest you go to reception and make an appointment or leave a card with me.' She eyed Claire frostily. 'I will see that she gets it.'

'I would feel more comfortable if we spoke to her sooner rather than later.'

When Alice made no attempt to answer, Claire spoke again, a grin spreading across her face. 'Perhaps you could go and knock on her door?'

Alice's eyes grew darker, in keeping with her mood. She looked reluctant at first but relented under Claire's gaze.

'Please wait in Reception. I will be with you shortly.'

*

They sat in silence, in dark-blue tub-chairs, watching people coming and going from the building. The furniture was modern with clean lines and minimal fuss, but the period details of the old building had been made into feature points throughout; a neat balance between old and new, which was tastefully done.

Claire noticed that the reception desk was really busy. The phones were ringing constantly, as well as the bustle at the front desk. The receptionist they had spoken to earlier looked harassed but seemed to have everything under control.

Claire leaned back in her chair, crossing her legs. 'How much do you think people pay for this crap?'

Stefan pulled a face, shaking his head and bending forward towards the coffee table in front of them. He picked up a leaflet and passed it to her. 'Why, you interested? Didn't you decline counselling after—'

He broke off in an instant when her face dropped, her eyes penetrating his.

'After last year? That's what you were going to say, isn't it?'

Stefan gave a sympathetic smile.

She ignored him as she scanned the selection literature. 'Let F. B. C. nurse your soul,' she began to read aloud. 'Let us help you take back the control in your life.' She paused and tossed the leaflet back on the table. 'Load of bollocks.'

Stefan laughed, but regained his composure when a man wearing stylish glasses appeared with a tray.

'Hello, I'm Lucas, from Admin and Bookings,' he said, reddening. 'Mrs Hathaway thought you might like some drinks while you wait.' He placed the tray on the table. Stefan eyed the biscuits and steaming tea with some relish.

'How long will Mrs Hathaway be?' Claire asked, glancing at her watch.

'Not long, I shouldn't think, but she did ask that I make sure you're comfortable,' he said. 'Is there anything else you need? Perhaps you want to go through the basics of what we have to offer here at Focus Being?'

Stefan went to speak but Claire gave him a sharp kick in the ankle under the coffee table.

'Yes, please do.'

Stefan shot her a surprised look.

It was clear that Alice Hathaway hadn't informed her staff there were two police officers sitting in the building. Their plain clothes, although not the normal attire compared to the other clients filtering in and out of the building, obviously didn't give them away. Usually, Claire found most people could tell she was someone of authority by the way she carried herself, and by the way she dressed.

Lucas beamed. 'Excellent. I'll go let Joseph know. He's in charge of making the bookings. I'm shadowing him today.'

'What're you doing?' Stefan said through gritted teeth as Lucas disappeared behind the reception desk.

'I just want to get an idea of what goes on here. They may be more honest if they don't know we're police.

*

Lucas sat opposite them both, taking notes, while next to him sat a tall man with dark wavy hair, who looked eager, his folder resting on his knees.

'I'm Joseph Green,' he said, offering Claire and then Stefan his hand. 'It's my job to make sure would-be clients understand what we offer at the centre.'

He smiled at Claire. 'Don't be scared to ask questions, that's what we're here for.'

Claire made herself return his smile. Stefan bit his lower lip.

'OK,' he said, handing Claire the same leaflet she'd looked at earlier. 'Here at Focus Being we offer counselling and psychotherapy for people from all social backgrounds, with help they feel they need in their life. That could be a loss of direction or purpose in life.'

Claire felt like he'd rehearsed this speech so many times, it sat like a file in his head that he could find and recite at any time with ease. He sounded like he was pitching some business proposition to a board of clients.

'Our psychotherapists have recognised qualifications in a wide variety of specialised subjects, including mental health counselling, and marriage and family therapy. We provide help on an individual basis or for couples, and for children.

'We're regulated, and we pride ourselves on using new and old tried-and-tested methods to suit each individual need. We provide a safe and secure environment for clients to express themselves freely.' He sucked in a deep breath, and smiled at Claire.

'Problems discussed are diverse,' he continued, and started to tap his fingertips with his pen, listing examples off one by one. 'Anxiety, psychotic breakdown, or problems with confidence, for example, are all quite common.'

'We're more interested in marriage counselling,' Claire said, trying to cut through the sales pitch.

Joseph paused. He looked at them both in turn, then smiled. He gestured with his hand, pointing between them both. 'You're married?'

'To each other, yes.'

Stefan choked on his biscuit and swigged back some of his tea. It practically scorched the back of his throat. He spluttered and looked at Claire, his eyes watering.

'Claire, perhaps—'

'Not now, honey,' she said, cutting him off. She turned to Joseph again. 'What type of problem qualifies as needing marriage counselling?'

Joseph looked a little bemused. 'Anything really. There are no rules, and we certainly don't wish to label or alienate potential clients.' He flexed his fingers together and handed her a printout from his folder.

'Here are some examples of what we typically deal with in relationship problems.' He used his pen to point to different sections on the paper. 'Sometimes we have incidents of financial worry, or each person's 'role' within the relationship.' He hovered over another point with his pen. 'Sometimes there are... intimacy issues.'

His face flushed a little as he spoke.

From the corner of her eye Claire saw Stefan bury his face in his hands.

'I can make an appointment for you both with our senior psychotherapist for an initial assessment, if you'd like?'

He opened the first leaflet that sat resting on Claire's knees. 'The price breakdown is listed here and we're open until quite late, so we're flexible and you can book a time that suits you.'

Claire watched his eager face. She guessed he was in his mid-thirties, despite having quite a baby face, but he had sharp eyes. He was slender, but she could tell by the fitted cut of his shirt that his shoulders were well defined. He was quite well-spoken and she guessed this was one of the main reasons he was a 'front of house' employee.

He seemed a little unnerved by her gaze, and she realised she was staring at him. He flushed red again. 'Do you have any questions?'

Claire smiled. 'Are there many couples that have this type of counselling?'

He looked a little taken aback. 'For marriage counselling? It's fairly popular, I guess, sad as I am to say it.'

'I suppose you get to know the regular faces, being in reception.'

He shook his head. 'No, not as such.'

He looked to Lucas, who gave him a look of encouragement.

'I've only just moved up to this role to cover maternity leave.' Claire nodded, smiled a little. Then she saw Alice Hathaway emerge from a corridor.

She looked angry. Claire acted fast. 'Do you know Gregg and Sara Thornton?'

Joseph looked confused. 'Who?'

Alice stormed over towards them. Stefan saw her and swore inwardly, but it didn't faze Claire.

She looked between the two men. 'Gregg and Sara Thornton. They're clients here.'

Lucas shook his head. 'We might know their faces if they're regulars, but not by name.'

'I'm only just starting to get to know the clients, putting names to faces,' Joseph said.

Alice was seconds from them.

Claire rose and handed Joseph her card. He looked confused. 'What's this for?'

'You're about to find out.'

Alice was beside them.

'Chief Inspector, you are here to speak to Mrs Curran. The rest of the staff are under my authority.'

Joseph looked surprised. 'You're cops?'

'Police,' Stefan corrected. He hated being referred to as a cop – it was too American for his liking.

'Cool,' he said, looking at the card Claire had given him. 'I wouldn't have put you two together anyway.' He didn't seem too concerned that she'd misled him. He was more intrigued than anything else. He looked at Claire again. 'What's Steph done?'

'Mrs Curran,' Alice broke in, 'has not done anything.' She eyed Claire warily. 'She's merely helping the police with their enquiries, on a voluntary basis.'

Stefan spoke this time, making eye contact with Alice. 'She'll see us then?'

Alice stiffened as she gave a curt nod.

Claire turned back to Joseph. 'If you remember anything—'

'No matter how irrelevant?' he said, excitement in his voice.

Claire nodded.

Alice bristled then, and stepped between them both. 'It will not be for very long, Mrs Curran has another client in ten minutes.'

'That's long enough,' Claire said. 'Lead the way.'

CHAPTER 30

Stephanie Curran didn't appear fazed at all.

Claire and Stefan sat opposite her at her desk and explained Sara's disappearance and their visit to Gregg. Stephanie listened at first and patiently waited until they finished before she said in a well-spoken voice, 'Our sessions are private. I cannot discuss anything without their written consent… consent from the both of them.'

'I need to know what they're like as a couple,' Claire said.

'Can't you ask Gregg?'

'You've been in a position to observe them from the outside. Sara is missing and we need to do all we can to rule out certain possibilities.'

Stephanie smiled, as if she'd just solved a great mystery. 'You mean you want to know if you can rule out any involvement by her husband.'

Claire remained silent.

'You can speak plainly here, Chief Inspector.' When no further words were forthcoming, she sighed and went to her filing cabinet. She unlocked it with a key from her trouser pocket, and searched for the Thorntons' file.

As Stephanie flicked through the manila files, Claire watched the sharp edges of her shoulder blades protruding through her thin cardigan. Stephanie was a tall, willowy stick of a figure, clad in designer clothes. She was in her mid-forties, although at a glance, you would be forgiven for thinking she was much younger.

Her long chestnut-coloured hair was piled high in a messy ponytail, strands hanging down, framing her thin face.

Her blue eyes glanced over each file, then paused when she found the right one. She flicked through it, but didn't bring it back to her desk. She read a few of her personal notes, then replaced it, locked the cabinet and sat back in her seat.

'The last session was no different to the others.'

Her words were met with a wall of silence. She sighed, rolled her eyes then added, 'I haven't seen anything within the marriage that would suggest the possibility of foul play. They do love each other. They've just… lost their way.'

'So no financial worries?'

'They both come from rich backgrounds, Inspector, and are in very well-paid jobs,' she said, addressing Stefan. 'Neither needs money to the degree they are willing to kill for it.'

'We have every reason to believe Sara is alive, Mrs Curran,' Claire said.

Stephanie shrugged. 'Kidnap with a view to murder… whatever the motive, I wouldn't believe Gregg was involved. I see a lot of people from every walk of life passing through my office. I can easily weed out the bad eggs from the good ones, and believe me, there are some bad ones, but Gregg isn't one of them.'

Claire stared at her and Stephanie grew uncomfortable under her gaze.

A sharp knock at the door broke the silence.

Someone opened the door before waiting to be invited in. A middle-aged man of average height, with dark hooded eyes and a mop of dark hair, walked in, carrying an air of arrogance with him.

'Anything wrong, Steph?'

'Nothing I can't handle,' she replied, looking at Claire. 'Chief Inspector, this is Mitchell Curran, the senior psychotherapist.'

'Curran?'

A smug look appeared across Stephanie's face. 'Yes. My husband.'

Stefan looked surprised as Mitchell offered his hand to them both.

'What's this all about?' he said, as Claire took his hand. 'I hope my wife is not in any sort of trouble.' He laughed, half meaning it as a joke, the other half deadly serious.

'They're here about that missing woman,' Stephanie said. 'Sara Thornton.'

His eyebrows rose. 'Oh?'

'They think maybe I know something.'

Claire shook her head. 'We're just trying to get a clearer picture of what's going on in Sara's life. We think her disappearance may be linked to the death of another girl.'

Mitchell looked surprised. 'Sounds ominous.'

Stefan's face was serious. 'Do you know a Nola Grant?'

Mitchell flinched, a very small gesture, which would have gone unnoticed by the untrained eye, but Claire and Stefan saw it immediately.

'Should I?'

'Do you watch the news, Mr Curran?'

'What sort of question is that?' he asked, folding his arms across his chest. 'Sometimes I do. Mostly not, it's too depressing, and I get enough of everyday woes in my office.' He smiled, an attempt at humour that failed to stir so much as a twitch.

Stefan explained Nola's death and the link between the man caught on CCTV abducting Sara.

'I really don't know what to say,' Mitchell said when he'd heard everything. 'I've never met or even heard of a

Nola Grant, and I doubt Sara would associate herself with a prostitute.' He shook his head again. 'I'm sorry I cannot help you.'

'What about you, Mrs Curran?' Claire said.

'Never heard of her.' She rose from her chair. 'I hate to rush you but I have clients to see. If we're finished?'

She gestured towards the door.

*

In the car driving back to the station, they remained quiet, with only the sound of the radio playing softly in the background. Stefan parked the car back at the station, and walked to the big glass entrance doors. Claire pulled on Stefan's arm before he could go into the warm.

'You saw his eyes, didn't you?' He knew instantly she was referring to Mitchell when they'd mentioned Nola Grant.

'Yeah, I saw it.' He leaned up against the wall by the entrance. 'You think he knows something?'

She nodded.

'He may have paid her at one time, you know. Maybe it's all innocent.'

'Curran? With a prostitute?' she said, sceptically. 'Why deny it?'

'Maybe he's embarrassed? And I doubt he'd say anything with his wife standing there.'

She shook her head. 'No, that's not it.' Stefan shrugged and looked longingly at the warmth of the station.

'Can we at least talk about this inside?'

CHAPTER 31

David Matthews had been chosen to break the news to Claire. He stood waiting for her to react, and he gripped the back of the chair opposite her desk, praying she wouldn't shoot the messenger.

Claire looked stony-faced, her eyes dull, staring down at her desk. She accessed Google via her BlackBerry, and saw the news was spreading across all the tabloid newspaper websites.

Sara's disappearance had gone national.

'They've started talking about Nola Grant as well. Nothing's been confirmed or denied of course but we've had journalists ringing up non-stop since news broke,' Matthews said, trying to gauge her reaction. 'Donahue has set up a press conference.'

'He's done what?'

Matthews looked away.

'When?'

'In a few hours.'

'For fuck's sake.' She looked at her watch:

12:03 p.m.

'How'd the press know about the link to Grant?'

Matthews avoided her eyes. Claire's eyes seemed to ignite. She knew there was nothing good to be said as soon as she saw his face. Inside she anticipated what was coming next but wanted to hear it from his own mouth.

'Out with it.'

'Press know Grant was pregnant. I wish I knew how, but—'

'I'll tell you how, Matthews,' she exploded, cutting him off. She pointed out to the incident room. 'Someone out there fucking leaked it.'

CHAPTER 32

Claire paced the room. She eyed every man and woman on her team and scowled. 'I want to know which one of you is responsible.'

Her eyes shot back and forth, from face to face, but saw nothing she could glean from her team, other than a look of dread.

'DI Matthews has informed me we've had prank calls relating to this already and a few men ringing in claiming they were the bloody father of Grant's child.'

She raised her hand and began firing off points, tapping each finger in turn as she went. 'Time. Money. Manpower. More statements that probably won't amount to anything but a waste of police time, not to mention extra pressure for fast results.'

She paused for breath. 'One of you,' she said, pointing to no one in particular, 'leaked it, and I want to know who.'

Silence.

Claire eyed Elias closely, but he remained poker-faced throughout. Claire had worked with every member of the team before, except Elias. Right now, he seemed the likely culprit.

'Claire,' a voice said behind her. She turned around and saw DSI Donahue. His face was grey, his eyes heavy with shadow as if he'd been up all night. 'I need a word, please.'

*

Donahue stayed close to Claire as they walked towards his office. 'Any thoughts as to who did it?'

'If I said DS Crest, would you believe me?'

His eyebrows rose. 'You have proof?'

She shook her head as they entered his office. 'I don't have any proof but I do know that everyone else on my team is trustworthy. Obviously, Crest is new… if I had to hazard a guess, I'd say him.'

Donahue sat in his chair and offered her a seat, flexed his fingers, then rested them on his belly. 'I'm not going to jump to conclusions. Right now I'm more concerned about how you handle the press conference.'

Claire pinched the bridge of her nose, trying to focus. 'I think we shouldn't reveal too much at this stage,' she said at length. 'I don't want to drive our man underground or push him into harming Sara. If he thinks he's cornered or running out of time, he might panic. There's nothing more dangerous than a cornered criminal. Sara's my priority.'

Donahue nodded, but looked deep in thought. Claire briefed him on everything they had so far – what leads they were following up, which were dead ends, and the talk she and Stefan had had with Stephanie and Mitchell Curran. She mentioned Mason Clarke, and said there were no obvious links between Nola Grant and Sara.

'No one cares much about Grant,' Donahue said. 'No family has come forward, and if it wasn't for the fact she was pregnant, she would be getting hardly any airtime or column inches.' He paused and stared at her hard. 'Sara Thornton is the golden girl here as far as the press and public are concerned.'

'Nola was a person too, Cliff. We're as much trying to bring her killer to justice as we are trying to help Sara.'

'Yes,' he said, frowning, 'but you know how the public feel about girls like Grant. I'm not saying her death is less important or less tragic—'

'I know what you're saying.' She sat forward and looked at him hard. 'I'm not going to let the media sway the public's emotions on this, Cliff. It's dangerous. It's playing with fire.'

She sat back in her chair. 'We need to agree on how much we're putting out there today and stick to it.'

CHAPTER 33

20th November

Twelve agonising days. That's equal to 288 wretched hours or 17,280 unbearable minutes... 1,036,800 crushing seconds.

This was how long it had been since Gregg had last seen Sara, and it was killing him, eating him away from the inside out. It felt like an eternity of having his body ripped apart and stitched back together, only to have the misery relived at the start of each new day.

Since the press conference, which he had attended with his in-laws, his mother and Mason, there had been little progress. There had been no more sightings of the man who took Sara. There had been no ransom note, so kidnap with a view to extort money was quickly ruled out.

The police had been in touch with Gregg constantly and he had a regular FLO, but nothing could ease his mind, and the longer it went with no news or leads, the more a little piece of him seemed to die every day.

He sat with Mason most evenings, when they weren't working on the business. Some nights they barely spoke and there was some kind of emotional strain between them. It'd crossed Gregg's mind several times that maybe Mason wanted more with Sara. It was no secret to him that Mason fancied his wife.

She was pretty, successful and intelligent. What wasn't there to like? Still, he could never quite find the inner strength to ask him about it. He was afraid of what he might hear. He'd already lost his wife; he didn't want to lose a friend as well. He didn't know how much longer he could go on pretending he was OK, and his mobile never left his side, in case Sara might ring, telling him she'd escaped and that she was all right. Frightened but alive.

The press had spent the last twelve days blaming the police for not finding Sara, and they'd had a field day exploiting the pregnancy of Nola Grant. There had even been a reconstruction on Crimewatch for the night Sara had disappeared, and although Mason had watched it, Gregg could not bring himself to. He blamed himself for her disappearance. If only he'd stayed on the phone to her, and not caused a row.

He'd spent hours beating himself up about every little thing before that night, blamed himself for everything, and there was nothing that could pull him out of his own self-pity.

The search for Sara had well and truly run cold.

Claire and her team's spirits were all but broken. No one had admitted to leaking any information to the media, and Claire's attempts to prise any incriminating information from them had been fruitless. She still suspected it was Elias, but she didn't openly admit this to anyone, although sometimes her eyes betrayed her true feelings. This had not gone unnoticed by Elias, who did his best to keep his head down. For Claire, this only confirmed his guilt.

DSI Donahue had also become more involved, and he and Claire had both assumed it would only be a matter of time before their man would kill Sara, if he hadn't already. Claire knew in her gut they were looking at a serial killer, and this only frustrated her more and lay heavy on her shoulders.

Iris had thought about going back to Spain but decided she would stay on until Christmas, as she'd originally planned.

For once she felt too much guilt at the prospect of leaving her daughter, when she felt Claire needed her most.

Everything Claire had on the investigation was being scrutinised. By the end of it all, she felt completely worn down, like she'd been chewed up and spat out.

While most murderers are caught through a process of elimination, after detectives follow up every lead, the man they were looking for had simply vanished. He'd gone from being brazen and arrogant, snatching both women in public places, and being knowledgeable about where the CCTV cameras were located, as well as about the women's movements, to suddenly dropping off the radar.

After the initial wave of prank callers regarding the paternity of Nola's unborn baby passed, all had gone quiet. To say Claire and her team were deflated was a huge understatement.

'Bayley's is a dead-end.'

Claire paced the incident room floor, arms folded, face determined, but her eyes revealed how tired she was.

'I spoke to the manager,' said Elias. He was standing opposite a huge whiteboard, staring at the key information collected on the case, his hands on his hips. 'Turns out their security cameras are just for show. Nothing's recorded.'

'What about the employees?' Stefan asked.

Harper said, 'Not a lot to go on. The girl working the counter doesn't remember him.'

Claire ran her hand through her shoulder-length hair in frustration. 'Matthews,' she said, 'where are we with Sara's mobile?'

'Recovered but smashed to bits. SIM card was shattered on the roadside and the records from her service provider haven't shown up anything we didn't know already.'

Claire stared at the still photographs on the wall of Sara and the man, taken from the CCTV footage.

Her eyes were scrutinising every inch, every line, every gesture. *Sara, where are you?*

CHAPTER 34

21st November

Sara Thornton was a clever woman. She'd excelled at school and later through her university years, and sailed into her current job. There was no doubt in anyone's mind that she would go on to do great things and, ever shrewd in her business life, this translated well to her personal life as well.

Being trapped against her will in the basement had tested her, more than she could ever have imagined. She'd learned in a small space of time that this man who abducted her was easily angered. He would appear incredibly charming and, dare she admit it, likeable one minute – but devoid of any reason or conscience the next. He never told her his name, not even a fake one for her to use, no matter how much she begged him to give her a name.

Any name.

She did, however, know he was familiar to her. She couldn't place him but couldn't shake the idea that their paths had crossed either. She felt fairly sure she'd never have socialised with someone like him, yet she knew him somehow.

That aside, she'd learned that to survive, she had to play his game and bide her time. Every day she would oblige him and respond well to his 'teaching'. He tried to mould her into his idea of a perfect woman.

He gave her little essays to write, all based on some kind of moral dilemma, then he'd check and scrutinise her answers. He tried to analyse her, and teach her everything about science and psychology. It almost made her feel like she was back at school. Most of the time she wished she was and this was all some horrible nightmare she had yet to wake from.

Thoughts that he wanted her for sexual gratification, thankfully, seemed unrealistic now; he treated her with the utmost respect when she was compliant with his rules and agreed with everything he told her.

Some days she thought he was close to letting her go, but then he seemed to change his mind almost instantly. The very real possibility had struck her that he might never be able to let her go.

She knew too much.

But what would be the point in keeping up the charade? She'd been gone for quite some time, although she couldn't be sure just how long. The man never responded when she asked him the date or time. He just became withdrawn and quiet, but she could tell deep down he was seething.

She gave up asking.

There had been one time when she had answered him back and he had struck her hard across the mouth. She had spat blood on the stone floor, once by accident, twice on purpose.

Leave DNA behind, no matter what.

After that he'd left her without food or water for some time.

Another lesson learned the hard way.

He told her she was spoilt and had lived a life of privilege, not knowing or caring how it was in reality for most people in life. She swallowed his sermons and lapped up his words of wisdom, for appearance's sake, but deep down, she was always plotting.

She had started making mental notes about when he left the house. Although she had no clock, she had estimated how long it would be after he brought her breakfast before she heard the floorboards creak when he walked past the basement door.

That path lead straight to the front door, and since she never heard the floor creak for long periods in between, she assumed he'd left the house. There would be silence for hours, then he would reappear, bring her lunch, then nothing until dinner.

The first time he had let her out of the basement was two days ago. Usually, she had to make do with a bucket to use as a toilet, but after some careful planning, she had gained enough trust for him to unlock her restraints and let her go upstairs to use the small toilet at the end of the hall.

He'd been very guarded, even strapping a knife to his belt, and she'd kept her movements small, not wishing to upset him. She hadn't been embarrassed when she told him she was on her period. He had looked away from her after checking she was telling the truth, then handed her some sanitary pads he'd already bought for this eventuality, but rather than feel ashamed, she'd relished his discomfort.

After she'd finished, he'd taken her back downstairs and she had kissed him on the cheek as a thank you.

He had recoiled at first, tension evident in his face. She had gauged his reaction, the flicker of emotion she caught in his eyes that told her he'd liked it.

Later that same day, he'd taken her upstairs again, this time to wash. In the first week she was a prisoner, she had to strip wash with water and soap from a large plastic mixing bowl in the basement, and he'd never left the room. He would sit with his back to her until she said she was dressed again.

When she'd first had to do this, she'd been terrified. She imagined that at any moment he would turn on her, assault her… and do other things she just couldn't bear to think about.

When nothing had happened, she felt like crying in relief, but she remained guarded the next few times regardless, just in case. Despite everything, he'd brought her some clean underwear and clothes, while he washed the dirty ones. She couldn't believe her luck when he'd allowed her to take a proper shower that morning.

But he never let her upstairs to the next level. He had a toilet and shower room downstairs, just off the hall, near the basement door. The house had obviously been adapted for either a disabled or elderly person. She noticed the old metal handrails dotted around the walls. It was odd. Something didn't add up.

Since he didn't appear to have any impediment and was certainly not old, she wondered how he'd come to live here. Her thoughts on this were brief. The prospect of hot running water was too great to think of anything else at the time.

She took her mind back to that morning…

*

He gripped her arm firmly, but was careful not to bruise her pale skin, as he steered her towards the tiny bathroom. She was naked under the rough, threadbare bath sheet he'd wrapped around her. He stood close behind her in the doorway, his breath hot on the back of her neck.

She felt fear creep up her spine, and her old fears that he might rape her came flooding back.

'I've removed the lock on the door,' he said. 'I won't be far from the bathroom.'

She gasped as he pushed her forward and slammed the door shut. She'd expected she wouldn't be able to lock the door, but she had no plans to escape just yet anyway. She needed to work out the layout of the house and where the potential exits were.

She saw there was no window in the plain cold bathroom, and when she saw he'd removed any razors and similar items from the medicine cabinet on the opposite wall, she felt like abandoning her idea of escape.

Deep down she knew she couldn't.

She had to fight if she wanted to survive this, and she didn't know how long she had left to plan an escape or get word to someone, somehow. The burning desire to just break down right there on the spot was overwhelming, and that desire had often plagued her during those lonely hours spent in the semi-darkness of her prison. Her own personal hell.

She silently shed her tears under the warmth of the shower. She cried so hard that her eyes stung. She hugged her arms tightly around her body as she slid down the tiled wall. She sat under the water for what seemed like an eternity.

Then he knocked on the door.

That was all he did.

He didn't speak. He didn't need to. It was a warning to her not to try anything and a reminder he could come in at any time.

She shut off the shower.

She was all smiles when he led her back to the basement. Just before she descended the stairs she caught a glimpse out the kitchen window, and saw enough of the garden to know it wasn't overlooked and had a tall gate at the end of the boundary fence.

She guessed the back door was kept locked and she would have to find out where he kept the key. Either that or she could always try to smash the window and get out that way, but she had no guarantee that she would be able to get out in time.

She'd seen the front door. There were several locks to negotiate. The back door was her best bet so far. She knew there was a landline somewhere; she'd heard it ring a few times. She thought it came from the living room, which was off limits. She also knew he wouldn't be so careless as to leave a mobile phone just lying around either. She needed to search for a key and that meant being allowed up in the house for more than just a toilet or shower break.

*

It was a few days after her first proper shower when she seized her chance and said she wanted to cook him dinner. His eyes searched hers for some hint of rebellion but she'd perfected the art of keeping her face neutral. She buried her fear deep inside herself. When she thought she might falter, she bit the inside of her cheek, for courage. It was a stark reminder to stay focused.

'Why would you want to do that?' he said, his eyes still dissecting her.

Sara forced a smile. 'I want to say thank you… for all you've done for me. I just wanted to show you how much I appreciate the lengths you've gone to.'

His eyes narrowed. He was sceptical, yet the conviction in her voice was undeniable.

Are you truly thankful?

'I don't know about that.'

'I won't try to escape,' she said. 'I owe you so much.'

He hesitated.

She drew closer to him. 'Please…' He felt her warm breath on his face, as she looked up into his eyes. She smiled. 'It's just dinner.'

CHAPTER 35

Sara was shown the kitchen properly for the first time. She saw the clock on the wall ahead:

7:32 p.m.

She felt like crying.

She didn't think there could be anything sweeter in sight right now. She still didn't know what day it was but just to know the time, after weeks of living like she was in a timeless existence, almost brought tears to her eyes.

The kitchen was nicely decorated and although a little old-fashioned, it felt homely, which was strange. She was half-expecting some kind of torture chamber.

The man was right behind her and moved her to one side. He went to the back door.

He tested the handle.

It didn't give. It was locked as expected, but she sensed he knew that and the gesture was merely for her benefit.

Actions speak louder than words.

He wanted her to understand he was still being vigilant. He was still in control and she didn't have his complete trust. Not yet.

He looked back at her and smiled. 'I did some shopping today.' He went to the plastic shopping bag on the kitchen table and pulled out a few tins. Sara frowned when she saw there were pre-cut vegetables and two cans of potatoes.

He looked up and saw her face. 'Don't be disappointed, Sara. You must understand I can't give you a knife.' He walked towards her and pushed a strand of loose hair back behind her ear.

She wanted to recoil but forced a smile instead and nodded. He finished putting out what she might need on the worktop, then sat perched on a rickety old wooden stool in the corner by the kitchen door.

He was taking no chances.

*

Almost an hour later, Sara had cooked a simple dinner, not the extravagant meal she had initially hoped for. She had wanted to create the 'wow' factor and lure him deeper but he hadn't been completely drawn in by her.

He was showing her he trusted her to a point but was careful to show some reluctance as well. He wasn't completely convinced about her motive for wanting to cook. They ate their meal at the dining room table in a dark little room, with patterned mauve wallpaper, just off from the kitchen.

He'd watched her closely while she cooked. He tried not to make it so obvious that it made her uncomfortable, but whenever she went to get more utensils, he moved like a predator, stalking its prey, looking over her shoulder, or passing her what she needed himself.

He'd laid out plastic spoons and the cups their wine sat in were also plastic. She'd managed to convince him to light some candles though, and he inspected her closely as she poured him another cup of wine.

He watched the shadows cast on her face by the flickering candles, and the way they danced over the walls and ceiling. They looked like swaying demons and the darkness made him sleepy.

He took a sip of wine and sat back in his chair, his eyes looking past her at something on the sideboard behind her.

She turned in her seat and saw many family photographs in ornate silver frames. There were two photographs of a pretty girl aged around six and another of the same girl aged about sixteen.

Sara wondered who she was. Maybe she would have asked if her eyes hadn't been drawn to a more poignant photograph from the man's past. It was of a woman, roughly in her thirties with her arm around a small boy aged about seven years old.

Sara recognised the same eyes that she had come to know so well over the last few weeks. She turned to face him and saw sadness in his face.

'Is that your mother in that photo?'

His face changed instantly. He hadn't meant for her to catch him in a moment of weakness. He avoided her eyes at first. She put her wine down, hoping he hadn't noticed she hadn't drunk nearly as much as he thought she had. She'd been taking small sips so she could avoid suspicion, but he'd taken full advantage of the bottle on the table.

'You can tell me,' she coaxed.

He let out a loud sigh, rubbed his forehead, and nodded. 'Yes, that's my mother. I was nearly eight in that picture. One of the happiest days of my life.'

'She looks happy.'

She smiled when he looked at her. Then he thought he saw sincerity in her eyes. He'd had so many feelings bottled up inside him for so long that he felt the urge to tell her everything.

'She was never really happy,' he said. 'My father left her when I was two and we never heard from him much after that. He came in and out of my life, on and off. Then he stopped completely, as if I no longer existed.'

She looked away, avoiding his eyes. 'I'm sorry. I didn't mean to pry.'

He ignored her and carried on, his eyes distant. 'I remember that day so vividly.' He closed his eyes, remembering a happier time. 'We were in Dorset. I begged my mother to take me to the beach, so she drove us to Bournemouth and we sat on that beach all afternoon... Ended up staying in a little B and B for a few days.' He looked back at Sara and managed a small smile.

'There was this family on the beach next to us. They looked so happy. The teenage daughter took that photo for us. That was the last time we ever went on holiday together. My grandmother took me away with her each year for a while, before her health started to decline.

'It was like my mother didn't want to spend that time with me any more. She took a few holidays on her own, and left me with my grandmother.' He paused, reflectively. 'Strangely, I didn't mind it so much. My grandmother was a fantastic woman – so strong. She taught me so much. She always had great stories to tell, especially about the time she was evacuated during the war.'

Sara looked at the table. She didn't know how far to go. She still didn't know where the key to the back door was kept. She guessed it was probably on him. She'd seen him with a chain of keys often enough, dangling tantalisingly just out of reach. She had two choices: go back to the basement and start the process again or delve deeper.

'Does it surprise you?'

'What?' she said, with a certain amount of wariness in her voice, which she couldn't hide.

'That I should have so much affection for my grandmother?'

'Why would it surprise me?'

He laughed. 'Because of what I've done to you.'

She held his gaze but was silent.

He leaned closer across the table. 'You're probably thinking I couldn't have a single sentimental bone in my body. That I'm incapable of feeling love for someone, even if it is family love.'

She shook her head. 'No. How could I be, after the kindness you've shown me?'

'Kindness?' he said. 'Is it kind to leave you in a basement, away from your family, your friends... your husband?' He paused, his face looking sad in the soft light. 'I wonder if I've done the right thing.'

She leaned forward and opened the other bottle of wine on the table. He eyed her suspiciously as she unscrewed the top. She hadn't expected this from him. She needed to bide some time, while she figured out how to play the scene out.

He caught her wrist as she poured the wine into his cup, spilling some of it on the table. She went to wipe it with her napkin with her other hand, but he caught hold of that too. 'Have I done the right thing, Sara?'

Her eyes met his. She nodded but it wasn't enough for him. He released her, slouching back in his chair. 'You don't mean that.'

Silence.

'What must I do for your approval?' he snapped. She heard the slight slur in his words. She reached over and continued pouring him more wine. She handed him the cup.

'I know you mean well. Perhaps I needed this,' she lied.

He snatched the cup from her and swallowed a large mouthful of the bitter liquid. 'You can't mean that.'

'At first, admittedly, I was scared. I hated you. I looked for a way out, but then you showed me how to be a better person.' She moved her chair close to him, her eyes unflinching. 'Tell me more about your grandmother.' She smiled, reached out her hand and rested it on his. 'It clearly gives you pleasure to talk about her.'

*

The next half–hour seemed to travel faster than the blink of an eye. Sara had managed to coax a great deal from him and she felt sure she could push him further, maybe get him to reveal where she was exactly. There was one window in the dining room, across on the far wall. She could see the faint light from a street lamp, glowing through the curtains, but she didn't hear much traffic.

She could be anywhere.

The man had opened up to her, and as he did, she would top his glass up every now and again, until she felt he was only another glass away from being really drunk.

He was letting his guard down and she meant to help him.

He told her how his grandmother had been fairly well-off and she'd taken him under her wing. In the end, she became more of a mother figure to him than his biological one, who by his early teens had all but disowned him.

He told her his mother had been successful in her job as an executive in a bank, and she had complete financial freedom and would be kept by no man, despite having many failed relationships over a short space of time. She had become cruel towards him, and barely acknowledged his presence, except to hurl insults at him.

She'd blamed him constantly for his father leaving her, and she bitterly resented the bond he had with his grandmother. Despite her misgivings at home, his mother was well respected and liked at work. She eventually earned enough to pay off the mortgage on the house Sara now sat in.

She was surprised when he revealed that this house that had been her prison was in fact his family home. He was still careful not to let slip any clues as to what town they were in. Then came the part in his life when Sara guessed he might have cracked.

His grandmother died the day before he turned seventeen, and his mother had flown into a rage once she learned the contents of her mother's will. His grandmother had left everything to him. Her home and all its contents were to be his. She had two bank accounts, holding just over £250,000 when combined, that also went to him and not his mother.

The house and money were to be held in trust until he reached eighteen; that didn't stop his mother contesting the will, but she lost her battle. After that, she'd tried a different tack. She tried to rebuild her relationship with him, but deep down he knew she was never sincere. Her drinking had become steadily worse and she became a shadow of her former self. She only kept her job at the bank because the CEO was an old friend, but she did come close to being sacked several times.

She'd previously threatened to change her will, whenever she was in a violent drink-fuelled rage, whereby he would get nothing in the event of her death, but he soon discovered this had merely been the drink talking. It kind of made up for a few of her misgivings in strange sort of way.

It was at this point in the story when Sara thought he might stop and dismiss her back to the basement, but he didn't. He told her that during a fierce thunderstorm, nearly a year after his grandmother's death, his mother had been killed behind the wheel of her car. She'd ploughed into a tree after swerving to avoid a cyclist in the street.

The toxicology report determined she'd been three times over the legal drink-drive limit, and he was now on his own. He inherited not only his grandmother's house and money, but also the family home where he had shared a turbulent life with his mother.

Sara was shocked, and guessed he'd left out some parts of the story. There were a few holes and one or two things that didn't add up, but she knew better than to stop and question him. By the end of it, he looked as if he had lifted a great weight off his shoulders, and she found herself feeling pangs of guilt over what she was about to do.

It was stupid, she knew. How could she feel anything other than revulsion towards the man who had kidnapped her and kept her prisoner? It crossed her mind that maybe he'd taught her something after all. Maybe he wasn't quite as mad as she thought he was in the beginning.

Suddenly, she didn't feel quite so selfish.

Any thoughts she had of softening towards him for real soon evaporated when he pushed himself up from his chair and stood looking down on her.

Predator eyeing its prey.

It became all too apparent that despite his revelations, she was still his prisoner.

'Time for you to go back below.'

His speech was slow. He was definitely drunk and she couldn't abandon her plan after so much hard work and effort. She stood up, raised her head and looked him hard in the face.

'I'm not going anywhere.'

CHAPTER 36

'I don't want to hurt you, Sara…'

The words that followed were sobering – but she held her resolve – '… but I will if I have to.'

She seized the chance; it was now or never. Her hand shot up, covered his mouth and hushed him. His reaction time was considerably delayed and when he tried removing her hand, she shook her head.

'You can't tell me all that about your childhood and not feel anything for me,' she said, raising her voice. If she tried hard enough, she knew she could possibly squeeze out a few tears as well. 'You must feel something for me to be able to open up to me like that.'

He frowned, pushing her hand from his mouth. 'I do feel something for you. Why do you think you're here in the first place?'

'Then don't put me back in the basement. Making me grateful by keeping me down there won't work.'

'I have to, you're no different, and I can't treat you as such.'

'No different from what?'

'From the others!'

Sara couldn't speak. It took every ounce of strength to hold back her tears.

He saw the look in her eyes.

'I've told you too much. I should never have agreed to this,' he said, gesturing to the empty dinner plates and candles. He pushed her back. 'This was a mistake.' He pushed her again, back towards the kitchen door.

'Don't say that.'

Act now in case you never get the chance again!

All reason seemed to be sucked away and it was as if she had no control over her body. She pushed his arms down, threw herself onto him and forced her mouth against his. She felt his resistance. His hands caught her forearms, trying to force her back but she pushed forward, her body now hard against his chest.

When she pulled back she looked up into his eyes and smiled. He tasted good, ashamed as she was to admit it.

He looked unsure what to do. She went to kiss him again but he turned his head. His breathing had quickened and she could feel his heart hammering inside his chest. She reached up, touched his cheek. He felt her breath hot on his skin, but he couldn't bring himself to look at her.

'Tell me your name,' she whispered. There was a small flicker in his eyes, but he said nothing. 'If you do nothing else, just tell me your name.'

He shook his head. 'I can't... and you mustn't ask it of me.' He swallowed hard, pushed her back, but she gripped his shoulders. 'Go back to the basement, Sara. Don't make this harder than it has to be.'

Deep down she could see him brooding. He was angry with her but he was trying to suppress it. Suddenly, she was unsure. However well she thought she'd got to know him, she realised she hadn't even scratched the surface.

She hesitated, but her voice was defiant. 'No.'

His eyes snapped towards her. They looked darker than before.

'I see the way you look at me.' Her voice rose. 'You can't keep this up forever.' She tried to kiss him again, but this time he anticipated it.

He gripped her face with both his hands and squeezed. She began to scream under the pressure. He grabbed her by the hand and dragged her back through the kitchen.

She pulled her body down to the floor, yanking his arm. Her feet began to slide across the old linoleum. She fought like a wild animal until he couldn't hold back any longer. He balled his right hand, then smashed it into her ribcage. She fell back like a sack of cement.

'Look what you made me do!' His face was red with rage. 'This is not who I am, Sara. I keep fighting it but girls like you make it so goddamn difficult!'

He turned his back to her.

'I know about the man you've been seeing at work, Sara.' He turned to face her again, grinned when he saw the shock on her face. 'Oh, I heard you on the phone to him, planning your next meet up.'

'I can't… I don't understand,' she said.

'Gregg was trying to make your marriage work, Sara, and even then you started sleeping with someone else.'

Sara shook her head, but couldn't find the words. She felt disgusted with herself.

'Fidelity,' he said. 'Have I not taught you anything?' He cocked his head to the side, looking down on her. 'Your plan wouldn't have worked.'

She whimpered, clutching her chest. Through squinted eyes, she looked into his.

'Kissing me?' he said. 'That's adultery. Gregg's given you a life worth having. A life worth living. Why weren't you ever grateful?'

And then it happened.

Like the light bulb moment you always hear about.

She knew him then. 'A life worth living…' she spluttered.

He turned around to face her.

'I know you… I remember the day you spoke those words to me… to Gregg.'

He paused. 'Bet you wish you'd listened to me then.'

He raised his hand and slapped her hard in the mouth. Before she could recover, he roughly encircled his arms around her torso, lifted and hauled her out through the kitchen, into the hall.

He swung the basement door open.

When she saw the stairs descending into the darkness below, she pleaded with him. She screamed and tears streamed down her face, but it fell on deaf ears.

With one surge forward, he shoved her through the doorway, and she hurtled down the stairs. Halfway down she managed to stop herself, clutching the rail for dear life, but he was soon down on her, raising his foot and slamming it into her chest.

As she fell down the final steps, her elbow caught the rough brick on one side of the staircase. She lay crumpled on the floor at the bottom, bleeding. Her elbow was grazed and stung like hell but she ignored the pain and climbed to her feet.

Her head swung back.

She let out a defiant scream.

He slammed the door, locked and bolted it. He stormed into the kitchen and drove his arm across the cluttered worktop, sending everything crashing to the floor. In the dining room he grabbed the candles, not bothering to extinguish the flames, and chucked the lot in the kitchen sink, blasting them with cold water from the tap.

He left it running as he went back to the dining room. He hurled both the empty wine bottles at the far wall, sending broken glass everywhere. He switched on the main lights, then sent his fist crashing into the picture frames on the sideboard. He picked up the one which held the photograph of him and his mother, and hurled it across the room, screaming so loud his throat ached.

How could I have been so stupid?

Down in the basement, Sara had climbed back up the stairs and was beating her fist against the door. She was screaming every obscenity she could think of.

Mentally, he'd been stronger than she'd thought. He hadn't taken the bait. She'd even been ready to give herself to him if it meant the chance of escape, despite knowing she would hate every minute of it, but he'd rejected her. Something Sara wasn't used to. It was alien to her. And now she knew who he was, every minute of her life in the last year came rushing into the forefront of her mind and she cursed every goddamn memory.

The man was now sitting amongst the broken plates and bowls on the kitchen floor. His eyes were transfixed on the basement door.

Inside he was ablaze with anger.

*

She didn't know how long it'd been before the pain in her hands had grown too much. Sara's knuckles were now bloody and bruised. She'd taken the top layer of skin off by hammering the basement door in a blind fury. She'd heard the man crashing around elsewhere in the house. He'd usually been more controlled but the drink had lowered his defences and affected his rational thinking considerably.

She sat perched on the top few steps, sucking at her damaged skin. All had gone quiet and she jumped with fright when she heard his voice somewhere in the distance. He sounded so angry.

Then nothing.

She felt as if her heart would give out with fright when someone hammered a fist on the door to the basement some time later. The thick wooden door vibrated violently.

Then silence again. She couldn't have spoken even if she'd wanted to; she was too scared.

She strained her ears.

She heard the faint sound of the back door opening, then footsteps coming closer to the door.

She backed down a few steps.

The lock on the door clicked. The bolt was drawn back.

The door slowly swung open.

She froze at what she saw and it scared her so much, she couldn't even scream.

CHAPTER 37

December 1987

'Be still… be as silent as a ghost.' He watched his grandmother's mouth, lined with wrinkles, pucker. 'Control your breathing.'

The boy was twelve and the grandmother had long promised to take him to the woods she'd known since childhood, when he came of age.

As a small girl she'd often laid primitive traps for small woodland animals. She'd then lie in wait, sometimes for hours, hidden under a bush or watching from a ditch, like they did in the movies. On the occasions she did catch something – a hare, usually, her favourite – she'd laugh, and clap and sing.

Sometimes she'd let the creature go.

Sometimes she didn't.

The days she came back with blood smeared across her rosy-red cheeks, caked under her fingernails, with soil encrusted on the hem of her dress, her parents would laugh their concerns away.

The boy never grew tired of his grandmother's stories or dark secrets. It showed him she was human. That she'd lived. That she wasn't afraid. Something to be admired, it was. Something almost sacred.

The frozen ground was solid against his chest, and the wind was bitter, taking bites at his flesh. He shivered, pulling his woolly hat down lower, covering his ears. He felt his throat contract, and he raised his gloved fist to stifle a cough.

'Shh,' the grandmother hissed, her icy-blue eyes snapping to the side, throwing him a warning glare. She raised her finger to her dry cracked lips, then pointed in front of her over the rim of the ditch. 'Over there, in the bushes.'

His eyes were watering profusely but he could still make out the salt-and-pepper-coloured fur and the long ears scrambling through the decaying undergrowth. He saw large, wide eyes.

The grandmother smiled. 'Any minute now.' Her breath was like dry ice escaping from her lips. 'It's near the snare. Come on, just a little closer.'

Snap.

The cable pulled tight. The hare scrambled frantically, its hind legs hammering the cold earth in panic.

The grandmother smiled.

The boy followed her out over the ditch. He watched her long brown skirt drag the floor, mindful not to step on it. She looked like some kind of nomad or mystic with her dark flowing clothes and meaningful stare. Even the spidery veins on her bony hands looked more prominent.

He hesitated, stopping in his tracks when her foot pressed on the taut cable. The hare's movements became more laboured, the cable biting through its fur. Drops of dark-red blood spattered the floor.

'Unusual to catch them this time of year.' She sounded breathless when she crouched down and drew her knife. 'Come, hold it down.' The boy watched the knife sway back and forth in her hand.

He gazed at the hare.

Its eyes penetrated his.

'Grab its legs.'

He did as he was told. She sawed the knife quickly, back and forth until the cable snapped. The hare didn't even attempt to run. Instead, it just lay there quietly, as if awaiting the inevitable and accepting its fate.

The grandmother waved the knife in front of him. 'It's your turn.' She smiled.

'Mum asked me not to.'

The smile faded.

'She has no say here, you know that.' She thrust the knife into his hands. 'Do it.'

He eyed the knife, then the hare. He shook his head. 'I can't.' the grandmother rolled her eyes. 'I can't, Nanna. Please don't make me.'

'It's just an animal.'

'I don't want to.'

'What if you were starving?'

He frowned.

'What if you were stuck out here in the wilderness, no chance of being found for a long time? You need food and water to survive... Would you do it then?'

He tried to answer but his voice stuck in his throat. She squeezed her hand around the hare's neck. 'Would you do it to survive?'

'Yes, I guess so... but this isn't the same thing.'

The grandmother wasn't listening. Her head shook violently. 'You're not grateful for what nature has provided us. Living off the land is the most natural thing in the world.'

'I don't want to eat it.'

'This is your mother's doing.' She ripped the knife from his hand. 'Have I got to do everything myself?' She pulled the hare up by its hind legs and drove the blade into its belly.

'She's selfish. Ungrateful and spoilt!' she raged, thrusting the blade in faster and faster with each swing. 'I won't have you growing up the same way.'

He watched each savage movement open-mouthed. The blood stained the ground, her hands and clothes. Her face looked like a snapshot of a mad frenzy, each stab her way of taking out her frustration about his mother. It didn't seem real, yet somehow it felt normal, as if he was part of it. As if it felt right. He realised he didn't feel any sadness for the animal either.

When she finally stopped, dropping the hare's mangled corpse to the ground with a thud, a sound he'd never forget, she wiped her forehead with the back of her hand, smearing blood across her skin.

She raised the knife, pointing it at his gut. 'Next time, you'll do it.'

And she was right.

The next time she took him to the forest, he killed at her request. Over time he grew to like it. Maybe he always had? The feeling crept up on him so quickly, he couldn't be sure.

At first it had taken some mental strength to be able to make the first cut, but over time, that soon disappeared, like his grandmother had said it would.

'Soon it will become second nature,' she told him. And as usual she'd been right. That was the only time he'd seen her behave like that. Only when she was in that forest trapping animals. It seemed to be for no reason other than pleasure. Back at home it was different. She'd always teach him to help others. Not in the typical sense but in her own way, whether the help was wanted or not.

He was the pupil and she was the teacher. Soon, she told him, it would be his turn. She told him not to fall into the self-loathing his mother had succumbed to and made him promise everything he would do after she was gone, he would do for the greater good.

CHAPTER 38

Deacon Hill was beautiful, exceptionally so in winter. Sitting off the B655 Hitchin Road, just over the Bedfordshire border, en route to the village of Hexton, Deacon Hill went unnoticed in a blink of an eye, but for those who lived close by, the picturesque trail to the top was breathtaking.

Many walkers took their dogs and cut across the cattle field, up towards the foot of the steep mound from which, after a short ascent, you could see miles upon miles of beautiful unspoilt English countryside. The surrounding land was littered with rabbit warrens, and birds of prey would soar high above, waiting for their chance to pluck an unlucky hare from the ground below.

In winter, it was mainly locals who came up here, or an artist trying to capture the beauty of the winter sun, but today, only one car sat off the road in the lay-by, and only one man stood upon the top of Deacon Hill.

Dressed in black, his large frame looked ominous against the white backdrop and the grey sky. The roads below were very quiet, and he'd managed to haul the body in the industrial-sized black sack up the trail, flanked either side with skeletal trees and bushes, towards the foot of the hill.

With little effort he carried the body up and leaned it against the side of the stone marker at the top of the hill. The large concrete sculpture was shaped like a pyramid. The base was made up of two large tiered squares, one slightly taller sitting on top of the other. The crowning top was a square pyramid in shape with a blunt top. Altogether, it stood at nearly seven feet tall.

The man breathed in the cold. It seeped into his bones, despite his thick clothes. He removed the black sack. He leaned the body against the structure.

The weather forecast earlier said there would be heavy snow in the early hours of the morning. This was good, not just because it would obscure or cover his footprints, but because of how it would almost transform the body.

Once the snow began to fall, it would give the illusion that the stone marker and the body were as one. A work of art.

He picked up the sack, reached the edge of the hilltop, and looked back. He smiled.

The naked body of Sara Thornton looked beautiful against the chosen backdrop. Her eyes were shut, her head leaning to one side, obscuring the deep gash at the side of her neck. She looked at peace. She looked like a sleeping angel.

A few flakes of snow began to drift down from the sky and the man caught a few in his gloved hand. After another look at the vast landscape around him, he disappeared down the hill.

PART FOUR

CHAPTER 39

22nd November

'Fallon!'

The familiar roar of her father's voice rumbled from down the hall. Richard Dockley stormed up the stairs towards his daughter's room. He burst through the door, not bothering to knock.

Fallon Dockley's skinny, boyish frame stood half dressed in front of her full-length mirror. Rolling her eyes when faced with her father's reflection, she half turned her head towards him.

'Don't you ever fucking knock?' She turned her attention back to the mirror, not waiting for a reply, and started to adjust her eyebrow stud.

'You got another speeding ticket, and this time I'm not paying for it or taking the points on my licence. You're nineteen, an adult, so start taking some responsibility.'

He waited for her to respond but she acted as though she hadn't heard him, busying herself by changing the stud in her eyebrow.

'Fallon.'

'I heard you the first time, Dad.'

'Then look at me when I'm speaking to you.'

Fallon swung her body around in a sulk, her face pulled into a sneer, her fingers pointing at her body. 'Mind if I get dressed first?'

It was only at this point that he noticed that his daughter stood before him wearing only her bra and jeans. Normally, he would have turned his head, embarrassed by seeing her exposed, but something caught his eye.

'What is that?' he said, pointing to her lower torso. Fallon looked down and remembered the latest addition to her pale body.

'Fuck…'

Richard shook his head. 'Fallon, we've been over this. How much more of this… this filth are you going to have inked into your skin?' He looked exasperated. 'Your mother won't approve.'

'Mum left. She has no say in how I live my life any more, and neither do you. I'm nineteen and I'll do what I want.'

'Whilst you're under my roof, you ungrateful brat, you will do as I say. I'm not paying out all this money for your education just to have you piss it all up the wall, wasting it getting inked up and pierced everywhere.'

Fallon ignored him and reached out for her top, yanking it over her head. She pulled the hem down over her tattooed belly and glared back at him.

'There, happy now?' She turned her back, grabbed a pot of hair gel and began working it into her dyed dirty-blonde hair, spiking her pixie-style crop. 'Oh, in future, with piercing, I'll just get done the parts of my body that don't show… I was thinking about my labia next time.'

Richard's face contorted with disgust. 'Don't be so repulsive. I never raised you this way, Fallon.'

'That's right. You barely raised me at all.'

Richard was visibly hurt by her words. How could he argue with that? It was true. Rather than being a real father to her, he'd spent most of her life investing all his time and effort into his property business and had tried to compensate for never being there for his only child by showering her with money and material things. It was no wonder she'd turned into a rich spoilt brat. It had been one of the many reasons his wife, Ellen, had walked out on them.

Fallon was unruly, selfish and plain spiteful, having no respect for anyone, and this was how she liked it. She thought she did no wrong. All she had to do was wind her dad around her finger and she could continue to work him to her advantage, like a puppet.

Fallon always held the strings.

She never worked for anything, and always got her own way. Why work and contribute when she had the 'Bank of Dad' at her disposal?

A look of defiance swept over her, when she caught her father's sad face in the reflection in the mirror. She grinned.

'Changing the subject… I need cash.'

Richard acted as though he'd barely heard her, and studied her face hard. 'It's for the party I'm throwing,' she added. Instead of the response she was expecting from him, Richard almost immediately produced his wallet from his trouser pocket, pulled out some notes and handed them to her.

She grabbed them, pushing them into her pocket. When she turned her back on him again, he knew it was her signal for him to leave. Like a whipped and beaten dog, he made for the door. Just as he was about to close it behind him, she called him back.

'My licence is in the Merc, by the way,' she said, now piling black eyeliner around her dark eyes. 'You wanna get me banned from driving, be my guest. It'll be your money you're wasting in the long run. You paid for all those hours of lessons for me.'

Richard looked down at the floor, sighed and shut her away out of his sight. He couldn't bear to look at her right now. She disgusted him.

Fallon smiled at her reflection in the mirror, knowing full well Dad would bail her out yet again.

Downstairs, Richard poured himself another large measure of vodka, his third for the morning, and knocked it back. He let out a long sigh. It had been three years since Ellen had walked out on them and since then she'd barely been in their lives.

She would send Fallon birthday cards, when she remembered, and they had received the odd Christmas card, but other than making a brief appearance, maybe once a year, she was estranged from her husband and daughter. And it never seemed to bother her unless she was trying to score points against him.

Richard poured another shot of the clear liquid into his glass, stopping short of drinking it when his eyes landed on a photograph of the three of them when Fallon was aged ten.

Those were happier times in the Dockley household. Sometimes he wondered what he could do to make his daughter love him again. He had lost count of how many times he had lain awake at night wishing she could be a better person, the kind and wonderful daughter she used to be.

As her iPod sounded a thundering beat above him, he raised the glass to his lips. The strong liquor burnt the back of his throat. These days he didn't seem to notice any more. He relished the discomfort. After all, he deserved it.

CHAPTER 40

As Richard Dockley pulled his car up the drive towards F. B. C.
and drove into a car parking space, he heard his daughter let
out a groan from the back seat.

He risked a glance behind him.

She'd slouched down in her seat, her legs now pulled up
towards her chest. One foot was pushed up against the back
of the front passenger seat, leaving a trail of muck from her
trainer sole, while the other was pulling against her open
seatbelt. The strap was looped over her foot and she was
stretching it to its full capacity.

Richard whisked his arm round and swatted her feet hard,
and she let out a yelp in surprise.

'What was that for?' She violently pulled her earphones
from her ears and sat forward as he parked the car. She reached
out and smacked him hard across the back of the shoulders.

She stared at the building ahead and groaned.

'All my friends are out getting ready for parties and where
the fuck am I? Here at this fucking nuthouse. I'm nineteen,
why do you have to treat me like a kid?'

Richard gripped the steering wheel hard, his knuckles
turning white. He remembered what their psychotherapist,
Mitchell Curran, had said at their last session about taking
deep breaths and working out how to defuse a potentially
volatile situation with Fallon before it escalated into a full-
blown fit of rage.

Whilst he knew the man was right in theory, he found it took every ounce of his strength to follow it through and put in practice.

'It's not a nuthouse. Watch your mouth and act your age,' he said, keeping his face focused dead ahead. 'Mr Curran is trying to help us and we would make more headway if you stopped putting up a brick wall.'

'I missed the Bonfire Night party my friends had and now I'm missing out again.'

'Shame,' he said.

Fallon was half out of the car, but his words stopped her. She glared at him, before a sly grin pulled across her face and she deliberately slammed the car door.

'Watch the paintwork.'

'Fuck the fucking paintwork.'

'Just get in there, we're already late. Our appointment started ten minutes ago,' he snapped, conscious that people in the grounds were beginning to stare.

Fallon began waltzing off in a strop in front of him. It took a few large strides to catch her up.

'You're supposed to be grounded, remember? You're not going anywhere.' He pushed her arm forcefully, moving her across the forecourt. 'Quite why you wanted to celebrate an act of terrorism the other week is beyond me.'

Fallon threw her arm up, exaggeratedly shoving his hand away, and said, 'What you on about?'

'All the money I've ploughed into your education and you don't know about the Gunpowder Plot?'

'Like, obviously I do,' she said, her voice childish.

'Then you know it was a failed act of terrorism. What's to celebrate? Now,' he said, pushing her through the entrance to the building, 'I don't want a repeat of last week. It's only an hour. Try to behave.'

*

Mitchell Curran sat with a large hardback notebook propped up against one leg, which was folded across the other. He was giving the impression that he was relaxed, in control, with his pen poised for action. He liked to appear as if he had all the time in the world but inside he wished the time he spent once a week with the Dockleys would speed up.

Staring at the sullen expression on Fallon's face made him feel depressed himself. She was spoilt, and very immature. She was baby-faced and, unless someone saw her date of birth on an official document, she could still easily pass for a lot younger than her nineteen years. She looked about fifteen.

Mitchell then gazed at her father, who sat awkwardly next to his daughter, fingers laced together and resting on his belly. His eyes were fixed on the floor.

'Richard, how about we start with you this week?' he said, willing Richard's eyes from the floor. 'How has your week been? Have you put into practice any of the exercises we discussed at our last session?' Richard looked back into Mitchell's dark eyes and forced a smile.

'It's been difficult, I'll admit. I have tried the breathing exercises and sometimes it works,' he said, then left a long pause. 'Sometimes not.'

Mitchell gave a short, sharp nod, then looked at Fallon, who was now gazing out of the large window to the side of her.

'Fallon, I'm interested to hear how you feel this week has gone. Have your father's breathing techniques helped how he responds to you? Is he thinking before he reacts?'

She turned to look at him. She studied his face as if it were the first time she had ever laid eyes on him and guessed he was around forty-five years old. Practically ancient, obviously.

His dark hair was well groomed, and he used the gym regularly, judging by his physique. She didn't hate him personally, but more what he represented. Her life had no meaning, her relationship with her father was virtually non-existent and she bitterly resented her mother.

The fact her father had enrolled them both at the F. B. C. had done little for her self-esteem. Outside, she portrayed the cocky, brazen rebel without a cause, but inside she was screaming, and she felt nobody could hear her, no matter how loud she cried.

'You don't want know what I think, Mitch,' she muttered, and stifled a yawn.

'That's Mr Curran, Fallon. You will address him as such,' said Richard.

Mitchell smiled at him and shook his head.

'It's fine, really. Mitch is as good a name as any.' He gestured to Fallon. 'Please, explain. I am here to listen.' She sighed heavily but didn't respond.

Mitchell decided to try another method.

'Here,' he said, getting up and placing a sheet of paper and a pen on the table on the far side of the room. 'If you have difficulty expressing yourself vocally, we can try writing things down instead.'

'She doesn't usually have that problem. It's getting her to shut up that's the trouble,' Richard scoffed. He folded his arms tight across his chest.

Mitchell shook his head. 'We're not here to get Fallon to 'shut up', Richard. Sometimes it's hard for a young woman, such as Fallon, to find her voice.'

'Believe me, she doesn't have that problem. She's just being stubborn, not to mention rude,' he said, turning to glare at her.

'You're not helping, Mr Dockley.' Richard noticed that Mitchell always dropped the use of his Christian name when he was losing his patience.

'Why are you making out that she's the injured party here?'

'Let's not start pointing the blame, it isn't helpful. I'm merely trying to bring your daughter out of her shell. To encourage her to open up and express how she feels.'

'Would you stop talking about me as if I wasn't here?' Fallon got up and marched towards the table. She picked up the pen as she sat on the chair beside the table. 'What do you want me to write?'

'I can't tell you that, Fallon. You alone must write what comes from here,' he said, gesturing to his head, then his heart, 'and in here.'

'What, just random words?'

'Yes, exactly. The first words that come into your head.'

She grinned. 'Can I swear?'

*

An hour later, Richard walked to the reception desk and waited patiently behind a young couple. When it was his turn, he smiled warmly at the man behind the counter.

'Hello, Joseph. I'd like to change my next appointment, please.'

'Certainly, Mr Dockley.' Joseph smiled as he tapped a few commands into the computer system, and scrolled through several pages. He glanced up and over Richard's shoulder.

'Hi, Fallon,' he said.

Fallon looked up from her phone. 'Hey, Joe.' Richard gave her the once-over. The only thing Fallon seemed not to mind about going there was chatting to Joseph, but today he knew not even he could keep her attention.

Fallon nudged him and held out her hand. He reached into his trouser pocket and gave her his car keys without saying a word. He watched her skulk out of the building and sighed, rubbing his fingers over his eyes.

'Today's session didn't go so well, I take it?' Joseph tapped further instructions into the computer. He looked up and saw Richard shake his head, too choked to speak. 'Give it time. Mr Curran is ever so good. You'll see.'

CHAPTER 41

23rd November

It had been barely eight the previous morning when Sara's body had been discovered by a man out walking his dog.

Her body had looked like a statue.

Heavy snow had obscured any chance of finding a footprint pattern to capture and lift. Claire knew their killer would've planned to use the terrible weather to his advantage.

As she addressed her team, she voiced what they were all thinking. 'I think he's just getting warmed up... Donahue's already talking about bringing in a bloody profiler.'

Murmurs of discord started to surface around the room.

As the SIO, Claire had to remain open-minded and focused, and she felt that bringing in someone to anticipate the moves and hazard a guess at the type of person the killer was likely to be, based on two murder victims, was rather pointless. She'd no intention of being blindsided by a set of 'rules' about a serial killer's profile.

These profiles had been compiled based on killers that had been caught and after their psyches had been examined. Then she always asked the question, what about the profile of killers that are never caught? There were no set rules for what could potentially be a new breed of killer. There was always someone waiting to bend the rules and become something the police hadn't seen before.

As members of the team started to all talk at once and raise their voices, Claire's voice rose several notches.

'Settle down!' All eyes fell on her. 'Let's look at what we know is probably the case,' she said. 'The killer's probably from a working-class background and may have priors for low-level crimes, and although intelligent has been an underachiever in life.'

She paused to stare at the map that was pinned to another board, with circles and pins indicating key areas of the investigation.

'If we think he's working locally, then he must be employed locally. He knows the surrounding areas well and he must make a living somehow. He's also, probably, very charming, maybe even respected. He blends into society perfectly and is able to gain trust easily.'

Elias leaned back against his chair and sighed.

Claire caught his eye. 'Something to add, Crest?'

'I'm starting to go with your theory that maybe this killer has no specific MO.'

A look of surprise flickered across her face, but quickly disappeared. 'I don't think the killer's been doing it long. Serial killers tend to work over a period of years, with gaps in between.'

'But he's killed two women in quick succession,' DC Harper said.

Claire nodded. 'Yes, and that's why we shouldn't assume he'll stick to any particular modus operandi. If he were an established killer he'd take his time.

'The post-mortem has confirmed we're looking at the same killer. We've got the same ligature marks around both Sara's wrists and ankles.'

She pointed to the photographs of Sara's body on the wall. 'She was suspended by her ankles, like Nola, and there were no signs of sexual assault. Death was caused by the same expert cut to the throat using the same knife.'

Stefan looked at the close up shots of Sara's hands.

'What about her nails?'

'Some were damaged but someone went to great lengths to clean them. Danika's taken swabs. With Nola, there was little to extract but Sara's body was looked after. No make-up traces, no dirt. Even the grazes and cuts on her knuckles and elbow had been thoroughly cleaned.'

Elias caught her eye. 'If the killer's taking the time to care for the bodies that may give us a clue to his identity or profession. It provides clues to his mental state.'

'But…' Stefan cut in, 'we don't know the types of women he's stalking. There're no similarities in lifestyle, appearance, or job that links these women. They're in their twenties, that's about all we've got.'

Claire shook her head. 'We can't fall into the trap of assuming there's no common link.'

'So what's your theory?' Elias asked, an air of arrogance in his voice.

Claire held his stare. 'They might have more in common than you think… both these women were broken women.'

'Broken?'

'Yes.' She pointed at the photographs of the two women. 'The killer has chosen an outsider, a prostitute. Someone who wouldn't really be missed. Then we have the solicitor. Sara was respected but her marriage was in trouble. Rachel Larson told us Nola's spirit had left her long ago… They were both in need of some kind of guidance.'

'Like therapy,' Stefan said.

Claire smiled. 'Exactly. We have to assume there will be more victims. We could further assume this broken vulnerability is how the victims are chosen. If it is, then is the killer disgusted at what he may see as a weakness? Or does he have a more profound interest that goes much, much deeper?'

Stefan shook his head. 'I'm not sure I get that theory. We have no proof Nola went to F. B. C.'

'So let's pay Curran another visit,' Elias said.

'What we need is some evidence,' Claire said, 'not blind theory. We need something we can throw at him.'

Stefan shrugged. 'Well, we need to do something before we have another body.'

After the team had been dismissed, Claire sat in her office alone and deep down she knew Stefan was right. She had that cold awful feeling that it wouldn't be long before the killer would take another girl off the street and this sorry mess would come down on her head.

CHAPTER 42

The Fox pub in the village of Pirton, just outside of Hitchin, sat where the high street and Crab Tree Lane meet at the crossroads.

It was late that evening when he went inside, and after a quick look around, he saw the girl hadn't arrived yet. He went to the bar and ordered a beer before taking one of the last remaining seats near the window.

The place was heaving. He'd only been in here once before and then he'd only used the toilet. He hadn't stopped for a drink but even then it had been busy. He noticed the blackboard hanging in the corner beside the bar advertising the night's entertainment: karaoke. A shiver travelled down his spine and he hoped the girl would be there soon.

He spent the next twenty minutes gazing out of the window. The thick snow outside made the beer garden look ghostly, but also beautiful under the moonlight. He sipped his beer, not really enjoying the taste. He wasn't usually much of a drinker. He blamed his mother for that. The demon drink had been a part of her for as long as he could remember.

Of course with Sara he had indulged in the pleasure of wine, but look how that had turned out. He needed to take control again and push his plans forward. Barely twenty-four hours after Sara had been found, he would take another.

His thoughts went back to the dinner with Sara.

He had been out of control that night.

His eyes grew dark and his brow furrowed. His mind wandered back again to those dark days with his mother. He saw her face spin from a mist and become clear in his head, and he drank from his glass, deeply this time, draining most of the amber liquid.

The bitterness he felt against his tongue evaporated instantly when he caught sight of his chosen girl coming up the steps to the entrance.

She was so pretty, but he knew she could never see it herself. He would try to convince her later on, after he'd explained why he'd chosen her, tell her why she was so special.

His smile faded when he saw she was followed by her parents and her older brother. He cocked his head to get a better look as they came through the entrance and headed to the bar.

Sixteen-year-old Felicity Davenport was glowing tonight; her long light-brown hair was tied back in the usual ponytail, which swung from side to side when she walked. Her bright blue eyes still sparkled despite the subdued lighting, and her clothes flattered her figure.

Her father ordered their drinks, then looked around for any free seats. He pointed Felicity towards a suddenly vacant space.

It was far away enough for him to go unnoticed, but he sank down lower in his chair nevertheless. Her parents and brother soon joined her, and he knew they'd be talking about anything and everything.

Inside, he envied them; he couldn't ever remember a time when his mother had asked him how his day had been, if he had needed help with his homework, or if he had any problems with bullies. She was usually too drunk to ask, but he guessed she wouldn't have bothered even if she'd been sober.

He watched Felicity as she talked, examining each twitch of her mouth, analysing every syllable. He knew she was lying when she told her mother she was happy and nothing was bothering her; this was, after all, the reason he'd chosen her. The reason why he felt the need to intervene in her life before it was too late, and it raised the hairs on the back of his neck.

He knew she'd grown lonely, disillusioned with her life. She thought she had the weight of the world on her shoulders. He knew it was all down to pressure. Pressure from her overbearing parents who placed their own ambitions on her shoulders.

Felicity felt she couldn't cope. She'd sought a new direction when she felt the depression seeping in. It'd terrified the man at first but he'd later taken comfort in the fact that if Felicity was the model student he thought she could be, he could easily set her back on track. He hoped she'd strayed just a little from her chosen path, and not enough to be completely lost to him.

He got up from the table, pushed through a sea of people and wandered out into the bitter night, down Crab Tree Lane, and stopped outside the house he had watched many times in the last few months.

Felicity's family home was beautiful.

He knew she came home most weekends from boarding school. He even knew which one of the many windows was her bedroom. The house was perfect; like her life, although she couldn't see it yet.

He only wished he could've had the good start in life that she had. Things would have been different for him, he knew that. He shook himself.

Don't dwell on the past. It isn't healthy.

He walked back to his car, parked in a neighbouring street, and waited. He pulled a blanket around his shoulders and kept his eyes staring straight ahead. He knew the family would be home by closing time, which was a few hours away.

He slouched down in the driver's seat and waited.

CHAPTER 43

24th November

The call came in just before 6:30 a.m. Claire's BlackBerry vibrated across her bedside cabinet, startling her from a deep sleep. It took her several seconds to register that it was her phone ringing. Her hand reached across, fingers hitting the Answer button.

'I think we've got another one.' Stefan's voice sounded strained.

He heard her voice catch in her throat. 'Christ, we've only just found Sara. He's not even giving us any time to breathe.'

'I know. It's what we feared.'

'Are we sure it's related?' Claire said. Somewhere in the back of her mind she hoped it had nothing to do with her investigation.

'We've had neighbours giving a description during the house-to-house of the same car used by our suspect, seen in the area.'

She shot forward in her bed, gripping the phone tight. 'Number plates?'

'I've only got a partial number – fake plates again.'

'Shit.'

'I know.' His voice mirrored the deflation in hers. He explained what they knew so far. The family had returned home from The Fox at around 11:45 p.m. They had all gone straight upstairs to get ready for bed, when someone knocked on the door. Felicity had volunteered to answer it, and her parents had thought nothing more of it when they heard her talking to someone. They had assumed it was someone who lived in the village.

When her mother had come down the stairs a little while later, she found the front door open, with no sign of Felicity. It was like she'd vanished into thin air. They'd called the police straight away. There had been desperate attempts to call Felicity's mobile but they heard ringing coming from her bedroom; her mobile was still on the bed where she'd left it.

Claire felt like a wave of ice was surging through her veins, chilling her blood, as she processed Stefan's words.

She swung her legs out of bed, pulling at her nightwear with one hand. 'Give me the address, I'll meet you there.'

*

Night had not yet succumbed completely to the light of day as Claire's Mazda pulled up outside Felicity's home. It was just after eight, and the sky was filled with dark clouds. The ice and snow under her feet showed no signs of thawing just yet.

She saw Stefan's car parked on the grass verge. He was already inside.

Claire rang the doorbell and a young man opened the door. He greeted her with sad eyes. His face was pale against his shock of natural scarlet-coloured hair. His green eyes were bloodshot from crying all night. He took a step forward, his tall, thin frame dwarfing Claire.

'I'm Wesley,' he said. 'Flick's brother.'

She followed him through the entrance hall and into the living room. She could hear a distraught voice coming from the kitchen down the hall. She looked at Stefan.

'Felicity's mother is with DC Harper, giving a statement,' he said, as if hearing her thoughts. 'This is Mr Davenport.'

'Call me Clark,' the man said, standing to shake her hand. Claire was a little taken aback but accepted his hand. He gripped her fingers tight and leaned in closer. She saw his eyes were red-rimmed from hours of crying and his breath had the sour twang of a hard spirit.

'DCI Claire Winters, Haverbridge CID.'

'Is it the same man who took the other two?' he said, ignoring her words. His voice was low, like he was sharing a secret between just the two of them. 'I must know.'

She stared back, pulling her hand until he reluctantly released it. 'We can't say with absolute certainty, Mr Davenport, but I understand we have had a few eye witnesses giving a description of the car which is relevant to the investigation… It's a possibility.'

Clark's eyes widened as his body began to shake. Wesley gripped his father's shoulders, helping him back to the sofa. He cried a fresh wave of tears and buried his head in his hands.

'Then all hope is gone. It's just a matter of time before she turns up like the other two… butchered.' His bottom lip quivered with the last word.

'We don't know for certain if this is related or not, Mr Davenport. I need to go through everything with you all, step by step, so we can help Felicity.'

'What more can I possibly say to you people?' he snapped, his face looking up at hers. 'You couldn't save the other two. What makes you think you can help Felicity now?' He stood and walked closer to her again. 'I've read about the case in the papers. I've seen the news. You've got nothing concrete and are no nearer to catching this man than when you first started, and now he has my Felicity.' Fresh tears rolled down his face.

'Please have a seat. You need to stay calm and focus. I'm going to get your wife, sit her down with you and Wesley, and we'll go through this a step at a time. You may remember something vital when we go through this again.'

*

DC Harper had left to continue another round of house-to-house visits and Hannah Davenport now sat opposite Claire and Stefan, staring at the floor. Clark was beside her, gripping her hand for support, while Wesley sat in the nearby armchair, legs crossed, twitching unconsciously, as he listened to his mother's words.

'I can't believe I let her answer the door late at night... What kind of mother am I?' She clasped a tissue to her mouth.

'You said so yourself, Mrs Davenport—'

'Hannah, Inspector,' she said, cutting Stefan off.

He smiled and gave a small nod. 'Hannah. You thought it was someone from the village. Everyone here knows everyone else. You can't be blamed for what happened. Felicity's sixteen, she's not a little girl.'

The room was silent.

'Perhaps you could tell us about what you did yesterday. I understand Felicity was home from boarding school this weekend?' Claire asked.

Hannah nodded. 'Yes, she comes home every weekend. Clark picked her up early yesterday morning from Kingsbrooke.'

'And this is a boarding school for girls?' Claire clarified.

A short, sharp nod. 'We spent the day together in the house, doing our own thing.'

'No one left the house and you had no visitors?'

'No.'

'What did Felicity do?'

'She was in her room most of the day.'

'She was on her laptop writing an essay,' Clark said. Wesley sighed, rolled his eyes.

'You've something to add, Wesley?' Stefan asked, keeping the tone of his voice casual.

'I have just told you she was doing her school assignment.' Clark had stepped in again, and it irritated Claire.

'If you could allow Wesley a chance to speak, I'd appreciate it.'

He shot her a cold look. 'My word not good enough, Chief Inspector?'

'Dad!' Wesley sat forward and held his hands out, shaking his head. 'The sooner you stop pretending like Flick was OK, the better.' He turned to Claire, and she saw nothing but truth in his eyes.

'Wesley, please,' Hannah said, tears rolling down her cheeks.

'No, Mum, we have to tell them.'

Clark stood and grabbed Wesley by the shoulders, pulling him from the chair. 'This jealousy of your sister will be the death of this family!'

Stefan took a firm hold of Clark's arm. 'Let him go, Mr Davenport.'

'You just don't want to see what's staring you in the face!' Wesley shouted, pushing his father from him.

Claire looked at Hannah, who had buried her face in her hands, consumed by grief. Her eyes crossed to Wesley. 'You need to tell us what you know if we're to help your sister.'

'I've been trying to help her for months,' he said, tears in his eyes again. 'I'm the only one who's really accepted Flick needs help.' He stared at his parents with disdain. 'Flick's suffering from depression... She was on The Way Out website yesterday, virtually all day.'

'Oh, God, please don't, Wesley,' Hannah said.

'What's The Way Out website?' Claire asked.

There was a heavy silence and all eyes were on Wesley. He swallowed hard before he spoke. 'It's a website for people contemplating suicide.' He paused. 'I can show you everything on her computer that she's been looking at.'

Claire looked to Clark and Hannah. Both avoided her eyes. Clark shook his head at his son. 'You can't face the fact she's making something of herself, can you?' He pointed a shaky finger in Wesley's face. 'You never took your studies seriously enough and now you want to interfere with Felicity's chances.'

Wesley's voice rose. 'No, you never took any of Flick's problems seriously. Now's the time for you and Mum to stop burying your heads in the sand.'

'OK,' Claire said, intervening. 'There're clearly some issues you need to make us aware of.'

'This is a family matter,' Clark snapped.

'Your daughter is missing, Mr Davenport,' Stefan said. 'We're not here to judge you as a family. We're here because your daughter's been kidnapped.'

Clark stared at Stefan for several seconds before he spoke. 'She had started cutting herself.'

'Why?' Claire asked. Hannah shook her head. When Clark also failed to answer, Claire looked to Wesley. 'Felicity confided in you, didn't she?'

He nodded. 'She couldn't take the pressure from our parents any more.'

'This is not our fault,' Clark said.

'I can show you where Flick kept her cutting kit. It's in a small tin in her drawer,' Wesley continued. 'She's vulnerable. She's scared and alone.'

'That's why I suggested the therapy,' Hannah said, cutting in. 'This isn't something we can handle on our own. It's not something I understand. I thought it was a silly phase but she wouldn't stop cutting away at herself.'

Claire exchanged glances with Stefan.

Broken women...

'Where were you going for therapy?' Claire asked.

Hannah's eyes met hers. She sniffed back her tears, looking embarrassed. 'We've been attending Focus Being in Letchworth.'

Claire felt her stomach pull tight. 'Have you been seeing Mitchell or Stephanie Curran?'

Hannah paused.

'Mitchell... how'd you know that?'

CHAPTER 44

Mitchell Curran sighed and massaged his forehead. He felt the beginnings of a migraine emerging from the front of his head, slowly creeping towards the back.

'I'll ask you one last time, Mr Curran, and if I were you, I'd think twice before you lie to me again.' He looked up at Claire and felt his stomach roll. 'Was Nola Grant a client of yours?'

He remained silent and glanced out of his window, planning in his head how to answer. 'She wasn't my client, but I did see her for her initial assessment.'

Claire and Stefan exchanged glances but said nothing. 'For data protection purposes, however, I—'

'There's an exception under the Data Protection Act 1998, Mr Curran, which no doubt you'll be aware of. It allows you to give information to the police in the event that it will help prevent or detect a crime, or catch or prosecute a suspect,' Claire said. He looked back at her and she raised her eyebrows.

Checkmate.

'I still have the right not to disclose anything, even under that law.'

'We can do this the hard way if you'd like, but I'd ask that you bear in mind there's a young girl missing, who was one of your clients. Need I remind you that Sara Thornton and her husband were also seeing your wife? ... Time may be running out for Felicity Davenport. The ball is in your court.'

He paused. He saw her eyes were serious.

'OK,' he snapped, throwing his hands up in the air. 'Nola wanted help to kick her drug habit and leave prostitution. She needed the mental strength.'

'And you referred her to someone else?'

A small nod.

'Who?'

Another long pause. 'My wife.'

'Your wife?' The confusion in Stefan's voice was audible.

'Why didn't you mention this before?' Claire asked. 'This is the connection.'

Mitchell sat forward, eyeballing her. 'You just don't get it, do you?'

'Apparently not.'

'Focus Being has been built by recommendation and reputation. It's not cheap, but people don't mind paying for quality. If anything got out in the public domain, linking our work here to these murders, it'd be bad for business.'

Shock registered on Stefan's face. 'People have died.'

Mitchell shrugged. 'Do you think that a business should suffer because of it? Nola Grant only came here for two, maybe three, sessions. Once with me, twice with my wife. She didn't want to change, not deep down, and I'm glad. Knowing where her money came from, we didn't want it.'

Stefan looked exasperated.

'Can anyone vouch for your whereabouts on the first and eighth of November?'

Mitchell turned to look at Claire, his face blank. 'Why?'

'I want to go over your alibis for the nights Nola and Sara disappeared. Just so we're really clear.'

'We've had this conversation before.' He stormed over to his office door, opening it with force. 'Why don't you go and ask my wife? She's in room three. She'll tell you I was at home with her all night, like before.'

'Both nights?'

'Both nights.'

'What about last night, when Felicity went missing?'

'I was at home.'

'Stefan,' Claire said, not looking at him, her eyes fixed on Mitchell. 'Please go and see Mrs Curran for me.'

Mitchell stood rigid when Stefan left the room. His eyes wandered back to Claire's.

'Why are the Davenports seeing you?'

Mitchell looked reluctant to answer.

'We could quite easily do this down at the station, I'm not fussed either way.'

'I haven't done anything wrong,' he said, taking a seat.

'Withholding information from the police, perverting the course of justice?'

He needed no more prompting.

'Hannah and Clark were worried about Felicity's behaviour. She was showing signs of depression and had started to feel suicidal. Felicity wouldn't reveal what the cause was and her parents just wanted things back to the way they were.'

'And there was nothing that gave you any cause for concern?'

A shake of the head. 'I didn't think Felicity was in any danger. It seemed she was seeking attention, although her brother suggested it was down to pressure from her parents to be exceptional. Felicity barely spoke in the sessions – she certainly didn't back her brother's claims. It was clear she didn't want to be here, and I didn't think she was the sort to find trouble.'

'But trouble has found her.'

He glared at her. 'I wasn't the cause of it.'

Stefan came in. He looked at Claire and gave a slight shake of his head as Stephanie Curran came into view behind him. Claire understood immediately.

Mitchell Curran had no alibi.

Mitchell looked alarmed and moved restlessly in his chair when his wife shook her head, and he caved under Claire's knowing stare.

'OK!' His hands banged hard on the armrests of his chair. 'I have no alibi. I lied.'

'Mitch… I'm sorry.'

'It's all right, Steph, it had to come out in the end.'

'You've both lied to the police in a murder and kidnap inquiry, Mr Curran. Anything else you want me to add to my list?' Claire said.

'Why don't you start by telling us where you were on the nights in question,' said Stefan, pulling up a chair directly in front of Mitchell. 'In your own time.'

Mitchell let his head fall into his hands. He sighed deeply and said, 'I was going to call you.'

Claire and Stefan exchanged glances of exasperation. It was not lost on Mitchell. 'Look,' he said, 'I know how this sounds, but it's the truth. I didn't want any of this to affect the business. We've already had a decline in clients over the last few years since the recession, and what with these self-help books, and the Internet… people will try and cut costs. That's the only reason I held back on the truth. I did it for the business.'

Claire remained stony-faced. 'You lied about being with your wife.'

'I was out on the nights in question,' Stephanie said.

All eyes fell on her.

'I work at the arts centre in town. I help out at the life-drawing classes. I was there all the nights in question, when Mitchell was at home.'

'We'll need the contact details of who was present on those nights.'

Stephanie nodded.

'This leads us back to you, Mr Curran.'

'I was at home, Chief Inspector, I assure you.'

'But no one can corroborate that.'

'And I know how that must look, but I'm telling you the truth. I had nothing to do with any of these,' he looked flustered as he searched for the words, 'horrible murders.' He paused. 'I keep thinking about Felicity. She must be so frightened. I wish in some way…' He trailed off, his eyes staring into space. 'I wish in some way I could help her. I wish I could save her… I wish I could've saved them all.'

CHAPTER 45

'Interesting choice of words he used there, don't you think?' Stefan said as he followed Claire towards the foyer.

'My thoughts exactly.'

'DCI Winters, wasn't it?' a voice cut in.

Claire looked up, and saw a familiar face staring back at her. She frowned, as she tried to remember his name.

'Joseph,' she said, after a beat.

'That's right.' He smiled. 'Glad you remembered me.'

Stefan gave him a half smile. 'Can we help you?'

Joseph shrugged. 'I just wondered if there was any more news?' he said. 'The local paper has posted an article online about the missing girl, Felicity.'

'Did you know her?' Claire asked.

He shook his head. 'No, not really. I recognised her photo online.' He paused. 'She always looked happy when I saw her here, I thought.' He reached into his pocket, and pulled out a business card that'd been folded in half. 'I kept this,' he said, showing Claire the card she'd given him. 'In case I do think of anything else.'

She nodded. 'One of my DCs will be in later to speak with you and the rest of the staff.' She stepped aside to walk to the exit, but Joseph stopped her, his hand lightly touching her elbow.

'I think Felicity slipped on a mask, you know.'

Claire's eyes flicked across to Stefan's quickly, then back to Joseph's.

'A mask?'

He nodded. 'I think she only pretended to get better.'

'Yet you said you thought she always looked happy.'

'She did… does,' he corrected himself. He looked over her shoulder, seeing Alice Hathaway watching them from the reception desk. 'I see a lot of people coming in and out of here. Usually they always look happy when they come in.'

'So… what are you saying?' Stefan said.

'Well, here's the thing,' Joseph said. 'How can they be happy if they are coming here? Surely they are coming here because they are unhappy with something?'

Claire's eyes narrowed. 'You think Felicity was faking it all, every emotion whilst here?'

Joseph nodded. 'Absolutely.' He took a step closer. 'Which makes me ask the question, why pretend? Why come if you have no intention in getting better, or healing whatever the reason is that brought you here in the first place?'

*

'He's got a point, don't you think?' Stefan said as they left the building.

Claire stopped and stared out across the car park. 'Yes and no.' She turned to face him. 'He's assuming Felicity was pretending. Maybe she was putting on a brave face? We know she's always trying to please her parents, or maybe that's just her face?'

Stefan frowned. 'Her face is always happy?'

Claire scoffed. 'I don't know, I'm just saying, perhaps there's nothing more to it. When someone's hiding something from the world, they try and act as normal as possible. Why would Felicity be any different? Normal for that family is keeping up the pretence, the appearance of normality, isn't it?'

Stefan nodded, mulling the information over in his head.

'And Curran?'

'We've not got anywhere near enough on him. It's all circumstantial evidence.'

'He has no alibi.'

'We need something more concrete.'

She checked her watch, then buried her hands in her coat pockets. 'Curran has met all three women. Nola and Sara for initial assessment, before assigning them to his wife. He looked after the Davenports personally. Felicity wouldn't have thought anything unusual in him appearing on her doorstep.'

Stefan thought for a moment. 'CCTV of Sara's abduction tells us what, though? Gregg didn't recognise him.'

'They met Curran once, like Nola. He's not that memorable, is he? Curran, I mean. He's Mr Average.'

He watched her face. 'What're you thinking?' he said, as they walked back to their cars.

'All we have is a theory, Fletch. Just a theory. We showed people in the building, clients and staff alike, photographs of our suspect and no one has seen him or anyone wearing those clothes from the CCTV footage.'

She slammed her hand on the top of her car. 'I'm buggered if I'm gonna be pushed into arresting the wrong man just 'cos the pressure's on for fast results.'

'So what are the options then?'

'Have a couple of DCs sent on a house-to-house in Curran's street. See if anyone saw him leave the house or if he had any visitors on the nights in question. Same for his wife. Have someone talk to the students who take the life-drawing classes and the tutor… If it is Curran, we'll find something and make it stick.'

CHAPTER 46

Felicity ran.

She couldn't quite believe she'd been able to escape, and she tore across the yard and into the pitch-black night, not caring about the cold biting at her naked body. She stumbled many times on the uneven ground, fear driving her on.

The shot rang out behind her.

She ducked.

Then came another and she fell to the ground so hard that her whole body jerked violently on impact, but she got to her feet and pushed on.

The ground underfoot was soggy and she heard him behind her, his boots crashing into the sludge underfoot. She couldn't see much in the darkness and had no idea where she was heading. She just kept going in a straight line in the vain hope she'd find a house or a main road.

Eventually, she saw a dim light ahead, maybe coming from a nearby cottage in the distance. She couldn't be sure but she raced on ahead as if it were a homing beacon calling her to safety. Tears washed her cheeks when she heard him closing in on her.

Suddenly her feet were pulled out from underneath her, and she crashed face first on the ground. He gripped her legs tight, pulling her back along the ground. She screamed but had little energy to keep it up. Her voice sounded like a moan of an animal in pain. Her hands reached forward, nails digging into the dirt, as if it'd make a difference.

It was no use.

She soon found herself back in the yard she'd run from, then being pulled roughly along the stone floor back to that scary place she had feared more than anything.

Soon she was hanging upside-down above the deep trough below. She saw him edge closer, knife in hand, and for the final time in her life, she let out a high-pitched scream.

*

The blood dripped from the blade onto the concrete like summer rain. The knife clattered to the floor, as the body hung there, blood flowing from the fatal wound, twitching. The man's eyes showed little emotion as the life of his latest victim ebbed away within a few seconds.

As he watched her body sway slightly from the suspension bars above him, he gazed down at her arms hanging down either side of her body with a dead weight. He could see the mud underneath her fingernails, and the cuts where she had fought him. She had been the most resilient yet and this had surprised him considering she was the youngest so far. She definitely had the fighting spirit when it came down to it.

Pity it'd come to this.

Looking down at the blood in the metal trough underneath the body, he briefly reminisced about the last few months, with some relish. He held up his left hand and used the fingers on the other to count out loud how many there had been since this had started.

After savouring the thought for a few moments, he thought back to the next one. 'Fallon Dockley,' he said, smiling, 'you lucky girl.'

CHAPTER 47

26th November

The lane not far from the village of Pirton was silent and peaceful. The snow was falling softly, landing on her body. She'd been cleaned. Hair brushed, mud removed from her face and body, then re-dressed. He couldn't bring himself to leave her naked.

Icy flakes began to melt, soaking into the fabric of her black jumper. A mid-length black skirt rested high up her thighs. She wore no shoes. They'd been lost in the struggle. Her feet were bare, nails broken and dirty.

Her hair was tied loosely behind her head, some strands fallen loose, tendrils curling around her frozen face. Her blue eyes looked as fragile as glass, an icy stare transfixed towards the sky.

The bushes flanking the lane were covered with red berries, giving the illusion of blood-red tears falling against the snow.

Her lips were blue, cracked, sore. Her skin looked like it would shatter under the slightest touch. Small droplets of blood soaked into the snow beside her.

Felicity Davenport was barely sixteen years old. She was well educated. Very sensible, although somewhat naïve, especially when it came to the evil that can lurk within others. She often walked down this lane, alone, to try to find some peace, to stop her dangerous thoughts of her life spiralling out of control.

The irony of this lane being her final resting place was not lost on the man who callously left her there, hidden from the main road, but soon to be found by one villager out on her morning walk.

May strolled around the corner, her Border Terrier pulling at the lead. She stopped dead in her tracks when her eyes caught sight of the body. In her shock, she dropped the leash, the dog bounding on ahead, stopping at Felicity's body. He bent his head, licked her hand and whimpered. He looked back at May, whose mobile was already glued to her ear.

CHAPTER 48

Claire was silent as she drove her car off Hexton Road onto the B655, Hitchin Road. Her eyes watched closely for the sharp turning that ran alongside farmers' fields, where the body had been discovered. She needn't have worried about missing anything.

The Beds and Herts Scientific Services Unit van – surrounded by SOCOs, almost camouflaged in their suits against the white backdrop – was like a homing beacon. Police tape cordoned off the area, fluttering in the cold wind on the horizon.

She slowed the car.

Her hands gripped the steering wheel tight. Stefan gave her a sideways glance. He felt as bad as she did. They knew the body would be Felicity's, even before they had a formal ID. Their man was taking his chosen ones fast and killing them just as quickly.

Claire pulled onto the side of the road. She and Stefan stared down the country lane, which had also been cordoned off by police tape. Elias was already on the scene waiting for them. He took a slow jog towards them through the snow. Claire rolled down her window as he approached.

His eyes said it all.

'Felicity?'

He nodded. 'There's no ID on the body, but she matches the pictures the Davenports gave us. She's not in the state of undress like the previous two. She's wearing clothes that match the description given by the Davenports. This is barely half a mile from where Sara's body was found. Can't be a coincidence.'

'What stage are we at?' asked Stefan.

'When the initial call came in, two CSOs arrived from Pirton village. Sergeant Millar is the senior officer on the scene. He's secured the area.'

'Same cut to the throat?'

'Yes, and the likely cause of death, but she was killed elsewhere. There's not enough blood at the scene. There are some traces of mud underneath her fingernails, but otherwise she looks very clean. Photographs and video have been taken, and the SOCOs have nearly finished, not that there's been much to go on. Any footprints have been covered by snow, but this route is popular with ramblers and people from the village.'

'Not in this weather,' Claire said.

Elias shrugged. 'There's only one fresh set of prints in the snow and it belongs to the woman who found the body.'

Claire unbuckled her seatbelt and got out of the car, followed by Stefan. The wind was fierce and she pulled her long black coat around her body. She folded her arms across her chest as she stared down the lane.

'This area is isolated from the main road. The lane is flanked by farmers' fields. If she was killed elsewhere, then our man would've had to transport her here using a vehicle. There must be tyre tracks? Something?'

Elias looked at her and nodded, his eyes squinting against the wind. 'Partial tracks. It snowed heavily last night, and Dr Schreiber thinks she hasn't been here longer than twelve hours.'

Claire wandered farther down the turning, towards the police tape, and Sergeant Millar nodded respectfully as she approached. 'DCI Winters,' he said, tipping his head. 'I think you have your serial killer. This one makes three, doesn't it?'

'I hoped I was wrong. He's killing them more quickly.'

Millar coughed into his hand and shook his head. 'She's so young. I've got a niece her age. It brings it all home to you, how fragile life is.' He turned his attention towards the incident tent far down the lane.

Claire followed his gaze.

The wind picked up again and the police tape vibrated in protest, the only sound she could hear, until black crows above her started squawking. She looked up, saw them circle, then come to rest on the branches of a skeletal tree flanking the side of the lane.

Spectators to the grim scene.

Claire's face looked pained, as if the Grim Reaper himself was resting upon her shoulder sharing a burden. Stefan shivered, his eyes fixed on the birds in the tree. They screeched, ruffling their black feathers. They cut a sombre shape in the grey skyline.

'A murder of crows,' Claire said, to no one in particular. Elias watched her face, set like stone, in a hard stare.

'Guv?' Elias said, eyebrow raised.

'That's what they call a gathering of crows,' Stefan said, thrusting his hands deep into his coat pockets. 'Fitting.'

Then they all heard the screaming.

They turned on their heels in unison.

Claire's eyes narrowed at the lady running towards them, who was swiftly followed by uniformed officers.

'Who's that?' Millar said. He pointed to another uniformed officer, now standing near Claire's car. 'She's breached the tape, get her back.' He strode forward ready to intercept her.

The woman didn't show any signs of stopping.

Then Claire recognised her. Following after Millar, she came up close beside him.

'What the hell does she think she's doing?'

'That's Hannah Davenport.' Millar turned to face her, his eyes questioning. 'Felicity's mother,' she clarified.

As Hannah ran closer to Claire's car, an officer in pursuit grabbed hold of her from behind, stopping her dead in her tracks. She dropped to the floor and wailed, her face chapped and slick with tears.

'Is it Felicity?' Her eyes were pleading, desperate. The officer who held her tried to pull her to her feet.

'This is a crime scene. The road is off limits.' She pushed him away, fell forward on her hands and tried to crawl from his grasp.

'They're saying it's my Felicity! Tell me it's not her. Tell me it's not my baby?'

Claire's eyes widened as Hannah's anguished cries rang through her ears. She felt the weight of the woman's desperation, her sorrow and her pain all at once. She bit her lip but couldn't tear her eyes away from the scene unfolding before her.

Millar was now running towards Hannah. Claire focused on his back, as if it might drown out the cries of grief.

But Hannah didn't stop.

Despite her voice growing hoarse, rattling from her throat, she wouldn't stop.

'Felicity!'

She screamed again and again, until Claire couldn't take it any more. She turned her back on Hannah.

Stefan was staring at her.

He watched her edge closer to him. Her eyes were staring beyond his shoulder, down towards the body, but her mouth was close to his ear.

'I want this bastard, Fletch.'

He turned to stare into her eyes.

Hannah's anguish seemed to engulf them both but Claire's resolve hardened again.

'I want this bastard.'

CHAPTER 49

27th November

The man lay back on his sofa watching the flashing lights coming from the TV in the corner of the room. The screen was filled with paparazzi, cameras flashing, then the screen changed to show a news conference. The sight of the Davenport family roused his interest immediately.

Clark, Hannah and Wesley Davenport sat along a large table with microphones attached to it. The news camera panned along their faces, moving on to the officers leading the investigation.

The man paid no attention to the news reporter speaking over the image. Instead, he read the captions running along the bottom of the screen: 'Breaking News – Concern grows as the body of a third girl is confirmed as that of missing schoolgirl Felicity Davenport, believed to be the third victim of the same killer attacking women in and around Haverbridge.'

The man scoffed when he read the caption.

He hated the fact the reports were making him out to be someone who just picked women at random for the sole purpose of butchering them, but he did like the fact the news had gone national. The time he'd spent agonising about the blood on his hands, the deaths of these women, seemed a long time ago.

He was growing and evolving.

The feeling that he was in control of a person's life, and had the ability to save it or take it away, excited him. He smiled, listening to the Davenports pleas for the killer to come forward. They could forgive him if he gave himself up and stopped the madness.

Cheek to call me mad.

He leaned back in his grandmother's chair. She'd have been so proud if she could see him now. She'd be able to see what he'd done. What he'd tried to do.

It wasn't his fault these women didn't want to change their lives, didn't want the help he could offer them. He'd tried. That's enough, isn't it?

True, he'd wept for the loss of Felicity but he hadn't any choice. After he caught her trying to take her own life in his basement, trying to open her veins with the sharp edge of broken china that was once her dinner plate, he knew she was a lost cause.

They'd all been responsible for their own fate. Felicity had been no different.

On the TV, Hannah Davenport had started to cry again. He couldn't be listening to that. It irritated him. He lowered the volume.

Then Claire Winters filled the screen.

He didn't turn the volume up, he didn't need to. She would be talking about the crimes, the victims, how he should give himself up... blah, blah, blah.

Keep telling yourself you're not interested in her... I dare you, he thought to himself.

True, he'd been captivated from the moment he'd first seen her, but she would be a big risk. She was the investigating officer, trained to track people like him down.

Things had got close for him already. He daren't risk it.

I'm not interested...

He'd done some digging on her already. He knew she would be perfect. Risky but perfect. A new thought flooded his senses. It rippled out into every limb.

Come on, it's not like you've not thought about it before.

He could find out more about Claire Winters, a great deal more than he knew already, if he wanted to. She looked hard, strong, but despite the intensity of her eyes, he saw what lay just underneath the surface. She had stories to tell, and flaws to be fixed before she could be perfect to him.

She would be worth getting caught for.

He reached out his hand and touched the screen tenderly.

Soon.

He'd changed his plans because of her and she was fast becoming his new obsession, he couldn't deny it. There was the other girl, true, but the more he thought about the possibility of cleansing them both, the more it excited him.

I could have her on her knees begging for her life.

He switched the television off, hummed to himself, and sat his laptop on his knees. He brought up Google, typed in Claire's name. A series of articles popped up in a list, both local news and national. He swapped to image results, smiling when Claire's face filled the screen.

They weren't particularly flattering shots. Most were taken of her leaving court or shots at a press conference, nothing to get excited about, but he still saved a few to his hard drive. He flicked back to the articles and selected one that had been about an investigation the previous year.

The murdered priest.

His eyes narrowed as he read the particulars again. There hadn't been any case to rival it before. It'd given Claire column inches and respect, but there was mention of less savoury accounts on that case, and her conduct.

This pleased him.

You're flawed, Claire Winters… beautifully so.

He knew he held the key to her salvation. He clicked on another thumbnail image, opened it to full resolution.

He went to save the image along with the others, but stopped.

He had never really believed in ghosts, but at that moment he did feel a sudden change in the air. The tiny hairs on his neck stood on end, and he looked over his shoulder to make sure he was alone.

He'd never understood it when people on the TV, or featured in magazines, said they had felt an other worldly presence come into a room, but he was beginning to understand it now.

He felt as if he wasn't alone.

He'd always thought that if ghosts existed, it would be his grandmother who would come to visit him.

If this ill feeling that was creeping into him was something real and not imagined, he knew it wasn't his grandmother.

It was his mother.

She'd never approved of him looking at women, but he would be defiant until the end.

He reached out to the laptop screen, touched Claire's face, fingertips smearing across the screen.

'Together we can learn so much.'

1991

His lungs were fit to burst.

Eyes were wide, stinging as he thrashed his head from side to side. His legs kicked out but skidded. Any moment now and he wouldn't be able to fight his body's natural reaction to open his mouth and just breathe.

He felt nails digging into his neck where her hand was clamped down with surprising strength, holding his head underneath the bath water.

As he struggled, his arms thrashing about in vain, water lapped over the side of the bath, soaking the floor.

His mouth opened then. His chest felt tight.

Then he heard a scream, muffled as it was under the water, but he knew it was her, come to save him.

The hand at his neck was wrenched away, his grandmother pulled him up and slapped his back. She was screaming at his mother, but he couldn't make out the words. He leaned forward and brought up bath water.

He then sat back into his grandmother's arms and wept. When he opened his eyes, he saw his mother clasping her face and a huge welt beginning to surface around her left eye.

He looked down at his grandmother's hands. The knuckles on her right hand were cut and he knew what she'd done to protect him.

His mother was shouting at her, at them both, then she reached for the toilet and vomited.

Another drunken binge on her part had ended in violence once again.

Sixteen years old, and here he was, reduced to almost nothing, cradled by the only person he knew how to love.

Five minutes later, and his mother managed to scrape herself up from the floor, and stumbled out of the bathroom without so much as a backward glance.

His grandmother turned to him. 'What did you do?'

He coughed, chest heavy, his throat burning. 'I answered her back.'

She looked down into his eyes. They looked alive with blood – bruised and bloodshot.

'She came in here when I was in the bath.' A tear rolled down his cheek. 'She's been—'

'Drinking,' the grandmother said. 'Yes, I know.'

He cuddled in close to her, breathed in her familiar scent. It gave him comfort. 'Why, Nanna? Why does she do this to me?'

'She's not worthy. When I think about all those poor souls who have no choice, who have to fight to survive in this world, I feel sick knowing she's wasting her life.'

He gripped her hand tight. 'She doesn't deserve the chance. That's what you're saying.'

She shook her head. 'No, she doesn't.' She looked to the empty doorway, heard the crashing sound of broken glass in the kitchen, knew her daughter had reached for yet another bottle of whatever she could find.

'But,' she said, glassy eyes returning to look down upon his, 'we teach, we steer, we influence the troubled, best as we can. One day, I won't be here any more and you'll be the only one left to carry on what I started.'

He kissed the back of her hand. 'I never want you to leave me.'

She ran her fingers through his wet and matted hair, but felt little warmth in her bones.

CHAPTER 50

30th November

Dress size 10, shoe size 7, aged thirty-eight and fast-tracked to a DCI. He also knew she hated peas. He'd managed to find that out on his own after following her to the local store and overhearing her irritating mother babbling on about veg.

He'd spent two days finding out what he could about Claire Winters and it'd been interesting to say the least. There weren't any surprises though, not really. One failed marriage under her belt, to another copper no less! No regular boyfriend, no real life outside of the job, nor friends who weren't fellow officers.

She'd put a girl in hospital once. Seventeen stitches to some bitch's head after a direct hit with a changing-room mirror at the local swimming pool when she was a teenager.

He'd smiled when he read that part. It'd been self-defence.

No one had bullied Claire after that, he reckoned.

Fitness. She liked to run and that was what brought him here, today, waiting in her local park. Shame it was so bloody cold.

He nestled down into the bushes.

It was early, just after 6:30 a.m. The snow lay thin on the ground where he hid, so he didn't mind kneeling on the ground too much. He'd become quite accustomed to the cold.

Dark thoughts turned back towards his childhood, where being cold was something he endured mentally as well as physically. He dismissed the thought. He didn't like going back there, the darkness inside his head, filed away, controlling him if he didn't keep it in check. Memories of his mother could be torture and he needed to concentrate.

Claire had left about ten minutes ago. He'd sprinted the opposite way, cutting across the neighbouring roads in the village and into the park, knowing he had around five minutes before she would come this way. From his vantage point, he would have the perfect line of vision.

He could watch her in her full glory.

He'd made good use of the last few days. Watching her movements, learning a great deal in the small amount of time he'd had. He'd even got to know her gestures. The way she unconsciously flicked her hair over her shoulder before getting into her car. The way she gave one last look out her front door before closing it for the night when she got home from the station.

Old habits that would never die.

He had loved every minute of it, but he wanted contact. He longed to hear her voice, to smell her hair and touch her skin.

The minutes ticked by.

He ignored one or two early morning joggers, dismissing their importance, as he adjusted his own tracksuit. He wasn't used to wearing anything like this. The material was cheap, felt nasty against his skin, but it would do. It was for appearance's sake anyway. He would dispose of it soon, once it served its purpose.

Another thirty seconds ticked by before he saw her. Blonde hair flailing in the light wind, a smart-looking grey tracksuit, and a determined expression on her flushed face.

*

Claire had taken up jogging as part of her fitness regime. What at first had started out as a chore, had now become something of an obsession. She worked out at a gym, but it'd been Stefan who introduced her to running in her local park, and despite the snow, Claire was determined to push herself.

Her face was cold, but the rest of her had worked up a sweat, her body feeling warm. When she reached the main entrance to the park, her pace slowed. She felt for the iPod secured to her waistband and turned the volume up.

She always listened to what her mother called 'angry music' when she exercised, and when the sound of the Chemical Brothers pulsed through her ears, she tore off into a fast sprint.

'*This is not what I wanted. I hoped you wouldn't remember this place.*'

The words spoken to her a year ago suddenly shot into her head so fast she almost lost her footing as the flashback of His face clouded her vision.

She shook her head. Not today, she thought. Go away.

'*Feel like pleading for your life?*'

Claire stopped dead in her tracks. 'Fuck's sake...' she hissed, her breathing laboured.

Why were His words coming back into her head right now? Was He going to taint her days now as well as haunt her nightmares?

'*Are you ready to die?*'

Claire remembered those words. Her reply would be burned into her soul for eternity.

'*Don't...*'

She felt saliva pool in her mouth and she thought she was going to be sick. She ran to the nearest cluster of bushes and emptied what little remained in her stomach.

Another jogger passed her, glanced, saw her cast him a cold look, so carried on in the opposite direction.

Claire wiped her mouth with the back of her hand. She wished she'd brought water with her this time. Her tongue felt thick in her dry mouth.

She stood with her hands on her hips, breathing slowing. She glanced at her watch, knew she couldn't stop the pace.

She forced herself on.

When she jogged past the children's play area, she didn't notice a man in a black tracksuit begin to follow her.

*

His eyes were trained on the back of her neck.

What the hell was all that about? She'd been sick? He hoped she wasn't pregnant. He didn't want another repeat of Nola.

This might be something he'd have to evaluate when the time came. He came out from the thicket of trees where he'd stood when he had seen her stop.

He carried on after her.

Despite his own fitness level being fairly good, he still found his body working overtime trying to keep up with her. It was difficult on the path. The ice was melting where many people had passed over it, but he still nearly lost his footing a few times.

He kept a safe distance behind so as not to arouse suspicion but even if he had been close enough to touch her, he doubted she would've noticed. She was lost in her own world, the music blaring in her ears.

He noticed her pace slow.

A quick look around confirmed they were alone.

His pace quickened.

She headed towards a bench which was coming up on the left. She slowed to a fast walk before putting a leg up on the bench to stretch it. She didn't bother to look behind her. Her head bobbed in time to the music.

He picked up speed, closing in on her.

She was almost within his reach.

Everything in his mind seemed to happen in slow motion when his hand reached out towards her.

Her back was to him and as he rushed past, he let his fingers brush through her hair. In an instant he caught the scent of her perfume. He felt euphoric, as the softness of her hair slipped away through his fingers.

Everything happened in under a second, but it would remain with him for a lifetime.

He didn't look back.

He picked up his pace and turned out of sight, off towards the street next to Claire's home, where he'd parked his car earlier. Later he would come back, watch her arrive home. He hoped the mother wouldn't be there this time. He wanted to enjoy the feeling he got when he knew Claire was all alone. Vulnerable and at his mercy, knowing what he could do if he wanted.

What he longed to do.

*

Claire's head shot up when something pulled through her hair.

She frowned, watching the man in the black tracksuit running ahead of her, never bothering to look back and apologise.

Creep.

She was feeling so pumped with adrenaline, it was a hard decision for her not to go after him and give him a piece of her mind. Instead, she watched him until he disappeared from sight and soon, out of mind. She finished stretching the other leg, before resuming her jog.

CHAPTER 51

Social get-togethers with colleagues weren't usually top of Claire's list of priorities, but since it was DSI Donahue's birthday drinks, she'd been dragged along. Donahue's favourite local wine bar was called Hedonism, which sat in the heart of the town's high street.

Decorated in gold and silver, with floor-to-ceiling glass windows at the front, Claire felt like she was in a car showroom rather than a bar. It was almost 7:00 p.m. and the place was busy.

'Clifton must be in a good mood,' she said to Stefan when he sat down, placing a small glass of wine in front of her. 'Open bar for us lot and spouses?'

'Shut up and drink.'

'I'm driving.'

'One won't kill you.'

Picking up the glass, she brought it up towards Stefan, met his pint glass with a loud clink, then downed half the liquid in one mouthful. As she put the glass back on the table, Elias sat down in front of them, swiftly followed by Matthews.

'Donahue said if you haven't lightened up by the end of the night, you're footing the bar tab,' Matthews said, his words already slurring.

He gave Claire a wink.

'If lightening up means ending up like you, Matthews, I'd gladly foot the bill.'

Stefan laughed. Matthews took a large swig of his beer and drunkenly pointed his finger at Claire. 'You need something to take your mind off the case. The Davenport girl in particular.' He gave Elias a playful dig in the arm with his elbow.

'I've seen her like this before, last year. There was this DS and he—'

'Matthews,' Claire said, arching her eyebrow. It was a warning, and Elias shifted uncomfortably in his seat.

'Let's drink to new beginnings,' Stefan said, raising his glass towards Elias, 'and to new colleagues?'

'I'll drink to that,' Matthews said, slapping Elias on the back. 'Even though you're a bit of a prick, you're all right most of the time.'

Elias lifted his glass. 'I guess there's a compliment there somewhere.'

They sipped their drinks and the table fell silent. Claire excused herself, took her glass and wandered off to the entrance of the bar. Matthews started talking about something so unintelligible that Stefan just made noises in what he hoped were the right places.

Elias followed Claire. He stood beside her, following her line of vision. She was staring out of the glass front towards the toy shop across the road, its windows twinkling with fairy lights and decorated in an old-fashioned theme.

'Reminds you of something out of a Dickens novel, doesn't it?'

She gave him a sideways glance. 'I don't do small talk.'

'I'm trying my best here.'

'Don't feel you have to.'

Elias stared at her, his eyes appearing darker than usual. He had something to ask her, and was unsure how to phrase it.

Seeing he was struggling, she forced her face to soften. 'What can I do for you?'

'Am I that transparent?'

She half smiled. 'You're not standing with me for my company, I know that much.' He didn't answer. 'What can I do for you, Crest?'

'This isn't related to the investigation.'

'Now I am worried,' she said, eyes widening in mock surprise.

'What have you told Stefan about why I'm here?' he said.

Claire noted the hard edge to his voice. He was serious; in no mood for games. He was trying his best not to sound confrontational, but failing miserably. His body language told her how uncomfortable he was.

Claire held his stare. 'Why you're here at Haverbridge you mean?'

Elias nodded.

Claire opened her mouth, sighed, then said, 'Nothing.'

'You're both close, so I find that hard to believe.'

Claire gave half a laugh, and shook her head. 'I think you've mis-read our relationship.' She paused. 'Stefan is one of my most trusted and loyal officers, but there are limits to what I share with him, and that includes what I know about your reasons for transferring from Merseyside.'

Elias took a moment to process her words, not sure if he believed them, and Claire remembered the reasons that had been passed to her from his old colleagues as to why Elias seemed to hate working under the authority of a woman.

Elias lived on his own, despite having a steady stream of girlfriends on and off. He preferred his own company.

He was born in London and spent most of his early years living – no, surviving – on a rundown sink estate in Brixton, sharing a cramped mould-ridden one-bed flat with his mother.

Elias's biological father had walked out when he was fifteen, and he hadn't seen much of him since then. When he'd found out Elias wanted to be a police officer, he pretty much disowned him. Elias's mother had then had a steady stream of boyfriends, all of whom had their own emotional baggage carried in tow.

By the time Elias's mother gave him the third half-sister since his father had left, Elias had quite literally had enough. He left home and moved to Liverpool, and soon took his first steps to becoming a police officer.

After five years in Liverpool South's CID team, Elias had wanted out.

'Has DI Fletcher said anything to you about why you came to this division?' she said at length.

Elias paused. He looked out the glass front again, focusing his gaze back towards the Christmas display in the shop opposite.

The official reason he left and transferred back down south was because he wanted to live and work closer to his family, but the real reason wasn't quite so clear cut.

Claire knew that. She knew pretty much everything.

Elias didn't like working under a woman's authority, that much was clear. A psychiatrist might argue that this is down to Elias's childhood and the way his mother raised him, but Claire wasn't buying into that.

His mother could've been the complete opposite of what she became and Elias would still resent her.

'Well?' she said. 'Has Fletch made any comments to you?'

He looked at her then and held her gaze. He shrugged. 'Not as such.'

'Meaning?'

'Meaning, he makes the odd dig… about my apparent problem with authority.'

Claire pulled at a strand of her hair that hung down over her shoulder. She twisted it through her fingers.

'Fletch, or anyone else for that matter, doesn't need me to spread gossip about your behaviour,' she said. 'You're not exactly an enigma to me, Crest. Your feelings are abundantly clear.'

'My file—'

'That only I and a select few have seen,' she added, cutting in.

Elias sighed. 'My file can't be read as purely black and white.'

'I know that.'

'You do?'

'Why do you think you were transferred to this team?' Elias didn't answer. His brow furrowed and Claire smiled. 'Despite what you may have heard or assumed about me, Crest,' she said, 'I tend to read past the paperwork, past what others say someone can or can't do.'

She leaned in closer to him.

'I judge from my initial first impressions, yes, that's true, but I'm not naïve. The cases you've worked on, the suspects you've helped catch…'

She sighed as she crossed her arms tight across her chest. 'You assume your file contains something questionable about your character…' Her eyes meet his. 'It doesn't.'

Elias frowned.

'If there had been anything untoward, you wouldn't be here,' she said. 'Your last boss, DCI Glass, she called me when she knew the details about the transfer had been approved.'

Elias felt the lump rise in his throat, tried to swallow it back down. He'd always assumed his file had contained details of what happened in Liverpool. What had been *alleged*.

An unreliable witness had made a complaint that Elias had harassed her about changing her statement. An argument with a neighbour had got out of hand. A man ended up dead after a known thug had smashed a glass bottle and slashed the man's neck, severing a carotid artery. The only witness had been the thug's mother, who was adamant she would stick by her son.

Elias knew she was lying and tried to pressure her, or so she claimed. She promptly dropped her complaint and Elias never did find out why. He assumed her son must have intervened because he later admitted to what he'd done.

The whole business had left Elias scared to an extent. He'd had enough and he wanted out of Liverpool.

His eyes met Claire's and he went to speak, but couldn't find the words.

'Professional Standards could've been involved,' Claire said. 'You'd never have been considered for transfer if they had. Your record is exemplary and you passed the vetting, the medical and fitness tests, and Glass gave you a good reference – fantastic, in fact.'

Claire turned to face him full on. 'She gave you a bloody get-out-of-jail-free card, Crest. Don't forget that.'

Elias's lips parted a little. He wasn't sure he believed what he was hearing.

Claire wasn't finished.

'What I heard, off the record, was that after the alleged harassment of a key witness, your relationship with your work colleagues broke down, and you needed a life line. After many meetings it was decided someone would give you that life line – the chance you needed, certainly not an easy ride, but a life line nonetheless.'

A slow realisation began to hit Elias full force and he wasn't sure what to think or how to feel. For the first time, he found he couldn't hold her stare.

He blinked, lowering his eyes.

'There were those privy to the incident that weren't prepared to take a risk on you transferring here.'

She let the sentence hang.

'Someone gave me the chance,' he said at last.

Claire nodded.

'That someone was… you?'

Claire's lips pulled into a hard line and she gave a small barely noticeable nod. Elias felt many emotions, but embarrassment was by far the most overwhelming emotion. He'd spent the last few weeks behaving like he had an axe to grind with her, and now he'd found out she'd helped save his arse, he didn't know how to feel.

'Truth is,' she said, 'it could've easily been me in the same situation as you ten years ago.'

'I really don't know what to say.'

Claire understood that feeling at least. 'Don't say anything. Not about this conversation and don't think that this makes us friends. In my eyes, you still have a lot to prove.'

He allowed himself an inward smile. 'Fair, I guess.' He looked back towards Stefan.

DSI Donahue had joined them with his wife. Her face was well-lined and her hair colour a perfect out-of-the-bottle auburn. Elias had met her briefly. She seemed all right, but he wasn't planning on getting too friendly with them.

Donahue had taken his side when he'd questioned Claire's actions regarding Daryl Thomas, which had surprised him, but still, he didn't know how far to trust the man.

That would take time, and despite what Claire had just revealed to him, he was of her mind.

He wasn't about to put all his trust in her either.

A raucous laugh erupted from the far corner near the bar, and Elias looked around and surveyed the drunken group of men and women, sharing a joke, and it was then that he saw her.

A young woman sat in the corner, her coat pulled right up to her chin and her hair partially covering her face, but despite this he could tell what she was doing instantly.

She was watching him.

He stared at her until she looked away. He thought nothing of it, until minutes later he caught her looking again. He leaned over to Claire, but as he went to speak, the woman in the corner got up and disappeared into the toilets.

'Something wrong?' Claire's eyes scanned the tables, following his stare.

He shrugged, turning towards her. 'It's nothing. You want another drink?'

'If you were paying the tab I'd feel more inclined to say yes and think that this was an honest attempt to get to know me.'

He frowned. 'Is that a yes or a no?'

She handed him her empty glass. 'I'll have an orange juice.'

*

The girl went into the toilet cubicle, locking the door behind her. Her heart was beating hard, and she flattened her palm over her chest to calm herself. She rested her head against the door and blew out her breath. She closed her eyes.

She thought about the fact there was nothing keeping her from walking away from this whole mess and starting a new life somewhere else, but then again she was born into this and there was no get-out clause. It was meant to be and the sooner she accepted it, the better.

*

When she came out of the toilets, Elias was waiting for her.

She took great care to hide most of her face when she swerved around him in between a large group of men.

Elias had an uneasy feeling deep inside his gut. This girl wasn't watching him because she was interested in him for company. She had another agenda.

As she neared the main door she risked a glance behind. She saw he was now going back to his table, grabbing his coat. He was coming after her. It was then she felt unsure about the whole thing for the second time that night.

There's no going back, not now.

It didn't matter how many times she told herself that, she was still fighting the urge to just run. Run now and never look back.

But she didn't.

She stepped out into the cold, pulled her hood up and headed down the high street.

*

Elias made his excuses and left Hedonism, pulling his coat collar up high when he stepped out into the bitter cold.

He looked in both directions and saw the back of the woman, a few yards away, heading towards the petrol station. He started to follow, pushing past the revellers spilling onto the pavement outside the clubs and restaurants. Then she stopped dead in her tracks and glanced behind her.

Stared right at him. Then she ran.

Elias gave chase.

When he turned a corner, she was already halfway down the road ahead of him. Despite her high heels, the girl could run fast. He pushed himself harder, picking up speed, skidding in the snow. She rounded another corner and slipped on the ice. She landed hard on her knees.

She scrambled on the pavement when he grabbed her shoulder.

'Take it easy,' he said, pulling her up. 'You're the one who was watching me, sweetheart.'

'Get off me!'

'Detective Sergeant Elias Crest,' he said, flashing his warrant card at her with his free hand. 'Why were you watching me? Why did you run?' She ignored him, pushing his arms, but he held tight. 'Answer me and I'll let you go.'

'All right, just get your hands off me!' He released her but closed the gap between them. He watched her adjust her clothes.

'I'm waiting.'

'And I'm fucking freezing. You mind if we do this somewhere else?'

He looked surprised, but nodded, taking a cautious step back. 'Don't try to run again.'

She glowered. 'Not in these heels.' She shoved past him. 'The Clover. You're paying.'

CHAPTER 52

The Clover was a greasy spoon just off the main high street run by a third-generation Irish family. Not the nicest of places, but it was cheap if not so cheerful, and it was warm, even if it did smell of cooking fat.

Elias had never been in there, but he'd heard of it – most policemen had. It wasn't uncommon for trouble to break out around here after kicking-out time in the pubs and clubs. The Clover was the only place that stayed open until 3:00 a.m., that wasn't a fast-food joint or kebab house.

Choosing a table in the corner, the girl sat down without removing her coat. The place was busy, mostly with groups of young men.

Elias ordered two mugs of tea, then sat watching her in silence until a grubby-looking man slammed down two steaming mugs in front of them. She reached forward and cupped one mug in her hands, breathing in the steam.

'Why were you watching me?'

Her eyes, smudged with black kohl, looked hard into his. She leaned in closer across the faded yellow table and glanced over his shoulder, checking it was safe to talk.

'I may have some information for you.'

He raised his eyebrows. 'About?'

'Before I tell you anything, I'm making it clear, I'm not going to the police station, or giving a statement, you understand?'

'Well that depends on what you know, doesn't it?' he said, folding his arms across his chest.

The girl shook her head. 'Nah, mate, I'm telling you how it is. I had second thoughts already tonight. I tried to walk away, but you came after me.' Elias didn't react. He just held her stare. 'You understand what I'm sayin'?'

'Why don't you just tell me whatever it is you know, and we'll see how relevant you are.'

The girl pushed her hair behind her head and scowled at him. 'I didn't have to come to you. I could've gone to any one of you lot back at Hedonism.'

'So why didn't you?'

Silence.

'How'd you know we were police officers? You been spying on us leaving the station or something?'

She took a swig of tea, but her eyes never left his. She sat in silence for an age, so Elias reached for his wallet and produced a folded note, shoving it across the table towards her.

She picked it up, unfolding it slowly. Her eyes narrowed.

'What's your name? You can tell me that much, can't you?'

'Mandy.'

'That's not your real name.'

'And you're a tight bastard,' she said, slinging the money back at him. 'I don't need your charity.'

Elias left the note on the table. 'How about some food instead?'

Her eyes lit up. She nodded. He went up to the counter, ordered her one of The Clover's all-day breakfasts. When he came back to the table she seemed more relaxed.

'I've got all night,' he said, 'as long as it takes.' She looked away and picked at her nails.

'It's about Nola Grant. The man you're after…' She trailed off, 'I know where he works.'

'What?' He sprang forward, arms across the table. 'Who is he?'

She shook her head. 'I don't know his name. I just know where he works.'

'Where?' He pulled out a pen from his jacket pocket and grabbed a white paper napkin from the dispenser next to them.

'He can't know who told you.'

'Let me worry about that, just tell me where.'

'He works in a slaughterhouse.'

Elias's face dropped. He looked at her, face stern. 'Which one?'

She shrugged.

'You don't know?'

Another shake of the head.

'So you know he works in a slaughterhouse, but don't know which one... Who knows how many there are in Heartfordshire? How do you know he even works in one? What's he look like? And more importantly, how do you know any of this?'

'I can't tell you.'

'Well you'd better start telling me something, darlin', 'cos I'm losing patience.'

A plate landed on the table with a loud bang. The grubby-looking man gave them both a weird look, then skulked back towards the kitchen. The girl gingerly picked up her knife and fork, staring at the food.

She looked at Elias.

'Be my guest.' He waited until she'd taken the first bite. 'Was he a paying customer?'

She threw him a dark look. 'It's that obvious what I am?'

'Hey,' he said, raising his hands, 'you don't look like you do a nine-to-five, put it that way.'

She stared at him. Then her face softened and she nodded, accepting his words. He was relieved she didn't just take off. 'OK,' he said, 'how does this man fit in with Nola?'

She wolfed down a slice of toast as if it were her last meal, then swigged her tea. 'I saw him with her the night she disappeared,' she said between mouthfuls. 'I'd been with him... privately. He told me things... fantasies he had.'

She stopped talking, eyeing the money on the table. He followed her eyes, then pushed the note towards her. She hesitated before stashing it in her pocket. 'He told me he had a fantasy, an urge, to take a girl, then see how long he could keep her alive before he killed her.'

Elias's face fell.

He reached across the table, grabbed her hand as she went to shove the fork in her mouth. He squeezed her wrist. His voice was menacing when he spoke. 'And you didn't think to tell anyone about this?'

'I didn't take him seriously.'

'Why not?'

She leaned forward, her eyes deadly serious. 'I've heard a lot worse, Sergeant, believe me. All these twisted fuckers out there cheatin' on their wives and girlfriends... Most of them have some kind of sick fantasy they get off on. I do things I don't always want to, just to survive. One man's turn-off is another man's dream. If I took it all seriously, I would've been in a loony bin long ago.'

'I don't care why you do what you do,' he sneered, 'but you got to do better than this.'

He sat back in his chair and stared at her. She looked a mess: bitten down nails, a dull look in her eyes as if her soul had been sucked out from her long ago. Her hair was messy and her cheeks were chapped from the cold.

'OK,' she said, pushing her plate away from her unfinished, 'he told me he worked in a slaughterhouse and after me, he was going to get some trash a few streets away. He'd picked her.'

'And you guessed it was Nola?'

'I knew it was.'

'How? Were you friends?'

A long pause. 'I don't have friends, not real ones. Not in this job.'

'OK, let's say I buy into what you're saying—'

'If you believe my story, then you'll know I'm telling the truth when I say I followed him. Right after we'd—'

'You did it in his car?' Elias cut in, now making notes on the napkin.

She shook her head. 'No.' Elias raised his eyebrows. She avoided his eyes. 'It was behind a shop, where I knew there were no cameras.'

Elias waved his hand, dismissing her, not wanting the gory details. 'So you saw him take Nola?'

'I saw her walk off with him. He didn't take her by force. I didn't follow them because I didn't believe he was serious, and she went with him willingly.'

The girl continued, telling Elias what time and which direction she saw them heading. Everything matched what they already knew, but it was possible she'd just got the information from the newspapers.

'You must have a good description of what he looked like?' he asked, as he sipped the last of his tea.

A rowdy group of boys piled in, taking seats by the window. Elias saw her cower, turning her head away from them. 'The man?' he pressed.

Again, she looked reluctant to speak.

He sighed, looking her hard in the eyes. 'Look, you came to me, remember? All I have to do is walk out of here and leave you and your conscience to battle it out together... Choice is yours.' When she remained silent, he pushed his chair out, scraping the legs across the floor.

'No, wait!' She reached for his wrist. She gave him a description of the man, and although it wasn't much, since it was dark when she'd been with him, the description of his clothing was an exact match for the man from the CCTV. He knew she could also have got this from the news.

'He's average height, average looks, average build.' He shook his head. 'Our man is like every other bloke on the street.' He walked towards the door. He heard her scoot from her chair.

'I can't do this formally. I know I sound crazy but you have to believe me.'

He looked amused and shrugged. 'Why?'

'Because I'm all you've got.'

He stared at her. He mulled over her words. He didn't even know how credible she was.

'What's in this for you?'

She shrugged. 'I guess I feel guilty.'

'Look, Mandy-that's-not-your-real-name, my hands are tied. I need names, places. Something better than what you've given me.'

'I can't give you what I don't know myself.'

'Well,' he said, handing her his card, 'when you've remembered more, including your name, give me a call.'

'I've just given you new information,' she protested, drawing glances from nearby tables. 'You're making a big mistake if you ignore me.'

Elias closed the gap between them. 'I think I'd be making a mistake if I took you seriously.'

She backed away from him. 'There's your dilemma.' He cocked his head to one side, waiting for her to finish. 'What if I'm telling the truth? He's taking them faster, isn't he? He's not wasting any time killing them either. What if another girl dies 'cos you didn't listen?'

CHAPTER 53

Elias made sure she took his card, telling her to call him if she remembered anything else. When he asked for her number, she'd been reluctant to give it to him, but in the end she'd relented, scrawling her number on his napkin.

He watched her disappear from view outside the café, then he pulled out his mobile, punched in the number, and waited.

Almost instantly he heard a loud beeping tone and an automated voice telling him the number he'd dialled wasn't recognised.

Just as he'd thought.

He shoved the napkin inside his jacket pocket and debated whether or not to go back to Hedonism and tell Claire about the mystery woman, or go home and see what leads he could find on his own.

It took a matter of seconds to decide.

Pride and ambition came to the surface, but a part of him also wanted to prove to Claire that he could do this, that her taking a risk on him was worth it. He walked back past Hedonism, towards the taxi rank.

*

When Elias got home, he poured himself a strong drink and switched on the television, but kept the volume low.

He couldn't concentrate in complete silence and had to have some form of background noise.

He unfolded the napkin he'd written on in the café, slumped down on his leather sofa, and read over the information again. The girl had refused to do an e-fit, or offer any further help for that matter, and he pondered her credibility. Despite his reservations, he felt there had been truth in her story. Somewhere.

He retrieved his laptop from the coffee table and booted it up. He accessed Google, typing in a search for slaughterhouses in Hertfordshire.

1,050 results with the key words.

He narrowed his search down a bit, hit Enter.

Jesus…

A long night ahead.

*

Elias woke with a jolt to the sound of drunken singing. He wiped a hand over his face and rubbed his eyes. The sound that had woken him was coming from the flat above. He glanced at his watch:

01:00 a.m.

He reached for the television remote, hit Standby and looked down at his laptop, which was balanced precariously on his knees. He logged back into his Internet, session.

He stared at the screen for a few minutes before a thought occurred to him. He thought back to what Claire had said. The manner in which the victims had died.

He opened another web page and accessed Google Maps, typed in another search. When the results sprang up, he minimised the screen and compared it to his first search results, which ran down half of the laptop screen. He leaned in closer, not seeing much at first, until he came to his last result.

His mouth felt dry. His lips parted a fraction. He made the map screen bigger again, stared at it awhile, then typed in two destinations, comparing the distance between them both.

He sat back and just stared at the screen.

Then an uneasy smile spread across his face as he realised the connection he might have just found.

Something so simple they'd been missing it for weeks.

CHAPTER 54

1st December

Felicity Davenport's autopsy had been conducted and samples taken to be analysed, and Claire had requested that Danika expedite the results.

'I'm putting you on loudspeaker. DI Fletcher's here with me. What've you got for me?' Claire asked, turning on the speakerphone in her office.

Danika paused. 'Well, it's all in the report but I may have something here.' They heard paper ruffle. 'Felicity was killed the same way as the other two, and there are the exact same ligature marks on the ankles, and marks on her wrists which are consistent with her being restrained. There were no signs of sexual assault. In fact, Felicity was a virgin... It appears she was washed, which I think was done before she died.

'There was a considerable amount of dirt underneath her nails, despite obvious attempts to remove it, and traces of soap. There are cut marks under the nails, tears in the nail bed, suggesting he tried to clean underneath them, with a nail file, or something similar. There are small abrasions and a cut underneath her thumbnail which is fairly deep and shows some signs of healing, which means it was inflicted before he killed her. I also think she put up a fight whilst he did it, hence the deep cut.'

More sounds of ruffled paper. 'There was also dirt under her toenails, but there was no obvious attempt to remove it. I don't think the killer was expecting her to get in that state.'

'Why attempt to remove dirt under fingernails, wash her body, but leave the toenails?' said Stefan.

'Exactly,' Danika continued. 'There was also a small amount of dirt in her hair, a smudge on her inner thigh that was very faint, and I found a small piece of sponge in the crease between her groin and thigh. The dirt found was considerable under her toenails, which leads me to believe she has been kept somewhere dirty or she crawled on the ground.'

Claire cut in at that point. 'You think our man just forgot to clean her toenails? Somehow that doesn't sit right. Why not kill her, then clean her up? Take his time?'

Stefan sat forward in his chair and offered an idea. 'Maybe time was against him. Maybe he was surprised? Maybe something happened that he didn't plan on, like she managed to get away, fell in dirt and he overlooked her toenails in his haste?'

'Actually, Stefan,' Danika said, 'that theory leads me to my next point… I sent swabs to the lab and although there was soil present, we found something else: animal excrement.'

Silence.

'Still there, guys?'

'You mean animal shit,' Claire clarified.

'Pig, to be exact.'

'Danika, you're telling me she was rolling around in pig shit?'

A nervous, uneasy laugh crackled over the speaker. 'Not exactly. A mixture of dirt and excrement, from the ground.'

'There wasn't anything like this on the previous two bodies,' Stefan cut in.

'No, which is why it would be a reasonable assumption that somewhere in the killer's plan, something went wrong.'

'Are there any properties in the soil that can be associated with a particular place or region?' Claire asked.

'I'm in the process of trying to find out where it's from, but considering the pig excrement, it's reasonable to assume farmland.'

Claire thanked Danika, who said she'd be in touch as soon as she had more information, and hung up with the press of a button. Her eyes met Stefan's.

'I want a list of all the farms in and around the areas our victims circulated in, see if there're any farms that keep pigs...' She trailed off, her eyes glazing over. Then a thought occurred.

Jerking forward, she hit redial on the telephone. Danika's voice cracked over the line when she answered.

'Danika,' Claire rushed into the mouthpiece, 'there's something you said, right back with the first victim, Nola Grant. The day of her autopsy, you said she'd been stuck like a pig.'

Danika paused. 'I was speaking figuratively.'

'I'm talking about a slaughter. The wounds inflicted on all the victims were a skilled cut to sever the main arteries... Like the method used in animal slaughter... Yes?'

There was another long pause.

'Yes, that's correct.'

'Thanks.' Claire quickly hung up. 'Stefan, I want a list of all the slaughterhouses in Hertfordshire as well. Our killer is a pro at what he does. He's had training. Danika said it herself; the cuts to the neck are performed by an expert. He has got it right each and every time, and it wasn't a fluke.'

CHAPTER 55

Claire had everyone together in the incident room, briefed them and assigned Matthews with the task of getting a list together of both the farms and slaughterhouses.

When she headed back to her office, she was followed by Stefan with Elias. She raised her eyes at them.

'Tell her what you just told me,' Stefan said to Elias. His voice was angry, which Claire knew was unusual in itself.

'Tell me what?'

Elias was quiet and he had a file underneath one arm, which he kept a tight hold of. 'Crest?'

'You're gonna be pissed I didn't tell you straight away, but I needed to clarify a few things first,' he said, taking a seat in front of her desk. He put the folder down in front of him.

'When I left Hedonism, it was because I saw someone. A girl.'

'A girl?'

'I saw her watching me in Hedonism when we had our…' He trailed off, glancing at Stefan. 'After our chat. She was hiding her face fairly well, then when I went to speak to her, she bolted for the door. Something about the whole thing wasn't right.'

'Then you left.'

He nodded. 'I followed her. She tried to run but I caught up with her, got her talking.'

Claire waited patiently as he retold the conversation, giving her a fleeting description of the girl. When he'd finished, she let her head slump into her hands, her elbows on the desk.

'I need to speak to this girl, Crest. It's important. Why didn't you tell me any of this before?'

'I'm telling you now.'

Her cheeks reddened. 'You're skating on very thin ice. This isn't a one-horse race, we're a team.'

Stefan frowned and waded in before Elias could answer. 'Nola's pregnancy.' The room fell silent. 'Were you the one who leaked it?'

Claire's face turned to Elias, eyes burning into his flesh. 'Answer the question, Crest.'

He was silent, not giving anything away. Then he took a deep breath. 'No.'

'I don't believe you.'

'Look,' he said, voice raised, thrusting the contents of his folder into her face, 'I don't care what you believe… I did this for you, for the team.' He thumped the sheets down on the table. 'I made a list of all the slaughterhouses in Hertfordshire, then I got to thinking about the way the victims were cut. I made the link between the whole slaughter-style executions. Tying the girls upside-down, one expert cut to the neck, and the bleeding out.'

His eyes rose and met her stare. She looked pissed, but he didn't waver. 'I then thought back to Felicity's body. I saw the muck under her nails. One of the slaughterhouses on this list is in close proximity to a farm. Alarm bells started ringing.'

He realised his knuckles had turned white with the pressure of his weight leaning on her desk. He eased off, and when he spoke again, his voice was calm.

'When you told us what Danika had found, I realised there was some strength to my theory.'

'None of the other girls had anything usable or relevant under their nails,' Stefan said.

'Yes, but there's the theory that Felicity almost got away. That she caught the killer off guard. She could've fallen and crawled but never made it.'

Elias laid out a particular sheet of paper for her to see.

'The nearest slaughterhouse in the area where all three victims were abducted and found is here,' he said, pointing to a name and address. 'Royston slaughterhouse. They process cattle.'

He placed another sheet in front of her. 'Here, two miles down the road from the slaughterhouse, is Hatcher Lodge... A pig farm.'

CHAPTER 56

Claire had organised two teams. DC Harper was to accompany Elias to Hatcher Lodge, while she and Stefan would visit the slaughterhouse.

Claire followed Elias, who was in the pool car, into Royston, a town about fifteen miles from Haverbridge, which sat near the army barracks of Bassingbourn. They drove through the main town and headed out into open countryside, where the snow lay thicker and almost unspoilt on the land around them.

When they reached the turning into Steeple Morden, Elias took a left, sign-posted for Hatcher Lodge, while Claire carried on, two miles ahead, turning into Ashwell Road.

The top of the slaughterhouse came into view, sitting just above hedgerows. They entered the visitor car park, found a space, then walked across the forecourt towards the entrance. The snow here had turned to a brown-coloured slush where many vehicles had driven over it, churning it up into deep ridges and furrows.

They walked through the doors and saw the reception ahead of them. Although it was incredibly basic, it was equipped with the essentials, complete with a smiling receptionist behind a large desk.

They showed the woman their warrant cards and she took them through a winding corridor to the site manager's office, a small, poky room, where the paint was peeling off the ceiling.

Calvin Reeves stared back at them. He didn't speak until after the receptionist explained why they were there.

'Well, when I headed off for work this morning, it never occurred to me that I would be sitting face-to-face with a pair of coppers from a murder inquiry.' He paused, glancing at Claire. 'I've seen you on telly… What can I do for you, Chief Inspector?'

CHAPTER 57

Two miles away, Elias and Harper were standing waiting for someone in charge to come and speak to them. Elias was leaning against the car, staring at his feet, when the wind picked up and his face wrinkled.

'What's the matter?' Harper said, kicking loose muddy snow from his boots.

'You smell that?'

Harper sniffed hard a couple of times and shook his head. 'Can't smell nothing.'

'Christ, it stinks enough.'

'What does?'

'Pigs.'

Harper smiled. 'My uncle's a farmer. I used to spend a lot of time up on his land when I was a kid. Guess I'm used to the smell of a working farm.'

'It must be a terrible thing to have to get used to it.'

'Put someone in a place or job for long enough and they'll soon get used to anything.' He pointed behind Elias. 'Looks like they've not forgotten us after all.'

Elias turned and saw a man in his mid-thirties heading towards them. He was dressed in tatty clothes, spattered with mud. Elias tried to ignore the smell as the man spoke when he approached them.

'I hear you're looking for the owner?'

Elias nodded. 'Are you him?'

'No, I'm Hal. You want Doug, Douglas Hatcher. He owns this place, but he's in Scotland. I'm in charge until he's back.'

'How long has he been away?'

'Let's see,' Hal said, scratching his head. Elias exchanged a funny look with Harper. Weird hick.

'He left end of October. His ex-wife is ill.'

'Ex-wife?' Harper said.

Hal nodded. 'They're on good terms.' He eyed both men, his eyes nervous. 'Doug's due back end of week... Is it important?' He wiped his hands off on a dirty-looking rag.

Elias paused before he spoke. 'Is it just pigs you rear?'

Another quick nod. 'Yeah, we rear them for slaughter. Free-range, our pigs, as well,' he said proudly, rubbing his belly. 'Better taste.'

Elias pulled his mouth into a thin smile.

'How many workers you got here?' asked Harper.

'About ten, usually. One is part-time, and then there's William, Doug's son, but he's not here all day.'

'Where's the son now?' Elias asked. He looked around at the farmhouse and many outbuildings. His face then shot straight back to Hal's when he didn't answer straight away. 'Something wrong?'

'No, no... William works a few hours away from the farm. Comes back by nightfall usually, but he's... How should I say it?' Hal looked at his feet, mulling over in his head for the word he was looking for. 'He's a little detached... I don't want to use the word retard, but...'

Harper's eyes narrowed. 'Detached? Like distant? Not involved?'

'Detached as in simple,' Hal said. 'I don't like describing him like that, but it's the only word I can think of. He's socially inept, I guess. Doctors can't agree on whether he's got some kind of autism, or if he's just plain odd, know what I mean? I tend to go with odd, though,' he said, grinning.

Elias felt a wave of anticipation shoot up his spine. 'Where does he work?'

'Two miles or so, that way,' Hal said, pointing behind them, to the road that ran past the farm, further north. Elias's eyes followed Hal's line of vision. He knew instantly where Hal meant.

'He works at the slaughterhouse.'

CHAPTER 58

Claire and Stefan had explained what had brought them to the slaughterhouse, and Calvin Reeves had spent the best part of that time biting the side of his cheek with the tension. When they were finished, he'd remained quiet for several minutes, processing all the information.

'I've been following this case closely,' he said at length, 'and I am of course willing to help in any way I can, but I still don't see what I can tell you about this place that you don't know already.'

'We're interested in the skill required for the actual process of slaughter,' Stefan said. 'Your staff, are they trained here or do they come here ready to go, so to speak?'

Calvin seemed to mull over the question awhile, searching for the right words. 'We tend to train in-house, although when I look at new potential employees, I keep an eye out for those who already have some experience.'

'And how do you hire?' Claire asked.

'Agencies mainly.'

Claire heard her BlackBerry ring in her pocket. She fished it out, glancing at the caller ID.

DS Crest.

'I'm sorry, Mr Reeves, but I need to take this call.'

Calvin smiled and gestured towards the door. 'Not a problem, Chief Inspector.'

Out in the corridor, Claire was hanging on Elias's every word.

'William Hatcher, aged thirty, has been working for the slaughterhouse for two years now, and it's textbook stuff... Socially inept, withdrawn, has difficulty building and maintaining relationships, and that's just for starters.'

He paused, took a deep breath. 'Here's the cherry on the cake...' he said, drawing it out, 'I've seen his bedroom... Hatcher has three separate pictures of all three women. Harper found them under the bed.' Claire was silent, taking in every word, processing it, fitting it all together. 'Still there, Guv?'

'Yes, I'm listening.' Claire looked through the glass window in the door to Calvin Reeves's office and ran her hand through her hair, while she thought. 'OK, here's what I want you to do.'

*

Calvin's face dropped when he caught the steely look in Claire's eyes when she came back into his office.

'You've a man working here by the name of William Hatcher.'

Calvin nodded, his face cautious. 'Yes, he's been here a couple of years now, good worker too.' When she remained silent, Calvin straightened himself in his chair. He looked uncomfortable. 'What's he done?'

'Does Hatcher work on the killing floor?'

Calvin gave a small nod, his face showing his unease.

Stefan caught on instantly. 'He makes the kill?'

'For God's sake!' Calvin shook his head. 'You're making it sound something truly awful and we get enough of that with the animal-meat-is-murder brigade.' He sat forward in his chair, looking them both square in the eye. 'The way we process the cattle is done in the most humane way possible. Each one is stunned using a captive bolt before they're—'

'Hung upside-down by their hind legs, before a jugular, carotid artery and trachea is severed, allowing blood to drain rapidly from the body,' Claire interrupted, finishing his sentence.

He stared at her, open-mouthed. 'Just what is going on here?'

'Mr Reeves,' Claire said, 'we need to speak to William, right now.'

CHAPTER 59

The killing floor, as Calvin dubbed it, was a fusion of bright lights, stainless steel, blood and stark white bone.

They stood on a long gangway above the area below, which had a set of metal steps leading down to where the workers were processing the cattle. The noise was almost unbearable, a mixture of clanking machinery and the fast-talking hum of workers. Claire peered down and saw a row of carcasses hanging up by the hind legs.

The workers below all wore full-length white aprons, covered by a plastic overcoat, white boots and blue hairnets and gloves. Some of them had facial masks over the lower face, blocking the smell.

'You see,' Calvin said, voice raised over the din below, pointing towards the dead animals, 'death is very quick. Then the head and feet are removed. Before the hide is separated, the digestive tract is removed, preventing faecal contamination, which takes skill.'

Claire stared at him and he shifted uneasily. She pointed below. 'Which one is Hatcher?'

Calvin looked down and after a several seconds, he reached out, pointing to a man with shaggy black curly hair. He was tall and wide, a mixture of fat and muscle. Even with the bulk of his overalls, it was obvious that he was a big and powerful man underneath.

He was about to cut into a cow hanging in front of him. Claire's eyes focused on the sharp knife in his right hand. She watched him slice into the animal's throat with one fluid motion, which lasted less than a second. The blood spilled from the animal, and she watched Hatcher stare at the trough below, mesmerised.

From where she stood, he didn't look similar to the image they had of the prime suspect caught on CCTV. Claire wasn't sure it was the same man.

'William!'

Claire's eyes shot back to Calvin, who was now leaning against the safety rail, trying to get Hatcher's attention down below. There was so much noise that Hatcher didn't hear.

'What the hell are you doing?!' Claire snapped, striding over to him. Calvin looked at her, perplexed by her expression.

'I can't allow you down there as you are. Health and Safety. *Regulations*, Chief Inspector.' He shook his head. 'It'll be easier to get him out of his overalls and we'll talk in my office.' He looked down again and shouted at the top of his voice, 'William!' A couple of workers looked up, and another went over to Hatcher, nudged his arm.

Pointed up.

Claire's breath caught in her throat as his eyes met hers. She held her breath.

Don't you dare run...

CHAPTER 60

Hatcher's eyes rested on Claire's a moment longer than planned. Then he bolted for the door nearest to him.

'Shit!'

Before Calvin could think about what was happening, Claire shoved past him and descended the metal staircase.

'Hey, you can't go down there!'

Workers on the floor below started jeering and shouting, some uncertain what was happening, others enjoying the chaos unfolding around them.

'Sorry, Mr Reeves,' Stefan said, pushing past him. He bounded down the stairs after Claire. He took the stairs two at a time, but Claire was faster. By the time he'd reached the bottom, Claire was already at the door Hatcher had escaped through.

He shoved a few workers out of the way and pushed the door open with force. He lost his footing and skidded across the shiny vinyl flooring that ran down a narrow corridor. He bounced off the wall opposite him and sprinted down the corridor, not bothering to look back to see if Calvin had followed them.

*

Hatcher looked over his shoulder as he ran down the winding corridor and into the men's locker room. He grabbed his coat

off the hook, sending others onto the floor, and ran back out
again. He pulled the coat around him.

'Hatcher!'

He looked and saw Claire running full speed towards him.
He bolted, running the other way, his breath now coming in
short sharp bursts, showing no signs of slowing down.

Claire shouted after him, but he didn't stop. As they turned
another sharp corner, she saw him running towards what
looked like a dead end.

It wasn't until she drew closer that she saw it was a fire
exit ahead. Hatcher pushed his arms out in front, his big
hands locking onto the bar across the door, pushing down
hard. The door flung open and an alarm instantly sounded
right above her head.

The door swung back in and she shot her right leg out,
kicking it back, as she propelled herself out of the door and
into the open.

*

Stefan had lost sight of Claire.

Then he heard the alarm go off, wincing at the sudden pain
in his ears. He followed the corridor round the bend and saw
the fire exit. He forced it open, running through it. He headed
around towards the car park, but he couldn't see any sign of
them.

*

Claire followed Hatcher as he ran out of the car park, but he
headed back around to the other side of the building, rather
than out of the main entrance.

She almost lost her footing a few times, her boots skidding
in the melting snow and ice. The grey of the building whipped

past her in a haze, as she sprinted onto snow-covered grass. Soon she was at the back of the slaughterhouse, where there was nothing but lines of barbed wire and open fields ahead, with another road off in the distance.

She paused to get her bearings. Hands on thighs, bent forward, panting hard. Heart slamming in her chest.

She saw Hatcher emerge out of the corner of her eye, but the realisation came too late. She turned just as he collided with her, his head bent, heavy meaty arms forcing her to the side, and she crashed hard, shoulder first, into the brick wall of an outbuilding.

The force sucked the wind from her in an instant. She slumped down to the ground, hands clutching her chest. She forced a large intake of breath. Spluttered. Her eyes misted over.

'Shit, are you OK?' Stefan was at her side, but she shoved him away.

'Hatcher, go after Hatcher!'

*

Hatcher was already at the barbed wire fence, pulling himself over it, but he snagged his jacket, leaving fine strands of cotton behind. He checked his mobile was still inside the inner coat pocket.

Then he ran. Ran faster than ever.

He knew the area well; after all, he'd lived here all his life. He knew if he could just make it out to the road ahead, he could go to ground, and slip back into the main town, keeping to the fields and country lanes.

There was no doubt in his mind they would find the things in the car back at the farm, the stuff in his bedroom. That didn't matter now. There were two more left. Two more that had to be saved, and if not, he'd end their lives, as he had the others.

CHAPTER 61

The evidence before them was startling.

William Hatcher's room was littered with evidence. Claire eyed the pictures of the three girls that Harper had found under Hatcher's bed and grimaced. Each girl was facing away from the camera, clearly unaware she'd been photographed.

Just how long had Hatcher been stalking these girls?

She walked outside.

'The car Hatcher drives is company owned,' Stefan said, coming up beside her.

She peered into the car Hatcher had been using when he wasn't at work. A beat-up, mud-spattered 2001 Range Rover SUV.

Wisps of light-brown hair were stuck in the backseat upholstery.

Felicity.

'Looks like he's our guy,' Elias said beside her. 'SOCOs have found a smashed-up mobile. Think it's Nola Grant's. SIM card's been burnt to a crisp though.'

Stefan waited for a reaction, but Claire's eyes stayed focused on the car in front of her.

'I've got teams out with the dogs, and a there's heavy police presence out looking for Hatcher. I've been in touch with his father, and he's flying back on the next available flight from Scotland,' he said.

Claire's face was unreadable. If she was relieved they'd had a break in the investigation, she didn't show it.

'I want more people up here to search the farm,' she said. 'Anything in his locker at the slaughterhouse?' she shouted over her shoulder at Harper, who was jogging towards them.

'Nothing in the locker. If he had a mobile, he's got it or he's dumped it somewhere,' he said.

'I want the surrounding fields cordoned off and searched,' she said. She rubbed her shoulder. Christ, it hurt.

Elias had remained quiet, but had noticed her rubbing her shoulder. He felt a surge of energy in his body and recognised it instantly.

Compassion.

And it was all for Claire Winters, which surprised him.

'We've had a look around the outhouses. There's a small building round the back… it's got a trough in there, and a suspension system above it. That farm hand, Hal? He says it's usually kept locked. Out of use,' Stefan said. He paused, watching the frown on her face. 'What's the matter?'

She raised her eyebrows. 'You don't think this is all too easy? All this evidence suddenly piled in our lap, all where Hatcher lives? Quite easy to find, too?'

He shrugged. 'I think it is what it is.'

'Yeah, fucking luck. It's a breakthrough, Guv,' Elias said.

'So why would he take so much time and care, watching over the girls, finding out their movements, the location of CCTV cameras, hiding his face, only to get sloppy when he killed Felicity?'

She circled them both, her arms wrapping tighter around her body when the wind picked up, raging across the open fields. 'You know it doesn't add up.'

'Given what we know so far, not all the lights are on up here,' Stefan said, gesturing to his head. 'Hatcher's messed up. Made his mistake. Felicity put up a fight, caught him by surprise, he panicked and tried to clean her up like the others, but missed her toenails.'

Claire prodded a finger into his chest, her face deadly serious. 'I find it hard to believe Hatcher could be clever enough to organise any of this.'

Stefan batted her hand away. 'I'd have thought you'd be happy. We've got all this evidence that's just landed in your bloody lap.'

'But no Hatcher!'

'It's only a matter of time before the dogs track him down.'

Claire started to speak but couldn't find the words. Instead she glowered at him. Elias pulled his eyes up from staring at the floor. He felt more than a bit awkward when he spoke.

'Douglas Hatcher has volunteered to come to the station and answer any questions we have for him. He's just as shocked as you are, Guv. Said William is incapable of masterminding something like this.'

Stefan frowned, turning to face Elias. 'You're going to ignore all the evidence here? Hatcher did it. End of story… and when it comes down to it, none of us really know what someone is capable of. None of us.'

Claire turned on her heels, ignoring him, and walked from the forecourt. She headed towards the outbuilding drawing the most attention.

'We're finished in there, if you wanna go in,' said Charlotte, the principle SOCO. 'You may want a face mask when you get suited up.'

Claire ignored her and pulled on the Tyvek suit given to her, along with her overshoes and gloves. She declined the face mask. She wanted to smell the place. Breathe it in. Experience what the victims must have felt and feared before drawing in their final breath.

She walked inside. Her eyes darted around, seeing the stains on the floor. Rust-red and brown.

Blood and shit.

The suspension bars above were also stained. She glanced into the trough. More stains. She sniffed hard, recognised the smell of blood.

William Hatcher's mind, she thought, must be one of the most depraved and scarred she'd ever come across.

'We've found more hair in here too,' Charlotte said, watching Claire. 'Human hair.'

Claire's eyes flickered over her face, then back to the trough. She shut her eyes.

She heard the screams of Hannah Davenport again, calling for her daughter, resounding through her head. She tried to bury them away, deep down somewhere else where she couldn't hear them any more.

For the first time in what seemed an age, it was something she couldn't force herself to do.

CHAPTER 62

The night sky was clear, except for another random flurry of snowflakes bouncing around in the wind. Claire watched the flakes batter against her office window, then returned her attention to the man sitting opposite her, her eyes taking in every inch of him.

A tired-looking Douglas Hatcher, with his well-lined skin, sat facing her, clasping his hands tightly in front of him on the table.

His expression was pained.

He shook his head and picked at the rough skin around each of his fingertips. His nails were filthy.

'That's not my son.' He pushed the image taken from the CCTV camera opposite McDonald's back across the table towards Claire. 'William is taller than this man, for a start.' His dark eyes met hers. 'Whatever you're accusing him of doing is…' He paused, searching for the right word. 'It's impossible.' He picked a lump of skin from his cuticle, flicking it to the floor. 'I've never seen him in these clothes before, either.'

Claire's mouth pulled into an icy smile as she leaned closer. 'How'd you explain the blood traces in the trough from the outbuilding on your farm?'

Douglas grimaced. 'I can't, can I?'

'What about the photographs of each victim in your son's bedroom? Then there's the hair, the colour a pretty close match to Felicity's, in the boot of William's car. The hair has been ripped out, root intact, we'll get a match. We're confident it'll be Felicity's.'

Douglas hesitated. 'It's a company car.'

'Which only you and your son actually drive… and you've been in Scotland since the end of October.'

Silence.

'Tell us about that,' Claire continued. 'Why didn't you take William to see his mother?'

Douglas grew angry. 'Have you ever seen someone dying of cancer, Chief Inspector? Let me tell you, it's not something I'd wish on my worst enemy, let alone my son.' He paused, pinched the bridge of his nose. 'I wanted to protect him. I didn't think he'd be able to cope, mentally.'

'Your son's got some mental impairment, I understand?' Stefan said, sceptically.

'It's been… difficult. William's never been diagnosed. I didn't want to keep dragging him from one doctor to the next when he was younger.'

'But you left him behind to tend the farm and work a normal job?' Claire said.

Douglas sighed. 'Look, I don't expect someone like you to understand. He's socially inept, not brain-dead.' He pointed a finger at her. 'I never left him in charge of the farm. Hal is my second-in-command but he tries to make William believe he has a say in things. And having the job at the slaughterhouse helps him. As far as the boss there is concerned he's just a little odd.'

Douglas wiped a tear away from the corner of his eye. 'I can't explain what's been found on the farm. I made Will promise to keep up his appointments though. I hoped it'd be enough until I got back from Scotland.'

'What appointments?' Claire's voice was full of unease.

'What, something you didn't know already?'

'Answer the question.'

He looked down at his fingers, picked away at a bit more skin. 'Tell me, Chief Inspector, have you heard of psychotherapy?'

CHAPTER 63

Claire found the home number for Mitchell Curran, and after the fifth ring his wife answered the phone.

'He's out, Chief Inspector.'

'Where?'

'Working late at the office, I should imagine.'

'Are you sure this time?' Claire heard the soft intake of breath. Exasperation probably, but Claire didn't give a damn what Stephanie Curran thought. She'd lied to her before. There was nothing to stop her doing it again.

'What do you mean by that?' Stephanie's voice was calm but there was a hard edge to it. She was pissed off.

'He's working late and you're not sure where,' Claire said.

Stephanie sighed. 'What did you want my husband for, exactly?'

'William Hatcher.'

'Who?'

Claire paused, letting the silence hang heavy. 'William Hatcher. Is he one of your husband's clients?'

Stephanie thought a moment. 'No, I don't believe so.' She gripped the receiver tighter in her hand. 'What's this about?'

Claire hung up without another word. Her hand rested on the telephone as she looked at Stefan, then Douglas. 'She doesn't know your son.'

Douglas shrugged. 'Maybe she genuinely doesn't know.'

'I doubt that.'

Douglas sat forward and buried his face in his hands, shaking his head. 'I can't believe this is happening.'

Claire's eyes remained cold. 'You'd better start believing… this is real.'

'I've told you already, my son couldn't mastermind something like this. Maybe he's been set up.'

'What, by Curran?' she said.

'Yes, why not? He can be linked with each victim, you said it yourself.'

She paused. 'And here's another theory. Maybe Curran picks them out, and your son murders them?'

'Now you're being ridiculous.'

'You can't argue with cold hard facts, and the evidence at your house and in your vehicle.'

'You're making an assumption.'

'And your farm was a killing ground for three innocent women, Mr Hatcher. If I were you, I'd stop clutching at straws and help us find your son before he kills again.'

Douglas broke down. His shoulders rose and fell with his grief.

She lowered her voice. 'Stefan, I want Mitchell Curran brought in. Now. Find him.'

'Yes, Guv.'

'Organise a warrant to search his house and office at F. B. C.' She turned to Douglas. 'Start singing… Where would William go if he couldn't come to you?'

He frowned.

'Tell me,' she snapped. 'Help us, help your son.'

CHAPTER 64

Mitchell Curran sat watching the news reports on the TV in his office, and the live updates streaming across the bottom of his laptop screen. He stared hard at the headline sweeping across the bottom of the page.

William Hatcher wanted in connection with the murders of three women.

This wasn't good.

Not for him, not for anyone. He knew people at F. B. C. would be asking the questions he feared, dreaded… If they weren't already, they very soon would be.

He went to his filing cabinet and his mobile rang. He stared at the caller ID and saw it was his wife. He let it go to voicemail. He knew she'd have questions. Questions he wasn't prepared to answer, not right now anyway.

She was probably wondering why he wasn't home yet, why he was staying so late. This was something he rarely did, but tonight he thought it was necessary.

He opened the filing cabinet just as his phone beeped:

1 New Voicemail.

It could wait.

He pulled out the files that were now fast becoming a ticking time bomb, about to destroy his life if he let them.

Four manila files altogether.

He brought them over to his desk and spread them out, staring at each one in turn:

Nola Grant.

Sara Thornton.

Felicity Davenport.

There was one more file staring back at him.

He hesitated, eyes fixed on the name neatly written on the front. A name that was going to mean repercussions. A name he'd rather forget for ever. It would change everything at the centre.

His fingers traced over the name, following every line and curve:

William Hatcher.

He found himself asking questions. Questions he knew the answer to but pretended he didn't.

How bad is this going to get?

He didn't want to go home. He couldn't, not yet. He needed to see an old friend, just until he got his head straight. His friend would know what to do. He'd always been there in times of crisis. It was his job, wasn't it?

See the friend.

Get his life back on track before everything he'd worked so hard for, for all these years, fell away and shattered.

CHAPTER 65

Fallon's toes curled forward, gripping the edge of the diving board. Looking down into the water, she jumped, tucking her legs up underneath her just before she plummeted into the deep end, letting herself sink to the bottom. The sound of the music from the side of the pool pulsated under the water, drowned out and muffled. When her toes touched the bottom, she pushed up, her head breaking the surface.

The pool party was in full swing, fuelled by drugs and alcohol. All her friends were there. All of them had money – naturally – or rather, their parents did. All of them were tanked-up to the brink, lounging around or dancing in their swimwear.

The indoor pool was flanked on one side by floor-to-ceiling glass windows that looked out into the vast garden. The cold outside, mixed with the heat of the pool room, caused the glass to fog, and it dripped condensation. The wall behind the bar had a mock-mosaic image of the Greek god Poseidon, pointing his trident down, a fierce look in his eye.

Fallon reached the side of the pool and was about to climb out, when a tall boy of around seventeen held out his hands and grinned down at her. She eyed his torso, his black swimming trunks and his wet messy blond hair.

She smiled. 'Julian.'

'Dockley,' he replied, as he gripped her hands and hauled her from the water. She grabbed her towel from a bar stool and wrapped it around herself.

'Jägerbomb?' she asked, drying herself. He grinned when she chucked her towel at him playfully and slipped behind the bar to mix the cocktail.

He eyed her torso as she poured him a drink and longed to see just how far the tattoo on her belly dipped below her bikini bottoms.

*

From his vantage point in the garden, the man had watched them all behaving like rabid dogs. Going crazy with the drink and drugs, and dancing around in time to the music like people possessed.

He'd stayed near the side of the pool house at first but as the condensation had taken hold of the glass wall, he'd edged closer. The air chilled him to the bone. The stars above were shining down, no clouds overhead. He watched his breath in front of him as he breathed out, a white fog circling his face.

He eyed the target.

She seemed to be all over some young toff at the bar. He remembered how to access the dressing room area joined to the pool house. He'd seen her use this many times before, when he'd been here in secret, preparing for this night. He knew it was only a matter of time before she'd go there to change. He also knew the lock on the door to the garden from the changing room was still broken.

He moved slowly through the snow. She had to go in there sometime. Taking her really did all depend on if she was alone. This was hit or miss. William could only run from the police for so long. Time was running out.

He played the waiting game.

*

Thirty minutes passed. Fallon found herself kissing Julian before they'd even made it into the changing room. They'd had a few drinks, shared some small talk, then got straight down to what they both wanted.

They stumbled through the door from the pool, laughing as they tripped over each other's feet in the semi-darkness. There was only one window letting the light of the moon seep inside, casting shadows around them.

Julian pushed her back onto a large leather sofa before collapsing on top of her. She was in fits of giggles as he clumsily pulled at her bikini top. She leaned forward, pulled at the string behind her back and whipped the garment off and over her head.

'I hope you've got something,' she said, as he planted passionate kisses down her neck, his tongue tracing the curves of its ivy tattoo. 'Julian?'

He groaned against her throat, pulled back and looked at her.

Her eyes narrowed. 'You're not getting near it otherwise.'

'Oh, come on!' He slumped to the side. 'I've not got anything. I'm clean.'

'I don't fucking care. It's getting knocked up. I don't want a bloody kid.'

'Aren't you on the Pill?'

'Obviously not,' she said, 'it makes you fat.' He sighed, looking down at her semi-naked body. That tattoo down her belly seemed to call for him. He dipped his fingers down the front of her bikini bottoms. She squealed, slapping him playfully around the face.

He removed his hand. 'Fuck's sake.' He paused, looking into her mischievous eyes. 'You'd better be worth it, Dockley,' he said, pushing himself off the sofa. He backed towards the door and pointed at her. 'Don't go anywhere.'

He opened the door to the pool, music flooding the room. It was so loud it rumbled around inside Fallon's skull.

She watched him disappear, slamming the adjoining door hard, then wrapped her arms over her chest. This room was colder than the pool room and she pushed herself deeper into the sofa.

The room span when she laid her head back. She heard the last music track end before the sound of the Chemical Brothers' 'Setting Sun' started to pound through the speakers. Her body twitched to the beat, willing Julian to hurry the hell up.

When she felt the icy draft come from the back door, she arched her feline-like body and tried to look over her shoulder.

She heard the wood floor creak and, turning, she saw him emerge from the darkness, as though he was seamlessly moulded to the shadows.

'Julian?'

The man stood, stretching himself up tall.

She screamed.

Springing from the sofa, she bolted for the door to the pool. She almost made it but he grabbed her, crushing her chest. She felt her whole body lift as he picked her up.

She screamed again, kicking her legs out, trying to throw him off balance. The music was roaring now – someone had turned it up – and the man grinned as he edged towards the back door ahead.

'No one can hear you scream, Fallon. Save your breath.'

She heard his voice, repeated it frantically inside her head.

I know you!

She tried to look at his face but he twisted it away. She bent her body almost in two, leaning forward, and found his flesh with her teeth, biting down hard.

He hissed a swear word and dropped her.

Scrambling on the floor, she pulled herself forward and back on her feet, bolting for the door to the garden, but he was right behind her. She felt the sheer force of him when he pushed her hard in the back.

Tripping over her own feet, she sailed forward, crashing into the cold glass window. Her face smacked against it, her teeth cutting into her lip.

She felt like a fly swatted against someone's hands and her head was swimming. His hands pulled at her waist, lifted her, and she was like a rag doll in his arms when he hauled her out of the door, across the garden.

Her feet dragged along in the snow behind them, leaving deep furrows. The cold air took bites at her skin, feeling like a million tiny teeth gnawing at her flesh. She shivered involuntarily, feeling gooseflesh pucker her body.

Her head hung heavy, looking down at the floor. She was barely awake and her eyes started to close. She embraced the blackout when it came.

*

When Claire finally got home, the first thing she did was switch on the television. A picture of William Hatcher shot up on screen, along with those of the murder victims, on Sky News.

Then she was startled by her BlackBerry ringing. She saw it was Stefan as she answered it.

'You need to come back in… We got him.'

Claire paused, not registering what he was telling her.

'We've got Hatcher, Claire.'

She bolted upright, but was speechless.

He smiled at the other end. 'We've got Hatcher and he's singing like a canary.'

CHAPTER 66

When Fallon woke, she couldn't move her wrists. She couldn't see either. Her eyes were open but everything was black. Her head was reeling. Then she got slung to one side, her body crashing into something hard, and she realised she was moving.

She was in a car that was negotiating sharp bends in the road. The reason she couldn't see anything was because there was a black T-shirt tied around her head. The reason her hands felt so numb was because there was cable wrapped tight around both wrists.

She sucked in a deep breath, suddenly feeling claustrophobic. Her chest rose and fell heavily, her breathing laboured. She tried to speak, but her breath caught in her throat. What the hell had happened? She remembered the man in the shadows. She remembered running towards the door to the garden. Then it all went blank.

The car slowed, coming to a halt. She heard the driver get out, then the back passenger door open, cold air rushing towards her.

She remembered she was naked except for her thin bikini bottoms and felt extremely vulnerable. When icy hands gripped her ankles, she let out a scream and bucked her legs. Then the car rocked under his weight as he clambered over the back seat on top of her, hands now squeezing around her throat.

'Shut up or I'll kill you.'

*

Fallon hadn't shut up because of his threat. She'd remembered the voice. She knew him. Jesus Christ, it was too much for her to even contemplate. Even when he'd sat her down in his kitchen and removed the t-shirt from her head, watching her reaction, she never spoke.

Instead her eyes bore into his, a look of defiance that was doing her more harm than good. She followed his eyes as they wandered over her naked body.

'Get a good fucking look, you sick bastard.'

The man looked away, left the kitchen, then came back with a bundle of clothes and threw them into her lap.

'Don't flatter yourself. Get dressed.'

'Does my body bother you? It never bothered you before.' He ignored her, averting his eyes. 'I thought you were trying to help me.'

He flung around and pointed at her, face twisted. 'I am trying to help you!'

'Doesn't look like it.'

'Stop talking or I'll be forced to gag you.'

'Bet you'd fucking love that.'

Without warning he flung his hand out and caught her hard across the temple.

Fallon's head lolled to one side and her body came crashing down off the stool, unconscious, hitting the floor hard.

He waited. She didn't move. His face was uncertain as he crouched down beside her.

A swell of relief flooded his body when he felt at her neck and found the soft thump of her pulse. He sank backwards onto the floor and stared into the hallway. He looked at the basement door off to his left.

He needed to move if his plan was to work. It was early yet, but he had much to prepare.

He cut loose Fallon's wrists and quickly dressed her, taking care not to look at much when he removed her bikini bottoms, replacing them with plain white pants. When she was clothed, he picked her up and carried her down the stairs and shackled her to the pipe, like it was second nature.

Then he left.

*

When he returned an hour later, Fallon was awake. He opened the basement door and saw her thrashing about in her restraints, kicking the pipe like something possessed.

He didn't bother trying to calm her just yet. He knew she'd tire herself out sooner or later, and then he'd make his move.

He offered her water.

She took the plastic cup, sipped, then spat it into his face. She laughed as the water ran off his face. He didn't want to risk knocking her unconscious again, not just yet, so he punched her hard in the gut. She fell to the floor spluttering, chest heaving.

He told her she wouldn't be fed until he was ready, as a punishment. That didn't stop her shouting and screaming at him. He pushed her obscenities to the back of his mind while he prepared for the next stage of his plan.

When he was finished, Fallon was slouched up against the wall with exhaustion, eyes barely able to stay focused. During her struggle, she'd managed to crack and rip off some of her nails on both hands. Where she'd thrown herself around in frustration, dark brown smudges from the dirty wall now adorned her face.

'You look like a sewer rat,' he said, as he removed the shackles and dragged her towards another pipe on the other side of the basement. 'You've made an exhibition of yourself.'

A sound gurgled from the back of her throat, and her eyes fluttered open to stare him hard in the face. 'When my dad finds out what you've…' She trailed off, as a surge of pain spread out across her forehead. A tension headache was taking hold, and she was so tired she couldn't finish her sentence.

The man locked her wrists in place and thought of what was to come. He had the rest of the day to put everything into motion.

The basement had room for one more visitor and it was only a matter of time before she came.

CHAPTER 67

Elias stood covering the flame from the light he'd offered DC Harper to light his cigarette, against the wind outside.

They'd captured William Hatcher trying to hide out in a kids' play area in the village close to the farm. The dogs had sniffed him out, and once Hatcher had caught a glimpse of an Alsatian, with its salivating jaws filled with sharp teeth, straining at its leash, he'd given himself up with relative ease.

Since he'd been at the station, he'd been eager to talk, but not a lot was making much sense to anyone right now.

They were now waiting for Claire to finish interviewing him. Until then, everyone was on tenterhooks.

Elias returned the lighter to his pocket and stared at DC Harper with questioning eyes. He'd had a gut feeling about Harper in recent weeks.

Something didn't sit right.

'I still say we've missed something with Curran,' Harper said, scrolling through his mobile phone. 'How many times have we questioned him? Everything seemed too convenient and what with his fake alibis, we should've nicked him long ago.'

Harper gave Elias a sideways glance when he didn't answer, and his face dropped. 'You're eyeballing me. What's up?'

Elias looked away, staring back towards the station's entrance, making sure they were alone. 'I've got questions, Harper.'

T.M.E. Walsh

He paused a beat. 'What about?'

'Questions with answers I'm not sure I'm gonna like.'

Harper smirked, and looked away then back again, to find Elias staring at him. His face dropped. 'I'm not sure I follow you.'

'Funny business that leak on Grant's pregnancy, wasn't it?' Harper swallowed hard, avoiding his eyes. 'There everyone was, quick to think it was me, the outsider, the one who had points to score against the Guv. No one thought to look closer, to someone else who had perfect opportunity.'

Harper's eyes shot back to his, face deadly serious. 'Everybody on the investigation had the opportunity.'

'It was you though, wasn't it?'

Harper scoffed. 'Damned if I know where you got that from.' He laughed nervously, turning his head to look across the car park. 'You're not thinking straight, Crest.'

Elias laid his palm on Harper's shoulder and patted it firmly. 'I don't care that you did it. Hell, I was this close to doing it myself,' he said, gesturing a small space with his fingers. 'There was only one thing holding me back.'

Harper turned to look at him. 'And what was that?'

Elias had almost called that journalist at the local paper, but something had stopped him, made him take stock of the situation.

Once he'd found out it was Claire who'd offered him a lifeline to transfer from Liverpool, he knew how close he'd come to really screwing everything up for himself.

Not that he was going to tell Harper that, despite the other man's eyes locked onto his, expecting some kind of answer.

Elias shrugged. 'I guess deep down I knew the Guv was right but I didn't want to admit it.'

'Doesn't mean I did it.'

Elias smiled thinly. 'I know you did... question is, why?'

Harper looked at his mobile, and then tapped it against his thigh nervously. His eyes shifted back and forth, over the skyline, anywhere but into Elias's eyes.

'I'm not gonna grass you up, Harper. I just wanna know why.'

Harper stumbled over his words. 'I did it 'cos I thought you were right.' He swallowed hard. 'I agreed with your theory and thought it would've been a risk worth taking.' He turned to Elias, eyes questioning. 'There're rumours about you. Reasons surrounding your transfer. Word going around is that you're a maverick. You don't do everything by the book, but you get results.'

Elias remained stony-faced. 'What else have you heard?'

'You want out with the old and in with the new.'

Elias eyed him suspiciously.

Some rumours really needed to be put to bed.

Many thoughts were going around in his head and the thought even crossed his mind that Claire had set Harper up for this talk, but then he reminded himself that it was he who'd called Harper's bluff. He rubbed his chin with his hand, scraping over his three-day-old stubble. He sighed heavily, shaking his head.

'Believe me, Harper, you don't know the half of it. I'd also be very careful where you go from here. Claire's not stupid. She won't let this go.'

Harper frowned. 'Since when are you an expert on the Guv?'

'Let's just say I'm learning fast. She'll see the leak as an act of betrayal, take it personally... best stop playing with fire before you get burned.'

CHAPTER 68

2nd December

The home video of Fallon was playing in the DVD player, her face filling the screen, pulling faces at her father, Richard, who panned the camera across to the rest of their house.

'I filmed this when Fallon turned sixteen. It was about a week before my wife left us,' he said, staring at the screen. 'This was the last video I ever took of her.'

Claire watched Richard. He was hurting. His face looked like a tortured soul, waiting for the relief of the end.

He scratched his chin, and paused playback. 'You've my permission to search her room, turn it upside down if you have to, whatever it takes. Just find her.'

Claire removed her gaze from Richard and didn't say a word. She was tired. It was the early hours of that morning and she'd been interviewing William Hatcher since she'd rushed back to the station after Stefan's call.

Hatcher had confessed to everything, except why he'd done it or how he chose his victims. He'd also confirmed he was Mitchell Curran's client. The same Mitchell Curran who'd since disappeared. And now another girl was missing.

Claire walked to the family photographs on a large sideboard at the other side of the room as Stefan appeared in the doorway holding a business card.

'I spoke to your wife about twenty minutes ago, Mr Dockley. She's on her way. I didn't realise she lived local.'

Richard nodded. 'In the next town, yes. I'd heard she'd moved closer a few months ago to be near her sister, but I didn't see the point in telling Fallon.' His eyes stared at the still frame on the television. Fallon was looking up at the camera, a present in her lap that she hadn't opened yet.

'Ellen Dockley – or should I say Morrissey? Last I heard, she was using her maiden name until I agree a divorce… She won't miss a chance to come straight back into our lives, after nothing for months, and tell me I'm a bad father to my face.'

'And are you?'

Everyone was silent and all eyes were on Claire. 'Are you a bad father?'

'So blunt,' Richard said. His brown eyes misted over. 'I deserve that. I could've been better. I was too involved with my property business when Fallon was younger. I tried to compensate for my absence by giving her anything she wanted, so long as it wasn't time… time that I couldn't afford to give her.'

'That was always going to be your downfall, Richard.'

The voice seemed to melt into the room from nowhere. All eyes fixed on the doorway and on the small, forty-something woman that now stood before them, rage in her eyes. 'Have you enough time for her now? Now she's missing?'

Richard looked away. Any tears he might have shed quickly disappeared. He looked at the woman, whose eyes were as dark as his own.

'That statement, my dear long-departed wife, is rich, coming from you.' His eyes fixed upon hers. 'Where have you been these last three years? Don't you dare blame all this on me. You haven't been here to pick up the pieces since the day you left us. If I'm not fit to be called a father, then you have no more right than I to be called a parent. A mother. You've become nothing to her, Ellen.'

Every fibre in Ellen's body seemed to rupture and before Claire or Stefan could react, she hurled herself towards Richard, arms raised.

'You let this happen!' Her fists pummelled his chest hard. He caught her wrists, pushing her from him. 'You bastard!' She pulled a hand free, smacked him hard across the face. 'I love my daughter!'

He sniffed at her in contempt and pushed her aside. 'Love? Don't make me laugh.'

She went to hit him again, but Claire caught her wrist, forcing the woman to look into her eyes. 'That's enough. This won't help Fallon.'

*

Richard Dockley studied the picture of William Hatcher in his hands, passed it across the table towards his wife and shook his head. 'I've never seen him before.'

Ellen's cold eyes studied the picture, then she shoved it back towards her husband. 'Me neither.'

'Are you sure?' Claire said, leaning across towards Richard over the kitchen table.

'This man is in police custody. He's confessed to those other murders,' he said, pointing to the picture. 'This is a waste of time. He can't be the one responsible for taking Fallon. He was in a cell when she was abducted.'

Ellen snorted and flicked her hair back. 'You're telling me they're wasting our time?' Richard ignored her. Her eyes shot to Claire. 'Well, isn't that great. What the hell are you doing here asking us about this monster, when it has nothing to do with our daughter?'

'Do you have any CCTV here?' Stefan asked Richard.

He shook his head.

'Excuse me,' Ellen said, clicking her fingers at Stefan, 'don't go changing the bloody subject. I want to know what you're planning to do to get my daughter back.'

Claire ignored her and faced Richard. 'Your daughter's photo was found in Hatcher's possessions.' She paused. 'Your daughter was a target.'

Richard's face rose in alarm, but he couldn't find the strength to speak. Claire's face softened a little. 'Was Fallon having any kind of therapy?'

She saw the flicker of recognition in his eyes.

'Yes.' His eyes lowered. 'We both were.'

'Oh, that's *great*,' Ellen spat. 'When were you planning on telling me she was seeing a shrink?'

'Richard,' Claire said, 'this is important.'

He hesitated, picked up his glass of water and emptied it. 'We were having psychotherapy here in Letchworth.'

CHAPTER 69

It was 7:00 p.m. when Claire got home. She traipsed into the living room, seeing Sky News on the television. William Hatcher was the main headline on pretty much every station. Claire stared at his mug shot, her mind ticking over.

It wasn't until Iris saw her in the doorway that she grabbed the remote and flicked to Standby. The picture went to black, but Claire's eyes remained glued to the screen.

'We've got the monkey, now we need the organ-grinder.'

Iris's brow furrowed. 'What?'

Claire pointed to the dark screen. 'Hatcher's not working alone and now he's clammed up.'

Iris sighed. 'I'll be glad when this case is over and that man's in jail for good, then maybe you'll snap out of this.' Her face turned serious. 'Your night terrors are getting more frequent and your obsession with this case isn't helping.'

Claire rounded on her. 'I'm the SIO! That means it's my arse on the line if I don't get results. I have to help bring justice to the victims, to their families. I can't just shut it all out when things get too much. I can't run and hide.'

'You've got a confession! It's all over the news.'

'Hatcher is not working alone, and the man I'm after has vanished into thin air.' She lowered her voice. 'This is far from over.'

'You need to let this one go. You've got a confession.'

Claire's eyes grew dark. 'Another girl is missing.'

Iris shrugged. She hadn't seen that on the news. She didn't know whether to believe it or not. 'It may be unrelated.'

'We've found a photograph of the missing girl amongst Hatcher's stuff. The real man behind all of this isn't finished yet. Hatcher's just a pawn.'

Iris lowered her eyes, staring at the floor. 'Can't DI Fletcher—'

'Stefan's working round the clock,' Claire cut in. 'We all are. I'm only here to catch up on some sleep.' She paused. 'And those dreams have stopped.'

Iris sneered and shook her head.

'They've *stopped*, Mum.'

'Post-traumatic stress,' Iris said. 'You've not been yourself since last year.'

Claire shook her head, pretending not to hear. The murdered priest case – won't it ever go away?

CHAPTER 70

A little while later, Iris came to find Claire. She entered the kitchen and stared at her daughter. 'I don't have to go out with Elsa tonight. I can stay with you. You look dreadful.'

'Thanks.'

'You know what I mean.'

Iris had arranged to go to the theatre with Claire's neighbour who lived across the street, and the taxi was due to pick her up from Elsa's house in the next fifteen minutes.

Claire avoided her mother's stare. 'It's OK. Go out and enjoy yourself.'

Today had sucked the energy from her. The fear of what might happen to Fallon Dockley if she got the next few hours very wrong picked away at her inside. It hacked at her soul and it took all her effort to climb up the stairs to the bathroom.

She began running the water and went into her bedroom to change. She heard Iris shout up to her from the bottom of the stairs and she pulled her dressing gown around her. When Iris saw the flimsy material and that Claire only had her underwear underneath, she tutted.

'You'll catch your death, girl. Go on upstairs, I have a key. I'll lock up after myself.'

Claire smiled.

Iris watched her disappear back up the stairs before letting herself out, locking up and trudging in the snow towards Elsa's house.

CHAPTER TEN

CHAPTER 71

The roll-top bath was nearly full. Claire balanced on the edge, staring at her reflection in the water. Her eyes were like dark pits. She fought back the visions of the dead women, blinking her eyes tight shut, especially when her thoughts turned towards Hatcher.

She leaned over and turned off the taps. She hung up her dressing gown and removed her underwear, tossing them to the floor, and lowered herself down into the water. She lay back, resting her head on the back of the bath.

She closed her eyes.

She lay there, still, feeling sleep beginning to take her almost instantly. She knew the dangers of falling asleep in the bath, but felt so drained of energy, she didn't care.

Then she heard a noise.

She opened her eyes.

Iris had already left, she was alone.

Am I?

She pushed herself upright in the water and stared at the door.

'Mum, is that you?'

She felt a shiver dance its way up along her spine, cooling her skin. She called out twice more, but heard nothing. Sensing something wasn't right, she got out of the bath, wrapped a towel around herself and stood as still as possible.

The stairs creaked.

The third stair from the bottom, to be precise. Creaking under someone's weight. Her heart skipped a beat. Instinct took over and she looked around for a weapon.

Someone's in the house.

She pulled on her underwear, covering herself with the dressing gown.

Claire always kept a knife in her bedroom, and she needed to get to it. She peered from behind the bathroom door, out on to the landing.

It was dark.

The lights had been turned out in the hall downstairs and in her bedroom.

She remained still but found it impossible to control her breathing. The sound seemed to reverberate around in her head, her ears, and her heartbeat quickened as she stepped out onto the landing. She slipped into her bedroom, found the knife in her drawer and gripped the handle tight. She glanced at the digital clock on her side table, the green digits glowing brightly in the darkness:

19:40.

Iris had only been gone ten minutes. Claire heard faint movement from the hall. She crept downstairs. Her body was crouched, keeping herself small, eyes dead ahead, waiting for the slightest movement.

She skipped the third stair from the bottom and when she hit the last one, she saw the shadow move in the living room from her vantage point across the hall.

She darted across the hardwood floor, feet smacking across the surface. The shadow was heading towards the other door to the kitchen and she doubled back towards the kitchen's other entrance.

As she came crashing through the kitchen door, she saw the shadow, frozen to the spot, at the other side of the room.

'Stay where you are!'

She couldn't see much in the darkness, despite the light coming from the moon through the windows to her right. It was enough, though, to see that the figure ahead of her was male.

The shadow cocked its head to one side, watching her.

She couldn't speak. Her voice lodged itself in her throat. She didn't know who he was or what he wanted. She heard his breathing though, coming in short sharp bursts, just as rampant as hers.

The adrenaline was running through her body.

She reached out and turned on the kitchen light.

As the overhead spotlights sprang to life, her eyes flickered, adjusting to the sudden brightness.

She raised the knife up and stared ahead at the man in front of her. She saw the wide grin spreading across his face when he saw she was shocked.

It took her mere seconds to place his face. She loosened the tension in the hand holding the knife.

'What the hell are you doing in my house?'

CHAPTER 72

Claire's eyes narrowed, staring back at him. Before, he'd had an otherworldly charm about him. He was not the type of person anyone would feel uncomfortable with, but now, as his eyes stared back into hers, there was nothing there but darkness, and it frightened her.

'What are you doing here?'

He smiled, almost melting away her fears for a brief moment. 'You remember me, Chief Inspector?' He nodded to himself. 'I like that. It means a lot to me.'

The knife in Claire's hand rose a little. She was shaking. 'What are you doing in my house?' She paused. 'How'd you get in?'

He took a step forward. 'So many questions.'

'Answer me!'

He looked at her, shocked by the bitterness in her voice.

'Your mother let me in.'

'My mother?'

'Inadvertently, of course.'

He rounded the island cupboards in the middle of the kitchen. 'It's dangerous leaving the front door wide open, unattended.' He toyed with the stem of an empty wine glass on the counter. 'Iris went to investigate a noise this afternoon.'

He winked.

'Poor cow left the front door ajar. Anyone could've got in. You can't be too careful these days. There's a killer on the loose, isn't there?' He stopped when Claire raised the knife. He tutted and shook his head.

'There's really no need for that, Claire.' She flinched when he spoke her name. 'I can call you Claire, can't I? I don't think it's too personal, since I feel like I know you quite well.'

She swallowed hard.

'I've been watching you. I didn't think about it much when we first met, but then you were on the news, with Flick's parents and that snivelling brother of hers. That's when it hit me. That's when you really got me thinking… you really are quite breathtaking.'

He edged closer.

'Stay where you are.' Her voice was controlled but her face flushed red.

He raised his eyebrows. 'And wait while you dial the three nines?' He held up her BlackBerry and shook his head. 'I don't think so. You've no doubt begun to work it all out. What my part is in all this, the brains behind it all.'

She remained defiant, standing her ground. 'I won't warn you again.'

He stopped, thinking back in his mind. 'I bet you're kicking yourself that you didn't see it before.' He grinned. 'Which surprises me, actually.'

He was teasing her and enjoying every second.

'It was quite easy when you think about it. After all, I did have access to all the information I wanted. I met each chosen one at least once. With Flick, I was in direct contact. I was careful, of course, not to let her family notice me in The Fox… and I spoke with Fallon most weeks. The others I watched from afar. I kept my distance.'

Claire took a step back.

'You, however… you were something else. I saw through your façade, Claire. I saw your weakness.' His hands rose towards her. 'You mustn't worry, I can help you if you'll only let me. Like the others. They would've thanked me, if they'd only applied themselves.'

Claire sneered as she spoke. 'Do you think those girls would ever give you a second thought? Do you think I thought of you? I'd forgotten you in a second.'

She saw his eyes narrow. She half laughed. 'My God, you actually thought they would care about you, your friendship.' He avoided her eyes. 'Where's Fallon? Is she dead too?'

'It shouldn't be Fallon you're concerned about.' He gazed at her. 'You're the special one in here,' he said, placing his palm against his chest, over his heart.

'Where's Fallon Dockley?'

She tried to keep her voice steady, despite the fear inside. In her head she was trying to find a way to subdue him, but despite the knife in her hand, she was vulnerable.

He was smiling at her now. 'If I gave myself up, would I still go to jail for a long time?' His voice was calm, but unnerving, a stark contrast from the first time they'd spoken.

'After what you've done, you'll go down for a long time. I'll make sure of it.'

He smiled at her. He cocked his head sideways, taking in every inch of her. 'I never killed anyone. That was William's job. Dispatch and disposal… something he's good at.'

'*Was* good at.'

'Ah yes, I heard he was in custody,' he said. 'I bet he didn't tell you anything though.'

'He told us more than you think. He's still being questioned. If William's not already admitted your part in it, he will do very soon, and then people will come looking for me.'

'Oh, Claire, come on, drop the charade. We both know that's not true.' He paused, lowering his eyes to her middle. Her dressing gown was barely hanging together around her body. 'You're shivering. Is it with cold… or fear?' He took a step closer, and she stepped back, raising the six-inch blade.

'I'll use this if I have to.'

'There's no need to fear me. I'm not here to hurt you.' He edged closer again and it was then that she seized her chance.

She bolted back down the hall.

She was inches from the front door when she felt his hand snare her hair, yanking her head back. She whipped her arm around, slicing into his thigh with the blade, before it clattered to the floor with the force. He groaned, falling sideways into the door.

Her exit blocked, she rushed into the living room, but he was on her again. He grabbed her around the waist, hauling her down on the sofa with one arm, his other hand clamping down on top of her mouth, muffling her screams.

'I'll only hurt you if you force me to,' he gasped, pinning down her arms with his knees. 'You're my project now, Claire, don't fight it.'

She bit down on his hand. He pulled it back, wincing with the pain, bringing down the other hand with a sideways swoop, smacking her hard across the cheek. It dazed her, pain tearing through her face.

He brought his lips closer to hers, and she could feel his breath hot against her. One hand rose up, gripping her by the throat, squeezing tighter, the other stroking away the stray strands of hair from her face.

'Don't you understand? The others, they were all a distraction. I wish I could've changed them but, in their hearts, they weren't interested in change. But you,' he said, kissing her cheek tenderly, 'you have so much more to offer. I've such high hopes for you. Don't let me down.'

She stared back into his eyes as his grip on her throat tightened further. 'I don't want to have to kill you, Claire, but I will if you make this difficult for me. With William in custody, I can't promise you the luxury of a quick death, like the others.'

He smiled as she spluttered for air.

'Do you know what it felt like to see the light go out of their eyes? I was there when William did it. Every time. I watched the life drain away and it was almost poetic.' Her eyes widened. 'I long to see it again.' She tried to scream again and his grip tightened.

Then they both froze.

The sound of a key in the front door was unmistakable.

He rolled them both off the sofa, landing hard on the floor. He pulled her towards him so that they remained obscured from the living room door, and she felt the knife she'd dropped earlier dig in at her ribs.

CHAPTER 73

She heard her mother's voice as the door swung open.

Iris craned her neck, looking up the stairs, and saw the light coming from the bathroom. 'Only me, Claire.'

Silence.

In the living room, Claire managed a muffled scream against his hand but he stuck the knife in a little, breaking the tender skin just under her ribs, and she froze.

'Say a word and I'll kill her. Do you understand me?'

Claire breathed in hard through her nose and gave a sharp nod.

Iris slipped off her shoes and wandered into the living room, continuing to call up to her daughter. 'I left my purse here. Think it's in the living room.' They heard Iris's footsteps come towards the coffee table and Claire felt him tense.

Iris stood mere inches away from seeing them.

She stooped towards the coffee table. 'I've found it,' she called out. 'I'd forget my head if it wasn't screwed on.' As she walked back towards the hall, Claire whimpered against the man's hand, hoping her mother would hear her, but he dug the knife in a little further.

Claire froze.

She felt a trickle of blood slide down her stomach. He seemed to have stopped breathing. He held on to her tight, his body pressed hard against hers, holding his breath.

They heard Iris open the front door. 'I'll be off now. I'll see you later.'

Assuming her daughter couldn't hear her from the bathroom, she locked the door after her, and got into the taxi that had just pulled up at Elsa's house.

Claire's heart went into overdrive when the headlights from across the street shone into the living room.

She looked into his eyes.

'That was close, wasn't it?'

She felt him relax, easing the pressure on her own body, and seized her chance.

Raising her elbow, she brought it crashing down into his chest, pushing him from her. She heard him groan but it didn't stop him. He ran after her into the hall. As she fumbled with the lock at the front door, he closed in behind her.

She saw his arm lurch forward with her knife gripped in his hand. She ducked as the blade landed inches from her head, embedding itself into the door. She shoved him back and bolted up the stairs. She ran into the bathroom, locking herself in. A few seconds later, he was kicking and punching at the barrier between them.

'You're trapped, Claire. Don't make this harder than it has to be.'

Inside the bathroom, she backed up against the wall, hitting her head against the medicine cabinet. She pulled it open, searching for anything she could use as a weapon. She pulled at the contents, sending them cascading to the floor, but found nothing. She swung around, eyes frantically searching for anything around the room.

She paused, her back now up against the bathroom door. She felt the force of a violent kick from the other side, and the door groaned.

He was coming in, no matter how long it took to kick the door down.

She looked at the mirror in the medicine cabinet.

She grabbed her bath towel, wrapped it around her right hand, and hurled her fist into the mirror, the glass shattering on impact. She prised out a shard of glass, not caring as it sliced into her skin.

Then a flurry of stabbing noises rained down from the other side of the door. He was ramming the knife into the wood, while his legs kicked in turn at the hinges, and the wood began to split.

She threw herself at the door just as it caved in. He tried to wrestle the barrier away from her, and she opened her mouth, screaming to the point where she thought her lungs might burst.

After a few hard shoves, he pushed the door aside from her grasp. She lashed out with the glass, catching him on the arm but no pain registered on his face.

He kicked the glass from her hand, lunged forward and gripped her around the wrists. She tried to headbutt him, but he anticipated the move, and encircled her into his body.

He pulled the rag from his trouser pocket and held it to her mouth and nose. It took seconds before she grew weak. Soon her arms fell down at her sides, her body slumping against his.

He gently laid her down on the cold tiled floor and pulled her dressing gown back around her. He went to her bedroom, pulled her duvet from the bed, then went back to wrap it around her.

He pulled her up under the shoulders and heaved her up over his shoulder. He went down the stairs, unlocked the front door, and stepped out into the snow.

Sleet came down in an icy sheet in the night air, melting when it hit his face and clothes. He walked down her drive, out into the quiet street.

Elsa's house was in darkness across the road, and there were no street lights on tonight, one of the council's money-saving ventures. Inside, he thanked them. It'd helped him and William on more than one occasion.

He turned towards the white van he'd hired earlier in the day and laid Claire down in the back. He secured the back doors, climbed into the driver's seat and started the engine. He looked back behind him, at her body sprawled out in the back.

He smiled.

He put the van in gear and drove up towards the main road, unnoticed, just as before when he'd arrived earlier that day.

CHAPTER 74

3rd December

It'd been nearly midnight by the time the taxi dropped them both home, and eager not to wake her daughter, Iris had discreetly let herself in and got ready for bed quietly in the en suite bathroom in the guest room.

The light was out in Claire's room and all was quiet. Given that the last few weeks had been erratic for her in terms of sleep, Iris had been silently grateful that Claire's night had been undisturbed. She must be sleeping soundly.

It was just after 8:30 a.m. when Iris woke – far later than she usually rose, but she was paying the price for the late night and the many G&Ts she and Elsa had been necking at the bar. She climbed out of bed and rummaged in her bag for some pills. She found an empty blister pack and grimaced.

Putting on her dressing gown, she ventured out onto the landing and towards the main bathroom, too tired to notice the drops of dried blood she stepped in as she went.

*

Stefan tried Claire's mobile several times before giving up and leaving a voicemail.

He sat at his desk, staring at his computer screen, then craned his neck around the workstation to see Elias.

'You heard from Claire this morning?' Elias shook his head but didn't look up from his screen. 'That's weird.'

'What is?' Elias said, still not looking. Stefan got up, wandered around and leaned up against Elias's desk.

'Claire's not answering her mobile, and we're supposed to be heading over to see Stephanie Curran, see if there's any sign of her husband yet.' He glanced at his watch again. 'And we're already running late. It's just not like her.'

'You saw her yesterday. She's probably passed out from exhaustion.' He looked up and saw Stefan's face. Saw the concern. 'Have you tried her landline?' Stefan shook his head, scrolled through his phone book, then hit the Call button. The line rang for less than four seconds before it was answered.

'Morning, Iris, is Cla—' he broke off, his face changing. 'Iris, calm down. Where's Claire?'

Elias saw Stefan's face drop. He could hear what sounded like a hysterical woman on the other end of the line and he swung his chair around, propelling himself to his feet.

'Where's the Guv?'

Stefan clasped his mobile tighter. 'OK, Iris, here's what I want you to do. I'm going to send officers around to the house. Do not disturb or touch anything else, leave everything as you found it. Just try to stay calm.'

A few comforting words later, Stefan hung up.

'Where's Claire?'

It took several seconds before Stefan could speak. His face had turned white and his eyes looked fearful.

'We've got a serious problem.'

CHAPTER 75

'What do you want us to do?'

Stefan was trying to keep his voice composed, but as he looked into Donahue's eyes, he knew he was projecting anything but a sense of calm. Donahue's jaw was set firm, his mind working over several things inside his head.

'Officers are at Claire's house now. The bathroom's a mess. Door was kicked in and there are what looks like knife marks in the frame.'

Donahue slammed his fist down on his desk in frustration, his eyes darting all over the place trying to make sense of it all. 'How the hell did Iris miss this?'

'You can't blame Iris. She came home late, she didn't want to disturb Claire, so she left the lights off and used the en suite in her bedroom. Claire's room and the family bathroom are down the landing from Iris's room.'

'And she didn't hear anything from Claire's?'

Stefan shook his head. 'She said Claire's been having disturbed nights lately. She didn't want to disturb her.'

'*Fantastic*,' Donahue said to himself. 'Is there anything useful, any clues about who took her?'

'There're several footprints on the bathroom door. They look like heavy-duty boots, maybe a size eleven, and there're spots of blood dotted in the hall, living room and upstairs.' Stefan paused. He dreaded the next few words that rushed around inside his head. 'Someone got hurt, Cliff. Someone got cut.'

Donahue's eyes looked into Stefan's and he felt his stomach knot.

'I want someone questioning William Hatcher right now. That bastard knows who has her and where they are.' Donahue then snapped his fingers, as if having an afterthought. 'What about Mitchell Curran?'

'Still trying to locate him, but we haven't anything but circumstantial evidence on him.'

'He was treating Hatcher… I want DS Crest to go to Focus Being and I want you on Hatcher.' Stefan nodded, heading for the door.

Donahue felt pain rising in his gut.

This was different. One of their own was in trouble, maybe even dead. The thought of losing Claire was so gut-wrenching he could barely allow his mind to contemplate the idea.

'It might not be hers,' he said, just before Stefan shut the door after himself. Stefan turned to face him. 'The blood, I mean,' Donahue clarified, 'it might not be Claire's.'

Stefan looked away. His voice was tight in his throat when he spoke. 'We have to face the possibility that it might be.'

CHAPTER 76

It'd been two hours since Claire had been reported missing. Elias had left for Focus Being half an hour ago and said he'd be in touch if he had anything that could help them.

Stefan was now finally sitting opposite William Hatcher in the custody suite interview room, hitting a brick wall, which he'd expected. The man's big frame dwarfed Stefan's even as he sat hunched over the table between them, his big hands clasped together. His hair was greasy, and his dark eyes held no light in them.

His mouth was set in a permanent snarl and his eyes cast a dark look at Stefan, as he chewed his bottom lip. He blinked hard, then glanced over at the duty solicitor, Sally Braithwaite, sitting next to him.

'You can help yourself by helping me, William. You know who has DCI Winters and where she's been taken. There may even be a chance that Fallon Dockley is with her,' Stefan said.

Hatcher stared up at him, peering out from under his thick black eyelashes. 'You can help them both, William,' said DC Harper, who sat beside Stefan.

Inside, Harper had very little faith that Hatcher would tell them anything. He felt bad for Stefan. He knew the bond he had with Claire was unmistakable. If he didn't get her back in one piece… well, it didn't bear thinking about.

*

Elias stood in front of Mitchell Curran, open-mouthed. 'Where the hell have you been?'

Mitchell shrugged, then smiled. 'Here and there, Sergeant.'

Stephanie was standing beside her husband, her brow furrowed. 'I've been trying to get hold of you,' she said, the tiredness showing in her voice. 'Where have you been? This lot have been calling non-stop. What's going on?'

Elias ignored her and brought his face close to Mitchell's. 'I'd start talking if I were you. It doesn't look good for you right now.'

Mitchell laughed. 'Are you going to arrest me? Please do. Then you can call my alibi and we can get this whole mess cleared up.'

'Mitch,' Stephanie sighed, running her hands through her hair. 'Stop this.'

He looked at his wife with disbelief. 'You actually think I've got something to hide, don't you?'

Silence.

'Jesus! You do, don't you?' He took a step back from her. 'How long have we been married?'

'I don't know what to think.' She paused and her body shook with frustration. 'All this secrecy, all the hiding. Just tell me the truth.'

Elias looked back at him. 'Well?'

Mitchell sighed. 'I've been with Father Paul.'

Elias stared at him. 'A priest?'

'Yes, Sergeant. A man who can vouch for my every move since William Hatcher was apprehended.' He paused, wiped his face with his hand, then motioned towards Alice Hathaway's office. 'Can we do this somewhere else? I'll explain everything, I promise.'

CHAPTER 77

Elias couldn't believe what he was hearing. He took the contact details for Father Paul from Mitchell's hand, his eyes narrowed.

'You didn't come forward because you, and I quote, 'couldn't get your head around it all and needed time before you could explain about William Hatcher'?'

Mitchell shrugged. 'Yes, something like that.'

'I don't believe this,' Stephanie said.

'I owe a duty of care and confidentiality to my clients,' Mitchell protested. 'I went to Father Paul for advice. With everything going on in the media, these deaths linked to the company, it could end us, Steph. Everything we've worked for, it's all for nothing if it all comes out in the press. I was intending to come in and clear all this up with Chief Inspector Winters this morning.'

Elias's face grew dark. 'Well, that's not going to be possible, is it?'

He explained Claire's disappearance, watching the Currans' reactions, not missing a trick.

'I had nothing to do with her disappearance, Sergeant,' Mitchell said.

Elias cocked an eyebrow. 'You sure about that?' He leaned into Mitchell's face. 'It wouldn't be the first time you've lied to the police, Mr Curran. DCI Winters is in trouble. There must be something that links her kidnapper to this centre and you're going to help me find it. I don't care how long it takes.'

Curran dropped his head into his hands, and spoke through gritted teeth. 'This is ridiculous.'

'What about this morning? Where were you?'

Mitchell sighed.

'I phoned ahead before I got here,' Elias said. 'The receptionist said you still hadn't been seen. Then you mysteriously arrived here before I did. Normally, if you know you'll be late in, you have to report it to Reception.' He let the sentence hang. 'Normally, you do that. Today, you didn't.'

Stephanie looked at her husband. Her brow furrowed. 'Mitch?'

Mitchell paused. He looked like a rabbit caught in headlights. The question had thrown him and he stuttered as he spoke.

'I have no answer for that.'

Stephanie broke in. 'What's going on? I just want someone to tell me the truth. I don't care how bad it is.'

Elias ignored her. He closed the distance between himself and Mitchell. 'If you don't know where DCI Winters is, then who does? Who has unrestricted access to all the patient files and databases?'

'Christ! We've been over this already. Only myself and Alice, and I trust her completely.'

Elias paused. He turned and looked out the glass panel in the door to Alice's office. He eyed the woman on reception.

A thought occurred to him. 'Have any staff not turned up today?'

*

Elias approached the receptionist and she recoiled as he leaned over her desk.

'Have any members of staff called in sick today, or not turned up?'

The girl looked flustered, shaking her head. 'No one's called in sick.' Her eyes widened when Mitchell and his wife appeared behind Elias.

'What about not turning up? Is everyone accounted for?'

The girl rifled through some papers, found the staff register and ran her fingers down the list of entries. 'I think everyone's here,' the girl said, feeling her face flush under the sudden pressure.

Mitchell looked behind her at the workstations back through to the admin office. His eyes ran over each person's face until he found one empty desk.

Realisation hit.

Things fell into place.

And suddenly, everything seemed to make sense in Mitchell's head.

CHAPTER 78

Stefan made his excuses and took a break from the interview room, leaving Harper with Hatcher and the duty solicitor. He ran his hands down over his face, through the sweat that beaded on his brow.

He took out his mobile. Elias had called him just seconds ago and left a voice message. Stefan listened to it. Elias had recorded just five words.

It's not Curran. Call me.

'What've you found?' Stefan said when he got through to Elias. 'Has Curran finally turned up?'

'I think we've been looking at the wrong person from the start. One of the employees hasn't shown up for work today. Curran has tried his home number and can't get through. Tried his mobile but it's switched off. He started working in a more senior role, covering maternity leave. That started in October, not long before Nola Grant was killed.'

Stefan's head was reeling. Not Curran? Then who?

Elias answered for him, as if he had read his mind. 'The man's name is Lucas Hall.'

And then it happened.

Stefan's stomach rolled. His mind replayed flashbacks from his meeting with Claire, when she pretended they were a married couple. Every look Lucas had given her, every gesture, every smile, was now going through his mind in glorious Technicolor.

It had been Joseph that had done most of the talking. Lucas had done all the observing he needed to. He never was shadowing Joseph. He'd always been observing Claire.

'Shit! He sat with me and Claire when we were enquiring about what the centre had to offer.'

Elias paused. 'You've met him?'

Stefan spun around and looked back at the door to interview room one. He ran his hand back through his hair while he debated what to do.

*

When Stefan came back into the interview room, Hatcher instantly knew something wasn't right. His eyes flashed with fear and then his worst suspicions were confirmed when the detective didn't pick up where he'd left off.

Stefan looked at Hatcher, leaned across the table and said, 'Who is Lucas Hall?'

Hatcher shifted in his seat.

Sally Braithwaite looked a little shell-shocked to say the least. Her eyes panned across between Stefan and Harper, then towards Hatcher.

'Have you some new information I should know about, Inspector?'

Stefan glanced at her, ignored the question and focused on Hatcher again. 'You know Lucas, right? He works at Focus Being. You came into contact with him several times, didn't you? He's the brains behind all of this, isn't he, William?'

Hatcher shuddered. His eyes remained locked with Stefan's but he didn't speak.

'I need a word with my client, Inspector Fletcher.'

'Whose idea was it all?' Stefan continued. 'It can't have been you, you're not bright enough to mastermind this whole thing. You were just the meat, the heavy. Isn't that right?'

Hatcher twitched.

'How'd he pick them?'

'Inspector Fletcher, I must insist—'

'You were the monkey, William. The loose cannon.'

Sally thumped the table in frustration. 'Inspector Fletcher!'

Harper looked at each one in turn, letting the scene unfold, not sure what the hell was going on.

'He has DCI Winters, doesn't he? You know where he's taken her. He's out there, while you're in here taking the fall for everything.'

Hatcher's eyes grew angry.

'You're going to take the rap for him. Was that part of the deal? He made sure you took all the risks, made sure all roads led back to you. Did he convince you that you had to take all the blame?' Stefan clicked his fingers in mid-air. 'No! Maybe he told you if you kept quiet about him, he'd be back to help you out... Is that how it was, William? He's left you in the shit though, you know that now, don't you?'

Hatcher's hands clenched into fists on the table top.

'Come on, William. It's on the tip of your tongue, isn't it?'

Hatcher spoke: 'No comment.'

'Why let him do this to you? Did he make you? Tell you he'd see you right if you cut those girls?'

'No comment.'

'He's got one of us now, William. You know that's not going to go down well. You can help us.'

Hatcher laughed.

'Where is she?'

'You won't find her,' Hatcher said, 'not without me.'

Sally started to speak but Hatcher gently placed his hand on her wrist, silencing her. 'If I'm going to help you, Inspector,' he said, quietly this time, 'I want some kind of guarantee of a reduced sentence.'

You're not as stupid as you like to make out, are you? Stefan thought.

'William, I would like to advise—'

Hatcher squeezed Sally's wrist. 'I'd *advise* you to keep quiet.'

'I can't guarantee anything, William, but it can't harm you to start giving me some answers.'

Hatcher was quiet. His eyes searched Stefan's and a smile spread across his face. He leaned back in his chair, crossed his legs casually.

'What do you want to know?'

'Everything.'

'Time's running out for them both. The secret of their survival is simple really.' He leaned forward again, raised a finger to his eyes. 'They must control their fear and not let their eyes betray them. They must learn for he must teach.'

'What are you, a poet now?' Harper said.

Hatcher looked to the floor, then back at Stefan. 'This isn't my puzzle to solve, it's yours… but I'll give you a head start.'

PART FIVE

She was there, in that place she'd come to dread. That same path, criss-crossed with melting snow and forest green. The air around her was cold, she could see her breath. She wasn't running this time, but felt she should be, as she sensed he was close.

'Don't let your eyes betray you.'

She heard it loud and clear. Her father's voice.

Her legs felt so heavy, she couldn't run, despite willing herself to.

'Don't let your eyes betray you.' Not her father's voice this time – it was His, the one whose death she could never bring herself to openly mourn.

She came out to the clearing, the same as before, and stopped. Turned around. This time she saw the lake ahead, frozen solid. The way back was blocked. The voice was closer, and she charged forward, her legs suddenly alive again, fear driving her on.

She slipped in the snow, her body crashing forward, skidding onto the ice that entombed the water below.

I have nowhere else left to run.

It is do or die.

Survival of the fittest.

Run, Claire, run.

Across the ice and never stop… Never look back.

CHAPTER 79

The spider crawled across Claire's face, pausing on her cheek, just as her eyes snapped open. It took her a while to see clearly. She felt dizzy, tired. She felt the crawling sensation on her skin. She raised her hand to swat the spider, but the shackles around her wrist pulled taut around the pipe.

It took a few moments for her to realise she'd been lying awkwardly up against the wall, and her back and neck ached. She looked at the shackles around each wrist, then the pipe, and felt her stomach roll.

She remembered the marks on the bodies of the dead women, on their wrists, on their ankles. Her own feet were free from restraint, and she managed to pull herself upright. The stinging pain came from under her ribs when she sat forward, making her gasp. She grabbed around her torso. She saw the dark stain on her dressing gown.

She held her breath as she peeled it back, frightened of what she might find. Her eyes tried hard to focus. She blinked her eyes tight, opened them again. She focused on the white gauze, a dressing, stuck crudely to her skin with what looked like masking tape.

She picked at it, pulling a section of it back, and saw a small cut, flaky with dried blood. It was only a flesh wound. She pushed the tape back down, then her eyes searched her surroundings.

She saw little. Only a single dirty bulb hung from the ceiling offering light. She saw a table with a jug of water, a plastic cup, and a lamp that was switched off.

Her eyes wandered up the steps that led towards a door, and she knew she was in a basement. Her body shivered when she caught sight of stains, almost black in colour, spattered on the concrete floor beside her. She was no stranger to those stains.

Blood.

She pulled herself to her feet, tugging hard on the pipe. The noise of metal against metal clattered, the sound seeming to engulf the space around her.

Upstairs, Lucas knew she was awake. A grin spread across his lips as he went to the hall. He stopped in front of the door to the basement and reached out his hands, resting his palms on the wooden barrier between them.

*

Claire pulled harder against the shackles, but she knew it was no use. She sank back down in a heap on the cold floor, sucking in large gulps of stale air. It was heavy, with a fetid smell that stung her nostrils. She could smell the sour tang of urine and vomit, and tried hard not to gag.

She closed her eyes when the pain of a tension headache began to emerge across her forehead.

Then she heard the bolt slide across the door at the top of the stairs.

She blinked hard when the door opened. She saw feet begin to descend the staircase.

She saw his face.

It was pale. Cold. His features were exaggerated by the shadows cast around the room.

'You're awake at last. You've been out a long time… I began to worry.' He watched her eyes, boring into his, and he glared back, drawing closer to her. He pointed to her middle. 'I dressed your wound. I'm sorry about that, it was a heat of the moment thing.' Her eyes remained unflinching when he crouched in front of her, his face drawing closer to hers. 'You can't say I didn't warn you beforehand.'

He pushed forward onto his knees.

'It's breakfast time, you must be hungry.' He saw her recoil as he crawled closer. He looked away from her, avoiding her eyes. 'You mustn't be scared of me, Claire.'

'Fuck you.'

He flinched, eyes growing dark. 'Watch your mouth.'

'My mother will have reported me missing by now. They'll be looking for me.'

'But they won't find you.'

Claire started laughing. 'After all the DNA and evidence you left in my house? You may as well have left a calling card.'

'Maybe.'

'*Definitely*. They'll find me – and soon.'

'Well, it's just as well you won't be staying here much longer, isn't it?'

Her face dropped.

Lucas smiled, pushed himself up from the floor.

She watched him. He was still wearing the clothes he had on when he abducted her and she saw the cut in the fabric at his thigh where she'd stabbed him.

A chink in his armour.

'You must be hungry.'

He started for the stairs, then glanced at her sideways, looked her all over. The look made her feel sick. 'You'll want a change of clothes, no doubt.' He climbed the stairs, not expecting an answer. She waited until he locked the door after him before getting to her feet, and tried the shackle chain once more. She tugged hard around the pipe.

'You're wasting your time.'

The voice came from the shadows.

Claire's head whipped around and stared into the far corner of the basement. She didn't know if her mind was playing tricks on her or if she had really heard a voice in the darkness. The effects of the chloroform had made her feel giddy and her head felt as thick as cotton wool.

'Hello?' she spoke to the darkness.

There was no reply.

She felt tension building in her chest, realised she was holding her breath, exhaled, and used what strength she had left in her arms to pull at the pipe again. She guessed Lucas could hear her from upstairs but she didn't care.

She pulled on it a second time, the strain visible in her face. The pipe groaned, but held fast against the wall.

'The pipe's never gonna give.'

This time, Claire walked as far as the shackles would allow her. The chain snapped taut after a few paces.

'Who's there?'

Silence.

'Fallon?'

In the dark corner she saw a blanket tossed aside, and a figure emerge, shuffling forward on its behind across the floor, until light from the bulb overhead revealed dirty-looking blonde hair, tousled with dried sweat.

A pair of chocolate-coloured eyes stared back into hers. Claire saw a nose stud and lip piercing catch the light from above and she knew then, beyond doubt.

'Fallon, you're alive.'

The girl lowered her eyes, then took in every inch of Claire's appearance. She frowned at the woman standing there in her underwear, only partially covered by the thin dressing gown.

'Who're you supposed to be?'

'I'm a police officer.'

'You're the cavalry?' she sneered, eyeing Claire up and down. She pushed herself back towards the corner she'd emerged from. 'I'd say we're both fucked.' She flipped the blanket over her legs with her cuffed hands.

Claire heard the sound of metal on metal. Fallon was chained to another pipe that had a longer chain on the shackles.

'We've been doing all we can to find you. Your father and friends… even your mother has come back to help us with our enquiries.'

Fallon sniggered. 'My mother?' She turned to look at Claire again. 'She hasn't been my mother for a long time. You haven't done your research very well.'

They heard the basement door unlock.

Claire ventured back towards the wall as Lucas appeared with a tray of food. There was only one plate and Claire stared at him.

'Where's Fallon's?'

His eyes shot up to the corner where Fallon was lurking in the shadows. His face relaxed. 'You've met.' He set the tray down on the floor near Claire. 'She'll eat when she's told to eat.'

He eyed her from head to toe, then went to the pipe and tested its sturdiness, followed by the chain of her shackles. He took one last look towards Fallon, then left them alone.

Claire was starving. She got down on the floor and uncovered the plate on the tray. There was some toast and a muffin. She picked up a slice and eyed it with suspicion.

'I doubt he poisoned it,' Fallon said. 'He needs you alive.' Claire looked towards her, then back at the food. It was all the encouragement she needed. She shovelled it into her mouth. She didn't know when she would have the chance to eat again, and she needed her strength.

She looked at Fallon, who was turned away from her, staring at the floor. 'You want some? When did you last eat something?'

'I dunno… maybe yesterday morning. It's hard to keep track of time down here.'

Claire held the plate out towards her. 'Here.' Fallon hesitated, then shuffled out from her corner. She picked up a slice of toast, and Claire noticed how dirty her fingernails were. She let Fallon eat a little before she spoke again. 'I'm DCI Claire Winters.'

Fallon stopped chewing, gave her the once over, then shrugged. 'Whatever DCI means?'

'I'm the detective in charge of the investigation into those recent murders – the three women?'

'And in charge of getting me back?'

'Yes.'

'Then you fucked up big time. Why the hell does he want you?'

'I don't know, but I need your help.'

Fallon held up her cuffed wrists. 'I'm no use to you.'

'You can give me an idea of what he wants, why he's doing this.'

Fallon shrugged again and took another piece of toast. They sat in silence, and after they'd spilt the muffin and demolished that, Claire wanted some answers.

'What did he mean when he said you would eat when you were told to?'

Fallon glanced up at her, licking her fingers. 'He thinks he can break me. He keeps trying but he can't. I won't let him.'

'Withholding food is your punishment?'

Fallon shrugged. 'I guess.' She dusted off her hands. 'He'll have to feed me sooner or later otherwise his plan won't work.'

Claire narrowed her eyes. 'What does he want with you?'

'He wants to change me. He thinks I need him… I can't believe I used to think he was OK.' Claire looked confused. She knew Fallon and Richard had been seeing Mitchell Curran, and the other victims had seen his wife, Stephanie, but none of them had mentioned Lucas.

'You know him?'

Fallon nodded. 'Yeah, he used to talk to me most weeks.' She saw the confused look on Claire's face. 'What?'

'We didn't think he made contact before he took the other women, except maybe Felicity. I'm wondering why you're different.'

Another shrug.

The door to the basement was unlocked.

Fallon crawled back to the corner and Claire pushed herself up on her feet. When Lucas descended the stairs, she saw he was carrying a pile of clothes. He stopped in front of her, glanced towards Fallon, then at the empty plate on the tray. Fallon saw him and looked away, wiping her mouth free of any crumbs.

He looked at Claire and threw the clothes at her.

'You fed her, didn't you?'

'No.'

'Don't lie to me!'

He stormed towards Fallon. The shackles at Claire's wrists strained as she tried to get closer. Lucas grabbed Fallon's shoulder and she screamed as he pulled her around to face him.

He slapped her across the face with the back of his hand. She shrieked, and he slapped her again.

'This is your fault.' He pointed his finger back at Claire. He grabbed a handful of Fallon's hair, pulling her face towards his. She spat at him, and this time he punched her, cutting her lip.

'Punish me then!' He looked back at Claire, his eyes wild with rage.

'You?'

'If it's my fault, punish me.'

He took a step closer to the light. Claire stood her ground. 'Don't sacrifice yourself for *that*,' he said, pointing back at Fallon. 'You're worth so much more than this spoilt brat.'

'Go fuck yourself.'

As the words escaped Fallon's lips, Claire sank inwardly. Lucas's eyes seemed set ablaze. He swung around and grabbed Fallon, wrenching her forward, screaming in her face.

'Make yourself sick, right now!'

Claire was screaming at him to leave her alone, as he forced Fallon's mouth open, sticking his fingers down her throat. Her gag reflex kicked in, her upper body convulsed, and she heaved forward and vomited onto the floor. She spluttered, coughed for air, and Lucas released her head.

He looked back at Claire. 'Get dressed.'

He pulled out a key and unlocked her shackles. He picked up the clothes from the floor, thrusting them into her arms. He glanced back at Fallon, who was now curled up into a ball, crying.

'Don't try anything stupid. There's no way out of this basement other than through that door and I'll be right behind it.'

CHAPTER 80

A bruise had already begun to appear across her cheek where Lucas had punched her, and she winced when she touched the side of her face. Claire helped Fallon sit forward.

'I'm OK,' she said, pushing Claire away. 'It's just sick.'

'I'm more concerned about the side of your face.'

Fallon shook her head. 'He could've done worse. He tries to control his anger but sometimes he can't. It gets the better of him.'

Claire looked around for something that might help them escape.

There was nothing.

She looked at the clothes he'd given her. A thin short-sleeved top and jogging bottoms, both navy and in her size. She felt loath to put them on, but she was cold, so forced herself out of necessity.

*

Once she was dressed, Claire realised the ache in her groin she'd felt for the last half hour was because she desperately needed the toilet. In all the chaos, she hadn't given it a second thought but now she felt the strain, fighting the urge to release the muscles stopping her bladder from emptying.

She looked around the basement again. Her eyes landed on Fallon, who was staring at the floor. She felt the weight of Claire's stare. Her eyes shot up to meet hers. 'What?'

'I really need to pee.'

'That's nice.'

Claire shook her head. 'You don't understand what I'm getting at. How'd you go to the toilet?'

Fallon grimaced. 'Same way you do.'

'I meant, where have you been going? Does he let you use the bathroom?'

'No, he's been bringing me a bucket. He doesn't even leave it down here for me. He makes me wait until he's ready. Bastard makes me hold it. I think he wants me to piss and shit myself to make me realise I need him.'

Claire pulled a face. 'Are you always this pleasant?'

'I'm the least of your problems.'

'What do you think would happen if I went and knocked on the door? I'm not shackled.'

'I wouldn't. He might lose his temper… and you know what he can do.'

Claire weighed up the possibilities. She had to do something. She climbed up the staircase to the basement door and hammered on it.

'You'll make him angry.'

Claire ignored her and kept on hammering with her clenched fist, until she heard him on the other side of the door.

CHAPTER 81

Stefan sprinted back to the incident room, closely followed by Harper. Stefan had his mobile to his ear, trying to get hold of Elias.

'How'd you know it was Lucas?' Harper said, matching Stefan's stride.

'I didn't, not for sure.'

'You took a gamble. You got that solicitor pissed.'

'Time's running out for Claire, we've not got time to do everything by the book. We have to find her.'

Elias answered at his end. 'I'm on my way back to the station now.'

'Hatcher's confessed it is Lucas Hall.'

'Then we've got him.'

Stefan shook his head, bounded up a flight of stairs, and entered the corridor that led to the incident room. 'Not quite. Hatcher wouldn't give up Lucas's location.'

'I got his address.' Elias read it out as Stefan wrote it down, handing the piece of paper to Harper. Stefan disconnected his call with Elias and got everyone in the incident room listening.

He stole another look at his watch for the hundredth time so far that day.

Hold on, Claire. Please hold on.

CHAPTER 82

Lucas had brought Claire a bucket but he didn't turn his back. When she'd finished, he took the bucket and put it in the far corner. He looked at the split, bleeding lip he'd just given her, five minutes before he gave her the bucket. He shook his head as he shackled her wrists.

'I really didn't want to do that. I felt bad when I found out William had almost dislocated your shoulder,' he said, running his fingers over the purple-black bruise up her arm and shoulder. He caressed it, then squeezed her shoulder hard, twisting his fingers. She masked a cry of pain.

He grinned to himself.

She stared at him in defiance, pursed her lips, and spat a glob of blood in his face. From her corner, Fallon laughed. Lucas's face shot towards her. 'Shut up!' His eyes went back to Claire's. He wiped the blood from his face. 'Don't lower yourself to her level.' He pointed at Fallon, but his gaze never left Claire's face.

'Just look at her body. That mess. She's disgusting.'

'And you think you can change her?'

Lucas's eyes seemed to flash just then with a hint of something other than anger. He crouched to her eye level.

'Do you know what it's like to watch someone's final moment, when they draw that last breath? I was there when William did it. I watched the moment the knife cut through sinful flesh. I was there… every time.'

Claire frowned. 'Sinful flesh? Felicity Davenport was barely sixteen. What did she do to deserve that?'

'She wasn't grateful for her life. She wanted to end it all, and for what? Her parents put too much on her shoulders? At least her parents cared.'

'Felicity was a teenager. She needed help and only her brother took her seriously. If you needed to punish anyone, it should've been her parents and the system that was failing her.'

'It wasn't my intention to punish. I am the teacher. It was William's job to punish if they failed to change, failed to learn.'

'And what now? William can't help you.'

He laughed. 'Just because I didn't intend to kill doesn't mean I won't.'

'Why Nola and Sara? They didn't deserve what happened either.'

His brow furrowed. 'Why Nola? Do you really need to ask? She was what is wrong with a lot of girls today. Her sin was her body and her misuse of it… With Nola, when I first saw her at Focus Being, I thought I saw something underneath her entire charade… I was wrong.'

Inside Claire's head was a fusion of curiosity and a sense of dread. She had to find out what made his mind tick and use it against him.

'She didn't even know you existed, did she?'

His face was stern. 'My role was mainly in the backroom admin. She looked my way once but she wouldn't have known me, and I had to change that.' He paused. A small trace of a smile twitched at the corner of his mouth.

'Sara was the same. She was a soul full of hurt. Her husband took her for granted and I would've left her to heal through the psychotherapy if I hadn't found out she was being unfaithful, whilst in therapy. That changed my view of

her. She was deliberately rebelling against the whole reason
why she was there in the first place! I spoke to her on the
phone soon after I read her file. I gave her a little advice. She
was someone worth saving until she tried to use her body to
fool me. She pretended to be grateful.'

Claire's eyes narrowed. 'Why the clients at Focus Being?
They're there for help, something you want to give people.'

He laughed. 'You really don't get it. These people, they
think the world in their head is all that matters.' He jammed
a thumb against his temple with passion. 'I got sick and tired
of watching these people breeze in and out thinking they had
the weight of the world on their shoulders.

'Look at the world around us. The world is fed on
suffering. *Real* human suffering and it pains me. War, famine,
rape, disease. That's the bigger picture. That's what these
people can't see. They can't see just how lucky they are...
Hell exists and it's right here on earth.'

Claire avoided his eyes. 'And where do you fit into all
this? You're one big contradiction. You say you want to help,
yet you've caused the death of three women.'

He shook his head. 'I wish you could see what I'm trying
to do here. I hoped you'd at least see the bigger picture. One
day people will thank me.'

'You're fucking crazy,' Fallon said.

He stared at her. The look made Claire's blood run cold.
She glanced at Fallon. 'What about her?' Fallon's face
showed her anger, but inside she was feeling sick. She didn't
want to hear the truth.

Lucas watched her as he spoke. 'She's beyond saving...
Daddy's spoilt little princess. Promiscuous, manipulative,
foul-mouthed. She's no better than a blood-sucking parasite.'

'I didn't ask for your help,' Fallon said.

'You've never been grateful for anything in your whole
miserable little life. You have a father who loves you, yet

you go out of your way to destroy him.' He pointed at her.
'The more I think about the reasons why I tried to help you,
the more I hate everything you've become. I'm glad William
can't be with us.' He grinned then. 'I'll have the pleasure of
killing you myself. I'll make you grateful for what you had,
right before I choke the last bit of life out of you.'

For the first time, the full gravity of the situation started to
hit Fallon full force.

'You're scaring her,' said Claire.

'And she should be scared.'

'When backed into a corner, people are dangerous, Lucas.'

He swung back to look at her. 'You included?' He sneered
and shook his head. 'You were scared last night. I could
almost hear the blood racing through your veins, and you
were very easy to catch.'

'Sorry to disappoint you.'

'On the contrary,' he said, the darkness leaving his voice.
'I find your weakness quite beautiful.' He paused. 'Tell me
your fears, Claire, it's all part of this process.'

'You need to stop this.'

'Are you still having those night terrors?'

Her whole body stiffened.

'You weren't responsible for what happened to him. You
do know that, don't you?'

'You have no right to talk to me about him.'

'I read up on the dead priest investigation,' he said,
ignoring her. 'What happened all those years ago, that whole
sorry mess, *everything*. There's no way you could ever come
back from that unscathed, without any scars.'

She looked away.

'You can't hope to heal without help, Claire, you do know
that, don't you?'

Claire changed tack. He knew her weakness and she was
damned sure that she knew his.

'Is it because of your mother? Is that why you're doing this?'

He flinched.

'She hurt me. She made my father leave. Everyone should be grateful for what they have; not many would've survived what I went through. I seek to make people thankful, and where they have strayed from the path, steer them back. Only then can they be happy.'

'Why target me?'

He smiled. 'You're flawed. You think people have to meet your standards. You think you can climb high without a care in the world. It's Claire's way or no way. That needs to change.'

He closed in on her, but she reeled back, raised her leg and brought it crashing down into the wound on his thigh. He buckled, and a guttural roar escaped his lips. He pushed himself to his feet. Saliva was hanging from his lip as he controlled the pain. 'That was stupid.'

He disappeared up the basement stairs, but not without pain in his step. When he came back he carried a pipe, uncoiling it from the kitchen as he came towards her. One end of the pipe was attached to the kitchen tap, back up the stairs. Lucas now pointed the other end at Claire.

'Don't get comfortable over there, Fallon.' Out the corner of his eye, he saw her flinch. 'We're moving to our final destination, Claire's test. It's going to be cold. He aimed the hose at her torso. 'Let's raise the stakes a little.'

Water began to dribble out onto the floor. 'If you're not careful, you could catch your death. I'll be your only hope of survival.'

He pressed the trigger and a jet of water shot towards her, drenching and soaking into her clothes. She cried out. Ice water, like tiny needles, lashed her skin. She pulled herself to her feet, but she couldn't avoid being completely soaked.

He laughed when she turned her back to him, as if it would make a difference. He aimed higher, blasted her hair, so it hung in limp vine-like tendrils, water dripping from the ends.

He released the trigger.

She turned towards him. Her face was red from the cold. She instantly began to shiver. She pressed her lips tight together, tried to stop herself trembling.

'You're soaked in the only clothes you have. You remember that.'

Claire didn't know what he meant, and right now she didn't care. Fallon, who had been stunned to silence, too scared to breathe, tried to stand when he came towards her.

He grabbed her, pulled a cloth from his trouser pocket, and pressed it over her nose and mouth. When she stopped fighting him, he let her slide to the floor with a thud.

Claire backed towards the wall when he turned on her.

'Come now, Claire.' He took a step closer. 'This won't hurt.'

CHAPTER 83

'Lucas Hall, age thirty-eight, five-ten, dark hair, dark eyes, wears glasses,' Stefan said, addressing the team. He circulated copies of Lucas's driving licence around the room.

'He's been done once for driving with no insurance, nothing else, but the PNC shows his car is a maroon Ford Mondeo, which is registered to a house in old Welwyn Garden City.'

Stefan looked up. 'There're also details, although they're limited, of another address, owned by Lucas, which the car used to be registered to – a house in the Lordship Estate, Letchworth, not far from Focus Being.'

He looked at Elias. 'Crest, I want you to take a team of officers over to the address in Welwyn, while I take a team to the Letchworth property. He's got to have taken Claire to one of these addresses. Maybe Fallon Dockley is with her too. William Hatcher has only given me Lucas's name as the brains behind the operation and that he'd targeted Claire. Other than that, we're on our own.'

He turned to DC Cleaver. 'Jane, I want everything you can get on Lucas: his background, any family that might be close enough to offer him shelter. Get me everything.'

'What about the media?' said Elias.

Stefan looked at him and shook his head. 'Not yet. If Lucas is keeping an eye out on the media, which I think he will be, I don't want him panicking. We need him to believe we don't know he's involved. That's the one advantage we can use to keep Claire alive.'

CHAPTER 5

CHAPTER 84

Despite the cold outside, Stefan was burning on the inside. It was the adrenaline, pumping through his veins, just at that moment before the Enforcer went hurtling into the hinges of the front door.

It went crashing to one side in one swoop, busting the hinges. Officers charged through the house, securing each room in turn. There was so much noise, Stefan couldn't be sure if they had found anything or not, until all fell silent.

*

Elias had been in the property in Welwyn less than two minutes and stared at each blank room.

'He lived here?' he said to Harper. They both stared at the peeling floral wallpaper in the living room. 'Is every room like this one?'

'Pretty much. I'd say no one's lived here for a long time, not properly anyway.'

Elias walked through to the kitchen, then went upstairs. There were a few photographs on a sideboard. He studied the pictures. He recognised those eyes that stared back into his.

Lucas.

*

Stefan's heart sank as an officer came up beside him, shaking his head.

'There's no one here.'

Stefan swore and banged his fist against the nearest wall. 'How can there be nothing?' He spun around on his heels. 'There's no way he could know we were on to him. He thought he'd manipulated Hatcher enough to buy him time.'

He stood staring into the living room, his mind working overtime. 'OK,' he said finally, 'let's get this place searched.'

Stefan looked at his surroundings. He could smell something. He sniffed hard. He was certain it was paint – maybe paper paste or something similar. It was a smell that lingered. He shook the thought from his head when his mobile started ringing.

'Fletcher.'

'It's Crest. There's nothing here. If this is Lucas's main address, he either hates DIY or he's deliberately made sure this house was used as a decoy. There're no clothes or anything that indicates he's been living here on a permanent basis.'

'He's been residing in his second home, which makes sense, it's so close to Focus Being,' said Stefan.

Elias sighed. 'No signs of the Guv?'

'Not yet.'

There was a long silence that hung heavy in the air. Elias walked through to the living room and saw a shelf on the wall behind the door filled with more framed photographs, covered with cobwebs.

'Crest?'

Elias was barely listening as his eyes scanned the photographs in front of him, his eyes coming back to one in particular.

A picture of someone with familiar eyes looking back into his.

A sinking feeling gripped his body. He grabbed the frame and made for the front door.

'Don't go anywhere. I'm coming right over!'

*

Stefan kept his mobile poised at his ear for a few moments after Elias had hung up. DC Cleaver came into the room.

'What is it, Jane?'

'I think we've found something.'

Stefan followed her back through to the hallway. From his original angle, he hadn't spotted it but from the new viewpoint, he saw it in an instant.

'Well, that explains the smell in here,' he said, reaching out his hand. His fingers touched the slightly damp wallpaper that covered one side of the hallway wall. It was light, fresher than the rest of the paper in the hall, despite the pattern being the same. His fingers touched a ridge, and he spread his palm out, ran it across the expanse and applied some pressure.

'It's a door.'

He pulled his car keys from his pocket and scored a line around the raised surface, cutting the paper.

'Shouldn't we wait for forensics? They'll want to take a video and photos.'

'There's no time. He took the time to conceal whatever is behind this door and we need to know why.' He peeled away a strip of paper, exposing a wooden door.

Jane swallowed hard. 'You don't think—'

'Let's not jump to conclusions.'

Stefan knew what she was thinking. Hell, he was thinking it himself. As the rest of the paper was peeled back, he prayed that if Claire was behind it, she was still alive.

The Enforcer did its job, breaking the lock as soon as metal hit metal. The basement door groaned and popped open.

The smell hit them first: a mixture of vomit, urine and sweat.

Inside, Stefan was reeling. He detected something else in the air and recognised it immediately.

The smell of blood.

He looked down. He saw the top of a wooden staircase that disappeared, winding down into an oily blackness that even the light from upstairs couldn't penetrate.

Jane passed him a torch.

He flicked it on.

He hesitated before shining it down the stairs.

*

It hadn't taken Elias long to get to the house in Letchworth and, when Stefan had shown him the basement door, he looked surprised.

'Down there,' Stefan said, pointing to the now brightly lit basement, 'is where he kept the victims. It's also where he kept Claire.'

'She's not—'

'We found her dressing gown – it's blood-stained.'

Elias paused. 'Do you think she's alive?'

Stefan nodded.

Elias thought back to the photograph he'd taken from the house, which he now held in his hands. The person in the photograph was someone who had drawn him in, lied to him, at least partly. The thought of what it could mean raced through his head.

'You need to see this,' he said, passing the picture to Stefan.

His mouth dropped open. 'Where did you get this?'

'Lucas's other house. This is the girl who gave me the information that helped lead us to Hatcher.'

Stefan's head shot up, a mixture of confusion and anger on his face. 'Crest, what've you done?' He shook his head. 'It can't be her.'

'What you on about?'

Stefan pointed at the photograph. He remembered the day she'd cried when presented with Nola's body on the slab. 'I know her, Crest.' His eyes turned serious. 'You'd better tell me everything, and fast.'

CHAPTER 85

It hadn't taken them long to find the girl.

They'd driven around Haverbridge town and around Hedonism, after they got no answer from her flat or the mobile number they had on file. It was when they had seemed out of options that Elias suggested The Clover.

After asking around inside, the man behind the counter knew where she was likely to be. He said he'd seen her in the town square most afternoons when he went out for his lunch.

Stefan then drove them to a side street beside the square and waited. 'How could you not realise?' he said, turning towards Elias.

'I never met her before the other night. You and Claire saw her once when she went to the morgue. It's not like her picture was in the incident room.'

Stefan bit his tongue. Right now, all that mattered was finding Claire and the girl.

It was nearly noon when they saw her. Stefan's mobile rang as he got out the car.

'I've found something,' said Jane when he answered. 'Hidden inside Lucas's mattress were some official documents. I have his birth certificate, and death certificates for both his mother and grandmother, but there's something else.'

'Jane, I've got to go. We have the girl in our sights, we need to move now.' Stefan's face was set rigid as Jane continued regardless. He couldn't quite believe what he was hearing. Never in his life could he ever have imagined the complexity of this entire investigation.

When he hung up, he turned to Elias.

'You approach her and see if you can get her talking. I'll head around to the other side of the square in case she runs.'

Elias was serious. 'What did Jane say to you?'

'Just follow the girl.'

*

She was in the middle of the square when Elias appeared in front of her.

'Hello again.'

She stared at him. 'How'd you know where to find me?'

'Since the mobile number you gave me was a fake,' he said, watching her face flush, 'I went back to The Clover. The owner knew where to find you. He didn't know your name though.'

'My name's not important, Sergeant.'

'Your name's just as important as what you know. That's why you chose me, isn't it? DCI Winters and DI Fletcher, they know you, that's why you couldn't go to them. But me? I'd never seen your face before.'

She shoved past him. 'Leave me alone, I told you all I know.'

'We both know that's not true.' He caught her arm. 'I need more. There's another girl's life at risk and DCI Winters is missing.'

She pulled her arm from him. 'You've arrested William Hatcher, charged him. I saw it on the news. It's in the papers. He *confessed*.'

She picked up her pace. Elias matched her stride.

'There's someone else working with him. Hatcher was in custody when the new girl went missing.' He shoved a photo in her face. 'Fallon Dockley. She needs your help. *I* need your help.'

She looked at Fallon's face for a few seconds before pushing his hand away. 'I can't help you.'

'You said you followed the man who we now know is William Hatcher, but he didn't take Nola, did he? That was a lie. A lie to help implicate him.'

'I should never have come to you.'

She broke into a run and Elias gave chase. When she ran towards where Stefan had parked, he came out of nowhere, his arms circling around her waist, pulling her back and slamming her up against his car.

'That was stupid,' Elias said, catching them up.

Her stomach was doing somersaults, especially when she saw Stefan's face. He looked down into her eyes and almost hoped none of this was true.

'Hello, Olivia.'

'Inspector Fletcher,' she said, out of breath, 'you should've said what you wanted, I'd have given you a reduced rate.' She winked, then bucked against his chest. He gripped her arms tight and spun her around just as Elias held up a pair of handcuffs.

'You coming quietly?'

'This is a mistake,' she said with venom.

Stefan lowered his mouth to her ear.

'No, helping your *brother* was the mistake.'

CHAPTER 86

Jane Cleaver's stomach had pulled tight inside her when she had found Olivia's birth certificate inside Lucas's mattress. It was a missing piece of the puzzle but it wasn't enough to satisfy Stefan.

She sighed as she gave him the bad news.

'There must be something?' he said. 'Anything that gives us a clue where he's taken them?'

'I can't magic it out of thin air. Olivia's the key. She knows.'

Stefan's breath felt as if it was catching in his throat. 'I know that, but it's gonna take time.' He shook his head. The stress was mounting up, time ticking by. 'Find me something, Jane. Find it fast.'

DSI Donahue laid his head in his hands when Stefan hung up on Jane. Stefan's eyes were alive with emotion. 'Even to assign Olivia a social worker will take time. Time we don't have.' Stefan's words cut through Donahue like a knife, and he found himself sweating despite the chill in his office.

'Has she denied Lucas Hall is her brother?'

'Like hell she has. She's practically broadcasting it now she's here. She knows she has nothing left to lose.'

'So all her ID is fake as well?'

'Jones is a fake surname. It's common, easy to overlook, that's why she picked it.'

'Why contact DS Crest? She risked a lot to make contact with him when he was with you and Claire.'

'That's what I need to find out, but getting the location of where Lucas has taken Claire is my priority. I need to question her now. It can't wait.'

Donahue looked deflated, his face lowered, staring at the floor. He nodded at Stefan. 'OK,' he said, standing up behind his desk, his face serious. 'Prise it out of the bitch.'

CHAPTER 87

Olivia looked up at Stefan, defiance in her eyes.

'Found her yet?'

Her voice was cocky. She sat back in her chair, crossing her legs. 'Time's running out.' She leaned forward again as Stefan and Elias sat in front of her. 'Tick, tock, Inspector.'

'Olivia Hall,' Stefan said. 'I can call you Hall, can't I?'

She gave a wry smile. 'I never liked Jones anyway.' Stefan stared at her, as Elias wrote a few notes.

'You understand why you have no one here to represent you and why you have been refused a phone call, don't you?'

She shrugged. 'Breaching my human rights?'

'Time constraints. You said yourself DCI Winters and Fallon Dockley are running out of time.'

'Fallon's probably dead by now. Lucas took quite a shine to your Claire, though.'

Elias pulled a face, drawing her attention towards him. 'You're not as stupid as you make out, arc you?'

She grinned, twisting a strand of hair around her fingers. 'Is it the blonde hair?' Her face then turned serious. 'It'd be stupid to underestimate me.'

Stefan paused. 'Just so we're clear, you have been refused a phone call and access to legal representation at this moment in time because DSI Donahue believes there's a real possibility it could lead to interference in the investigation and harm of evidence connected with the case, not to

mention the very real risk of harm befalling DCI Winters and
Fallon Dockley.'

Another sneer. 'Do your worst, Inspector,' she said,
flicking her long hair over her shoulder. 'I've got all the time
in the world to play your game.'

*

After committing the relevant information to tape, Stefan
wasted no time with Olivia, but she wasn't giving up where
Lucas had taken Claire and Fallon. He tried to trip her up. He
hoped she'd give her brother away by mistake if he got her
talking about their past.

'What made you come to DS Crest?'

She threw her head back, grinning. 'You fuckers couldn't
connect the dots.'

'You wanted to be caught?'

'William was meant to be Lucas's fall guy. He always was.'

'Why?'

'Because he trusted my brother. He was the perfect
candidate. He was stupid enough to believe the lies Lucas
told him and what he promised.'

'What did he promise him?'

She smiled. 'Everything.'

She leaned forward, pointed a bony finger to her temple.
'He got inside William's head. Made him believe he wasn't
worthless, that he could serve a purpose for the greater good,
and, more importantly, he could help fund private medical
care for his dying mother.'

Stefan and Elias exchanged glances.

'William's mother has inoperable cancer. William knows
that.'

She shrugged. 'People are prepared to show a little faith
in the impossible when it's a loved one's life at stake.' She

smiled again. 'It was William's weakness. His grief and pain. It made him easier to manipulate.'

Stefan shook his head.

'You think it's sick, twisted.'

'It is.'

'No,' she said, shaking her head, 'it gave William some hope. Light in the darkness. Something to absorb the pain that pills and therapy couldn't touch.'

Elias leaned towards her. 'Help us understand why you're part of this. Nola Grant was your friend.' Olivia lowered her eyes as if any reminder of her past pained her. 'Your brother has killed people. Doesn't that mean anything to you?'

Her eyes snapped up, angry. 'He hasn't killed anyone. That was William's job, but now he's locked up, so what happens next is your fault.'

Stefan's brow furrowed. 'How does that work out?'

'He's had to change his plans.'

'You led us to Hatcher,' Elias broke in, 'that was your doing. Your brother changed his plans because of what you did.'

Her face glazed over. She looked away and said, 'I had to. He left me no choice.'

Elias turned to Stefan. 'She's wasting our time on purpose.'

'Lucas wanted to cut me out,' she said, her eyes now concentrating on the table in front of her. 'He wouldn't give me the money he promised me.' Her eyes misted over in rage. 'Lucy was my grandmother too!'

She leaned across the table, her hands clenched into fists. 'And Nola wasn't my friend. She wasn't anyone's friend. She looked out for herself. No one else mattered. My brother wanted tortured souls, people who needed to change. I gave Nola the chance by sending Lucas her way. She fell on her own sword. She got what was coming to her and I don't regret anything.'

CHAPTER 88

Olivia sipped the water Elias brought her and ran her tongue over her dry lips. She set the plastic cup down, keeping her eyes lowered.

'Mum didn't want me. I was an accident and she made Lucas treat me like dirt. She said she hadn't wanted any more kids after she'd had him. Lucas was two when Dad walked out but that didn't stop Mum fucking around with him years later. That's when she fell pregnant with me.'

She frowned at the mention of her father. 'Dad didn't stand by her, accused her of seeing other men, which was true. He left before I was born. I've never met him. Lucas was seven when I was born.'

Her eyes narrowed into slits. 'My mother was a complete slut and off her head. When she came home from work, she'd slap me about if she'd had a few. She never really touched Lucas physically, but mentally she taunted him. Then Grandma Lucy stepped in, saved him… She didn't bother with me much. Lucas was her baby. Her favourite. I used to joke about it – Lucy and Lucas – it sounded weird, but they were like two peas in a pod. Shared the same traits, and I knew not to get on the wrong side of them.'

Olivia went on to tell them everything she remembered leading up to her mother's and grandmother's deaths. She explained how everything had been left to Lucas and she'd gone to live with her aunt.

'And you're bitter about that?' Stefan asked, without a hint of sympathy.

'Grandma Lucy was a fucking nut. Like a fucking evil gene or something. It was passed to Mum, and Lucas, although he's good at hiding it. He's been hiding it most of his life. There's a part of him that believes his own lies. He owes the art of deception to Grandma Lucy.'

She paused. 'She scared me shitless. I always did what she said. I helped out a lot when she was dying, yet she left me nothing in her will. I envied my brother. I still do. We had no love from our mother but Lucy, she gave him the love he craved while I was left with nothing, yet I still tried to please her, despite everything.'

Her eyes rose to meet Stefan's, stabbing her index finger down hard on the table top. 'I deserve a share of her money. He promised me. I want what's mine.'

'You've been doing this for your grandmother's inheritance?' Stefan said. 'That's blood money.'

'I was left with nothing, forced into prostitution after my aunt kicked me out. Lucas didn't want to help me. He left me to fend for myself. He told me I should be grateful for my life. Our grandmother was a stickler for being content with the cards fate dealt us.'

She wiped a tear from her cheek. 'I found myself struggling on the street. Me and Rach met Nola and she used to try and steal money, get Daryl pissed off with us, take the heat off her. When I asked Lucas the final time for money a few months ago, he said I had to help him and earn Lucy's money. Make her proud of me.'

Olivia broke down then, but Stefan pressed her further.

'Lucas controlled you. He left you with nothing. When you were at your lowest he said you had to help him. Help him kill.'

Olivia seemed to become agitated, defiant, when anyone spoke ill of her brother. They saw her change from a weak, broken woman, to an aggressive tyrant in a matter of seconds.

'He didn't set out to have anyone killed. My brother tried to help these women. He wanted to help them turn their lives around. He told me he'd been watching the women coming in to Focus Being. He got angry when he thought about how Lucy had worked so hard to bring herself out of poverty. She had a hard life, yet she never complained. Lucas wanted to offer these women one final chance.'

'And if they didn't conform, he'd have them killed,' Elias said.

'It would be a last resort, and not by his hand. He noticed William straight away at the centre. He was perfect.'

'Pretty handy his mother was dying and that he worked for a slaughterhouse too, though, I imagine.'

She glared at Stefan. 'You don't know us or how we lived. You can't judge. William could've walked away at any time, and Lucas planned to stop after the Davenport girl.'

'You made the choice to set William up, to let him take the fall for what was going on. It doesn't make any sense to abduct Fallon and Claire while William was in custody.'

Olivia buried her head in her hands. 'Lucas went too far. It was never supposed to happen but he told me he couldn't stop and that he wouldn't give me the money he'd promised.' Her eyes were alive with a sense of injustice. 'I wanted out but with my share.'

Stefan was sceptical. 'One minute you're defending him, the next you're ready to drop him in it.'

She avoided his eyes.

The anger inside Stefan reached boiling point. He slammed a hand down on the table, making her recoil. 'Stop wasting my fucking time... Where is DCI Winters?'

She matched his temper. 'I don't have to tell you anything. Lucas hasn't finished yet. He's got the taste. He wants blood. Who am I to stop that?'

Elias cut in. 'He has the money. Your share of it. He planned to stop what he was doing but he hasn't. Where's the pull of loyalty coming from? He stitched you up just as he did William.'

'No!'

'And you're letting him get away with it.'

'Those women had it coming, and so does Claire Winters.'

Stefan shot out of his seat, his chair slamming back against the wall behind him. He leaned across the table, invading her personal space. She could almost taste his breath when he spoke.

'Where is she?'

'It's too late. I won't tell you anything.'

Stefan paused. He felt reason and all of his training come into the front of his mind. He knew he had to control his temper. Anything that could be deemed aggressive when questioning a suspect could make any subsequent confession unreliable and then they'd have nothing.

Swallowing hard, he tried to control his voice and moved back away from her. 'Your brother's betrayed you. He's letting you take the blame along with William. He's played you both, can't you see that? You can stop this, Olivia.'

A smile spread across her lips. 'You don't get it, do you? I don't want to stop him, he can do what he likes.'

'Why?'

'Because I love my brother!' she screamed into his face, rising from her own chair. Her face was red, her eyes burning back into his. 'Family is family and I refuse to say another goddamn word.'

Stefan sneered. 'Do you really think he cares about you?' He watched her mouth twitch with anger. 'He doesn't give a damn about what happens to you.'

She shook her head. 'I know what you're trying to do.'

'I'm trying to help you see how little you mean to him. He's been using you your whole life. He's out of control.

If you tell me where he's taken them, your life doesn't have to be completely over.'

Olivia brought her hands crashing down on the table and shoved her face right up to Stefan's in frustration. 'This won't work on me!'

Elias quickly rose to his feet to restrain her but Stefan pushed him back.

'Drop the act. I've seen grown men tougher than you can imagine crumble at the thought of going to prison. You wouldn't last five minutes before someone cut you up just for looking at them the wrong way.'

Elias looked towards the camera in the far corner of the ceiling. 'Boss…'

Stefan ignored him, pushing his face closer to Olivia's. 'Just look at yourself. Some man's plaything.'

She shoved a finger in his face. 'You don't know anything about me.'

'I know you gave up another girl on the street for slaughter. Was Rachel Larson on the list as well?'

'I was only ever in this for the money. Those girls got themselves killed. All they had to do was play along and he would've let them go.'

'You're more stupid than I thought if that's what you really think. He could never let them go, they'd know too much, and he's finally realised that. It's just a game to him now. He's testing himself to see how far he can go before he has to kill, and you played your part in it.'

Olivia's right fist balled up at her side. She swung it towards his face but he blocked the punch. Undeterred, she launched herself at him, her hands grabbing at his shirt, knees crashing over the table top.

'Don't you judge me!'

Elias got behind her, trying to haul her back.

'Where's he taken them?' Stefan demanded. He grabbed her hands when her fingers clawed at the fabric of his shirt, tearing into his skin.

She then dropped to the floor as if the life had been instantly sucked out of her. She started crying, tears streaming down her face. Both men looked shell-shocked.

Then Stefan's mobile rang.

DC Cleaver.

'Jane?' he said, answering it.

'Starling Rentals in Letchworth,' she said. 'I found part of the invoice. He's rented a van but he's burnt the paperwork. I've managed to piece together some of the remaining fragments but we don't know the make or model of the vehicle.'

When Jane had finished, Stefan hung up. His face was flushed, but a sense of relief spread across his face. 'Get her back in a cell,' he said.

Olivia looked up at him.

'You going to tell us where that van's going?' He saw the flicker of recognition in her eyes. He crouched down, staring into her face. 'Last chance.'

She leaned forward and spat in his face. 'Go to hell.'

CHAPTER 89

Stefan and Elias drew worried looks from the admin staff as they showed their warrant cards to the manager, Elliot Starling, of Starling Rentals. He frowned at both men, reluctantly ushering them through to his office. He offered them a seat, but they declined. Elliot flopped down in the chair behind his desk, his face stern as they explained that Lucas was a person of interest. They were careful not to mention anything else.

'He used his real name,' Elliot said, running his finger across the entry in his log book. 'Hired a short-wheelbase Ford Transit van, white. Paid in cash. He came in yesterday and knew exactly which van he wanted.' Stefan frowned and Elliot's face grew serious. 'What's he wanted for?'

Stefan explained.

Elliot felt sick. He sat back down in his chair again. 'This isn't a joke, is it?'

'I'm afraid not.'

'Christ. Why didn't you say so? Look,' he said, now reaching for the keyboard on his desk, 'we have tracking devices in all our vehicles.' He pulled up a software application and typed in a few details relating to the van Lucas had hired.

After a few seconds he smiled, turning the computer monitor around. 'There you go.'

Leaning forward, Stefan and Elias saw a map, similar to those on Google, with a blue dot on the screen about fifty miles north-west from where they were sitting.

CHAPTER 90

Claire awoke to the sound of the wind howling. She felt the cold air gnawing at the skin of her bare arms. Her clothes were still sodden, sticking to her like a second skin. She shivered involuntarily. She opened her eyes a little more but saw nothing much in the shadows. There was only one shaft of daylight, which crept through a single boarded-up window.

The last thing she remembered was seeing Lucas and the white rag he'd held over her face.

Then she remembered Fallon.

She pulled her body upright. She was still bound at the wrists but with a thick white cord, which numbed her wrists. She tried to flex her wrists out. The cord wouldn't break but gave enough to allow sensation to flow through her fingers again.

She looked around the room. She made out the outline of a door opposite and a long shape on the floor not far from her feet.

'Fallon?'

There was a murmur and the shape rolled over. 'Fallon, is that you? You need to wake up.'

The figure rolled to face her. Claire could just about make out the outline of her face.

'You should've let me sleep. I just want this to be over.'

'We need to find a way out of here. Can you crawl to me?'

Fallon sneered. 'And what do you plan to do if we get our hands untied and manage to get out of this fucking shack? We're in the middle of bloody nowhere.' She rolled over to face the floor, her back towards Claire.

'You know where we are? I thought Lucas knocked us both out.'

'He did, but I woke up as he was moving us from his van. We're in some kind of wood or forest, nothing but trees around this derelict shack. He covered my face once he saw I was awake.'

Fallon stopped and thought for a moment. She turned her face back to Claire's. 'Nobody's going hear us scream when the time comes, are they?'

Claire stopped pulling the cord at her wrists, slowly raising her eyes to Fallon's. The thought made her blood run cold. Despite the darkness, she still saw the fear in the girl's eyes.

'We're not done yet, but you need to help me. You need to think if you want to survive this. What else can you tell me about where we are?' Fallon pulled her body up until she was sitting opposite Claire.

'I've told you already, we're surrounded by trees. I only caught a glimpse of this building. I don't know how many other rooms there are.' She sniffed, her nose now blocked where she'd been crying.

Claire looked towards the window and saw it was covered with wooden board, crudely nailed into a rotting frame. She saw the small gap at the bottom, which let a small shaft of light into the room.

Pulling her legs under her body, she got to her feet, stumbled towards the door ahead of them and tried the handle.

Locked, as expected.

She went back to the window and ran her fingers around the rough board. The wood was damp, splinters of it coming away under her touch. It would prove a little difficult to manoeuvre with her wrists bound, but if she could force her fingers up under the gap at the bottom, she might be able to pull the board away from the window frame.

She began working her fingers into the gap, sliding them up. She winced when the flesh on her knuckles tore, scraping on the frame just beneath where the wood panel ended. When she had enough leverage, she gripped the board and pulled with force.

The wood groaned as it started to give, and after a few minutes of pulling, a nail popped from the bottom. The other nails quickly followed, and the board soon came away in her hands and she threw it to the floor. Light from the window flooded into the room.

From the floor, Fallon raised her bound hands to shield her eyes. When her pupils adjusted to the light, she watched Claire looking out at their surroundings.

'That window's too small for you to get through. You've cut your hands up for nothing.'

Claire looked down at her hands; they were smeared with thin trickles of blood, drying on the knuckles, and her fingertips were red raw. She brushed splinters from her fingers, and turned to Fallon.

'I might be, but you're not.'

'I'm not going through that window. He could be out there waiting.'

'His van's gone. I can see the tyre tracks in the snow leading along the dirt track between the trees.'

'So where's he gone?'

Claire shrugged. 'I don't know but this may be our only chance to make a break for it. If we can get you through the window, you can go around to the front door and unlock the one to this room.'

'And what about getting this cord off our wrists? We won't be getting far like this.' Claire looked down at her wrists, then around the room. Fallon glanced at her. 'Didn't think about that, did you?'

Claire took in their surroundings: rough concrete floor, dark dank wooden walls, like a garden shed, pitched wooden roof, one door, and one window. Nothing she could use to cut their bonds.

Shit.

She returned to the window and looked outside again, cocking her head left then right, gauging the size of the shack. It couldn't be very big. Maybe there was a kitchen where she might find a knife. Her breath steamed up the window, and it was then that she remembered just how cold it was outside.

She glanced down at her clothes, still wet. They smelled musty and clung to her every curve. She realised they wouldn't get far in the snow if they were in the middle of nowhere. She looked at Fallon and the thin jacket Lucas had made her change into before Claire was brought to his basement. It was barely giving any warmth.

Fallon glared when she caught her staring. 'What?'

'We need to break that window.'

'So break it.'

'You've got protection in that jacket. My arms are bare. I need you to get up and use your elbow to put through the glass.'

Fallon looked at her jacket, then the window. She shook her head. 'Nah, you smash it. I'll give you my jacket.'

'How you going to get the sleeves over your bound wrists?'

There was a brief silence.

'I could cut myself.'

Claire lost her patience. 'It's either that or the alternative. You know what Lucas is capable of.' Fallon looked at the floor. 'Question is, are you ready to die yet? 'Cos that's all he has planned for us. Torture, then death. Make your choice.'

Fallon scowled.

'He could be back at any moment. If I'm going to die, I'd rather it be trying to escape.'

It wasn't until she heard the words escape her own lips that it really hit Claire. Hit her hard in the pit of her stomach. She was likely to die out here.

End of the line.

Fallon seemed to shake off her self-pity and heaved herself up onto her feet.

Claire nodded and pointed to the window.

'Once you're outside, head around to the left. I think that part of the building that juts out is the entrance. We need to get this door open. Now,' she said, pausing, looking at Fallon, 'short hard jab with your elbow, here.' She tapped the middle of the glass. She caught Fallon unconsciously rubbing her elbow. 'It'll be OK. You can do this. The glass is old and thin. It won't take much to put it through.'

Taking a few long deep breaths, psyching herself up, Fallon raised her right arm, turned her head away, gritted her teeth and lashed out, her elbow crashing hard into the glass. Claire winced at the cry that escaped Fallon's lips as the window gave way, sending large shards of glass cascading out onto the snow outside.

She saw the streaks of red left on the broken glass shards still wedged into the wooden frame.

Fallon's breathing was coming in short sharp bursts as she stared at her elbow, still raised in the void where the glass had been moments before.

Claire pulled at her arm and looked down at the dark stain that had seeped into Fallon's green jacket, making the blood appear black. The fabric had torn and a long fragment of glass was embedded in her skin about an inch down from her elbow. Claire touched it and Fallon flinched, yanking her arm from her grasp.

'That hurts, you fucking sadist!'

'I was trying to see how deep it was. Here, give me your arm, I can pull that out.' Fallon backed off when Claire went to touch her again.

'No.' Fallon paused. 'I'll do it myself.' She raised her elbow at an angle, and managed to slowly pull the glass shard from her skin, using the middle and index finger of her left hand. She winced at the pain, cramp shooting through her hand, until the glass slid out and dropped to the floor. She inspected her wound, which she quickly deduced wasn't life threatening.

Claire knocked the few remaining shards of glass from the window frame. The icy-cold air rushed at her face, causing her breath to catch in her throat.

Fallon stooped on tiptoes and peered out the window. She raised her bound hands, her fingers gripping the window frame, and pulled herself up further.

She looked down at the ground. The snow looked thick and the drop was about four and a half feet from the window.

'I'm going to need a bunk-up,' she said.

Claire cupped her hands as best she could, the cord cutting deep into her flesh, lowered her arms and braced herself. Fallon wedged her foot into Claire's palms, gripped the window frame and, ignoring the pain in her arm, hauled herself up until she was hanging out of the window. She misjudged her balance and fell forward, landing head first in the thick snow below.

She swore, pulling herself upright, the cold drawing deep into her jeans. It made her shiver. She looked up and saw Claire's head poking out through the window.

'Try the entrance, see if it's unlocked. See if you can find something to cut the cord with and some blankets or warm clothes.'

Fallon ran towards the far end of the building. Inside, Claire ran up to the door to listen out for her.

Fallon found the entrance. The door was literally rotting away, the wood old and weathered. The building, shack-like in appearance, seemed to be a mixture of old and new. Patches of different decades sewn together.

She gingerly approached the door and tried the handle. To her surprise it opened after she gave it a sharp jolt. She tapped the door open farther with her fingers and, with caution, peered inside.

Satisfied the room beyond was empty, she went inside, closing the door behind her. The air was thick with the smell of damp and she quickly went into the next room, which had a small dirty-looking sink, a wall-mounted cabinet and a small table with old newspapers on top. The papers were dated five years ago, she noticed on closer inspection.

She looked inside the cabinet on the wall, which contained a few dirty plates. She looked behind her. She saw there were two more doors ahead of her. Claire called to her from behind one of them.

'Anything?'

'Just a minute, there's another door, another room next to yours.'

Fallon edged closer and tried the handle. The door bounced open and inside was a cabinet next to an old iron-framed bed. There was a brown blanket, covered in mould, thrown over the top of a dirty mattress. Off to one side was another door within the room, which was a W.C. The toilet, Fallon noticed, was filthy, and the hand basin wasn't much better. She didn't linger.

She went to the door where Claire was waiting behind it. 'There's nothing here,' she said.

'Nothing to cut the cord or warm clothes? There can't seriously be nothing.'

'Look, I'm telling you there's nothing.'

From inside the room, Claire swore to herself, looked around the room again, despite knowing it was pointless, then stared at the door in front of her. She remembered Lucas breaking into her bathroom.

'Stand back,' she shouted. 'I'm going to try forcing the door.'

CHAPTER 91

Stefan stared at the dot pulsating on the screen. 'He's in Buckinghamshire?'

'In a wood?' Elias added.

Elliot took another look at the screen and nodded. 'He's moving through Black Hill Forest by the looks of it, which is strange.'

Elias's eyes narrowed at the screen. 'I've not heard of Black... Forest, or whatever it's called.'

Elliot looked at Elias with a wry smile on his lips. 'Black *Hill* Forest. It's big but as far as I know, there's no access to the public, which is why I said it's strange.'

'But there's vehicle access through there?' Stefan asked, leaning across for a better angle on the screen.

Elliot shook his head. 'Not as such. It's all dirt tracks... Look, I've not been there for eight years, easily.' Stefan went around to Elliot's side of the desk, taking over his computer.

He accessed Google and searched for Black Hill Forest. There was no official website for it, or much else for that matter, but he did find a small section on an online encyclopaedia with a few details.

'It's closed to the public. It used to be open, but there isn't much information other than that, and it doesn't mention why it closed. Just goes on to say there's a lake at the far end of it.' He trailed off, read a few more lines. 'There's an old map still available to download.'

Elias was now hovering at his shoulder while Stefan downloaded the PDF file. After a few tense seconds, it opened.

The image had been scanned from an original drawing and colour-coded with pencil. It showed the lake, and a mile to the south of it, there was a small building, labelled as a Warden Station, with a first-aid logo beside it. There were a few small walking trails, but not a lot else.

Stefan printed the map and studied it carefully.

'How far is the forest from here, according to the tracking system?'

Elliot ran his hand over his chin, while the other clicked away at the mouse, opening and closing a few files. 'Approximately fifty miles. The van seems to be moving deeper into the forest.'

Elias shook his head, looking at Stefan. 'If he has Claire and Fallon in that van—'

'We don't have much time. I know,' Stefan said, finishing his sentence. His mind drifted, and pictured Claire's face. Just as quickly, he saw the soulless expressions of the three murdered women. Claire could easily become the next victim. Another face, another name, another bloody statistic.

He made a decision.

'We need air support.'

'You won't be able to land down there,' Elliot said. 'There are too many trees.' Stefan held up the map of the forest.

'There's a clearing by the lake, and another by the Warden Station. We've got to take the chance. Just the sight of the helicopter might be enough to frighten Lucas into submission.' He turned to Elias. 'Contact the station. Put out an alert on the van Lucas is driving, in case he moves.'

Elias blinked hard. 'And where are you going?'

'Where *we're* going: RAF Benson.'

CHAPTER 92

It hadn't taken Claire long to force the old door, but the cold was starting to take its toll on her body. She was hungry, thirsty and tired. Her head pounded and her body felt like it could quite easily shut down at any moment; she was running on nothing but her instinct to survive and pure fear. Fear of either dying by Lucas's hands or by Mother Nature's relentless winter cold.

Fallon had got a shard of glass from the broken window and after a few minutes of clumsy sawing, they'd cut through the cord at their wrists.

Fallon watched Claire shiver uncontrollably. 'There's an old blanket in there,' she said, nodding her head towards the other room.

'I think I'm getting too cold to care any more.'

Fallon went into the other room, retrieving the mould-covered blanket. 'Here,' she said, wrapping it around Claire's arms before she could protest.

Claire managed a smile.

Then they heard something.

The sound of tyres crunching on the frozen ground, coming up the trail towards the shack, was unmistakable.

The look on Fallon's face betrayed many emotions, but fear was by far the most obvious. She looked eaten away by it. She froze to the spot, waiting for the vehicle to appear.

'It's him, isn't it?' Her breath was now coming in short sharp bursts.

Control your fear.

Claire heard her own voice in her head and tried to put it into practice. She opened the door a crack, stared outside, and gripped Fallon's wrist hard and waited. The noise grew louder, then the front of the hire van pushed through the snow ahead.

Claire pulled Fallon down to the floor out of view as she kicked the door shut, letting the blanket fall from her shoulders. 'We've got to make a run for it.'

'He'll see us.'

'We'll go back through the other room, and you go out the window. You'll be obscured from his view, once he's out of the van.' She pulled Fallon up from the floor and through the door opposite. 'Wait here for me.'

'What're you doing?'

Claire ignored her, kept herself low, and pulled the door open again just enough to see Lucas.

He'd just switched off the engine and she saw something in his hands.

Her eyes widened.

Lucas swung the shotgun over his lap and Claire knew he was loading it. Her stomach somersaulted. She bolted towards Fallon and shoved her forward towards the window with some force.

'He's got a fucking shotgun, now move!'

Fallon's face lost all colour.

She ran to the window and grasped the ledge, ignoring the broken glass sitting like teeth still wedged in the frame, cutting her palms.

'Not yet,' Claire said, gripping her arms as Fallon went to jump. Claire went back to the front door. Saw Lucas climb out the van.

He turned towards the shack.

She sprinted back inside the room and helped Fallon up and out of the window. She guessed they had ten, maybe fifteen seconds before Lucas was in the shack… God knows how long before he knew something was up. She guessed he'd check on them first.

'Run,' she whispered to Fallon, who had ducked down low in the snow below.

'Are you crazy?'

'I'll be all right, just run… and don't look back, no matter what you hear.'

*

Lucas propped the shotgun he'd taken from William's farm up against the wheel of the van, then fished around in the glove compartment and pulled out the bag of extra cartridges. He swung the handles of the cloth bag containing the cartridges onto his belt and buckled it up again.

Then he checked his knife.

It was still there, nice and secure.

He picked up the shotgun and swung it across the back of his shoulders, supporting it with one arm.

Claire saw him approaching and just made it into the second room with the bed, threw the blanket on the mattress, and tucked herself behind the door. It wasn't until Lucas had stepped inside that she realised the door to the room she was in had been shut before.

She prayed he wouldn't notice.

She watched him, through the gap in the door, put the shotgun and the keys to the van on the table by the newspapers.

He had his back to her.

Fear kept her firmly rooted to the spot.

She saw the top page of one of the newspapers on the table begin to flutter. In the other room, the wind was circling through the broken window and under the door to where he stood.

He turned, stared at the old paper.

He looked away… then back again.

He saw the splinters of wood on the floor.

His eyes wandered to the broken lock.

He dived for the handle, pulled the door open wide, and Claire seized her chance. She threw herself around the door where she hid, grabbed the keys to the van, and charged through the entrance and never looked back.

CHAPTER 93

The door to the van was inches away when she heard the first shot. A spray of snow exploded just to the left of her, pellets narrowly missing her legs, but she didn't risk a glance behind. The van was unlocked and she threw herself into the driver's seat. She pushed the keys into the ignition.

Then her eyes met his.

He was running towards her, shotgun by his side. He had no intention of killing Claire by gunshot. That'd be too easy. He wanted to feel what it would be like to use his knife, tear through her skin, feel her warm blood on his hands. Wounding her by gunshot, however, was different.

He'd seen Fallon's tracks in the snow under the broken window, heading deep into the forest. He'd then seen Claire running to the van, and knew he could catch up with Fallon later. The forest was too dense, too isolated, for her to go very far in the cold, barefooted, without any warm clothes, food or water. If he didn't kill her, the cold most certainly would. Claire, however, had to be stopped.

And fast.

He swung the butt of the shotgun at the windscreen. She screamed as it crashed into the glass, but it held fast. He swung it again, and this time cracks appeared. She slammed her foot on the accelerator. The van bunny-hopped forward, narrowly missing him. He backed off, anticipating her next move. The snow was thick and uneven and the van's wheels spun around idly in the snow.

She looked up into Lucas's eyes and he grinned, swinging the gun barrel to face her head on.

She ducked as he fired, shielding her eyes as a sea of glass rained down on top of her.

Then all was still.

She slowly looked up. He was reloading. Then he took aim and pulled the trigger again.

She ducked down just as shot radiated out above her shoulder, striking the back rest. She let out a guttural roar, through gritted teeth, but it sounded like it came from elsewhere. An animal sound deep from within herself that she didn't recognise.

She peered over the steering wheel. He took aim again, and she slammed the accelerator pedal. The wheels spun, screeching, catching traction, then the van shot forward.

Lucas fell to the ground. She knew he wasn't hit. She would have felt the impact. She panicked, put the van in reverse and it shot backwards down the dirt track.

Lucas scrambled to his feet and gave chase. The van was going too slowly, lumbering over the snow.

She willed it to speed up.

He raised the gun but this time he didn't fire straight away.

She slammed on the brake.

She revved the van, stared into his eyes, and drove forward, aiming straight for him. She found her voice, screaming, as the van hurtled forwards. She shut her eyes and braced for impact.

Lucas rolled to the side, off the track, but was soon on his feet again. The van careered back into the clearing towards the Warden Station and fishtailed around. It now faced the right way towards the track.

Claire slammed the pedal again and the tyres managed some traction across the snow. Lucas raised the gun once more and fired at the front tyre on the driver's side. It burst with a loud bang and Claire screamed, instinctively raising her arms to protect her head, as the van careered off the track, crashing into a tree.

CHAPTER 94

Fallon had managed to scramble forward, falling many times in the snow. She'd headed out right into the thick of the trees, where there was no path.

A risk, but a necessary one.

She heard the gunshots.

They rang around in her head and stopped her dead in her tracks. She felt, for the first time since she was a small girl, the pull of loyalty. The detective – she'd helped her, cared for her almost. No one, not since her mother had left, had really given a damn about what happened to her. Not when it mattered.

She was kneeling in the snow, a stitch in her side, the cold seeping into her jeans, debating whether or not to turn back and confront Lucas or just keep going and pray to God she made it.

Just keep running, don't look back. The voice of reason in her head was clear.

She knew there was a very real possibility Claire was already dead. There had been several shots and she doubted Lucas was a gun-toting novice.

Go back, you coward. Her conscience tore away at her. She pushed herself to her feet and ran.

She ran until she was alongside a deep long-winding ditch, littered with dead leaves. The snow lay less thick here, the density of the tree branches overhead had seen to that.

Instead, the ground here was more of a brown sludge. She slipped in it and crash-landed in the ditch.

She felt a dull ache travel along her body when she pushed herself up on all fours. She got to her feet and looked around. The ditch was deep enough to obscure her from view if Lucas came after her from the way she'd come. Besides, the ditch would be hard to climb out of, the banks either side being steep and sodden with sludge.

She trudged a few feet ahead before the smell hit her, stopping her in her tracks. Edging forward, hand clasped to her nose and mouth, she pushed ahead.

The scent of something rotting hit her, and she forced what was left of her stomach contents back down her throat. She guessed there was a dead animal lying somewhere close, so she trod as carefully as she could, but ever mindful that Lucas could be close behind. It was then she saw the mound, partially covered with dead leaves.

The smell grew stronger the closer she got, but there was no way around it, other than climbing over.

She approached cautiously. She saw the familiar shape of a hand, and stopped.

It was a body.

She inched closer. She saw the body of a woman. What was left of her anyway. She was partially decomposed, and her skin was torn at the face. Her lips looked as if they'd been chewed.

Animals, Fallon thought, fighting back more bile. The body of the woman, whoever she was, had very dark skin, was maybe in her forties, but Fallon couldn't be sure due to the state of her.

God knows how long she'd been lying here. Fallon knew cold weather would've slowed decomposition, but she suspected the body had been here long enough in the heavy October rain before the snow had come. The corpse made an exquisite source of food for the local wildlife.

She saw a long gold chain around the neck, covered with filth. She stooped and pulled at it. It was a locket. She tilted it towards the light. There was an inscription on the front:

> *To Mummy*
> *Love*
> *Isabelle & Jasmine*

Fallon felt sick as sadness gripped her.

She popped the delicate catch and saw the picture inside. Two small girls, smiling happily for the camera. She felt like crying.

She held her breath, bending closer to the woman's body. She found the lobster-claw catch, released the chain and pushed the locket into her jacket pocket.

She crossed herself, although she didn't know why since she wasn't in the slightest bit religious. She took a deep breath, held it again.

She ran back the way she'd come.

CHAPTER 95

Her head pounded and her throat was dry with thirst.

Claire had passed out when she'd hit her head on the steering wheel, and now the pain surged across her forehead.

She looked up.

The front of the van was rammed against the tree, but the engine was still running. Her lower face felt wet. She touched her nose, and winced in pain. There was blood on her fingers, which she wiped on her trousers.

Then she remembered Lucas and the gun.

She shot around in her seat, seeing nothing at first. She looked in the rear-view mirror and saw him circling the van, gun raised. She'd only blacked out momentarily, and had seconds to move. She opened the door and dropped from the seat.

She hit the ground hard, rolled over, then was up on her feet. She managed only a few paces before she was shoved forward. She landed face first in the snow, the hard ice nearly knocking her out again.

'Don't fight it, Claire.'

Lucas pointed the gun at her as she got to her feet.

'Fallon will bring help,' she said.

He smiled. 'She won't get far in this forest. There's nobody around for miles.' Claire didn't speak. Her eyes began to close, pain and cold willing her body to shut down. He motioned with his head. 'Move. We can't have you blacking out just yet.'

Claire's eyes fluttered open. She shook her head. 'No.'

'No?' He lowered the gun, pointing it at her stomach. 'Do you know how painful a shot to the stomach is?'

'You're not going to shoot me.'

'I wouldn't be so sure. I only narrowly missed your head back in the van.'

She stared at him, not knowing if Fallon was any closer to bringing help or not. For all she knew, the girl was lost, which could easily have happened. This forest all looked the same.

He stared at her. Her feet were bare, red from the cold. Her trousers were heavy with damp, hanging low on her hips. Her top was stained with dirt and sweat. Blood trickled from her nose, over her chin, down her throat. One eye was bloodshot.

Her hair was dirty and matted, hanging limply around her face and shoulders. Her face was flushed, making her blue eyes more prominent. She held his gaze, never faltering.

She'll never break. Such a shame I can't leave her alive.

He pointed the gun beyond her. 'Down there.'

She looked over her shoulder and saw the ground through the trees sloping down. She had no idea where it led. She knew it would be nowhere safe. He wanted her further out in the wilderness. No chance of anyone finding her. She looked back at him. He aimed the gun at her knees.

'I said move… unless you can make do without your kneecaps?'

She turned and slowly headed through the trees lining the track and down the slope. She saw the ditch running along the bottom, not knowing how far it stretched. She scrunched her fingers tightly into a fist.

As they neared the ditch, he dug the barrel of the gun into her back, between her shoulder blades. She kept her eyes low. The ditch was steep and deep. She longed to fall into its belly, swallowed whole. Away from pain. Away from fear.

She scanned the horizon and saw the sun beginning to set, dipping low behind the skyline in the distance. The glow of red and orange swirled above, like oil in the sky.

It was stunning.

'Blood on the snow,' he broke into her thoughts, 'is so beautiful, I've always thought... the red and the white.'

Claire sucked in her breath. Held it until her lungs screamed.

'I used to come to this forest when I was a kid. My grandmother, Lucy, used to bring me. She taught me how to shoot, can you believe that?' He smiled at the memory. 'She started me off shooting tin cans. When I started getting good, we tried animals.'

Claire felt a sickness hit her stomach.

'Sometimes we would spend hours waiting for anything, for some little animal to come along. We mostly used snares but I preferred a gun.' He smiled. 'The first time I shot a hare, I nearly died from the excitement. It was snowing then too... blood on the snow... so beautiful.'

He watched her carefully. She showed little reaction to his words. This wasn't good enough for him.

He wanted her running scared, out of her mind. His arms grew heavy under the strain of the gun. He hadn't actually killed a human with his own hands before and he longed to experience it, but at the same time, he didn't want the game with Claire to end.

'How about I give you a sporting chance?' he said, grinning. 'We'll hunt... you're the hare.'

She took a few paces back. Biting back tears. There was no way she'd give him the satisfaction of crying.

'You're mad.'

He smiled. 'I guess it ran in the family... You've got until the count of twenty.'

His face turned serious.

'Run, rabbit, run.' He pointed beyond her, towards the dense block of trees ahead. 'Make it count.'

CHAPTER 96

Fallon's pace began to slow. Her body ached with the cold, and the stitch in her side was becoming unbearable. For a short time, she heard nothing but the sound of her own breathing.

Then she heard the snap of twigs.

Her head shot up.

She braced herself, frozen to the spot, as something drew closer. She held her breath as a figure came into view, crashing around the corner ahead.

It was Claire.

She fell at Fallon's feet.

'He's not far behind me. We've got to move.' Claire's voice was hoarse, as if each word was painful to speak.

'There's nowhere to run to. I couldn't find a way out of the trees. I've been going around in circles.' She pulled Claire up on her knees and gripped her arms to steady her.

'Just help me up. He's right behind—'

CRACK… Thump.

They heard the shot ring out, and pellets hit the ground just behind Fallon, spraying a mist of snow over her legs.

She looked up and saw Lucas trying to negotiate the steep terrain which sloped down towards them. Her eyes flew back to Claire's, just as she shoved her forward.

Seconds later another shot was fired.

Fallon cried out.

Claire felt the weight of Fallon's body pulling her down. She looked at the blood oozing through the girl's fingers as they pressed tightly to her right calf.

As Fallon sank to the ground, her eyes rose and met Lucas's as he lowered the shotgun. He grinned and began to walk towards them.

Claire moved Fallon's hand away to check the wound. Her jeans had a small hole where the pellet had entered, and the fabric was stained black. Blood trickled onto the snow.

'Oh, shit,' she whimpered at the sight of it.

Claire didn't have time to think ahead. She grabbed Fallon under her arms, pulled her up and staggered towards the ditch and helped Fallon down into it.

She ripped the sleeve of Fallon's jacket and tied it hard around the girl's leg. Her hands were shaking as she tied the tourniquet.

'What're we going to do?' Fallon said.

Claire stopped and looked into her eyes, which were like liquid, brimming with tears.

Claire stood up. *What can I do?*

'Please don't leave me.'

Claire flinched at Fallon's words. *Don't make this harder than it has to be. Please.*

'I'm scared.'

'He didn't follow you before. It's me he's after. I'll make sure he follows me. I'll get help, just keep pressure on the wound.'

'But what if you don't come back?'

Claire had to move. Now. 'I will come back for you.'

Fallon wasn't sure she believed her, but the pain in her leg was too great for her to argue. She would die out here if they didn't get help. Her only hope was that Claire could outrun and outsmart him. She had to believe this or else she may as well die right here and now and not prolong the agony.

She nodded and Claire got to her feet, keeping her body low. She ran further before pulling herself up, out of the ditch.

As soon as she was on her feet she ran as fast as she could. She risked a look back. Lucas was coming after her. He'd taken the bait. She prayed Fallon could hold on that bit longer. She didn't know where she was going. She saw the trees begin to thin out a hundred yards or so ahead and ran towards them.

*

It hadn't been a difficult decision for Lucas.

He guessed Fallon was passed out in the ditch. If she wasn't, she soon would be. He could come back for her, and if he found her still alive, that'd be a bonus.

It was Claire he wanted.

He raised the shotgun when he saw where she was heading.

He knew there was another clearing that way, which led to the vast lake. He knew this forest like the back of his hand. Whilst he knew nobody came here any more he knew all she had to do was follow around the lake and it would lead to a trail, which would soon lead onto farmland and to a main road.

His heart sank. He took aim and fired.

*

The pellets zipped past Claire's shoulder. She swore, risking a glance behind her. She saw Lucas run. She sucked in a deep breath and pushed herself to go faster.

She was nearly at the line of trees ahead when she caught sight of something large and white beyond them. She soon realised it was a frozen lake.

She found a new surge of energy, bolting forward. As she broke out from the trees, she stopped at the frozen edge. She couldn't be sure how thick it was.

Would it take her weight?

Her eyes scanned the trails that ran either side of the frozen water. It would take her longer to go around but if she risked it on the lake, Lucas would have a clear shot at her. That's if she didn't fall through the ice first.

As she agonised over the cruel twist of fate that lay in front of her, she heard another shot. The spray hit the ground by her feet, and instead of running she turned to face him.

He stepped out from the trees and a cruel smile spread across his lips.

CHAPTER 97

'You can't run forever, Claire. You've come as far as you can. You mustn't be upset,' he said, edging closer. 'You had a good run.'

She edged back towards the lake, and he paused, staring at her cautiously. 'I don't want to shoot you in the back,' he said, taking a step forward, hand raised towards her. 'But I will if you go out onto the ice.'

'You scared to take a chance out there?' She gestured to the lake behind her. 'I'll go down fighting. I won't make this easy for you.'

'I doubt that. It's been pretty easy so far.'

'You had William before. You've never known what it's like to take someone's life.' She sneered at him. 'I doubt you've got it in you. It's been too easy to manipulate William, bending him to your will. When it comes down to it, you're nothing. A nobody.'

The slight change in Lucas's demeanour was small but Claire noticed it. He was having doubts and she had every intention of using that to her advantage. 'You chose badly when you picked me and Fallon.'

'Don't worry yourself about Fallon. I'll take good care of her after I've dealt with you.'

She laughed at him. 'You think I won't take a chance on the ice?'

'I know you're scared but you're not stupid.'

'Maybe you're the scared one. Maybe you don't know me at all.'

Before he had a chance to answer, she turned and tore across the ice as fast as she could. Her bare feet felt like they were burning on the dry ice but she didn't stop. Not even when she heard the creaking under the strain of her weight, when she started zigzagging across the ice.

Lucas stood dumbfounded at first, then aimed the gun. He couldn't get a clear shot, as she ran from left to right, straight ahead then left to right again. He could hit a moving target generally, but a target that moved all over the place? Near impossible.

He lowered the gun and fired at the ice.

Claire swung around at the sound of the shot. She was nearly out into the middle now. Her eyes widened when she realised what he'd done. The shot had hit the ice wide from where she stood and when she heard the cracking sound, she realised she hadn't been the target this time.

Her eyes looked back towards him.

His face grew hard, and he took a few tentative steps onto the ice, then broke out into a sprint after her. His feet slid a few times, throwing him off balance, and Claire turned on her heels and ran. He fired another shot, this time at her leg. He missed but the pellets hit the ice to the side of her.

The ice was beginning to thin out the closer she got to the middle and her mind flashed back to Bonfire Night at Haverbridge Lake. She remembered Harry falling through the ice into the freezing water. He'd only just survived.

She prayed it held. There would be no one to pull her out.

She could hardly keep up the pace. The lake was a lot wider than she'd previously thought and her legs began to grow heavier with each step. She willed herself to run faster, but she was slowing down. She hit halfway and it was then she heard him close behind her.

She knew she should have trusted her instincts and looked back. If she had, she could have prevented what happened next.

CHAPTER 98

His hands slammed into her back, propelling her with force across the frozen water. When her body hit the ice, it groaned under the strain as she skidded across the surface.

When she pulled herself up, he reached for her.

She kicked out, striking him in the thigh where she'd wounded him earlier. He buckled, landing hard on his knees, crippled with pain. The shotgun, hanging on its strap, fell off his shoulder and skidded across the ice.

'You bitch!'

He lurched forward, grasping her legs. She frantically twisted and turned, her arms reaching out trying to gain leverage on the ice. He grabbed her by the waist, pulling her towards him. Her body shot back, sliding down between his legs. She saw the knife secured to his waist and reached for it.

She pulled it from its sheath but he caught her wrist and squeezed.

The ice beneath them began to groan.

A few cracks began to appear beneath Claire's head, radiating out. Her eyes were wide with fear, but he was grinning.

'We need to get off the ice!'

He tried to prise the knife from her hand. Claire held on tight, and the cracks in the ice spread out fast.

She prised her wrist from his grasp and swung the knife across his cheek, cutting deep into the side of his face.

He cried out, grasping his cheek, blood leaking through his fingers. She raised her knees up towards her chest, then out, shoving him back, her feet kicking him in the ribs. He crashed back against the ice so hard it cracked underneath him.

Claire scrambled back as the cracks in the ice began to splinter out towards her. Her hands slipped over the cold surface, then she felt freezing water rise up and slide over the ice. With her last ounce of strength, she rolled over onto her stomach, pushing herself up and forward just as the ice gave way underneath Lucas.

He plummeted down into the water, leaving nothing but broken slabs of ice floating on the surface. Claire carefully edged away, distributing her weight across the weakened ice. She waited, eyes transfixed on the spot where Lucas had been mere seconds ago.

Thin cracks still radiated out from the hole and she backed up further towards the other side of the lake. Then she heard a rush as Lucas propelled himself up, his arms flailing at the slippery ice. He screamed out, and his eyes bore into hers.

'Claire!'

His voice was strained and she knew his pain would be unimaginable as his body began shutting down against the cold. 'Help me!' His screams pierced her ears, and she shut her eyes tight, trying to drown them out.

She shook her head violently.

I can't. I just can't.

She heard him splutter and risked a glance, almost afraid to watch. His head kept disappearing under the water, then he'd surface for a few moments, spluttering for air.

He managed one final push for the ice surrounding him.

'Claire, please!'

There was a small part of her that told her to slide across the ice, grab his hand and pull him out, despite what he'd done. Despite the fact that Fallon was still in danger.

She knew she risked falling through herself, but that was not what pulled at her conscience.

It was the faces of the other women who had died because of him. She thought of Fallon lying in the ditch, shot, freezing and likely to die if she didn't get help.

She saw the dead face of Felicity Davenport, and her mother's cries of anguish rang through her ears.

She saw Gregg Thornton's face when confronted with Sara's lifeless body.

She thought of the unborn baby in Nola Grant's womb.

She looked back at Lucas. His eyes were pleading. For a moment she thought they looked kind.

Then she remembered the evil and the sheer hatred.

Don't let your eyes betray you.

His certainly had.

She watched as the strength left him. He let out one final scream, before sliding back down under the dark water.

CHAPTER 99

The silence was eerie. The cold felt like an evil entity, its fingers tearing away at her flesh. She drew breath and it hurt like hell. Her legs were completely numb. She tried climbing to her feet, but came crashing down, her chin hitting the ice. She couldn't risk it breaking. She tried to slide herself towards the other side of the lake, but her body was now fighting against her. Against sleep.

She found herself rolling over, falling back, resting on the ice, looking up at the sky. Her eyelids were heavy.

She let them close.

*

The noise from the rotor jolted her awake.

One eye opened slowly. Saw the landscape lying sideways.

It was dark. The sun had disappeared, taking with it the beautiful colours of the sunset.

She felt the chill down one side of her face. Felt the tingling pain in her hands. She rolled off her side, onto her back again and remembered where she was.

Everything was numb.

She had no idea how long she'd blacked out for. All she knew was that there was a deep rumbling in the distance of something drawing closer.

Then the thundering sound was above her, before she saw a light illuminating the sky. Her eyes flickered as the wind picked up.

Then the noise was almost deafening. Soon a light shone down so intensely, she shut her eyes tight.

It was then she heard it.

A voice in the void.

It told her to remain calm. At least, that's what she thought it said. She wasn't sure. In the bright light, noise and confusion, all she wanted to do was give in and sleep for eternity.

Opening her eyes one more time, she saw the belly of the police Eurocopter above her.

It hovered.

She blacked out.

*

She could hear lots of noise. Running. Shouting.

A sense of urgency.

Her eyes fluttered open.

She saw a man looking down at her. He was saying something, but it sounded muffled. The ceiling was rushing past his head. She realised she was moving.

They hastily turned around a corner. More ceiling, lights, noise… The man was leaning down again, telling her something.

She shut her eyes.

The light hurt and sleep was calling her again. She heard a clatter and a force underneath her body jolted her awake again. She realised she was on a bed… being wheeled along winding corridors.

There was a woman hovering over her now. The ceiling was rushing past her head too. She wore a uniform. She looked like a nurse.

Claire felt like she was floating. It felt comforting. She closed her eyes again and drowned out the sound around her.

She concentrated on the voice in her head. She heard her mother's words. Words spoken a long time ago, when she was a child.

It gave her comfort.

'*If I shall die before I wake, I pray the Lord my soul to take...*'

CHAPTER 100

4th December

His watch said it was nearly two in the morning. Stefan guessed he'd had maybe an hour's sleep at most. He got up from the sofa, stumbling in the darkness. He heard a noise and stopped.

It was Iris. She was talking in her sleep upstairs.

Stefan had driven her back to the house from the hospital once the doctors had stabilised Claire. Iris had wanted to stay by her side, but she'd been persuaded to get some rest herself, and Stefan had promised to stay with her.

He found his jacket, thrown over the back of a chair, fished his mobile from the pocket, and checked the call list:

1 Missed Call – Elias Crest.

'Crest, sorry I missed your call,' Stefan said, when Elias picked up at the other end. 'I fell asleep. I've lost an hour.'

'We found another body.'

Stefan's face was white. 'What?'

'We found a body not far from where we picked up Fallon Dockley. All we know so far is that it's female… we think.'

'You think?'

Elias sighed and shook his head at what he'd seen – the body lying in a heap on the forest floor. 'The body has been there a while. It's been exposed to the elements, not to mention the wildlife.'

'I get the picture.'

'There's more… Fallon had a locket which she found on the body. It has an inscription on the back. We're running a check with Mispers.'

Stefan heard Iris stir upstairs. Her feet landed on the floor and moved towards the landing. Soon he heard the third stair from the bottom creak.

'Keep me updated,' he said, about to hang up.

'Wait,' Elias said.

Pause.

'How's Claire?'

'She's… stable. For now.' Elias closed his eyes, letting the silence drag out. 'I have to go, Crest.' Stefan hung up just as Iris pushed open the living room door.

'I heard you talking. Was that the hospital?'

Stefan looked into her worried, tired eyes and shook his head. 'No news is good news,' he said, setting down his phone. 'Did you get much sleep?'

'I can't really sleep knowing Claire's in ICU.'

'She's made of strong stuff,' he said, smiling. 'She'll be OK.'

'What if you're wrong?'

Stefan looked away. *Look on the positive side, love,* he thought. 'I'm not wrong.'

'You make this sound trivial. How can you be so sure?'

He looked away, down at his feet.

He felt his throat pull tight.

'Because I have to be.'

CHAPTER 101

4 days later

Claire sat up in the hospital bed. She thought about how just days ago she was near death. Hypothermia had set in, clutching at her body, not willing to let go without a fight. Somehow she'd battled against the odds. Somehow her body had fought back and physically she was recovering well. How she was coping mentally, though, was a different story and only time would tell just how fragile her mind had become. Right now, all she felt was the swell of relief. Relief at being alive.

She flexed her toes and winced.

Chilblains.

She had them on her fingers as well. Red, itchy, blister-like sores, which felt like they were burning. She started to scratch at them, unaware that a man was approaching her bed.

'Don't scratch them, you'll make them worse.'

She looked sheepish when she saw Stefan's face. 'I just want to claw my skin off.'

'You're lucky this wasn't worse. I thought maybe I'd lost you.'

'Unfortunately for you, I'll live,' she said with half a smile.

His face remained serious. 'You could've died.'

The smile faded from her face. She gave him a small nod but didn't speak.

She couldn't.

Behind her tough exterior she was like a little girl running scared. She'd almost died. She'd somehow survived against that monster, yet despite the initial relief, she'd then realised she had no energy left to save herself on the ice.

She thought she'd die there. Alone.

She wanted to offer Stefan thanks, but she thought her voice might falter, betray her inner suffering if she revealed just how much loyalty she felt for him.

She couldn't even bring herself to thank him. The risk of crying was far too great.

He sat on the chair beside her bed. This was the first time Claire had seen or spoken to Stefan properly since everything had happened.

'How's Fallon?' she managed, breaking the tension.

'She's OK. The shot to her leg looked worse than it was. She had mild hypothermia but she went home yesterday to a very relieved father.' He paused. 'Even her mother has been staying in the family home the last few days. I don't think it'll be a bed of roses but she is trying to make things right… The mother, I mean.'

Claire nodded, but kept her eyes trained on the floor. She had so many questions but didn't know where to start.

He filled her in on Olivia.

She felt sick and couldn't bring herself to speak. She didn't ask any questions, just listened. Then his voice changed and his eyes came over all dark.

'I've seen that look before, Fletch. It never means good news.'

He sighed and pinched the bridge of his nose. 'We found another body in the forest.' He let Claire's eyes wander over his face before he spoke again. 'Her name was Roberta Parry. She was Hatcher's first victim. Lucas's first chosen one.'

She paused. 'You've lost me.'

'Hatcher has given us his version of events… Roberta Parry was married with two young girls. She lost all of them in a car crash a year ago. She disappeared at the end of October and her sister reported her missing. She said Roberta was being treated for depression and she feared her sister may have taken her own life. Roberta never forgave herself for the death of her husband and children.'

Claire raised her eyebrows.

'She was driving but it wasn't her fault. A drunk driver crashed into their car. Roberta escaped with a few broken bones. Her husband Anthony and their daughter Jasmine were killed instantly. Isabelle died a few days later.'

'God, that's horrible. How does Hatcher fit into all this?'

'He came into Parry's life purely by accident.'

'Some accident.'

'He's been pretty sketchy on the details,' Stefan said. 'He says he tried to help her with her grief, but I showed the sister a photo of Hatcher and she said she'd never seen him before and she was with her sister most days since the accident.'

Claire sighed. 'So he's lying to us.'

'Not exactly. Hatcher came across Parry because she attended Focus Being as well. Lucas chose her, just like he chose Hatcher.'

'That place needs a health warning itself.'

'God, your jokes are bad.'

'And ill-timed?'

Stefan's smile was faint. 'Just a little.'

'I do that when I'm nervous. There's more you're not telling me. I can feel it.'

Stefan pulled his chair a little closer to her. 'I've not been able to find out who leaked Nola's pregnancy. The team's tight. Maybe the press got wind of it elsewhere.'

Claire shook her head. She couldn't accept that. The idea that there was someone she couldn't trust on the team made her restless. She demanded loyalty and she knew she'd track down who betrayed them no matter how long it took.

Stefan watched her face, gauging her reaction. There was more to tell her and she looked apprehensive.

'Olivia wants to see you.'

Claire grew concerned. 'Why?'

He shrugged. 'I think she wants to apologise.'

'That bitch can shove her apology.'

'I thought you'd say that. Told her as much but she was still adamant that you go and see her.'

Claire stared at the blank white wall ahead. Her brow furrowed and her hands balled up into tight fists, gripping the sheets tight.

'What do you think I should do?'

He sat back in his chair and shrugged.

'It doesn't matter what I say. You'll do what you think is best… you always do.'

CHAPTER 102

6 weeks later – HMP Holloway, London

As Claire sat down in front of the table, she instantly felt her stomach turn as Olivia smiled.

'How are you?'

Claire blinked at her. Her mouth was set firm and it took every ounce of strength not to hurl her fist into her lying, treacherous face. 'I mean it,' Olivia said, hope in her voice. 'I was glad when they told me you survived.'

'Were you?' Claire shot back, her voice cold. 'The way I heard it, you were pretty much gunning on your brother murdering me.'

Olivia looked away. 'I've changed. Being in here waiting for the trial is teaching me what's right. What's important.'

'You suddenly have a conscience? You can't just magic that out of thin air.'

'My childhood was one massive fuck-up,' she said with venom. 'People like me don't have a choice. Sometimes we do things, evil things, to survive.'

Claire gave a mock laugh. 'Mummy gave you a bad childhood, your brother screwed you over and everyone else in society has to accept what you did, and support the families left behind.' She shook her head. 'You're a fool if you think I'll accept that. Even more so if you think you can convince a jury you were just as much a victim of your brother as the others.'

Olivia's eyes grew dark. 'I thought you'd understand me.'

Claire leaned forward across the table. 'What I don't understand is that your brother ruined and took away lives.' She paused. 'He nearly took Fallon's… He nearly took *mine*.'

Olivia was stony-faced.

'I don't give a fuck about you, Olivia. I don't care about your childhood. I don't care how your mother made you feel or how Lucas used you. All I care about is getting justice for the families you helped destroy.'

'Then what're you doing here?' she said. Her voice had a cruel edge to it. 'Why did you come?'

Claire's eyes met hers, until Olivia looked away. Claire didn't waver. 'I know there's more to your story.'

Olivia shrugged. 'Is there?'

'Oh, there's a hell of a lot more. You helped your brother and William more than you've admitted to so far.'

Olivia leaned across the table. The tone of her voice was almost seductive. 'And do you have any proof?'

Claire remained silent.

Olivia smiled. 'It's what you can prove in court that counts.'

'I wouldn't count on William keeping your secrets. He has no reason to save your neck. Not now he knows you helped to set him up to take all the responsibility for those murders.'

A sickly smile spread across Olivia's face. 'Is that why you came? To tell me that?'

'I came for two reasons.'

'I'm all ears.'

'I came to see if I could see through your lies.'

'And what do you see?' Olivia raised her eyebrows, eager for an answer.

'I see a frightened little girl who thinks she can lie her way out of this. But I know different, and deep down so do you. I see through your lies and so will a jury.'

Olivia let out a little laugh, still cocky as she said, 'And the second?'

'I want to know the real reason you helped your brother. It was more than just money.'

A long pause hung heavy in the air before she answered. 'He was family.'

Claire stayed silent.

'My turn,' Olivia said. 'How did it feel for you, watching him die? You could've saved him.'

Claire's eyes flickered. She swallowed hard. Hoped Olivia didn't notice. 'I passed out on the ice. There was nothing I could've done.'

Olivia's face was serious. 'Now I can see through your lies.'

Claire held her gaze a moment longer than she should have, giving Olivia an unspoken answer, confirming all she needed to, before she pushed her chair back with a loud scrape across the linoleum floor.

Olivia raised her eyebrows in surprise. 'You're going?' Claire ignored her, instead nodding her head towards the prison guard to let her out.

'I'm glad he didn't kill you.' Claire stopped, turned. Olivia was grinning. 'Out of them all, I'm glad you survived.'

'Fallon's alive and well.'

Olivia sighed and shook her head. 'I know… unfortunately.' Claire's eyes narrowed at the coldness in her voice. 'Still,' Olivia continued, 'I bet you're grateful now?'

'What?'

'You heard me: I said, "I bet you're grateful now?" After what my brother did, it forced you to see how things could've turned out. But now you're grateful for the life you have. You passed a test. Maybe Lucas taught you something after all.'

Claire thought back to the look in Lucas's eyes before he drowned. It was a look that would be burned into her soul for the rest of her life. Professionally, she'd made the wrong choice. She should have tried to save him so he could stand trial. It was, after all, why she did this job. Wasn't it?

Yes, professionally, it had been the wrong decision. Deep down inside her, however, if she had her time over again, could rewind to that split second in time, she'd let him die a thousand times over and over again if she could.

There was one nagging question though.

If she'd made the right decision, why did her conscience pull at her inside? Did letting Lucas die make her any better than him?

Mercy… It's what makes us human.

'Did I touch a nerve, Chief Inspector?' Claire was shaken from her thoughts as Olivia grinned.

Claire strode towards her and slammed her hands down as she leaned over the table. Olivia recoiled back in her seat. 'Why'd you do it? Just tell me that much. The real reason you helped Lucas.'

'You really wanna know?'

'I won't ask you again.'

'What if you're not satisfied with my answer?'

Claire's face looked pinched, almost cruel. She smiled faintly, shaking her head, and turned on her heels, walking back towards the door. 'See you in court, Olivia.'

'No, wait!' Olivia said, standing up from her seat. 'Don't walk away from me.'

'You want an audience.' Claire barely turned as she spoke to her. 'I'm not giving you that satisfaction.' The look in her face was calm, unsympathetic, and her voice was unyielding.

Cold.

Heartless.

Just as Lucas had been to her and all of the other victims.

Claire Winters had a conscience but it didn't extend to murderers and their accomplices. Any doubt she had about

Lucas's death was rapidly fading just as quickly as it had surfaced.

'It's simple, Chief Inspector.' Olivia paused as Claire turned to face her. 'My brother, he…' She trailed off. She took a deep breath again, as if the next words to come out of her mouth would take all her effort to speak.

She sighed, raising her eyes back to Claire's.

'It's simple really… He got inside my head. He twisted it, danced around in it, leaving nothing behind but bad memories and bloody footprints.'

EPILOGUE

January

Harwood Park Crematorium was a peaceful and beautiful place. Even in the darker months of winter the vast memorial gardens were well tended and, in a strange way, still of comfort.

Situated on the edge of Stevenage, a large town about a thirty minute drive from Claire's house, it was surrounded by open countryside.

The sky was a mix of deep gun-metal-grey clouds, intercut with hazy sunlight, peeking through any break in the clouds.

There weren't many people around today. The rough winds had kept many at home. The darkness of the clouds threatened rain.

The squawk of a crow above reminded her she wasn't alone in the world.

Claire's eyes rose to the sky, saw the bird dipping, then heading towards the horizon.

She buried her hands deeper into her coat pockets, and lowered her face, burying her chin into her scarf. Despite the patchy sunlight, the ground still sparkled with early morning frost.

Claire watched as a lone woman tended a stone vault, clearing the leaves and twigs that the wind had brought to rest on a loved one's memorial.

Many people chose to have flower vases, or benches, stone memorials or a simple plaque.

In Claire's case, she'd chosen the latter.

Black with gold writing, raised slightly from the ground, resting on pretty coloured pebbles.

She stared down at the inscription:

In loving memory of...

She didn't want to read His name today.

She blinked water away from her eyes. She wasn't sure if they were tears or just her eyes watering in the bitter wind.

'Did I do the right thing?' she said.

She thought back to the look in Lucas's eyes, the lasting image of terror caught in that final moment when he'd realised his fate, before he sank down into the dark cold depths.

The lake was still being dredged. His body had yet to be found in the murky waters.

Claire hoped it stayed that way.

'Was I wrong?'

She laughed to herself then. Was she really expecting a reply? To hear some voice, His voice, echoing around her. Would he reassure or condemn her for not saving a soul, even if it had been evil?

'I still think of you,' she said. 'I never think about... well, I won't speak her name, not after what she did.'

She paused a beat. She heard a cawing.

The crow was back.

This time it landed, about ten feet from her. It cocked its head, beady black eyes watching.

She smiled then and it felt like genuine happiness.

She stared back at the crow. 'I may not always make the right choices... but I make them for what I believe to be the right reasons.'

As if on cue, the crow ruffled its feathers, and took off again.

Claire heard Lucas's cries for help in her head. She squeezed her eyes shut. He might have made her grateful, that much she couldn't deny, but she was determined to never feel in his debt.

'I did the right thing,' she said, opening her eyes.

She cast one last look at the simple memorial she had chosen for Him, over a year ago, with a name that would always mean something to her, the memory not always pleasant.

She walked away.

As she reached her car, her BlackBerry began to vibrate in her coat pocket. Pulling her glove off with her teeth, she retrieved the phone and stared at the screen:

Unknown number.

She answered it.

'DCI Claire Winters,' she said. The wind blew a tangled mess of blonde hair about her face, and whistled through the phone. She had heard a voice, but couldn't decipher it.

'Could you speak up, please?' she said, pressing her finger against her other ear, in an effort to drown out the wind.

'Claire…'

'Yes. Who's this?'

Static fed back along the line, and then, 'It's me. Has it been so long that you don't recognise your own father's voice any more?'

Her body stiffened then and he sensed what she was about to do.

'Please, don't hang up on me.'

She swallowed hard, not wanting to hear his words. 'Dad,' she said. 'How'd you get my new number?'

A rasping followed down the line and she realised he was laughing in exasperation. The laugh soon changed into a hacking cough.

She closed her eyes, not wanting to hear any of this.

He soon composed himself and said, voice full of pain, 'I'm dying, Claire.'

Her eyes snapped open.

'I'm dying and there's something I want you to know…'

ACKNOWLEDGEMENTS

Thank you to the dedicated team at HQ. Special thanks to Anna for designing my fantastic book covers. You've captured the tone of the DCI Winters series perfectly. To my editor, Clio Cornish, thank you for your continued support for the series. Your advice and input on this novel has been invaluable.

Further thanks to my husband, Daniel, for everything you do that allows me to write full time. To my daughter, Eden, you can never have too many books and I am SO proud of you. To my parents, Sandra and Stewart, thank you for the love and constant support. My crazy in-laws, Jackie and Phil (with a little help from Kevin) huge thanks for all the laughs!

Finally, the biggest thank you must go to my friend Willow Thomas. You've been there since the 'early days'. I will always be eternally grateful to you.